# DISPLACED

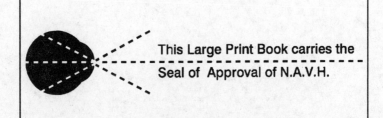

This Large Print Book carries the
Seal of Approval of N.A.V.H.

# DISPLACED

## STEPHAN ABARBANELL
### *Translated by Lucy Renner Jones*

**THORNDIKE PRESS**
A part of Gale, a Cengage Company

Farmington Hills, Mich • San Francisco • New York • Waterville, Maine
Meriden, Conn • Mason, Ohio • Chicago

LIBRARY OF CONGRESS CIP DATA ON FILE.
CATALOGUING IN PUBLICATION FOR THIS BOOK
IS AVAILABLE FROM THE LIBRARY OF CONGRESS

ISBN-13: 978-1-4328-4522-3 (hardcover)
ISBN-10: 1-4328-4522-5 (hardcover)

Published in 2018 by arrangement with Harper, an imprint of HarperCollins Publishers

Printed in the United States of America
1 2 3 4 5 6 7 22 21 20 19 18

It is as though the space between us were time: an irrevocable quality.

William Faulkner, *As I Lay Dying*

■ ■ ■ ■

# JERUSALEM

## JAFFA ROAD

■ ■ ■ ■

# CHAPTER ONE

Dusk was already beginning to fall when the bus came to a standstill in a dip between Deir Ayub and Bab el-Wad. The driver struck the steering wheel with the flat of his hand, jumped up from his seat and grabbed a canister of water. He threw open the bonnet of the Dodge and tried to unscrew the hissing radiator with a handkerchief wrapped around his hand. None of the passengers on board said a word. The fanning of newspapers and the chirping of crickets were the only sounds that broke the silence. Flies had found their way in through the open door, along with the heat that peeled away from the ground on June days.

She glanced up the hillside, scanning the rocks and scrub. The trees were doubled over as though they were dying. Sweat ran down her temples. She gathered up her hair and tied it into a ponytail, then went back to clutching the cap in her lap. Up on the distant ridge, she spotted a shepherd and his son, a mangy dog with a mottled coat skulking around their heels.

She hadn't taken much notice of the man beside her until now. When the bus had stopped in Tel Aviv, and she'd got on at Carmel Market, she'd sat in an empty row, and spread out her things: her rucksack, the cap, a tin flask of water and a book from the kibbutz library in Hanita, way up north in the hills, her hideaway for the last three months. Soon afterwards, she hadn't been able to keep her eyes open. Had she fallen asleep? Light had filtered through her eyelids — something flickering, like far-off signals — and her head had bumped against the window whenever the driver changed gears.

The man stood up, walked down to the front of the bus, and got out. Through the window, she saw him talking to the driver who was standing, arms akimbo, by the open bonnet. The stranger pulled his shirt loose from his trousers, wrapped the front tails around his hand and opened the radiator with a quick twist. With the other hand, he took the canister. A short while later, the engine started up, the two men climbed back on board and the bus set off. A breeze blew in through the open window; a passenger murmured a prayer. The man sat

10

down again next to her. He had white teeth, a dark, rakish shock of hair and a handsome profile. He brushed the damp hair off his forehead and wiped his hands on his trousers.

'Shaul Avidan,' he said, introducing himself. 'And what is your name?'

'Lilya,' she said, and reached out her hand.

'Lilya — and what else?'

'Wasserfall.'

He watched her, as if he were still waiting for something. How often had she been through this? *You're not a Jew then, not one of us,* he was now thinking?

She sighed. 'Lilya *Tova* Wasserfall.'

He smiled. 'Nice name, suits you.'

'Thank you.'

He looked down at her lap. Only now did she realise that her fingers were wrapped tightly around the cap. She tried to hide the dark, almost black stains on it. He took out a clean, neatly folded handkerchief from his trouser pocket and offered it to her. She thanked him and pressed it to her forehead and temples, then rubbed her neck and hairline. He seemed to watch her as she did this, with curiosity and a sort of detached interest as if he wanted to check whether his handkerchief was doing its duty.

The bus was on a flatter stretch now, the

slope gentler. The driver kept turning his head to one side, leaning forward and listening to the engine.

'So you're leaving the country and heading for the Holy City? You know Jerusalem?' he asked, tucking the handkerchief back into his trouser pocket.

'Very well, although I haven't been there for a while.'

'You'll be amazed how our city is thriving despite all the violence. It's a miracle.'

'Miracles are beautiful. But they tend not to happen in the places they're needed — with a few exceptions, like in this case . . .' Lilya tried to sound nonchalant.

She didn't know what to make of Shaul, but she was enjoying their conversation and the distraction he provided. She wanted to carry on talking, and drift in thoughts and sentences as weightless as the wind up on the crest of the hill. At the same time, she felt what a huge effort it took. She went back to looking out of the window; the city wasn't far now.

The bus had slowed down again. The driver was gripping the steering wheel with one hand, his arm outstretched, and pulled hard to the left. They turned into a bus station. People immediately got up, pulled down suitcases and bags, pushed, shoved and were thrown back and forth as the bus continued moving. With a jolt, they suddenly halted. The engine shuddered once more, then died. The driver pushed the door open and jumped down.

Lilya and Shaul were the last to leave the bus. When he reached the door, he turned around again.

'*Shalom,*' he said, fixing her sharply for what seemed like eternity, and then turned and disappeared, striding off into the crowds.

She looked around the bus station, her rucksack slung over one shoulder. Later she could think about who Shaul was, and what his penetrating gaze meant but now she was already on the lookout for British soldiers. As a member of Haganah, the underground defence force fighting for an independent Jewish state, she could never be too careful. She had escaped three razzia so far and here she was again on a secret mission. But there were just squatting traders hawking falafel, coffee, spices and jewellery. Newsboys waved the evening papers in her face, and Arab children ran alongside her, their hands thrust out. The stench of diesel, soot and burned mutton lingered in the air. Storytellers, readers and travelling dentists hunkered by the roadside. The poorly lit Jaffa Road led her into the city.

Elias Lind: the forgotten writer. Tomorrow she would meet him, get it over and done with and leave the city again. It was an order from Shimon Ben Gedi to go and find him. Although she'd only received her orders from Ben Gedi the previous day, it already felt like an eternity ago. In her mind's eye, she saw her commander leaning over the table as she entered the room. She had tried to resist when he rolled out his plan before her, but without success. She had lacked strength and Ben Gedi had known that.

She walked past the Mahane Yehuda market to her right, the stalls, booths and shutters looking like disassembled theatre sets waiting for the next day. Cats nosed at empty food cans. From the direction of the Old City, Bedouins came towards her laden with baskets and bags on the way to their stores outside town.

Behind the main military post, the street fell away steeply and led to the Old City and Jaffa Gate. She had to keep to the right now. The apartment was in a side street in Nahalat Shiva; it couldn't be much further from here. It lay in a courtyard that reeked of mould and dankness, a home to bats on summer nights. But it was convenient. When her parents had left the city to start their new life in the coastal town of Netanya way up north, they had rented this little apartment cheaply and filled it haphazardly with objects from their large house in Jerusalem-Rehavia, where Lilya had grown up. Everything they had wanted to leave in the city, whether useful or useless, was now harboured in this little place. It was a pied-à-terre, a place of refuge, a home and a storage unit rolled into one. Lilya would seek shelter there for a couple of days, meet Elias Lind, then leave the city.

The key lay in the agreed hiding place and her hands shook as she touched it in the dark. She hesitated, opened the door and entered.

# CHAPTER TWO

The morning light was falling into the room through thin slats, sketching bright stripes on the wall. Lilya turned over and tried to read her watch, holding it towards the light. At ten o'clock she was meeting Elias Lind in Café Levandovsky, close to the apartment in King George Street where Lilya, her parents and Yoram had all lived together before they moved to their big house in the Rehavia district of Jerusalem. That was in 1934 when she was ten years old. They had taken in Yoram in 1931 after his parents — the Lippmans — were killed in a gun battle between Arab insurgents and the British police, who maintained order in British Palestine. Yoram had witnessed the event, and was the sole survivor.

To her parents it was immediately obvious that they would raise their friends' son as their own. Yoram was troubled, barely spoke, barely ate, and Lilya's mother had to strip his wet sheets every morning. She lavished all her attention on him, dragging him along to the ageing psychoanalyst Dr Kitteler, who silently examined the boy, but he had no idea what to do either. *Yoram this and Yoram that* — soon Lilya could not hear it any more. Her parents' love was still hers, but their anxiety, which often seemed greater, belonged entirely to her new brother. The situation silently withered her father's humour as if his soul lacked water, sunlight and fresh air, and he became more serious with each passing day. And her mother, once a blend of love, warmth and diligence, grew increasingly strict.

Yoram was a good-looking boy. Lilya watched him grow up with a mixture of confusion and, later, curiosity; she watched him read and study, make new friends and grapple with the rousing and violent fight for independence. His attacks of melancholy became rarer. She liked his reserve; she thought it showed depth. And eventually, long after men and boys had started staring at her with that ravenous, dog-like yearning, she was sure that she, Lilya Tova Wasserfall, and she alone, was in a position, even destined, to infiltrate and tap his reserve. Yoram's earnestness aroused her. Was it love? It turned into love, yes: but a love without redemption that she kept hidden from all other men.

She tried to stop her thoughts racing: it would be better to get up now, get dressed, and leave. Instead she sank back into the pillows, closed her eyes, and curled up. She saw herself in the garden of their big house, lying on a blanket with a book, her chin propped up on her hands. The trees in this country were sturdy and closely planted together, forming a protective canopy. Somewhere in the house, the clattering of a typewriter could be heard. Doctors, professors and artists lived on Haran Street, but that sounded like Father on his typewriter; he wrote tirelessly in his spare time — petitions, submissions, concepts for the common state of Palestine. Piano playing reached her ears from a window of the house next door, and soon afterwards a high-pitched violin could be heard from the other side: arpeggios, scales, opening sequences.

'Bach on the left, Debussy on the right. That's a recipe for disaster. One of them will have to give in,' Yoram said.

He was lying next to her on the grass, a pile of newspapers in front of him: *Palestine Post, Davar, Yediot Ahronot, Haaretz* and the

Arabic *Al-Difa*. He was cutting out articles with a large pair of scissors.

'And who's going to win?' she asked.

Yoram laughed without looking up. 'The better one, of course. Ofer, he's the greatest.'

The piano fell silent.

'That's the way it should be,' said Yoram. 'The muses are fair. Bach wins.'

She looked across at him. His dark, almost black hair hung over his face, his shirt was unbuttoned to nearly halfway down, showing a tanned chest, and his beautiful hands deftly cut out the selected articles. He smelled of leather and lemons. The sinews on his right arm were taut. If he lifted his head, he'd notice that she was staring at him. This thought made her blush. Perhaps he had long noticed her staring, but, if so, he didn't let it show.

She rolled on to her back.

'What will you do when one of your notebooks is full?'

'I'll buy myself a new one. And another . . .'

Swiftly and mechanically, Yoram flicked through the newspapers until he found what he was looking for: every single article about an attack, hold-up, detention or abduction; police reports, background reports, appeals, commentaries and photos; snapshots of car explosions, collapsed buildings, the injured, dead and the maimed; photos of unearthed stashes of weapons and prisoners sentenced to death. The black notebook was for articles about attacks by Arab groups, but also British strikes, raids and invasions; the white book contained articles about the Irgun's violent or even terrorist activities against the British and the Arabs as well as those performed by other Jewish activists. Yoram cut them out, stuck them into one of his notebooks, and added the date.

'The British want to abolish punishment by flogging in Palestine,' he said. 'Eighteen lashes and a sentence of eighteen months will become a thing of the past. They want to turn it into twenty-eight months' imprisonment under the harshest conditions. Now *that's* what I call justice.'

She couldn't tell from his tone if he was angry or sad and despairing. Both, she thought. And his anger will win.

She sat up, and raised her hand to touch his face. Even though she knew it was wrong, she brushed his hair back from his eyes. He froze. Her heart hammered. She leaned forward.

He returned her kiss timidly, then vigorously; he grabbed her around the waist, and pulled her towards him. Quite abruptly, he let her go again, and turned away.

'I'm your brother,' he said.

'No, you're not,' she replied.

'Lilya . . .'

'You're Yoram Lippman.'

'There are no Lippmans any more. Ehud and Deborah are my parents, and you're my sister.'

She noticed a slight tremor in his voice, an uncertainty that gave her hope, a chance to slip through the gap. He loves me, she thought. He will, he must love me. Our happiness depends on it.

In one of the cupboards in the small kitchen she found tea, and soon lit the small gas cooker. She smoothed out her clothes and took a closer look around the apartment. There the shell lay, between the bookends, and it gave Lilya a jolt. Carefully, she picked it up — it was lighter than she remembered — and held it to her nose, inhaling deeply. At the time, when she had given it to her father to say thank you, it had smelled of sea and salt. But now the scent had faded.

They had hiked, just the two of them, for five days on the *Yam-el-Yam* trail, from sea to sea. She had been sixteen and Yoram had just left home to start an apprenticeship in Haifa. Mother had wanted to intervene, saying the journey was too dangerous, and that they should avoid the Arab villages at least. She was right, no doubt, but Father waved her concerns aside and, in the end, he got his way. They had hiked from Kinneret, the Sea of Galilee, all the way to the Mediterranean, with just rucksacks and caps, and by the end their shoes were worn and lopsided from all the walking. Along the way they talked, fell silent, sang and laughed: never before and never again would she have her father to herself like that. On the last day, Mount Carmel stood in front of them and when they reached the summit, just before the low mountain range fell away to the coast, they saw the ocean. They hugged each other and Father didn't seem to want to let go again. South of Haifa they reached the sea, and there in the sand she found a particularly beautiful shell, as pale as Carrara marble, criss-crossed with dark lines as if painted by hand. She picked it up, breathed in its scent and gave it to her father.

Shortly before their return, she realised somewhat bitterly that her father had had an ulterior motive for spending time together like this. That, like her mother, he was worried about Yoram. Yoram had started doing weapon practice in the evenings, and mixing with types whose impatience was written all over their faces: young men who spoke Hebrew and carried guns, who felt Haganah, even the Palmach, were not doing enough. Would she follow Yoram's path, her father wanted to know, would she too resort to violence to liberate Palestine and claim it for the Jews?

Just before ten, she left the apartment, crossed the courtyard and stepped out on to the teeming street.

Ascher Levandovsky's Café was situated on upper Ben Yehuda Street, right next to King George Street. Over the years it had become run down. It didn't surprise her that Elias Lind had chosen this café, of all places, to meet. Here, at the end of the street, time stood still: it could have been any period before the war. It was 1946, and an entire world had vanished, but not here.

Over the past few months, there had been no good news. Even if the newspapers often embellished the facts, some thought that there was now no choice but to believe them. In the Steimatzky bookshop missing persons' notices hung next to American, British and French newspapers. Many fears had received bitter confirmation: parents, siblings, cousins, friends and schoolmates had indeed disappeared. The full scale of what had happened in Germany and Europe was gradually becoming apparent but this knowledge was still too vast for most to take in.

She went up Ben Yehuda Street: it was surely not far now.

She was following Ben Gedi's order. She had always respected her commander. He was dedicated to the creation of an independent Jewish state like no other, and had a sense of proportion, was flexible, severe and skilful. And he had been a good teacher, perhaps the best there was. The British in charge of Palestine feared him yet sought him out. They knew he couldn't be trusted, but knowing that he was unpredictable made him reliable in a certain way — you just knew where you stood with Ben Gedi. When she entered his secret office he glanced up at her briefly, and his expression seemed to say: *I knew that you would come.* He had changed as a person since her Palmach training, when he had taught her and others in the elite Haganah combat unit how to fight for the right cause with honest means: cunning, rigour and a range of weapons. She studied him: his shoulders looked stiff and angular as if time had gone to work on his bones. His cheekbones seemed larger, and his eyes lay deep in their sockets, embedded inside his skull. He was well over forty, but was still athletic; he wore an open-necked white shirt, its sleeves rolled up casually, and khaki shorts; his reading glasses were a new addition.

He asked her to approach the table, looked up briefly, smiled and said, '*Shalom.* And thank you for coming.' He pointed to the map lying in front of him. The words *Deutsches Reich* stood at the top right-hand corner, emblazoned with a swastika underneath. In the lower part of the map, Ben Gedi had marked circles; now he tapped them with his pencil.

Germany, he said, was one big waiting room, and he pointed to the places he'd marked. Jewish survivors were escaping into Bavaria. Thousands and thousands from Eastern Europe were desperately seeking shelter from new violence and pogroms in the countries now under Stalin's rule, but Britain was still placing an iron hand across the gates to Palestine, the only safe haven for them. In Landsberg, Feldafing and Föhrenwald, huge refugee camps had been set up by the US Army, and more and more Displaced Persons were expected. The situation was getting out of control. Hunger, typhus and other diseases were beginning to take their toll. People with little hope can be unpredictable and fear of violence in the camps was widespread. Ben Gedi needed a detailed and clear-cut report about the biggest one: Föhrenwald. Sharply written, concise and with a strong political perspective. 'Consider the report as a weapon, not a piece of paper,' he added.

Before Lilya had properly understood what this was all about, or could ask if Ben Gedi intended to send her to Germany, he had placed her ID papers on the table. American Jewish Joint Distribution Committee, the Joint for short. The Joint was one of the biggest aid organisations for Jewish refugees, and it would take Lilya under its wing.

'Welcome to the Joint, Commissioner Wasserfall,' said Ben Gedi.

'It's all above board,' he said, 'and everything's been prepared.' The British would let her leave Palestine with this stamp on her papers as a farewell kiss. In a few weeks, she'd be back and no one would even have noticed she'd been gone. She felt the urge to get up and leave the room. Even though she had learned during her training that orders were to be followed and not questioned — after all, without a reliable command structure, their struggle could not be won — it was hard for her to accept. She would have liked Ben Gedi to ask her if she was prepared to travel to Germany. Especially after all she'd been through and everything he knew about her. She was offended by his failure to mention the work she had done from her hideout in the north: concepts, designs and plans for the Haganah's Operation Markolet, which would destroy all bridges and access roads into the British Mandate of Palestine. It was going to be a decisive blow against the British, and a big step forward in securing independence. She had been convinced that this was why he'd summoned her: because he had read and liked her material. But now he wanted to send her away. The message was plain: Ben Gedi clearly thought she was still too weak for the pending operation. Not fit for service, not resilient enough. He presumed that she would not survive an interrogation behind British walls. She had been struck off his list, at least for the time being. Lilya Tova Wasserfall was too great a risk in his eyes.

Is that what her commander was telling her?

'Sit down, you don't look well,' he said. He brought her a glass of water, stopped talking, and looked at her for a while. She had forgotten how to interpret his look. They exchanged words — she couldn't remember any of the details — but at some point she had heard the word *order*. It had cut through the air like a cold blade. He sat down and then began to explain the Lind case. Since she would be in Germany more or less officially, she could also do some work behind the scenes: research on a very specific case.

Elias Lind, the famous writer? she asked. Her parents had given her his novel *Joseph Sternkind* some years ago after having read it themselves. For weeks, the book had sat untouched among maps, schoolbooks and her diary. But when she finally picked it up, almost in passing, she wasn't able to put it down again.

Ben Gedi nodded. Lind had received a message a few days previously from two representatives of the British Mandate: the Nazis had allegedly murdered his brother Raphael, an acclaimed academic in Berlin. But Elias had evidence that Raphael was still alive. The news of his brother's death had roused Elias's suspicions and he had sought out Ben Gedi, a trusted friend and experienced soldier. And, yes, a devoted reader of Lind's famous book, just like her.

'Go and meet Elias Lind,' Ben Gedi had said at the end of their meeting. 'I am sure you'll find something in Germany that we can use against the British; something that will increase our pressure on the occupiers and make them shiver. What happened to Raphael Lind? They know. They lie. And we will find out, soon. Something must have gone wrong in Germany back then, I can sense it, and they are trying to sweep it under the carpet. Besides, times are going to get harder after Operation Markolet. We'll need all kinds of new weapons — one of which could be public pressure. And you, Lilya, can deliver the ammunition.'

'Why me?' she asked. 'Is this supposed to be a test? To see if you can trust me again?'

Ben Gedi smiled but didn't say anything.

'What if I fail?'

'You won't.' He leaned forward. 'And it's not about trust, Lilya.'

He then explained to her that the day would come when he might have to pull out, resign, settle somewhere in Galilee and hand his job over to other people.

'Younger people, people like you, Lilya. But you have to show that you are strong enough.'

Outside Café Levandovsky, Lilya spotted a

29

tall man seated by the window. She guessed he was in his mid-fifties. But the times had taken their toll and left him haggard. She pushed open the café door and went inside.

'I asked Ascher to keep the seats by the window free,' the man said, standing up as Lilya walked towards him. 'I need light, you see, as much light as possible. And from here you can see what's going on outside, and spot any further acts of discrimination in the street. We will not have to wait long, I fear.'

Lilya stared at him, lost for words.

On his nose rested an unusually heavy pair of tortoiseshell spectacles that magnified his eyes, making them huge; it was as though he were peering out through the bottoms of two milk bottles. His hair was still full and thick, just a little sprinkled with grey. His threadbare grey suit was too big, cut in a European style, and had been tailor-made a long time ago. He held a stick in his hand that was too slight even for a stroll through the city, but his bearing was upright.

'Come on. We do have an appointment after all. I've already ordered coffee.'

Elias Lind pulled out a chair from the table, waited until she had sat down, and took his seat again facing her. He leaned the flimsy stick against the empty chair next to him, where a black briefcase was already lying.

'The stick,' he said, 'is my third eye. My doctor expects that my eyesight will continue to deteriorate in a not altogether negligible way.'

He took the stick in his hand again and briefly tapped the table leg.

'So? What do you think? Cedar? Perhaps pine. Definitely conifer. It'll never be a match for eyesight in any case.'

Lilya followed his every move, not sure what to make of him. So this was the great writer Elias Lind? She knew that as a young man, many years ago, he had fought for Germany, his country, in the Great War. After he was severely injured and disillusioned with Jewish life in Germany, he'd turned his back on his country in the early twenties. And went to Palestine.

'Lebanese cedar has almost no scent, by the way — at most, a very faint one, slightly aromatic, like fresh wood. Here, smell this.'

He leaned forward and sniffed the wooden surface of the table. Lilya also bent her head, but paused halfway without Lind noticing.

'And?' he said, looking up again. 'Not much smell, is there? But enough of all that. Let's talk about the matter in hand. Shimon

Ben Gedi told me . . .'

He looked at her, half amused, half serious, the corners of his mouth pulled down.

'Ben Gedi — my God, yes — he came up with a plan straight away, of course. Not a week has passed since I went to see him, and here you are already, sitting in front of me. He is taking whatever can help his cause and turning it into a weapon. A weapon against the British. Or should I say: your cause too? He once fought with England against Hitler, side by side; now he has turned against Prime Minister Attlee and the hated Foreign Secretary Ernest Bevin — and even some people in Whitehall.'

'So you think that the British lied when they told you the news about your brother? A lie from high up? Whitehall?'

'I wouldn't call it that. I think they told their version of the truth, and I'm searching for mine,' he said.

'But there can only be one truth. Either your brother Raphael died, as the British claimed, or he's still alive.'

Lind raised his eyebrows and smiled indulgently at Lilya.

She waited to see if he would carry on, but instead he took his briefcase from the chair, opened it, pulled out a flat packet of documents, and laid it on the table. He fiddled with the knot in the string, trying laboriously to open it, then reached into his pocket and fished out a magnifying lens almost the size of a whale's eye. With the lens in one hand and the string in the other, he managed to untie the knot.

'From a friend in Germany,' he said, nodding in the direction of the package. 'She inserted a charming letter too, which might be beneficial for us. But I'm afraid I've left it on my desk at my office. Sent from the American Sector in Berlin. Please take a look.'

Lilya turned the packet over in her hands. The address was written in large, sweeping handwriting; Lilya was reminded of blossoms, something ornamental. 'How long did it take to get here?'

'Not even three weeks.'

She whistled appreciatively. 'May I look inside?'

'That's why we're here.'

Wrapped in the paper lay a thin, leatherbound book with a gilt coat of arms inscribed on the cover. She traced it with her finger: it was an owl with closed eyes, perched on a pedestal made of three standing scrolls. At its feet, printed in big script, were the letters C.F. LIND.

'That's a bookplate that belonged to my

father, Chaim Friedrich Lind. He had the book made shortly after the Great War in 1918. It's a catalogue of all his books: papers, folios, slipcases of collected works — thousands of them. His *Book of Books*. An infinite treasure. Meticulously executed and cherished. Father named his kingdom *Alexandria,* and he mapped it out with this book. That kingdom was in Berlin, Spittelmarkt, on the third floor facing the street.'

He paused as though wondering whether to go on. 'But in the end, this book was Raphael's, my brother's.'

'Why?'

For a moment, Elias Lind seemed embarrassed. 'That's a long story. My father bequeathed everything to my brother Raphael. His entire property, including *Alexandria.* This *Book of Books* is my brother's. But open it, right at the first page.'

Lilya opened it carefully, and the leather creaked.

At the bottom left of the first page, she discovered a stamp, the letters *ERR,* and underneath it, a handwritten date: *18 October 1941.*

She looked up at him.

'Nazi gibberish, all these awful abbreviations. But the stamp is special,' he said.

'You'll have to help me out here.'

'Alfred Rosenberg and his people. ERR stands for *Einsatzstab Reichsleiter Rosenberg:* Rosenberg was the Führer's main thinker. But also his biggest thief, stealing any cultural artefact of value, Jewish property — books, art, musical instruments.'

'Is the book looted property?'

'I'd say it's the only possible conclusion.'

She ran her fingers over the pages. They contained indexes and catalogues of hundreds of books, first in order of titles, then in order of authors. She looked again at the stamp.

'It all seems to fit. October 1941. They came for your brother and took his books too, along with this catalogue.'

'I have a slightly different theory — there's a lot more to it than that.'

He paused. Lilya hoped that Elias Lind had nothing concrete to go on. All she had to do was listen, then lead him, like a placid guide dog, to the right door, back out into the light. Then she would let Ben Gedi know that this whole affair was a dead-end; and besides, it was absurd, not to mention unpolitical, to put too much effort into individual cases. She would need less time than Ben Gedi had anticipated.

'If we're going to make any headway, we'll need facts,' Lilya said. 'Tell me what you know about your brother, about the past few years. What was he like? What made him stay in Germany? And if he really is still alive, why is there no sign of life from him?'

'Of course. Facts,' he said and stared at the book. 'But what in the end are facts? Interpretations of facts are what matter. Look at this.'

Elias moved his coffee cup to one side and placed a photo on the table in front of her. 'This photo was stuck inside. It fell out when I opened the book.'

Lilya picked it up. The photo was of a large house made of dark wood somewhere at the edge of a forest. Smoke was billowing from the chimney. One of the windows was open, the room behind inviting the viewer to look inside.

'Where is this?'

'I don't know. What's more interesting is the writing on the back.'

Lilya turned over the photo and tried to decipher what little she could make out. The letters, written in pencil, were smudged. 'Well?'

Elias Lind looked at her expectantly. 'See the little note down there?' he said, almost impatiently.

He offered her the magnifying lens.

'Are you sure this is your brother's

writing?' she asked, as she held the lens over the letters and figures.

'No doubt about it.'

She read the numbers 9-12-5: 50. They were framed by a thin, hand-drawn box. The rest was illegible — perhaps other numbers, or letters, or perhaps even formulae.

'I would never have discovered the symbols if it wasn't for the lens. I use it to read everything, in case something escapes my notice. The letters in the box. You'll know what they are. It's your speciality, after all. It was Ben Gedi who sent you, one of the best, he said.'

She sensed that he was watching her eagerly while she continued to decipher the signs.

*A Test. Failed. Trust. Ben Gedi's smile.* She pushed away these thoughts.

'Raphael and I developed an arcanum with an abbreviation in the middle,' he continued, 'and that's what put me on the right track — as well as causing me some sleepless nights.'

'A secret language,' she said, and looked up.

Lind raised his eyebrows.

'So we need to try to work out what it says in plain language.'

'Plain language,' said Lind and smiled

thinly. 'I like that phrase as much as I like facts.'

'The figures correspond to the order of letters in the alphabet,' she said.

'That's right,' he replied.

'Only the order of the figures is reversed. A useful and simple trick.'

'9-12-5. Let's look at them the other way round . . .'

*'Eli,'* she said.

He lowered his voice and looked at her through his thick spectacles. 'My letters, even the ones I sent Raphael, were always signed *Eli* — that's what they called me at home. My parents, Raphael — I was Eli to them all. Raphael loved brainteasers and puzzles. This one's quite easy compared to his usual ones.'

She held the lens again over the box.

'And the 50 after the colon? It could refer to your age. How old are you now?'

'Fifty-two, I'm afraid,' he said.

'So your fiftieth was in . . . ?'

'In 1944.'

Lilya leaned back. 'The British claim that your brother died in 1941?'

'I don't want to deny that it's possible,' he said, 'and there's a great deal to confirm it. But if the symbols refer to me, I wonder why my brother wrote down my birthday

38

three years before the event. It doesn't make sense. My fiftieth birthday was in 1944. So much is fact.'

'So you presume that your brother Raphael might still have been alive in 1944?'

He leaned forward and placed his arms on the table.

'I don't know if the British lied to me intentionally, but the fact is that they came looking for me officially to tell me the news of his death . . .' Elias Lind paused.

'It looks like they wanted to be sure that you believed what they said and didn't start going around asking questions. Do you have any explanation for that?' she asked.

He had asked himself that question over and over again, and was unable to find an answer. At the same time, he hadn't been able to get Raphael's puzzle out of his mind. He had held out for two nights, then visited Ben Gedi.

'I haven't seen Raphael for some years. Now and again he'd write a postcard on my birthday or at New Year, before the war. I expected him to ask me for a visa so that he could come to Palestine after all the things that I'd heard were going on in Germany. But then I thought: Perhaps he's too proud. Eventually he stopped sending cards. I feared the worst and blamed myself for not doing anything. I tried to persuade myself that his reputation as an academic would have secured him a chair abroad. But if that were the case, wouldn't he have been in touch to say he was out of danger? Then the package from Berlin arrived with his *Book of Books,* and just when I hoped that Raphael was still alive, the British arrived at my door. The package was from my old and very dear friend Desirée von Wallsdorff. She was Raphael's friend as well — probably more than just a friend; she still lives in Berlin.'

For a moment it seemed that memories and thoughts had carried him away. He looked up again, blushing slightly, she thought.

Lilya placed the photograph back on the table and waited to see if Lind would carry on.

'I want to tell you something that I haven't dared tell anyone so far — not even myself for a long time.'

His voice had changed; his tone was deeper now.

'I'm not grieving for Raphael. But he and I are the only ones left in our family. It's as though my brother were watching me, day and night. Sometimes through the eyes of my father. When I wake up in the morning,

I don't know if I have been sleeping or dreaming, or if I'm still dreaming. I see Raphael in front of me all the time — he looks at me silently and questioningly. One day runs into the next. There is no release, no tomorrow. Just a huge chill that gradually spreads from the depths of my soul. Life needs certainty and release, otherwise it isn't a life. We both need you, Raphael and me.'

His hands were trembling. Lilya felt the urge to hold them. But she didn't.

'I'm preparing some papers for you to read. It's not been easy for me and I can't claim that they will contain plain-speaking facts but they might be helpful to you. I'll let you know once I've finished and then we'll meet again. Come to my office at the Jewish Agency, you know where it is,' he said, standing up, and reaching for his stick.

# CHAPTER THREE

When Lilya had passed Jaffa Gate, she left
the souk behind that smelled of cardamom,
coffee, spices, meat and rotten leftovers. She
felt that she was being watched. The man
was looking at her quite blatantly from the
other side of the street. She saw his bright
teeth and shining eyes. The stranger from
the bus: she was sure it was him. Carts and
wagons kept blocking him from view; then
trucks, buses, jeeps and camels. He was
standing in the entrance to a building.

She had known that the man from the bus
would catch up with her. She recognised his
athletic, striding gait. He would follow her
like a shadow until she had told him what
he wanted to hear. Why hadn't she seen
straight away that he was one of Yoram's
people, and that he had been sent to find
out whether they could count on her?
Whether she was prepared to join their
cause, even without Yoram? Their goal was

not a state for the Jews, but a Jewish state, country, soil and people: a single entity. As Yoram had once said to her, the path to this goal could only be through armed conflict, an underground movement, ambush and terror. At that, she'd shivered. Ben Gedi and the others still tried to fight by reaching out a hand, but not Yoram.

He had suggested that they walk up the Mount of Olives. They had crossed Kidron Valley and the Garden of Gethsemane, and when they reached the top, they sat on a wall high above the city and looked down. 'This is all ours,' Yoram said, 'and ours alone.' He had lifted his hand, as though he wanted to touch the roofs. The houses, alleys and walls were bathed in a honey-coloured light, but up here, even though a light breeze was blowing, she thought she could still feel the heat from the bricks. She had wanted to contradict him, but his expression and the tone of his voice scared her. *No,* she had wanted to say, *it might be our city but we share it with those who lived here before us.* In her mind, she saw them walking along Gaza Street, King George Street, past the pines, acacias, oleanders, palms, cypresses and bougainvillea, saw herself on the terrace of the YMCA, right across from the King David Hotel that shimmered reddish-gold in the evening sun. Several kinds of people came and went: British officers, dandified American travellers visiting the Orient, elegant women and industrious emissaries with bulging briefcases under their arms. Yoram had asked her for this meeting. Meeting? An awful, stupid word. She had wanted to see him again, to touch him. And what had he wanted?

'My mind is made up,' he said. 'I am going to join Zvi and the others.'

She knew what he was saying: he was going underground. The British would chase him, and Ben Gedi and his people would hate him. From now on, he would try to force victory with violence. It was the wrong path, and yet she knew she would never be able to dissuade him. The wind swallowed up his words. She wanted to say that her parents would never approve of his decision, and that he was about to trample everything underfoot that they had ever tried to teach him.

She had frantically tried to work out what to say. *You will die. Stay with me, for our sake. Don't do this to our parents.* But instead, she bit her lip and said nothing. Then he asked her if she would follow him. She hadn't expected this. She knew that he was not

44

concerned with having her close to him, but only with the cause and how she could help it. So she would lose him even if she followed him.

Or perhaps this was simply a ploy to get away from her. Perhaps he could no longer bear her love, her insistence. Her soul froze at this thought. He put his arm around her in a brotherly fashion. She pulled away, looked at him, drew herself up and began to scream at him: *he only thought of himself; he was a coward; he did not have the courage to commit to her; he was destroying everything.* Then she slapped him, hard and brisk, across the face. He didn't move a muscle. She sank to her knees, crouched in the dust and started to cry.

She hadn't noticed the two men standing behind her. Only when Yoram got up, and they all silently left to go back down into the city without once looking back, did she know that it was over.

She turned into HaNeviim Street, trying to lose herself in the Orthodox district. Mea She'arim, a hundred gates. A hundred ways to disappear, to go underground. She didn't want to join them, or have anything to do with them. She didn't know what Yoram would say now if he saw her here, and she did not even want to think about it.

Hawkers squatted at the kerbside, offering vegetables, spices, leather goods and knives. Their stands were nothing more than boxes on which they had spread rough sacks. From the balcony of an Ottoman-style house, the eyes of boys wearing kaftans and dark, wide-brimmed hats followed her.

She stopped in front of a shoemaker's shop and tried to catch a glimpse of movement in the reflection in the window — a shadow, a tuft of hair. Had he followed her all the way here? During her training in the Negev Desert they had been given mirrors on poles to peer out of ditches, windows and caves, and around the corners of buildings into unknown streets. *Hold it so that it doesn't catch the sun,* she'd been told.

The shoemaker, who was wearing a leather apron over his kaftan, looked up and smiled at her. He put down his work and came to the door. In his sidelocks and beard hung the remains of brown wood shavings. 'Keep going, straight on,' said the shoemaker, thinking her lost. 'You can't miss the exit.' He waved his hand up the street, said goodbye and disappeared back into his shop.

Suddenly a shadow appeared next to her.

'So a little tour through the Holy City after all?' he said. 'I can barely keep up with you. Why didn't you invite me along?'

She turned around. It was Shaul Avidan, just as she had suspected.

'Because our common path has no common goal,' she said, and turned back to the street.

'Stop! We haven't even started yet.'

She knew she would not be able to shake him off now. Had Yoram put Shaul up to this, just before he'd lost his life along with three other fighters — meaninglessly, pointlessly, through their own carelessness while building a bomb in some hidden cellar?

Shaul suggested that she accompany him to Jaffa Gate, and listen without interrupting him so that he could explain his business, which, as she must know, came from the best source. Then he would say no more and she would be free to decide; he would accept any decision on her part.

She hesitated for a moment. 'No, forget it,' she said.

The big secret mission, Operation Markolet, destroying all the bridges, putting even more pressure on the British — she already knew about it. And she also knew that Ben Gedi would not want her to get involved with these people. Her hands were trembling. On the other side of the street, not even a hundred yards away, a jeep, clearly a patrol, was moving slowly towards them. A driver sat inside, with two soldiers, carbines propped between their legs. Shaul looked briefly down the street, sizing up the situation. Just a few steps from the shoemaker's shop was an opening in the wall, beyond which was a narrow alleyway.

'Your friends,' he said, jerking his head in the direction of the jeep, but before she could answer he had sloped over to the opening and, with three or four strides, he disappeared.

She turned to leave, first slowly, then gradually speeding up. The soldiers did not seem to be interested in her; she saw the jeep turn around and retreat into the distance.

She would reach Jaffa Road via HaNeviim, and then vanish into the crowd. She would have a drink, collect herself, and afterwards set off in the direction of the agency.

She wouldn't let him get as close to her again.

When she arrived at a café in Jaffa Road, taking a seat at the bar to drink a glass of cold water, her thoughts turned to Elias Lind, and she felt herself tense. She wanted to bring the business with him to a conclusion in her way — gently, yet firmly. But all of a sudden she wasn't sure what this conclusion would be. If there had been the slightest hint that Yoram might still be alive, what would she have done? She had asked herself this many times since her first meeting with Elias Lind. The answer was painful: everything.

Even the impossible.

# CHAPTER FOUR

The Jewish Agency building resembled an ancient fortress: a semicircular complex constructed around a large courtyard. It was built of large, cleanly hewn bricks in light-coloured stone; a portico above the entrance rested on square columns, upon which there was a balcony and a podium from where speeches were delivered. A long drive led visitors between two crescent-shaped patches of parched lawn.

Lilya went up the few steps and entered the hall. Inside it was cool. A security man sitting behind a wooden desk folded his newspaper, stood up and looked at her.

'I'm looking for Dr Lind,' she said.

'Is he expecting you?'

'Yes.'

He looked her up and down. 'Any weapons?' he asked.

She pretended to check, running her hand around her belt. 'Don't think so,' she said.

He left the desk, and came over to her. 'You don't think so — good, good,' he said.

She was wearing her khaki-coloured trousers and clumpy shoes; her skin was dark from working in the fields in the sun, and her hands were rough.

The guard laughed and, rather too nonchalantly for her liking, sauntered over to a noticeboard that hung next to the stairwell. He was much taller than she had supposed, and an odour of stale cigarette tinged with sweat hung about him.

'Lind, you say? All the way to the end of the hall, left wing.'

He told her the room number, placed his outstretched index finger on the board a little longer than was necessary and then checked the clock, saying, 'At this time of day, you'd better go in quietly. Or you can wait here if you like.'

His eyes probed her again, not searching for a weapon this time. Whatever he meant by *this time of day,* she did not want to wait to find out. She thanked him, the guard watching her with feigned disappointment, and then she left, heading for the stairs. As Lilya walked along the corridors on the ground floor, she could hear the sound of her own shoes. Doors opened and closed again, and a young woman, who was pushing a squeaking trolley stacked with transit files, barely glanced at Lilya. Two men carrying briefcases came out of a room. She heard voices, footsteps and the clattering of typewriters behind closed doors. She passed an overcrowded conference room whose door stood wide open, the men and women inside thronged around a large desk. The mood was tense.

A few yards further on, it was quieter; the corridors emptied. She looked around, but there was no one to be seen. It had to be around here somewhere.

Eventually she found the sign with Lind's name on it. The door to the office was ajar. She peered through the crack and saw the tips of someone's toes, and a pair of shoes on the floor.

Gingerly, without making a sound, she pushed open the door. In the middle of the room stood a table with three chairs; lying on it were sheaves of papers, dossiers, newspaper cuttings and a magnifying glass. Despite the open window, the heat of the fading day was stifling in the room. She saw books on the shelves, files held together by string, a store of medicine — dropper bottles, tinctures — a pile of clean handkerchiefs and an open spectacle case.

■ ■ ■ ■

Elias Lind was lying on a divan with his eyes closed. Despite the heat, he had a blanket spread across his midriff. His heavy spectacles sat like a huge sleeping insect on a chair next to him. Lilya looked at his high forehead, his long neck, and his eyes without their opaque screen for the first time. He moaned, but did not wake up. It was not right simply to creep in here and watch this sleeping man, she thought.

'I have found the letter. You know, the one that was in the package from Germany.'

Lilya started. His voice was raw from sleep, and frail; he must have realised she was there without being able to see her.

'But please pass me my spectacles first.'

She held them out to him: he lifted his head and fumbled them awkwardly into place on his nose, putting one earpiece on at a time. His features relaxed.

'I must ask you to be lenient with me for greeting you here like a penniless poet. Normally a quarter of an hour nap suffices, but this lunchtime I wasn't feeling well. Would you mind if I remain in this position a little longer, even if it is not conducive to receiving guests?'

'I didn't mean to be impolite; the door was ajar.'

'Politeness is for times of peace. In this country, that will take another few centuries. In any case it was not impolite of you to simply come in — it was extremely practical.'

He sat up a little.

'I fear that you have only come to say farewell. I would not think badly of you, and can understand your point of view very well. Your way of thinking is political and strategic. This country needs building. Searching for an old scientist, who simply should have left his country in time, only holds you back.'

'That's not it. I just don't think there's enough to go on to make this mission a successful one. Even the photo of the house in the woods, wherever it was taken, throws up more questions than it answers.'

'Facts. Theories. There is nothing in between. *Hypotheses are not facts.* That's what Dahlia always said. You would have got along well.'

He sat up again and cleared his throat.

'Since my wife died, I often feel that I've lost my bearings, my sense of direction and my courage too. We don't really have anything to go on, you're right. But I've been having quite different, daring thoughts.' He grinned, looking mischievous all of a sudden. 'If you do find something over there, I would set off and join you. I'd poke around in the rubble with my stick to look for Raphael.'

'A stick wouldn't be enough,' she said.

He looked at her steadily. *No bearings, no courage,* is what he'd said, and now she realised he'd been teasing her.

'Nonetheless, there would be two of us — your eyes and my memories. What a team! Unbeatable.'

'Would you really travel to Germany?' said Lilya, not sure how seriously she should take him.

He hesitated, glanced down and then up again. 'No, I couldn't. But read the letter that I told you about.' He indicated an envelope lying on the table in front of her.

'I have to warn you that it details very private matters. But the business at hand requires you to know. So please read it and decide afterwards if you want to help me.'

Berlin, 26 May 1946

My dear Elias,

In times like these, who knows if you will ever receive this letter? Or if you

55

even remember or want to be reminded of me? Everything happened so long ago, there's a great divide between us and everything we once had — even each other. But I had to send you this book. I made my mind up the moment I came across it.

I discovered it in the hands of a black-market trader. It was a sheer co-incidence. And then again, how can it be! It was worth nothing to him, but for me it was like a summons: *Alexandria,* the library of your esteemed father, and part of Raphael's inheritance.

It wasn't easy to find your where-abouts, and I was about to address this letter to 'Elias Lind, Palestine'. It's such a small country, after all. But an Allied officer friend of mine helped me by sending the package via military post. I have forged a good understanding with the Allies over the years.

This book is Raphael's, there's no doubt about it. As you know, your brother and I were very close, and for a while, there was even more to it than that, even though our union wasn't blessed with happiness — we both re-alised that. I have often asked myself what happened to Raphael after his disappearance on the day they turned up at his house in Dahlem. I was visiting him at the time — we had long since become good friends again.

On the afternoon of 8 October 1941, SS officials rang the doorbell. Five o'clock tea was already laid out for us by the housekeeper, and Raphael had gone into the garden to check on his roses because of the early frost. They demanded a list of his belongings. Most of all, they wanted a complete inventory of his books, essays and lectures, and all his documents, they said. They would be back.

From then on, every morning from half past four, he sat at his desk in a suit and tie, waiting for them to come. But they didn't.

I told him he had to leave the country, that he could perhaps still make it. He had money, connections — maybe it wasn't too late. But he wouldn't hear of it.

He decided to stay.

So I set about preparing things on my own, without his consent. I made enquiries, visited administration offices, queued in front of cash desks, customs investigation centres, exchange offices, and negotiated with high-up officials, low-down officials, even the lowest-of-the-low officials.

He barked at me down the telephone. He said I should stop. That he knew what he was doing. About what was just and right. I started crying but I said no more.

A few days later, he disappeared. They must have come for him at night. Trucks drove up and they seized all his books. They took everything; his entire life.

Wiped out.

I would be so happy if this book reaches you, if it returns to the home where it belongs. Please write to me and let me know if my note arrives. And how you have been. Should you ever find your way back to this dead city, dear Elias, please know that you are more than welcome. I still live in Kleiner Wannsee; my house is bearing up, although it is really too large for me. And if anything should happen to me before then, my niece knows what you mean to me.

With affection

Lilya held the letter and didn't say a word. *Wiped out.*

She could sense the strength of this elderly lady, Elias and Raphael's dear friend, between the lines. And it matched Elias's well-hidden, yet deeply solid will. Could it be true that lost hope might not be the end of the road, but might well be the beginning of something else, something new, unheard of? she thought. As long as you are strong enough to face it and you have the courage to do things that you wouldn't have expected. For the sake of one you love.

*The impossible. Failed. You won't.*

She looked at Elias Lind but he seemed to be lost in his thoughts.

Almost to himself he said, 'Desirée von Wallsdorff. She wrote me this letter. I confess that I adored her more than anyone in the world before I met Dahlia — perhaps too much. But it was not reciprocal. She belonged to *his* circle of friends, and she was beautiful, clever, worldly and at ease. In those years, she epitomised Berlin to me: by day and at night, Berlin in the early hours when the newspaper vendors teemed out on to the streets, and the S-Bahn scraped and rattled into a tunnel in the early morning. And the milkmen with horses and carts went from house to house, rubbing shoulders with night revellers who pushed past them into their houses as though they were afraid of the light. Raphael had an affair with Desirée, but she didn't suit him and all his airs and graces.'

He paused for a moment.

'But she wanted him, not me. Perhaps I wanted to set her free with my desperate love. But she didn't need setting free. She was always free. What a woman!'

He shook his head a little, lost in thought.

'The photograph of the house in the woods. The box with the secret numbers. There's no mention of them in her letter. Not a thing,' Lilya said.

'I don't think she knew the photograph was in there.'

'It would have been useful to hear her thoughts on it.'

'Yes, you're right. Perhaps we would already be a little further on.'

'*Joseph Sternkind,* what a book!' she had said to Elias Lind before leaving. 'Why make your readers wait so long? The story has to go on.'

'Have you ever tried writing a book?' he had answered.

'Texts, essays, shorter academic papers. But no, not a book.'

Elias Lind smiled at her cryptically. 'Imagine you wrote a novel. A young, pretty soldier comes across evidence that saved a life, many lives, thanks to a blind old man. *Whose life?* you would ask. *Well, that depends on your story,* would be the answer.'

What was he trying to say to her?

'Imagine that were true, but you wished that you'd never even dared consider it and so you wasted an opportunity. An opportunity to change things for the better. To save not only one but many people; waiting, longing for freedom. To make our foreign rulers in Palestine change their politics — or leave. Leave! I know that's what you are fighting for, the same as Ben Gedi and all the others. Helping me is part of the struggle. Your struggle. You will see, but first you have to be willing to start.' He smiled at her complacently. 'Think about doing what is right and then we will meet again.'

*The impossible. The possible. For the sake of one you love.*

■ ■ ■ ■

# LONDON

WHITEHALL

■ ■ ■ ■

# CHAPTER FIVE

The brakes squealed; the doors flew open. Marble Arch, at last.

Up on street level she had a perfect sense of direction. But down here, deep below London, it often failed her. When the Central Line train had glided from the platform into the tunnel, her inner compass stopped working for a few minutes. The walls of the carriages seemed to be closing in on her, and the tunnels were so narrow that she fancied she could hear the sound of metal grinding on stone.

Lilya thrust her way out of the carriage, took deep breaths, and scanned the crowded platform for the stairs to the exit. A muggy, warm wind announced the approach of a train on the opposite platform. The smell of smouldering cables hung in the air, mingled with cologne from lawyers and business-men; somewhere, a child was screaming. She walked towards the exit and looked up at the steep escalator before getting on.

She had memorised Dr Albert Green's address. It was a few minutes' walk from the Underground station. Whether Green would talk or be a dead-end trail, she wasn't sure. But she seemed to be on to something. She had visited the British Library to get an idea of who Raphael Lind was; his research and scholarly papers had been published in Britain, as well as in Germany. In doing so, she had come across the name Albert Green. He was a professor, a biochemist and a doctor. In Germany, the family had still been called Grün, but that had been a long time ago. In London, where they settled in 1910 before the Great War, they had changed their name to Green.

Many of Green's early academic essays were written in German but his publications in English were what roused her curiosity. She noticed that a certain Professor Albert Green often wrote on the same subjects as Raphael Lind: biochemistry, protein research, chemical resistance, but above all, gaseous compounds. She wasn't able to explain this connection between Raphael Lind and Albert Green so she had set off to meet him from her lodgings in Clapham to try to find out more.

Buses as high as the buildings on Jaffa Road shunted their way down Oxford Street. Black sedan cars, taxis and army vehicles coursed along the streets. She was happy to have solid ground under her feet again. Travelling by sea was not for her. Neither were journeys through manmade tunnels in rattling tin boxes. Nonetheless she'd had no choice but to take the route via London.

'Why England?' she had asked Ben Gedi.

He'd laughed. 'There'll be no problems. At home the British behave quite decently. You could even say they have a democracy.' Besides, there was no direct route from Palestine to Germany.

Ben Gedi told her to report immediately to the Joint office in London and ask for her transfer to be arranged to Germany. A ship was usually scheduled every few days, or she could fly. The US Air Force had set up a shuttle across the Channel. *There will be a lot to take in,* Ben Gedi had said, adding that she should use her time in the capital wisely, researching and observing their British friends. After all, they had kept the Führer from the throats of the Palestine people; they alone had carried on fighting when Hitler had seized nearly the rest of Europe. This commanded respect. 'We'd be dead without the British. But with them, life is impossible. That's the fate of us Jews,' Ben Gedi had said.

On the ocean crossing from Haifa, she had felt as if she were in a living nightmare. They had docked for a night in Limassol harbour on the southern tip of Cyprus and she had not been allowed to leave the ship. British soldiers stood guard all night in front of the gangway. Goods were loaded and offloaded. She saw wooden crates against the dark backdrop of the sky; floodlights streaked across the ship, traders peddling wares called out, and trucks drove up to the quay, then rumbled away again. She soon realised that the dockers' cries and the cursing of the loadmaster were going to carry on all night. Her cabin was right next to the crew's berths and barely larger than a travelling trunk. It was unbearably hot below deck and even though her porthole was open, she was scared she might suffocate.

The next morning when she heard the bell ringing, orders being called, and the hum of the engines running shortly afterwards, she went up on deck. The sun was beginning to appear over the horizon, and there was not a cloud in the sky. The freighter seemed to be moving at an angle, tilting to one side as though unsure whether it dared sail back out on to the open sea, which was spread before them like a smooth cloth. And she realised for the first time that she had indeed left home. She would do everything she could to return as soon as possible.

'You have to leave your country to rediscover it — not everyone's opinion, but for me it's true.'

The stranger had appeared at the stern railing quite suddenly, and was looking out to sea next to her, as she tried to shield her eyes from the bright June sun. She wasn't sure if he had spoken to her or just aloud to himself. He was the only passenger on the freighter besides her and usually seemed only to leave his cabin for meals. When he ate, he did so silently and without looking up, spooning soup into his mouth, or stirring about in the colourless stew, cutting his bread into slices with the broad, jagged blade of his knife. On his left hand he wore a glove made of thin, brown leather which did not seem to hamper his movements. His reclusiveness suited her only too well; yet she often had the feeling that he was watching her from the corner of his eye.

'You don't talk much.' He now turned and looked her in the face.

'I wasn't sure if you were speaking to me.'

'I was,' he said. 'Well, at least now I know that you can talk.'

She hoped that this would be the end of their conversation. And the man did in fact fall silent, and looked out to sea.

'You like this spot, don't you? The wind's not as fierce here as on the bow, and you can see what's behind you. I haven't introduced myself. Colm O'Madden,' he said, and gave her a guarded look. 'From Ireland. And yourself?'

Lilya told him her name, feeling that it was a mistake.

'The Orient,' he said, and looked at her. 'No offence, but in my opinion there's not much to it. It's one big disappointment. Just sand, heat, crazy leaders and people from all over the place at each other's throats. Can't wait to be out of here.'

He fished a cigarette out of a pack and tried to light it, asking Lilya to shield the match from the wind. Trying not to show that she felt uneasy, she took the matchbox, and with practised skill pulled the matchbox halfway out, and then held the kindled match in the hollow. She invited him to light his cigarette. O'Madden stared at her in amazement.

'It's a useful trick,' she said, 'and it doesn't

70

show up in the dark either. A glowing cigarette always gives away where your head is.'

O'Madden inhaled deeply, and then blew out a cloud of smoke that flew up in the wind.

'Solid training,' he said.

'A tip from friends . . .'

'They had your best interests at heart.'

The following day, he sat down next to her in the mess without being asked, and poured some water. Where would she be going next, if they actually managed to get to England, and what would she be doing there? he wanted to know. She was taken aback by his directness.

'In England? Nothing in particular,' she said.

Would she be travelling on from there, perhaps to Germany? He carried on cutting his bread with his knife.

What made him ask that? she thought. He looked expectantly at her. And when she didn't answer straight away, his expression grew cold. The veins on his temples bulged as if he were struggling with something.

She decided to turn things around.

'Have you been there, or did you fight against the Germans?' she asked, looking at him, widening her eyes.

He hesitated for a moment, then stuck one leg out from under the table, and rolled up his trouser.

'A bullet, clean through my calf, with a bone lesion. Summer 1940,' he said, 'aerial gunner for the RAF.' After that, the war had been over for him.

She looked at the scar. It was too small for that type of injury. A machine-gun strike on board a plane would surely have ripped his leg apart. And what about his gloved left hand?

That was the last time they spoke. For the rest of the journey she managed to stay out of O'Madden's way. When they reached Southampton, and he disappeared into the crowds on the quay, she gasped with relief. She hoped never to see him again.

Before she had set off on her journey, she had met Elias Lind twice more and let him talk — of his time in Berlin, his childhood under the Kaiser, of Chaim Friedrich Lind's *Alexandria,* which had become Raphael's after his father's death. His only bond with his brother was their shared surname, Lind stressed, and after the war, his parents' belief in the future and their German values had come between him and them too. For

Elias, the only future lay in Palestine. That is where he met Dahlia, fell in love with her, and they had lived happily together until her premature death. After that he began writing.

But Lind's memories provided very few clues as to where Lilya should start looking.

What he had brought was a photo, on the back of which was written 'Berlin, 1932'. It was almost fifteen years old, but better than nothing. It showed both brothers, staring in surprise at the camera, each in his own way. Raphael was wearing a dark, tailored suit, the height of fashion during the period, and a watch was sticking out of his waistcoat pocket. He was as tall as Elias, and had the same full, black hair, slicked back with brilliantine. He wore a monocle, and his expression was proud, self-assured and haughty. It was as though he wanted to fill the photograph all by himself. His brother, in his too-large suit, stood next to him with slightly stooped shoulders as if he were trying to conceal his height, or had ended up in the photograph by accident, and was looking for a way out. Lilya had seldom seen brothers look so different from one another.

On her last visit, Elias had pushed a sheaf of loose papers into her hands.

'My life's journey in sketches. But I'm

afraid you won't find too many answers to the questions you might come across. It's rather so that you understand what our life was like back then. Raphael's and mine, and our family's.'

In London, not long after her arrival, she had spent a few days buried in the British Library under the arched dome of the large Reading Room. The Joint had told her that it would be six days until the next available flight — at the very least. Officer Cordelia Vinyard, who was supposed to brief Lilya about her work, had looked through her papers, smiled at her warmly, and then sized her up from top to bottom. And sizing her up was precisely what she was doing: the uniform division was in the neighbouring building and stored everything from skirts and shirts to boots and ties. A dark badge had been sewn on to the uniform sleeves with A.J.D.C. in large, highly visible letters. *American Joint Distribution Committee.* Cordelia put together a well-fitting combination for Lilya, and helped her knot the short necktie with a practised hand.

Looking in the mirror, Lilya had the fleeting suspicion that this uniform, even the blouse and socks, had been sewn by Cordelia herself. She didn't feel like herself in these clothes but Cordelia said that from the outset of her journey to the Continent, a uniform would be obligatory. Then she looked almost reproachfully at Lilya's rough hands and fingernails.

'The country air gives you nice red cheeks,' said Cordelia, winking, 'but you have to groom the rest yourself.'

Lilya took the hint. Finally, Cordelia shook her hand and promised that she would soon be in touch about her transfer to Germany. She was looking forward to working together, she said, and Lilya should certainly visit her again. 'There is so much I have to tell you,' Cordelia added. 'And I can show you around the city while we talk.'

The American woman's openness and friendliness was almost too much for Lilya. With her uniform under one arm, hastily stuffed into a canvas bag, she and Cordelia had said goodbye.

'Perhaps we can travel together,' Cordelia called out after her. 'I'm waiting for the next flight to Germany too. Just so you know, I'm terrified of flying. It'd be nice to know there's someone to hold my hand. I'll be thirty soon — then perhaps it'll stop. Something has to get better with age.'

After that meeting with Cordelia, Lilya

started on her research: Lind, Raphael, scientific papers, books, research descriptions, expert reports. She ordered all the available editions of *Die Naturwissenschaften* and pored over them in the pale light of the British Library's Reading Room. It had once been the German answer to the acclaimed *Nature.*

Lilya took each year's editions of *Die Naturwissenschaften* and noted all the essays that Raphael Lind had written. Then she ordered *Nature* to find the essays he had published there before the war. And this was when she made her discovery about Professor Albert Green — by accident, but also thanks to her trained eye. As well as writing about the same subjects, some of the formulations and phrasings in his language were very similar to Raphael Lind's, almost as if one had copied the other. Could it be true?

At first, she cast this possibility aside. But again and again, she came across stylistic and structural similarities — as though many of the essays had been written by the same author. But there didn't seem to be a plausible explanation for this, no matter how hard she thought about it. Perhaps Professor Green would be able to supply her with one; but for that, she would have to go in search of him.

She tried looking him up at random in the London telephone directory, and found at least a dozen Albert Greens. But there was only one Prof. Dr Albert Green, GP, and it seemed very likely that this was the man she was looking for. His doctor's surgery was only a few minutes' walk from Great Cumberland Place. When she called to make an appointment on the pretence of being sick, Green's assistant seemed to be under orders to fob patients off rather than help them. No, she was told, the professor was not taking on any new patients. Lilya described her condition as 'acute'. She made it sound like an emergency. That way the doctor couldn't refuse her.

She left Marble Arch station and turned right into Oxford Street. A newspaper vendor amputee on a small wooden cart rolled along beside her: *Republic of Italy declared!* he cried out. *Interim government in India fails due to Congress Party!*

She came to a large, light sandstone building. A helmeted knight looked down at her from the eaves. This was the house she was looking for.

After she had glanced around, she went into the entrance hall. Only the echo of a rattling motorcycle filtered inside: it was cool and quiet. A lift made of wrought iron resembling a birdcage was waiting in the lobby. No thank you, she thought. Dr Green's surgery was on the third floor.

She took the stairs, which had a lingering odour of lavender and fried fish; like a *laterna magica* from a distant childhood, she passed pictures of Greek myths on the walls as she went up: Dionysus with his pitcher and grapes, Hermes with his winged helmet, Artemis carrying a bow and arrow, and, finally, Apollo with his lyre and laurel wreath. This is what it must have looked like in the Lind household in Berlin's Spittelmarkt before the Great War. She imagined two boys with leather satchels, short trousers and wrinkled socks storming up the stairs; a daily race that Raphael won every time no doubt.

She gripped a well-worn knocker in the form of a lion's head, embedded in a brass hollow in the centre of a large door, and rapped. The receptionist, a violet-scented elderly woman, greeted her coolly. Lilya recognised her voice from the telephone.

Somewhere she heard the ticking of a grandfather clock. In the hallway stood a vitrine in which cups and porcelain figures were lined up in rows. A half-opened sliding door revealed the library on the right-hand side. None of this looked like a doctor's surgery.

When she entered what the receptionist referred to as the consultation room, Green was standing with his back to her in front of a bookcase that reached all the way to the ceiling.

Consultation room, she thought. Well, we'll see about that.

Green turned to her. He was balancing a pile of books in his hands, and held out his elbow to greet her.

'Nothing is more permanent than provisional arrangements,' he said. 'When you move, unpack everything straight away — otherwise it becomes a life project.'

He deposited the pile of books on a wooden stepladder, crossed the room to his mahogany desk, which was covered with an array of papers, busts and pipe-smoking utensils, and invited her to sit down. In front of the desk stood a dark green leather armchair: the patient's chair.

'Have you been here before?' he asked, looking at Lilya while he rooted around on his desk for a fountain pen and a blank index card.

He was a small man with thinning, almost white hair, and he spoke with a German accent that hardened the edges of his words.

*Yekke* English.

'You are still out of breath. Mrs Richards will call the caretaker about the lift . . .'

She waved away his suggestion.

'So what can I do for you?'

'I have come here from Jerusalem,' she said.

She had thought long and hard about how to approach Green. In the end, she had decided to come straight out with it, presenting her hypothesis as fact, and see what happened. Lind and Green must have known each other, perhaps even very well. This was her starting point.

'Europe is very far away. And the war has made travelling particularly difficult,' replied Green, rather impatiently. 'But you said your pains were *acute*?'

Lilya sat up straight. 'I am healthy, as far as I can tell, not being a medical expert. But I'm here for a different reason. To see you as a scientist, Dr Green, rather than a doctor.'

He raised his eyebrows.

'First of all, Elias Lind asked me to pass on his regards.'

'I am sorry to say that I do not know an Elias Lind. And my journey in life has so far never taken me to Jerusalem. I am afraid you have mixed me up with someone else.'

'Elias Lind — Raphael Lind's brother.'

Dr Green seemed immobilised for the blink of an eye, but regained his composure straight away.

'Lind? We were colleagues for a while. He was a great scientist. I didn't know that he had a brother. We barely spoke about private matters.'

'Elias Lind received the news a few weeks ago that his brother is dead.'

'That, to be honest, I had already feared. Please offer him my sincere condolences,' Green said.

'I am here in the hope that you can help Raphael's grieving brother and me with some information about the years before he died. In Palestine, we're cut off from almost everything.'

Green took off his glasses and looked at her severely. 'What is it that you want from me?'

'Your help. I am looking for information about Professor Lind's final years — what he worked on last, what he spent his time doing, when he had to stop working. I know that you are not obliged to tell me anything, but —'

'My help?' Green interrupted her. 'First you sneak in here on the pretence of acute illness, then you send me regards from a stranger — and now you want to march through the German history of science? Everything I have to say has been published. You can find it all in the relevant libraries. Once you have read it, we can gladly meet again for a professional conversation.'

'I have already read your work,' Lilya said.

'Sorry?'

'Not all of them, but many of them — yours, and Raphael Lind's essays, in English.'

'And you are disappointed to find that essays are not autobiographies? They talk about facts — not friendships. They follow the path of reason.'

Green stood up suddenly.

'Lind and I have not been in contact since the war.'

It was imperative for Lilya to be on guard now. She couldn't afford to make a false move. The professor was on the point of asking her to leave.

'Professor Green, I sat in the British Library for several days. I cannot claim to have understood everything I read — formulas, compounds, aggregate states, useful materials, dangerous materials; what do I know? I'm not a natural scientist. Yet it made interesting reading — I'd go as far as to say it was fascinating.'

'I'm happy to hear it. I always took great pains to write in a way so that even those who were not familiar with the material could gain something from it.'

Lilya paused for a moment. Then she pressed on.

'What surprised me the most was that yours and Lind's research findings were so noticeably similar.'

'Scientists are not monads who live in the dark. Research involves communication, exchanging views. Even stimulating adversaries.'

'My impression was not that there was a scientific race going on between you, but that you were a very tightly coordinated research team.'

'Research team? I'd have liked nothing better. It's just that the times weren't conducive to it. We were at war, and I am English. And a Jew. What's more, Lind was banned from working from the mid-thirties on. How could we have managed it?'

'He might have left for England in time?'

'I invited him, and the Society for the Protection of Science and Learning also made him offers several times. There was even a personal letter from our chairman. That door was wide open. He would have been a credit to England and our research.'

'So why didn't he take up the offer?'

He gave her a guarded look. It was obvious that he didn't want to reveal any more information, and wanted to end the conversation as swiftly as possible. But something drove him on against his will. From his expression, she sensed that he was afraid of something, but at the same time was looking for her guidance. He sat down again, sighed, lifted his hands, then let them sink back on to the desk.

'I have no answer to that question. I have asked myself many times.'

'Did he believe in Germany to the very end?'

'Raphael wasn't naïve.'

'He could have saved his life and continued his research in freedom.'

Green straightened up and leaned forward slightly. 'I wouldn't say that I know it from personal experience, but as someone who has seen something of life, I know that there are all kinds of reasons why people do things that seem to contradict their interests. Or even put themselves in danger, in a way that inevitably catches up with them.'

Lilya wondered what he meant. But Green carried on.

'Some people want to make up for something. Their motives, if you like, are shame, guilt or love or perhaps all three. But as I said, Raphael Lind and I were not even in contact as scientists for all those years.'

'Which makes it all the more surprising that your essays up to 1941 sound as though you and Raphael Lind — putting it carefully — coordinated your research. But that was hardly possible, the way you describe the situation.'

'Coordinated? What leads you to make such a ludicrous assumption?'

'What I've read. The similarities in the structure of your texts. Lind and Green, Green and Lind. Two sides of the same coin. I can't fathom it.' Here she paused for a moment and looked Green in the eye. 'But I am hoping that you might be willing to help me understand. It's not about you. It's for Raphael Lind's sake. To find out what happened to him. You see' — and here she paused for a second, pondering whether she should say it or not — 'I wonder if he's still alive.'

Green blanched. He steadied himself on the desk, stood up, crossed the room and closed the large double doors. Then he went over to the window and stared out on to the street with his back to her. Lilya heard something like a dull humming sound, and watched Green take out his handkerchief to blow his nose.

'It is —' he said, and then broke off.

The telephone on Green's desk rang. He didn't seem to hear it. Still facing the window, he said quietly, 'Lind wrote for us in the thirties, and was published in *Nature*. In 1937 the journal was banned in Germany. It was even banned in university libraries under the Third Reich. They said that English science had attacked German science, and insulted it. Ridiculous.'

He turned back to her.

'About two years later, in early 1939, I received a surprising, but let's say *official* summons to ensure Raphael Lind continued to be published in *Nature*. But he wasn't allowed to publish under his own name any more. Not in Germany, nor in Britain. I asked how I was supposed to manage this, even if we would have been only too glad to use his research results.'

Green blew his nose again and sat down at his desk again.

'They insisted that I gave him access to the journal. They would have his work delivered to me from Berlin. Someone there was still in contact with him, and that's how Raphael began publishing under my name, with my agreement. His subjects, his theses, his insights. They wanted him to continue publishing in Britain, but anonymously. It was a kind of signal.'

'They? Who asked you to do this?'

'If only I knew! It wasn't the universities, that's certain, and not the scientific world either. They must have been top people — Baker Street or Whitehall, I don't know. I did what I was told. There was a war going on and by the end of 1941 Britain was fighting alone against Germany. No one knew how long we would hold up. What was I supposed to do? I saw it as my duty. And I even gained recognition and acclaim. For Raphael's ideas and thoughts! It was terrible.'

'I'm afraid I don't understand.'

'There were people who needed Raphael's research results. And I was his mouthpiece.'

'What do you mean by that?'

'*Über die bei der Bestrahlung des Urans mittels Neutronen entstehenden Erdalkalimetalle.* "Concerning the Existence of Alkaline Earth Metals Resulting from Neutron Irradiation of Uranium". Does that ring a bell? It was published in 1939.'

Lilya was startled to hear Green speaking in German.

'No, I'm afraid not.'

'I'll help you along. That's the title of an article about the path to the German bomb.

But the amazing part was that everyone, all over the world, could read it — and that may have been intentional. Specifically, Paul Rosbaud, the chief editor, saw to it that it was published, and he knew what he was doing. But nothing could be proven; what's more, he was believed to be a Nazi, and loyal to the cause.'

'A smokescreen?'

'Let me put it this way: Rosbaud wanted those who read the treatise to understand where the Germans stood, and where this path could lead. Einstein and many other exiles were alarmed when they read the essay. They understood.'

For a moment, Green scrutinised Lilya as if he were trying to read her expression.

'I, a German Jew, had to show my new country where I stood, more than most. Perhaps I've been able to help you a little. And if so, probably more than I should have done.'

'Did you turn your back on science then?'

Green gave a bitter laugh. 'After the war, when it transpired that I had published the research of a colleague under my name, I was advised, regrettably, to renounce all academic honour and privileges. I had stolen someone else's research, deceived people. Whatever the reasons.'

He gazed at Lilya with a blank expression.

'It wasn't my idea, but I had to keep that to myself. Since then I have been running this surgery.'

He stood up.

'What are you going to do with this information?'

'I don't know. It's all very confusing. But I'm very grateful for your openness.'

'Openness? You are only free when you have nothing left to lose. But as one who has witnessed many things, let me tell you this: sometimes it's better to leave things alone. What's done is done. We have to look forward, and there's no going back. Ever.'

Green saw her out. When they came to the door, she stopped again for a moment.

'Could you tell me when you last had direct contact with Raphael Lind?'

Green replied so quickly that it seemed as though he'd been waiting for her to ask.

'Before the end of the Blitz.'

'In 1941?'

'It must have been the summer. A postcard came from Berlin for my birthday, unsigned. But I knew his handwriting. A few weeks later, it was leaked that his last article was published under my name.'

Lilya reached into her bag and pulled out the photo of the house in the woods, showed him the back, and asked if he recognised anything apart from the figures.

Green went over to his desk, and came back wearing his reading glasses.

'With the best will in the world — it's illegible. It's as if someone has written something and rubbed it out again. Not a chance.'

'Are you at least able to tell me if it's his handwriting? The legible letters, I mean.'

He took his glasses off again and held the postcard at arm's length. 'I wouldn't rule it out.'

Scientists, she thought to herself: they searched for as long as they could for a navigable path between what was falsifiable and verifiable, right and wrong. Did that mean yes or no? It was so simple.

'Is that a yes or a no?'

'A yes, but —'

'But?'

'The empirical material is too thin to build a hypothesis on. In other words, it's completely illegible.'

'What does your heart say?'

Green gave her an enigmatic look. 'No answer.'

'Elias Lind is sure that it's his brother's handwriting.'

Green gave her back the photo.

'Then believe him. But in the end, you already do. Otherwise you wouldn't be here.'

She found herself back on the street, exhausted. Her assumptions had been right. And yet after this conversation, it seemed even less likely to her that Lind was alive. Green hadn't heard from him since 1941. Had her visit been nothing more than a waste of time and energy?

She thought about going back to the Joint office and sending a telegram with Cordelia Vinyard's help addressed to the Jewish Agency, Jerusalem, last door at the end on the right. As though her conversation with Green had never taken place:

*REGRET+STOP+SEARCH      LACKS RESULTS+STOP*

She imagined Elias Lind sitting at his half-opened window in his office, bending over her telegram with his magnifying glass. Warm air would be streaming in, the scent of pines, blossoms, the sounds of the city, a police siren in the distance, the rattling of tank tracks. She chased away the idea of the telegram, stood still for a moment and breathed deeply. She had made a promise and she would keep it. Not to mention her conversation with Green: it had finally roused her curiosity.

*A Test. Trust. Will not fail.*

She made her way back towards Hyde Park's green lawns, and looked for a park bench. On Speakers' Corner, pigeons fluttered up into the air, and she heard the distant yet distinct cries of a man.

She found a bench, sat down and closed her eyes. She needed to calm down and think.

'It wasn't easy finding you.'

She opened her eyes.

A man was sitting next to her on the bench.

'I had to follow you for an awfully long time,' he said, 'just to be sure it really was you. I know it wasn't very courteous of me, but it was my only option.'

He had a conspicuously straight nose, an almost youthful voice and was wearing a light grey suit and hat. He sat with one leg crossed over the other, turned to face her and handed her a business card.

Major Desmond Terry, Foreign Ministry.

'We'd like to invite you over. To Whitehall.'

Lilya looked quizzically at the stranger and Major Terry smiled, a little patronisingly.

She felt her strength returning.

'And to what do I owe the honour, Major?' she asked.

92

'A friend of a friend of yours would like to get to know you.'

'I didn't know I had friends with connections in the British Foreign Ministry.'

The stranger laughed. 'Your friend Ben Gedi has had the best connections to Sir Lucius Honeywell for years. And he would like to meet you for tea.'

'With or without handcuffs?'

He smiled and leaned back slightly on the bench. 'With sugar. And if you like your tea English-style, then with a little milk.'

'When?'

'Tomorrow. A car will pick you up in Clapham. From there, it's just a stone's throw to the city. Shall we say ten o'clock?'

'Do I have a choice?'

'You may say no.'

'And what if I do?'

'A different kind of vehicle will come and pick you up tomorrow. This time without leather upholstery and chauffeur. Sir Lucius can be awfully stubborn. Believe me, I should know.'

# CHAPTER SIX

She turned off the light and fell asleep, but woke again a short while later and listened to the rattling of the trains. To get back to sleep, she tried counting the carriages that she could hear rumbling over the railway tracks at Clapham Junction station. The noises were like a distant, unintelligible knocking as if someone were trying to send her a message. The moon cast a cold light on the floor. The walls seemed to lean in, and a silver platter with lavender blossoms on the table looked like a toad shimmering in the moonlight. Her room was on the first floor in a narrow street not far from the station. Laura Todd was a widow and in need of money, like so many in these times. Lilya had spotted her note pinned to a tree, a little slip of paper in meticulous handwriting that suggested the fragrance of biscuits, wilted flowers and peace. No one would guess she was here, she had thought, hidden among

the narrow rows of houses and chimneystacks black from soot. And so after a brief
negotiation about the price, she'd taken the
room.

What time could it be? She pulled the
blanket higher, shivered and let her thoughts
drift: she was back in the desert, lying in a
tent, waiting for Yoram and not knowing if
he would ever come. It was a deep, inky-
blue night; there were no clouds in the
starry sky, and the air was fresh and clear.
Next to her, Shoshana was breathing softly
in her sleep. Through an opening, she could
see the silhouettes of the other tents, hills,
rocks and sparse trees. How many hours
away was morning? There was no lamp in
her tent: the light would have given her
away.

A stick was leaning against her camp bed,
which was used in place of a real weapon
during exercises. She wasn't allowed to drop
it; she had to run, climb, crawl on her belly
and stalk, all without losing it. If she did,
she had to do the exercises all over again as
a penalty.

When dawn broke they would start proper
shooting practice — first with blanks, then
real bullets, firing single shots.

Since she'd been told this, she hadn't slept
properly. Would Yoram be among the Pal-

mach, the secret army instructors, who came to train them out here in the desert?

Early in the morning, they saw a cloud of dust approaching from the valley below. It was their jeep. The sun was rising over the crest of the hill; in an hour, the heat would be unbearable.

The men walked towards her. First came Shimon Ben Gedi, then Udi. And finally Yoram. His hair was shorn, his shoulders were broader, and around his neck he wore a light blue, washed-out scarf. Shmuel, who ran the camp, pointed to a hollow behind the tents: a *wadi.* Yoram nodded. Ben Gedi and Udi went to the vehicle and fetched the weapons. *Come, help them carry the gear,* Yoram's expression said.

Lying on the ground, propped up on her forearms, she could smell the weapon grease. He showed her the rear and front sight, and the safety release catch that could fire single shots or, when shifted, up to 500 rounds a minute. They would load the ammunition later. That day two magazines were planned, no more. Ben Gedi stood with his binoculars on a rocky precipice scanning the landscape. British patrols seldom found their way here, but they had to be sure.

As if it were the most natural thing in the

world, Yoram laid his hand on hers, guided her finger to the trigger, and explained. She felt the warmth of his skin on her hand, his breath on her neck, and, for a moment, her impulse was to put down the weapon and touch him. Just for a second, so that she could feel him instead of the cold gun steel. The weapon went *clack*. 'When you fire grip it tighter, otherwise it'll start jiving all over the place,' he said, before standing up and going over to Shoshana. She heard her friend and him laughing. Shoshana knew all about the two of them, her unrequited love for Yoram. But she had no idea how much it hurt to be so near him without being allowed to touch him or nestle against him.

They lay all day beneath the cloudless sky in the hollow except during the midday heat; then they had to run, weapons in hands, throw themselves on the ground and shoot at a stationary target. Before dusk fell like a black scarf thrown across the hill, they fired at a dead tree stump from different angles with live ammunition. Her shoulder throbbed, but she hit the target several times in a row. They stood in a circle around the tree stump to wait for Ben Gedi's reaction to their performance. He delivered a short speech, gave some warnings, praise and then handed things over to Yoram. They'd done a good job. *Well done,* he said.

At supper, which consisted of dried fruit and a canister of water, she could feel his eyes on her. The following morning, the men would be setting off once more. She wouldn't be able to sleep again that night.

Bed Gedi had ordered some of the group to go on a night march. They wouldn't be back until dawn. She had been allowed to stay. 'Lucky you,' Shoshana said, hefting her khaki-coloured rucksack on to her shoulder.

Lilya lay in her tent, Shoshana's empty bed next to her. Was this sleep? It was as if she were swimming and diving, plummeting headlong. But there was no one to catch her.

Then she heard a noise, very faint foot-steps, and her blanket got lighter for a moment. She was lying facing the wall of the tent. She suddenly felt his touch. He crawled under the blanket, and put his arm around her belly, very gently. He just lay there without moving. She felt his sex against her, smelled his skin and breath. She laid her hand on the hand that was holding her.

'Yoram,' she whispered.

'Yes,' he said.

She wanted to turn towards him, search for his mouth and give what he wouldn't ask for. Her body shuddered as if a warm brook was rising up to the surface, finding its way out of her pores and moistening her skin. Gently, he held her close.

'It's good this way,' he said tenderly, pressing his lips to her neck. 'Let's sleep.'

'Miss Wasserfall, breakfast!' From the kitchen a floor below, the BBC fanfare to *Music While You Work* blared from the radio. A broadcaster announced Henry Hall's 'The Teddy Bear's Picnic' and a song by Les Paul and Mary Ford.

'Thank you, Mrs Todd,' she called through the closed bedroom door. She heard footsteps on the creaking stairs.

A cup of instant coffee and two wafer-thin slices of bread spread with margarine and artificial honey were waiting on a tray outside her door. Weekly rations of butter, cheese, sugar, milk and meat were limited, and you had to be registered with a shop before you could buy groceries there. Eggs were in scarce supply. But if you were lucky, you could buy a tin of Mullins powdered eggs from America. Or Sweet Today powdered milk. On the leaky ship of the great British Empire, food stamps were almost the only way to buy groceries. Even to buy the brown, calcium-enriched, bland National Loaf, two slices of which Mrs Todd had placed on her plate.

Over the window in her room still hung the thick felt curtain that Bernard Todd had fixed there during the blackout before being killed on the beaches of Dunkirk. Lilya had noticed a black-framed photo that hung in the hallway. In it, he was wearing a tight-fitting sergeant's uniform, and his face bore an expression of surprise at his new role, a premonition that it would result in his premature death and he would become a silent guest in a lonely house.

The British would leave Palestine, she thought that morning. A country that doesn't have enough bread for its own people won't want or be able to wage war on others. But what would happen if they withdrew overnight while she was still in Europe? That would mean war, and what should she do then? But what did the British want from her now? Why this curious invitation and the mention of Ben Gedi? She thought of Green. He had scarcely finished telling her that high-up people had been behind the *Nature* affair, when a shadowy employee from Whitehall had turned up next to her on a bench in Hyde Park, inviting her to a talk over tea — if it could be called an invitation. Was it her meeting with Green they were interested in? Or Lind?

She prepared her Joint papers, which should protect her if necessary, checked her ID again and glanced at the clock. The car was due to arrive at ten o'clock. She poured water into the basin and began to wash. The cold water did her good. She glanced at herself in the mirror: had she changed since her arrival in London? Her skin had got lighter, and she looked tired. She pulled up her shirt, turned to one side and viewed her breasts in profile. Then she stretched, took a comb, and tied her hair into a ponytail.

After dressing, she peered out of the window. The coffee had gone cold and tasted bitter. She ate a slice of bread, stirred her coffee again, this time with a spoonful of artificial honey, but it wouldn't dissolve. There was no one to be seen. It was only nine o'clock.

She still had time and took out Elias's texts to read. CHAPTER 1 in bold, crooked letters headed the first sheet. The text itself was written on a typewriter. It was an outline of his early life, and his brother's, Lilya realised as she leafed through it, and an attempt to understand the paths that his and Raphael's lives had followed; an attempt to orient himself, and a sketch of

Lind family life at the same time.

Perhaps you are at sea, standing at the railing. The sun is still low over the horizon. You look back in the direction from which you have come — or forward to whatever the future holds. It is invisible, merely a sensation. Even for those who can see. Seagulls follow your ship a little longer, then fly back to land. You are alone, and you still don't know if you're doing the right thing. This feeling will linger for some time. I am all too familiar with it. Every step we take is between two eternities — memory and hope. Where do we belong?

Or perhaps you have already arrived in London, which I have never seen but was my brother's intellectual home — one that might have saved him.

Here in London, your search could begin — our search. If it didn't already begin a long time ago, which seems likely if you'll excuse my presumption.

All wisdom begins with a question, as does every search. But every answer throws up a new question: often many similar questions, some new, unknown, unsuspected or unforeseen. You can get caught up in them if you aren't careful. I want to try to make things easy for you. But I don't have many answers.

Our first part is a last one of sorts: my meeting with Raphael in October 1932 in Berlin. After that I never saw him again.

In June 1932 I received a telegram from Berlin with the news of our father's death. A few weeks later a second one arrived, this time announcing Mother's death. Our parents died quickly and unexpectedly, first one then the other, as if they had run away from the ugliness about to rear its head in Germany.

I felt numb during the days that followed. Like a sleepwalker, I wandered through the streets of Jerusalem, waiting for the tears to come. But they didn't. There was just a hard knot in my belly. I wanted to believe it was grief, and began to feel ashamed that I didn't feel more affected. But something held me back from the emotions that sons are supposed to have when their parents die.

In the autumn, I decided to go to Germany. Perhaps at my brother's side in Berlin I would be able to grieve. And I secretly hoped that the death of our parents would bring us closer together.

In the meantime, Raphael had made all the necessary arrangements: the notices, the funerals and the thank-you cards for the condolence letters.

He had sold our parents' apartment on Spittelmarkt. It was too large for him as a pied-à-terre in the city centre. I had wanted him to wait until I arrived before he did this, but it was already too late. My father's bitter will, written in a shaky hand in 1925 before I emigrated and left for safekeeping, now took its full effect: Raphael was the sole heir of my father's estate. Our father had wanted it that way.

I left the ship in Hamburg and took a train to Berlin. Telegraph masts flashed past like matches in the wind. The meadows were green, the trees, fields and farms so neat it was as though they had been cut with a fretsaw. It was shortly before the elections and flags were hanging from windows.

Raphael picked me up from Lehrter Bahnhof. He looked as elegant as ever, just a little more filled-out, and he was wearing a fine suit. From his waistcoat hung the golden chain of a pocket watch — our father's. The scar on his left cheek that ended just above his upper lip shone lividly.

We shook hands. He suddenly pulled me towards him as though he wanted to embrace me, then stopped midway and pushed me away again.

The next time I travelled to Berlin, he said, I would be able to cover the stretch in one and a half hours with the *Fliegender Hamburger* train. It might even be possible before the Reichstag elections in November. Science and technology would make it possible.

I had thought for a long time about whether I should travel to Berlin without buying a ticket. I'd needed a suit for the journey, and even that was too expensive for me. Dahlia had wanted to give me her savings, but I'd refused. She should save them for times to come.

Raphael had come to the station in his new Wanderer, a black convertible, with a brown wooden trim, leather seats and what I thought were unreasonably large headlamps.

He threaded his way through the traffic down Invalidenstrasse towards Weißensee, and explained that the car was as good as new — he'd just had the headlamps replaced with these larger ones because Berlin was so dark at night. He laughed, but then his tone changed.

'It's nice of you to come, Eli. Better if you'd come earlier, but never mind,' he said.

He didn't wait for a reply, but asked how my journey from the Orient had been. And whether there was a faculty of natural sciences or even biochemistry at the Hebrew University — he called it 'your university'. Judging from its publications, he said it must be quite rudimentary.

There was a horde of people standing on a square. A uniformed man was giving a speech on the bed of a truck, and policemen wearing shako caps watched indifferently from the sidelines.

Raphael noticed me looking at this scene: quite abruptly he said that things weren't so bad. Every government needed good scientists, even bad ones. Jews were good German scientists: Otto Warburg, Richard Willstätter, Fritz Haber, Otto Stern and all the others. His place was here, in Dahlem, and the Kaiser Wilhelm Society was like a family to him. Governments came and went — that's just how it was in these times — but science would always stay.

We parked the car at the entrance to the cemetery. We walked down the avenues lined with tall trees, and the nineteenth century was everywhere, in all its blissful ignorance. According to tradition, there were stones lying on the graves. There were a great many lying on Father's grave.

'Every time I come I take two stones — one for me, one for you,' said Raphael.

'Why one for me?'

'To show them you haven't forgotten them, Eli.'

'Me? Forgotten them? That's ridiculous. It was Father who —'

'All right, Eli, let's not discuss it now.'

There were suddenly tears in Raphael's eyes. The corners of his mouth turned down.

He took a handkerchief and wiped his eyes. It surprised me to see him that way and at the same time I sensed he wasn't just grieving for our parents. For a moment, he seemed awkward, as though something were weighing him down but he didn't want to talk about it — certainly not to me. I didn't dare ask.

We went back to the car in silence. He pulled himself together and we walked alongside each other. He held his head high and there was a spring in his step, just like always. But he seemed tense.

'Let's take a photograph,' he said, trying to sound nonchalant. 'We have to record this historical reunion of ours. Who knows when the next one will be?'

Studio Baumüller was on Schönhauser Allee. Raphael had often had photographs done here for friends and family, but mostly for congresses and journals: as a doctorate student, at a lectern dressed in a black suit and a band collar, then later in a doctor's coat, in his laboratory with a microscope on the table. He said he'd either give me the photo, or send it on.

When we arrived back at the car, I suggested we go somewhere. Even though I didn't think that Raphael would go along with it. But I wanted to rescue something, build on it, without being sure what.

We had always been completely unalike. Our similarities in height and hair colour were deceptive ever since we were boys: they had obscured our differences. Raphael was four years older than me and in charge of our universe. He was a born leader, purposeful and decisive, and I had little choice but to bow down to his authority. Or withdraw deep inside my world, which no one could enter. Later, when we were older and our horizons broadened — to taking part in society and meeting young ladies — all the women fell in love with Raphael. He was witty, charming, stylish in both manners and clothing, and had a great career ahead of him. Young women like Desirée, from good families, whom I myself loved so dearly, sought my company and conversation. But Raphael was the man they preferred: I was Raphael Lind's little brother. Nevertheless, in a certain way, he was loyal to me, took me places, and wanted to show me the world — even if it was his world. And I admired him, and wanted to please him. Perhaps it wasn't so much his love that I wanted as his respect. And to be close.

In summer 1914 war broke out and everything changed. Father signed war bonds, and on 1 August he stood with Raphael, waving his hat among the cheering crowds in front of the Crown Prince's palace on Unter den Linden. Raphael's research at the Kaiser Wilhelm Institute had taken a new, 'patriotic' direction, as he called it. As for me, I wanted to do my part, and signed up for voluntary conscription. At our reunion in Berlin, I didn't want to accept that we'd lost the intimacy of our childhood and youth for ever. Why had I made this long trip that I couldn't even afford?

My suggestion was both ridiculous and futile. I remembered the Iron Lake and the Luna amusement park in Halensee. Little electric cars would drive around in a circle on the Iron Lake, and you had to try not to collide. The 'lake' was made of steel. There were bars, a hippodrome and the famous Shimmy Stairs which had a fan that blew out ladies' skirts.

Father had stolidly refused to take us children there. But our mother gave in after we begged her for a long time. She put on her 'sports clothes', as she called them: a dark blue anorak, underneath which her smart skirt looked oddly out of place. As if there were two mothers — one on the surface and one below. The upper one laughed and screamed when she stood on the Shimmy Stairs and the fans were switched on, or when she narrowly avoided a pile-up in the electric cars, her sons to the left and right.

'Halensee? You must be joking!' Raphael

retorted. He had to go to the institute. We were no longer children, he said. We'd meet at suppertime.

I stayed in Berlin for three weeks at Raphael's house in Dahlem. He had a large parlour with a conservatory, three bedrooms, a separate bathroom for guests, and a servant's room. He had begun to cultivate roses, and proudly showed me his garden. Most of the time, however, he was at the institute, and I didn't see much of him. I have to admit that that was fine by me, and he probably felt the same. Our conversations were difficult and tense. Raphael had always been concentrated and diligent, but now he came across as driven and restless; that autumn in 1932 he almost seemed like a lone hiker in an open field, looking into the distance and hearing thunder. We went out a few times and met his friends, both old and new. Among them was a strikingly beautiful young woman, a Dane, Desirée's successor, or so I guessed. She had an aura of melancholy about her, which only made her more intriguing. Raphael was not the type for serious relationships, let alone marriage; he was much too caught up in himself, and not one to make compromises. He would never have declared his love for a woman in public. But the way he looked at her and sought her out in a crowd left me in no doubt that she was more than an acquaintance.

During that time, I walked for hours through Berlin. The city had changed: it had got bigger, louder, more crowded and busy, and on the streets uniforms were everywhere to be seen. I soon felt a pang of homesickness for Jerusalem, and knew for sure that I belonged there, not in Germany.

When we said goodbye at the station one morning, with a certain feeling of relief, he gave me the catalogue — *Alexandria* — to take home. I couldn't understand why. 'Please, Eli,' he said, and I noticed that the corner of his mouth was twitching. He pressed it into my hand, embraced me, and left.

A few weeks later, I sent it back to him: I didn't want it. It had been Father's book, and now it was his, not mine. Wrapped in newspaper, and tied up with string, I brought it to the post office on Jaffa Road.

She put the text to one side and took out her catalogue of questions; under the section *Characteristics*, she wrote: *Scar (!), left-hand side red, to the corner of mouth.*

After she had packed her papers into her rucksack, she looked out of the window again.

A large, black car was waiting in front of

111

the house.

*Talk without saying anything:* that was her plan. She was nervous about the meeting, but curious all the same. *Tov,* she thought, as she shut the door behind her.

The front windscreen of the car reflected the pale, scudding clouds. In the driver's seat sat a man in a chauffeur's grey uniform, his gloved hands resting on the wheel. A small, rotund bald man was standing next to the car, looking at his watch.

'Miss Wasserfall?' he said. 'Mason's my name, from His Majesty's Government chauffeur services. Please do get in.'

He opened the door, let Lilya settle in the back, and then got in himself.

Noiselessly, the car set off. They drove past the station at Clapham Junction. Women with baskets, rucksacks and disused prams were standing in a long queue in front of a bakery, holding food stamps. The wind had died down and London's sandy-grey skyline — the streets, shopfronts, chimneystacks, garages, churches, warehouses, post offices and hospitals — seemed to be glazed in a thin sheen of Technicolor.

'Nice car,' said Lilya, after she noticed that Mr Mason was watching her with ill-disguised curiosity.

'Oh, yes,' replied Mason.

They drove across a bridge. On the left-hand side the Houses of Parliament appeared: there was a gaping hole in the roof.

'The Germans,' explained Mason.

At the archway of King Charles Street, they were stopped and a sentry greeted them through the open window, waving them in after casting a quick glance inside the car.

Mason led her through lobbies and corridors, before finally leaving her alone in a large vestibule. She examined the oil paintings on the wall. They depicted battles at sea, navy parades and views of harbours. Five chairs upholstered in red velvet stood along one wall, uninviting, as if cordoned off.

Through an open door she saw two men standing at a round, brown table, looking at her expectantly. She walked past the valet who had opened the door and entered the room.

One of the men was Desmond Terry, whom she had already met in Hyde Park. He was wearing the same well-tailored grey suit.

The other had to be Sir Lucius Honeywell. He was gaunt, tall and about Ben Gedi's age. He had a red, pointy nose and small, sparkling eyes. He was wearing a pair

113

of beige-coloured slacks and a tweed jacket with a dark grey handkerchief peeking out of one pocket. His shoes were thickly soled as if he were in the habit of strolling around his estate like a lord, or cutting roses in a remote part of his park. Honeywell introduced himself, shaking Lilya's hand and then indicated one of the chairs with a reserved, aristocratic gesture.

Desmond Terry gave her an inviting look, waited until she had taken her seat, and then sat down himself.

'I trust we haven't caused you too much inconvenience,' said Honeywell, who was now sitting across from Lilya, 'but it would have been downright rude not to invite you at all.'

Lilya looked around. Next to the meeting table, she saw a bookcase that ran along the wall and stretched up to the ceiling, in front of which stood two leather seats and a somewhat oversized globe resting on a wooden lion's foot. Between the books was a portrait of a man in an old-fashioned wig. To the rear of the elongated room stood a desk covered with a leather blotter that looked as if it had never been used.

'The car journey was comfortable and very short,' she said. 'London is a remarkable city.'

'Is this your first time in the United Kingdom?'

She nodded.

A valet poured three cups of tea from a silver teapot, which he brought in on a tray with artistically twisted antelope horns for handles. He placed milk and sugar on the table, and then vanished, as if erased from view by magic.

Honeywell dropped three sugar cubes into his tea with a pair of tongs, gazed down at them for a moment, then looked up.

'We are interested in an exchange with you,' he said, 'which is why, I admit, we rather insisted on inviting you here.'

He paused as if to examine whether the expression *insisted* had ruined the careful balance of their discussion.

'Palestine presents us with many puzzles,' he said finally. 'Perhaps you can help us arrive at a better understanding of the country and its inhabitants.' Honeywell's features assumed a rueful, rather strained smile, then he sipped his tea.

'Your friend Ben Gedi is also causing us a spot of bother,' said Terry before she could answer, earning him a scolding look from his superior.

'I'm sorry to hear that,' Lilya said coolly, looking Major Terry straight in the eye. She turned back to Honeywell.

'When our major here speaks of "bother",' explained Honeywell, steering the way back into calmer waters, 'what he is referring to most of all is how we coexist in the Mandate. Particularly when we look ahead to the near future. We'd all do better to come to an arrangement. Not to jump the gun.'

'But I'm in Europe right now,' she said, 'so you've come to the wrong person with your concerns, whatever they may be.'

'I know Ben Gedi, my old comrade from wartimes — he's always three moves ahead. The war in Europe is barely over, the corpses only just totted up, and he's already envisioning the national flag waving over Mount Zion. We were friends, once, but now he has too many wrong ideas and plans we cannot approve of . . .'

Operation Markolet: had they got wind of it? Or were they just taking a stab in the dark?

'I'm not aware of any plans,' she said. 'And you seem to know Shimon Ben Gedi much better than I do.'

'Inasmuch as one can know him at all,' said Honeywell, giving a short laugh, then glancing at Terry, who returned his look with a weary smile. The major was leaning back in his chair, his legs crossed, and was surveying Lilya with interest.

'Now, I see that you're not keen on talking to us about Ben Gedi and his plans,' Honeywell remarked, 'and the old soldier and patriot in me completely understands.'

He took another sip of tea, crooking his little finger, set down his cup, and leaned back.

Terry took a silver case from his jacket pocket, flipped it open, and offered Lilya a cigarette. She declined with thanks, but her hands shook, and she wondered whether she should have taken one after all.

Since she didn't respond to Honeywell's remark, he spoke again.

'Well, perhaps you'd prefer to talk to me about your travel plans instead? I hear that you're travelling to Germany?'

'Where the need is greatest,' she said, without showing that his question had startled her.

'I see. Your country wants to lend people a hand there. Yes, the need is immense. And it needs them too, as long as they can hold a shovel or a gun.'

He paused, and gave her a probing look.

This was an abrupt change of tack: so he knew she was on her way to Germany.

'I take it that you and Albert Green talked a little about his old country?'

Lilya started this time. She hoped that neither of the men had noticed. She waited a moment before answering: 'I went to see him about my sinuses.'

Terry stifled a laugh. Honeywell paused for a moment, frowned, then leaned forward and smiled almost paternally at her.

'You are travelling alone to a country that cost many armies to conquer. You have no idea what the situation is like over there. Don't expect too much of yourself. You may be faced with circumstances — or should I say dangers — that you have never encountered before. It can't be ruled out.'

He stood up and so did Major Terry.

'Well, in case you change your mind and would like to talk to us about your trip to Germany,' said Honeywell, 'or if we can be of service in any way, don't hesitate to contact us. You have Major Terry's card.'

Terry saw her out to the gate. He was about to wave over the car that was already waiting, but she thanked him politely and said she was in the mood for a walk.

As soon as she was back on the street a short distance away, she stopped and leaned against the wrought-iron railing that bordered the pavement. She breathed in and out deeply, slowly letting the strain of the last hour ebb away. Now she was sure she was closing in on something that Whitehall wasn't too happy about. But she still had no clue what exactly it was.

I'll have company from now on whether I like it or not, she thought, and set off for the closest Underground station.

# Chapter Seven

When Lilya entered the departure hall she heard voices, talking, laughter; some travellers were sleeping upright on the benches, their temples beaded with sweat. The air was stifling and damp. A ceiling fan ploughed its way through thick clouds of cigarette and pipe smoke. The hall was slowly filling up, and the jostling constantly increased.

The thunderstorm came like salvation: but it meant that they were stranded on the ground for the time being.

Lilya put down her rucksack and looked around. A US Army clerk thrust her way through the throng of waiting people with a clipboard in her hand. 'Wiesbaden Airbase, new departure time seven p.m.,' she cried out, and then again for the army personnel: 'Nineteen hundred hours! Please do not leave the departure hall!'

The crowd murmured in response.

Cordelia Vinyard was sitting on one of the benches facing the airstrip, engrossed in a book. Lilya was relieved to see her.

The two women had met twice in London at the Joint office to talk about the details of their trip, and to familiarise Lilya with the conditions in Föhrenwald, which were worsening every day. Cordelia advised Lilya to register not only at the Joint office on her arrival, but also at the UNRRA, the United Nations Relief and Rehabilitation Administration, which was responsible for running the camp. And it was the only place where all the information converged. For some weeks an American officer, David Guggenheim, had been running the South Bavarian office.

As well as meeting at the office, Cordelia had taken Lilya to Camden Market. When a market stand near them tipped over, and the trader shrugged and muttered, 'Jesus!', they helped him set up his stall again. As they walked away, Cordelia suddenly burst out laughing and said that, thanks to their help, *Jesus had been raised from the dead.* Lilya started laughing too, and soon the two of them had to stop, doubled over and gasping for air, while the tears ran down their faces. Just when one had calmed down, the other would shout 'Jesus!' which set them off again. Cordelia linked arms with Lilya and guided her into a pub. They were the only women, and they could feel the inquisitive looks of the drinkers. Cordelia ordered two glasses of lager, foamless and filled to the brim, and they sat down to drink them at a small table strewn with ash. The barman eyed them warily.

'Women don't drink beer. Especially not in public,' Cordelia said, winking and lifting her glass. 'That's the way the world is. But we'll show these guys they're wrong. After all, we're rebuilding the world they have destroyed. Here's to Jesus and our journey to the Dark Continent.'

In the airport departure hall, Lilya weaved her way through the crowds to where Cordelia was sitting. A fat man offered her his seat and she sat down next to Cordelia and stared out of the window at the airstrip. The rain was still lashing like sea spray over the aeroplane, which was fixed by ropes to the ground at the wings and tail like Gulliver tied by Lilliputians. The storm already seemed to be moving away, and the horizon was brightening up, the thunder just a distant rumble.

Cordelia glanced at Lilya, and, if her expression was anything to go by, she was proud of Lilya's makeover. She herself was wearing a Joint uniform that fitted like a glove, pulled in at the waist almost like a dress: there was no doubt it was tailor-made. She had black hair and almond-shaped eyes. Her lips were painted red. She gave off a scent that Lilya couldn't name — American somehow, Lilya thought: fresh and bright, powerful and excitingly foreign.

'That man who just gave you his seat — he's Dick Troutman, a congressman from Dakota. He knows my father. Once, when I was still very young, Troutman called me "Daddy's little souvenir". I didn't understand what he meant by that but it was obvious to everyone, of course, that I was different from the other white-skinned, blue-eyed girls at school. I come from somewhere in the Far East. I never knew my mother. She died shortly after I was born. That's how I became a child of the military. As a general, Father had connections and money, and he could take me or have me brought anywhere. Until I started studying economics at Harvard during the war. He once said that if the war had gone on any longer, he would have employed me as a quartermaster. That way I could have worked for him like Mary Churchill did for her father, in Potsdam during the conference. I would have been his aide-de-camp. And everyone would have known that I was his daughter!'

She looked out at the airstrip. Still nothing was happening.

'In the end, my father became adviser to the commander in chief. When I told him at the end of the war that I was going to sign up with the Joint, because I wanted to travel to Europe and help there, he handed me a list of his comrades and contacts in Germany. Mostly high-ranking officers, people in the new administration or economy. I'm sure that he dropped some cables to a few people. Then he hugged me before I left and said something that I'd never heard him say before: *Good luck, darling. I'm proud of you.*'

'And quite rightly so,' Lilya said and smiled at her.

'I'm happy you're sitting next to me on the plane,' Cordelia carried on. 'People can't actually fly, and we sometimes forget that.'

She closed her eyes as if she were already practising her flight posture.

'Before I sit next to you in the aeroplane, sweating and not able to say a word, you have to tell me what you'll be doing in Germany. I mean, apart from the fact that you'll be writing a report, and putting the

124

world's nations under pressure to open Palestine's gates,' said Cordelia, opening her eyes again, and giving her an appealing look. 'There's something else going on in your life apart from world politics, I can sense it. So, come on, Commissioner Wasserfall, out with it! Is it a man?'

Lilya blushed.

'Come on. The Joint is helping you, and I'm helping you — so I've got a right to hear your story.'

Cordelia sat up and turned towards Lilya expectantly.

*Talk without saying anything.* She pictured Ben Gedi's sharp features in her mind. It would be a clear violation of orders to tell Cordelia about the task she had to carry out. But with Cordelia, it wasn't easy to pretend, not least because Lilya would have been more than happy to share what she'd been through up to now. It was confusing enough: her visit to Green, the subsequent invitation to Whitehall, the realisation that Honeywell knew she'd visited Green. She could no longer ignore that Whitehall was interested in her search for Lind, since it was the British who had delivered the news of his death. And after all, it confirmed her suspicion that Green had been in contact with Lind for a few years. But she couldn't work out exactly what was behind it all.

Perhaps the clever, worldly, wise Cordelia would have an answer to one of her questions, or at least an idea. She seemed beyond doubt the right person to take stock of what had happened so far. And her connections in military circles might be of benefit to Lilya. But still, she had to be circumspect, and could not blurt out too much in a crowded departure hall.

'The longer you sit there saying nothing, the more curious you're making me,' said Cordelia, tearing her away from her thoughts.

So Lilya began her story with Yoram's death, telling Cordelia about her time in Hanita, in the north, the work on the land and her nights of disturbing dreams. She told her about the orders that had brought her to Tel Aviv after all those months, the task Ben Gedi had set her, and her report on Föhrenwald. She didn't hide her disappointment at having been sent away from Palestine at a time when so much was happening, and when the outline of her own future was beginning to emerge.

Cordelia listened. Here and there she asked questions if she hadn't understood properly, or wanted to know something in more detail. Then she looked eagerly at

Lilya and smiled, her head tilted to one side. 'Is that really everything?' she asked.

Lilya wondered how far she dared continue, and, after hesitating briefly, she decided to go one step further.

Ben Gedi had also asked her to search for a missing Jewish scientist in Germany, she added shortly. Cordelia seemed to prick up her ears.

'It's a personal matter,' said Lilya, lowering her voice. 'The British claim he's dead, but his brother in Jerusalem believes he may still be alive.'

'The British claim he's dead? What has a Jewish scientist missing in Germany got to do with the British?' asked Cordelia, almost whispering.

'That's what I've been wondering too. And I want to try to find out.' Lilya paused briefly, then moved in closer to Cordelia. 'Not least because I was invited to Whitehall a few days ago.'

'This is getting more and more interesting,' said Cordelia, arching one eyebrow.

'They mentioned Ben Gedi,' Lilya continued, feeling the relief of talking to Cordelia, 'and later they made it perfectly clear that I'm under surveillance. They'd clearly hoped I would make a mistake and start spilling the details. And they wanted to show me that no matter what I do here, they'll find out and know where I am.'

'I don't like the sound of this at all,' said Cordelia, and reached into her pocket to fish out a black notebook, held together with a large elastic band. Paper clips flashed between the pages.

'I'm a child of the military, and that means I make a plan before starting anything. Up to now, you've worked with your intuition and instinct — very cleverly, especially in your talk at Whitehall. But perhaps that isn't enough.'

She opened her book. It was an alphabetical address book, but just a short glance revealed that it wasn't ordered by name. Quite randomly, Cordelia's finger was lying on the letter *H*. Below it was written *Honolulu.*

She explained that this book was like a map of her life. She sorted her friends by place and subject instead. She had lived in Honolulu with her father from 1937 to 1939, so this was where her childhood friends were listed. Under *B* for *Books,* there was a list of her few bookworm friends.

The pages with the letter *L* were held together by a paper clip, as if locked away. Cordelia smiled.

'Well?'

'*L* as in *Love,*' Cordelia explained. 'Only the best and only a few. I could have placed Jeff Clinton under *K* because he gave me my first kiss in Virginia at the tender age of thirteen. But he made it into *L* — the ultimate discipline of life. My God, he was beautiful. He smelled of almond oil.'

Under *V* were General Vinyard's contacts. Cordelia wrote some of them down on a sheet of paper: officers, the US military supreme command, army doctors, representatives of aid organisations. They might all be of use, according to Cordelia, if she needed help in Germany. But only if it was really serious, she added, and closed her notebook with a smile.

Things outside started moving: the ropes on the aeroplane were unlashed by the ground crew, and the boarding engineer walked around the plane, looked into the engine and turned the rotor blades. Then came the call to move towards the exit. Vapour started to rise from the puddles on the airstrip; the sun stood low and clear in the sky.

During the flight, Cordelia kept her eyes closed and wasn't able to speak. Lilya sat next to her by the window, glancing at her on and off. She saw the country disappearing below her: fields, church spires, the coast, and then the grey sea, choppy with wind. For a moment she hoped that the plane would change course and head south towards a different sea. She saw it all in her mind's eye: first Cyprus, then the descent along the coast, the shadow of the wings on the blue of the water. And then the wind from the desert, which would be like a velvet-gloved hand on her cheek once the cabin doors opened. To land on the soil of her beloved, restless country.

She must have fallen asleep. When the plane began to descend, she opened her eyes and saw dusk fall, watching the light sinking for the first time on this foreign country: meadows, forests, farms, the crest of the uplands, a street that wound its way uphill, scarcely a light, and everything in deep sleep. Could this be Germany?

The pilot prepared for landing when they were above Frankfurt, and for the first time the city was so near she felt she could touch it.

'Take a good look,' said Cordelia, without opening her eyes. 'You won't ever forget it again. Ever.'

Lilya stared out of the window. Cordelia was right. She had never seen destruction of such magnitude.

■ ■ ■ ■

# Bavaria

## CAMP FÖHRENWALD

■ ■ ■ ■

# CHAPTER EIGHT

As soon as they had landed, Cordelia's invisible hand had immediately guided Lilya to Wolfratshausen US Commando. Here she was allocated a small room in an attic in a building commandeered by the army near the bridge across the Loisach. It was little more than a compartment, but it had a window on to the street. Camp Föhrenwald was very close.

At the airstrip, she and Cordelia had parted ways. When they'd landed, Cordelia had opened her eyes, leaned over and they'd hugged. She said she hoped they'd see each other again soon, and that Lilya should stay in touch and keep her up to date on her *mission*. Cordelia, quite herself again as she retraced the contours of her lips with a dark red pencil and tidied her hair, lent this word an undertone. It suggested all the things that Lilya had not said, rather than those she had.

Lev Ancel, who had been assigned to her by the administration at Camp Föhrenwald the day before, was already waiting for her when she arrived. He was small and slightly bow-legged, and hid a large scar under his cap, which she spotted when he lifted it to greet her: it was several inches long starting from the top of his forehead. He wiped his palms on his trousers, but then didn't shake hands with her. He seemed shy and nervous, and spoke Yiddish to her as a matter of course. It was the camp language, he explained. He wasn't fluent enough in Hebrew, he apologised, but Russian or Romanian . . . They quickly agreed on German, which Lev also spoke fairly well. He puffed and panted hard as he carried Lilya's rucksack up the steep staircase to her attic. But she detected a different, invisible burden that bowed his legs and weighed down his body.

Upstairs, he put her rucksack down and looked around with undisguised curiosity, almost amazement.

The place smelled of floor wax or an acrid detergent. The little room was bare save for a bed, a cupboard, a table and a chair, over whose arms hung two neatly folded, clean white towels. On the way up she'd seen the bathroom on the floor below.

Lev seemed to be watching her as she looked around the room, fiddling with his trouser seams as he did so. Much of what she knew about war survivors came from stories, articles or reports. In Palestine, these people existed — and yet they didn't. You saw them everywhere — on street corners, in shops, cafés or on buses, standing next to dented suitcases or ripped bags — but many of them didn't seem to belong there. For some, they were the epitome of shame, even disgrace, manifestations of a horror that was too huge to bear. How long would she be staying, Lev wanted to know, and she saw his eyes sizing up the room. He touched the table, stroking its surface, before his hand went back to fumbling with his trouser seams.

'I'm not sure yet,' she said. It all depended on how quickly she gained access to the camp.

He had orders to drive her to Munich the following day, he said, so that she could apply for a pass to the camp at the UNRRA Regional HQ: without a pass, there was no way in. But the car wouldn't be available until the afternoon. Lilya thanked him and said she hoped she wasn't causing too much trouble.

He raised his hands, as if he were trying

to push something away. 'Tomorrow at five,' he said, raised his cap again and left.

She opened the window, took in deep breaths of fresh air and looked out, her ears pricked. What was that noise? Then she realised it was water coming down from the mountains: she'd never heard it before. For a while, she paused and lost herself in the unfamiliar rushing sound.

At five o'clock sharp the following afternoon, a car drew up outside the door. She had everything she needed: her papers, the ID card that Ben Gedi had given her in Tel Aviv, and confirmation from London's Joint HQ saying she should be deployed in Föhrenwald 'on a temporary basis for administrative purposes'.

Cordelia had told her that when commissions sent their reports to the top, to the very places that had requested them after weeks of enquiries in the camps, tiny miracles sometimes happened: food rations from American suppliers were suddenly approved, new apartments provided and new jobs created for camp occupants, equipped with shiny German machines straight out of the factory. The Makabi football club received a set of brand-new balls, the printing press was repaired for the camp newspaper

*Bamidar,* and the passport process that paved the way to a new life for many was speeded up faster than anyone had dared hope.

Lilya would do her best. After all, she had received orders. But any conclusions she drew would be more effective if she could put them into a wider context. More than a year after Germany's collapse the camp conditions still seemed scandalous. She would make that unmistakably clear. A report without vision was just a sheet of paper. Although she wasn't going to provide people with bread or new beds, she could conjure up a much bigger image: one of the future.

Lev Ancel was waiting next to the car, his right hand fumbling with the door handle as if inspecting it. They drove in silence for the first few miles but there was no awkwardness between them. The road rose and fell over gentle hills, and in the waning daylight the meadows and fields shone with a green that she had never seen before. Below them in a river valley lay a monastery, indicated by a crooked wooden sign that pointed down the road. Lilya quickly realised that Lev was an inexperienced driver. It took up all his concentration. Sometimes she thought he'd said something to her, but when she turned, he was only murmuring faintly to himself. 'Double-declutch' she heard him say, and 'accelerator' when he stepped on the clutch to change gears.

He had only learned to drive a few weeks ago in the camp, he explained tersely when they reached a long, straight road, gripping the steering wheel: Munich wasn't much further. They'd said he should take every opportunity to practise — something he hadn't had the chance to do until now.

Finally they reached the UNRRA garrison quarters in Siebertstrasse in the north of the city and pulled up in the shade of a beech tree. Lev turned off the engine and sighed. His hands looked like two creatures that he'd set free, no longer tamed by the steering wheel.

Through the car window, Lilya looked at the huge, miraculously undamaged buildings in München-Bogenhausen. That's what Cordelia had called it, as though it were a separate town. Like Jerusalem-Rehavia, thought Lilya and felt a stab of homesickness. She pulled herself together and got out.

A short gravel path led to the building that was fenced off from the street by high wrought-iron railings; their metal tips looked either like corkscrews or petrified flames. Lilya studied the building, which was like a small palace; it was both inviting and hostile at the same time. She paused for a moment, and then passed between the two stone pillars that marked the entrance to the grounds. The door itself must have been broken off during the war. Only the hinges were left, hanging uselessly on the pins fixed to the masonry.

The villa door was ajar. *UNRRA Team — South Bavaria* was written on an improvised wooden sign next to the entrance. She heard the clattering of typewriters, a telephone ringing and voices coming from somewhere deep inside the building. From the large garden, bordered by tall trees, strains of birdsong filtered to her ears, and a squeaking sound, probably made by a swing moving back and forth on rusty steel rings. Lilya went in.

The lower-floor corridor was wide and had a high ceiling. Two women in faded dresses were sitting in one of the wooden-panelled rooms. Perhaps it had once been the library or study, but now it served as a waiting room. The women were both gaunt with sunken eyes and were wearing worn-out shoes. Opposite them, a group of men anywhere between eighteen and seventy were slouched in chairs. Near the door, an elderly couple were waiting, huddled close together. They were wearing black armbands and not talking.

'Nathanson!'

The door opened, an officer peered out and ushered the couple in. Murmurs in Yiddish, Russian and Polish went through the room, and then died down again.

Was she too supposed to sit down and wait? When a uniformed employee walked along the corridor, she approached her and explained who she was, showing her papers and her ID card. The woman looked at her uniform and took Lilya to a large room overlooking the garden, which must once have been the parlour in this grand villa. There was no one there. On an armchair lay folders containing documents held together by coarse string. A uniform jacket hung on a coat stand that looked out of place; the room smelled of cigarette smoke. Pencils, a dented tin coffee cup and an ashtray lay on the table. A photograph of a woman was propped against an empty vase. Lilya guessed her to be in her mid-twenties. She was blonde and was wearing a dark, well-tailored dress with bright white polka dots. Her lips were curved in a cautious, almost graceful smile. She was extraordinarily beautiful.

Lilya waited for a few minutes, paced up and down the room, hesitated and then sat down.

Again, she heard the sound of squeaking drifting in through the open veranda door. She decided to follow the sound into the garden. And there, behind a hedge, she discovered the swing, its ropes swaying to and fro. Over the shrubbery, a mop of blond hair appeared and vanished again.

When she reached the swing, she heard a man's voice saying, 'One, two, three and fly!' A barefoot boy in short trousers, not much older than six, launched himself off the swing, went flying through the air, landed in a squat and did a forward roll. Neither of them noticed Lilya.

But when the boy did glance up and see her, he darted away, squeezed through the garden fence and disappeared into the neighbour's garden. David Guggenheim, the American UNRRA boss in charge of Föhrenwald, the Displaced Persons Camp, turned to face her. His eyes were sky blue, but there was something troubled in their expression.

Guggenheim was wearing loose-fitting olive-green trousers and an open-necked white shirt. He could only be a few years older than she was. His hair was slicked back with oil; he pushed a strand out of his eyes before shaking hands with her.

'Hannes visits me now and again,' he said. 'His father's doing time in Nuremberg, and his mother's disappeared without a trace. Only the nanny is left. That's the way it goes: "The fathers have eaten sour grapes and the children's teeth are set on edge." '

'Ezekiel 18,' she said. 'But it must have been more than sour fruit that shipped his father off to Nuremberg.'

'Yes, he was one of the big guys — a doctor who did experiments in hypothermia. Hannes will never see him again. But he probably won't forget him — and who's to say whether that's good or bad.'

His tone was casual, even self-assured, in a way that made her nervous.

He looked in the direction in which the boy had disappeared, now long out of sight. Then he turned back to her again. 'Let's go to my office,' he said. 'I expect you don't have much time.'

He gave her an appraising look which she couldn't interpret. Then he walked off towards the villa in silence. She followed him through the garden. He was averagely tall and tanned from the sun, his stride nonchalant yet purposeful. She could picture him only too well strolling across a sundappled campus in the United States — David Guggenheim Jr, Ivy League, East Coast — a top-notch diploma in his hand, looking out at the football pitch where he'd won trophies for the team with his quarterback skills. Then after high school came his good deed of going to Europe. A member of the US Army, transferred to UNRRA after the war ended to join the world's helpers and rescuers, as befitted a young man from a respectable family. He'd spoken German to Hannes with barely a trace of an accent, and now he switched to English. All very slick, she thought.

He offered her a seat at the large table and looked at her as if he had no need to prompt her into telling him what she was doing here. After all, he was someone who had already listened to so many people.

All the things that she admired in Cordelia — her aura of invincibility and worldly wisdom — made her inexplicably furious when she saw them in David Guggenheim. But what angered her more was that people like him — with their American notions of peace, complacency and spotless consciences because they were 'saving the world' — could get to her in the first place.

143

It took a great deal of self-control to hide these feelings as she briefly summed up why she was there. She wanted him and UNRRA to grant her access to the camp as a Joint representative. She placed her ID card on the table.

He barely even glanced at it: his eyes slid briefly across the photograph, while she felt a twinge of annoyance at the huge stamp covering the right-hand side of her face.

In Palestine, people were concerned about the situation in Föhrenwald and in the other American camps in south Germany, she continued.

Guggenheim listened to her without saying anything, but became visibly more agitated as she repeated the word 'report', spoke of 'possible maladministration', and the resulting 'political imperatives'.

'So you really want to help? By writing a report? One of your superiors seems to want to know exactly how dire the situation is here and what a lousy outfit UNRRA is. And he wants to show that we Americans aren't capable of putting the necessary pressure on the British Mandate to make the gates to Palestine spring open, as if freshly oiled. Papers here, papers there! Big ideas! What we really need is every hand on deck. Money, blankets, medication and, at some point, a political solution.'

He paused.

She took a deep breath, surprised by his outburst and the vitriol of his words.

'We're concerned that it's been a year since the war ended, and people are still being held behind walls,' she said, 'including children who have never lived in freedom. Our main aim is that these people find a country that they can call home, that the community of states finally wakes up and that this misery . . .'

He was looking out at the garden. Was he even listening?

'Community of states? Nice idea. But it's closed for repairs at present,' he said. 'Come back again in three years! No, better make it five, and perhaps the situation will have improved by then.'

He turned back to face her. 'If you really want to know how things are, put your pen down and stay for a few months, like many of your Joint colleagues who are now indispensable. You'd be very welcome. But not long from now, when we can't cope because floods of survivors fleeing from the East have overrun us in Föhrenwald, you'll be over the hills and far away. And your report will be neatly filed in some drawer. Thank you so much, Miss Wasserfall, a truly fine job. And your far-sighted perspective, how very thought-provoking!'

Lilya was taken aback by Guggenheim's vehemence. He seemed to hesitate for a moment, as if he himself realised that he'd gone too far. She thought that was the end of their discussion and that he'd show her out. But he was leaning back again.

'Ezekiel 2:1,' he said abruptly and smiled.

Her mind ticked over until she thought she knew what he was referring to.

' "Son of man, stand upon your feet and I will speak to you." Ezekiel's assignment.'

He smiled again, this time his eyes twinkling with curiosity. 'This is my offer: I'll grant you unlimited access to the camp. Come and attend our conferences, look everywhere and stir about in anything you don't like the look of. Oh, there's plenty to find! Write it all down and take your notes. Talk to people, even your own people. And if your report manages to work wonders — no matter how small — I'll come to Palestine, cap in hand, and look you up.'

She wanted to come back at him but instead remained silent, even though it was tempting to keep on arguing. But she'd achieved what she wanted. And it hadn't been her decision to come here armed with just a pen.

He signed the papers, looked her briefly in the eye as if trying to establish whether he could trust her, then got up and showed her to the door.

In the corridor, uniformed UNRRA personnel, two US Army officers and a man in civilian clothes with a brown briefcase under his arm were waiting; they jostled past her.

'Gentlemen, thank you for coming,' she heard Guggenheim saying in a steely voice. Then he closed the door behind her.

# CHAPTER NINE

The following morning, she wanted to set off for the camp straight away. Lev said he'd be waiting at the gate. Following the path that ran alongside the railway tracks, she walked from Wolfratshausen in the direction of the mountains, which seemed strangely close. The path led her past a wood and soon she spotted the endless barbed wire that fenced off the buildings. The entrance to the camp lay opposite the railway tracks and was guarded by US Army soldiers. On the other side of the road barrier, a few men were standing around. They were smoking and arguing loudly. One of them eventually looked across at her. It was Lev; he waved. After showing her papers, she was quickly let past the camp entrance. Lev came over, glancing furtively at the other men, as if he felt awkward meeting this pretty young woman.

'Welcome to Föhrenwald,' he said.

He'd drawn a map of the camp on a piece of card: the fence, streets and squares, the administration office, hospital, synagogue, cinema, playing fields, various stores and market place. The cardboard map was for her to keep, he said.

Surrounded by a group of barefoot, spindle-legged children with deep-socketed eyes who had appeared out of nowhere, they set off. Lev gently shooed away the little gang in front of them until the children grew bored and scattered.

She read the signs they passed: Michigan Street, New Jersey Street, Connecticut Street, New York Street.

'It used to be called Adolf Hitler Square,' said Lev, 'now Roosevelt Square. You have to move with the times.'

As they walked around, Lev constantly greeted people, doffing his cap and patiently answering their questions. She sensed that some of them only said hello or caught her up in conversation to get a better look: they were curious about Lev's new guest. But there was both hope and scepticism in their curiosity. A young uniformed woman with a notepad and pen could mean many things, among them perhaps a ticket to a new life.

The roads were narrow but the houses were made of stone, even though the plaster was crumbling in many places. Carts, wagons and prams were used by the camp occupants as means of transport: they filled them up with wood, carrots or potatoes, explained Lev, and on Sundays with goods that they hawked at the market.

A man shouldering a leather bag hastened towards them, greeting them before he hurried on. That was Ezer, the postman, Lev told her. This postman held sway over life and death, future and departure, freedom or camp, so people said. Ezer was the one who brought news of whether you had to make it alone in the world from now on, or whether there was still hope. People were afraid of him, yet they looked forward every day to his rounds, and were disappointed if he didn't stop at their house. Lilya had already realised that everything Lev told her also referred to himself.

Lev knocked on a door and they went in. He wanted to show her the living quarters, all of which had the same layout. They entered a plain, dark hallway. On the right was the kitchen, on the left the bathroom and at the end a bigger room, divided down the middle by a horse rug hung by crude hooks in the wall. Camp beds were set up in the room. Three on one side, two on the other, with barely room to walk in between.

Lev guided her around the camp for several hours. He showed her the bakery, where you could often get fresh bagels, and the Florida Bar right behind the synagogue, which served excellent coffee and soda. The Sunday market even attracted Germans from the surrounding areas. You could buy just about anything there, even American jeans, Lev said.

He showed her the tailor shop, telling her with undisguised pride that he ran errands for them now and again by car. He sat down at one of the brand-new machines, stepped on the cast-iron pedal and asked Lilya to take a look: it was a miracle of technology.

'Lev, a sewing machine isn't the same as a car,' said the tailor shop manageress, a plump woman with a Polish accent who must have overheard them from the room next door.

On a clothes stand hung trousers, dresses, blouses and pillowcases. And a dress still pinned at the seams, clearly intended for a girl. Lilya took a closer look.

Lev suddenly appeared next to her and stroked the fabric, running his hand over the hem again and again. 'Ruth,' he murmured, almost to himself.

'It's beautiful,' said Lilya. She imagined the kind of girl who would wear this dress:

a straw hat in one hand, she would run along a path beside a rapeseed field that stretched in endless yellow as far as the eye could see, while a bird circled overhead, plummeting and rising, its wings open as if in greeting. Lilya looked at Lev and froze. He was as white as a sheet. He turned away and left without a word.

'His daughter, Ruth,' said the woman. 'He lived for a long time hoping that she would wear this dress. His other daughter's name was Hannah . . . He knows there's no hope now.'

They walked silently back down New Jersey Street. Lev had returned to his normal self and wanted to show her the playing field: it was a special day, and nearly everyone was out there. Today was to be the day.

On the outskirts of the camp, where the wood began, people were already jostling their way along the length of an improvised playing field. The team from Camp Feldafing had arrived on a US Army bus that was parked a little way off in the blazing sun. Besides the camp occupants, UNRRA and Joint employees had turned up, along with US soldiers; they were all standing in small groups lining the pitch. Lev and Lilya thrust their way through the crowds, but no one took any notice of them: they were all waiting for the teams to arrive.

Suddenly, Camp Föhrenwald supporters started clapping as their team walked out on to the pitch. The Camp Feldafing players ran on to the pitch, jumped up and down on the spot, and stretched and clapped each other's hands in the air. Yelling over the din of the supporters, Lev tried to explain to her that Föhrenwald had often played against Feldafing but was always beaten. Today the tables would be turned.

More and more spectators surged towards the edge of the playing field. The game started and the ball flew down the pitch, landing straight in Föhrenwald's penalty area. The crowd roared. The game went back and forth, appearing very evenly balanced in strength and skill.

Lilya glanced at a group of uniformed men who had moved to the side of the playing field. Her eyes scanned their heads, and she found herself looking for David Guggenheim.

Lev tapped her from behind. 'The daily briefing in the camp cinema,' he said. 'You should go over and listen. There'll be UNRRA reps too. Come on, I'll take you there.'

The uniformed men set off and Lev fol

lowed with Lilya at his side. He would pick her up later to take her back to the game.

The room was dimly lit; it must once have been some kind of community room, and now it was the camp cinema, which was almost more popular than the synagogue, Lev explained before he left. There were chairs set out on a podium in front of the screen. Men and women from the independent camp administration had gathered in the auditorium: a doctor from the US Army who ran the infirmary, several representatives from Joint, as well as an envoy from an Eastern European aid organisation for refugees. He had come straight from Russia to Föhrenwald. A young woman called Lisa Strassburger represented the camp committee. Someone had laid a blanket for her on a chair in the front row.

A young army officer climbed up on stage and commenced a brief talk: the situation in the camp would drastically decline in the coming weeks. Exact figures were not known but a huge flood of survivors from the East was expected. Those who weren't trying to find a way to Berlin, he said, were heading to Bavaria. By now, this group made up the majority of the refugees. Most of them wanted to enter the American zone; assaults on Jews in the East were on the increase.

Some who tried to return to their old homes found other people had moved in and occupied them and they were driven away again. Jews were being attacked and robbed. Word spread quickly about even the most minor incidents, leading to panicked reactions. There was fear of a mass exodus to Germany.

'Föhrenwald isn't sufficiently equipped for them all,' said the officer. 'We have already far exceeded our limits.'

As the officer was talking, the door opened and three uniformed men entered the room: one of them was David Guggenheim.

The officer asked them up on stage and gave the floor to the UNRRA director.

'Thanks, Harold, and thank you all for inviting us to your camp meeting. Only a host of measures can help us in the current situation. The danger of starvation, typhus and TB is growing and we have to help more people leave the country so we can take in new occupants,' he explained. 'Please check camp supplies — food, clothing, blankets, medication — and I'll speak to the medical services of the 7th US Army again and put some serious pressure on them. New camp beds are on their way.'

Lilya saw that Lisa Strassburger was taking notes.

155

'And we have to bolster our training programmes,' continued Guggenheim. 'We have to prepare new occupants as quickly as possible for life outside the camp. We need books. I'll try to get in touch with the depot in Offenbach again. Despite excellent contacts, I've been banging my head against a brick wall so far. It's a setback, but that's the way it is.'

Lilya knew about the haven of looted Jewish books in Offenbach, set up by the US Army in an old factory building. As soon as she was done here, Offenbach would be the next stop on her list.

The young officer, the one Guggenheim had called Harold, looked around. 'Any questions?'

'Why books, of all things, when there's not enough for people to eat?' asked one employee.

Guggenheim's eyes searched the room for the man who had spoken. 'Books can feed people too,' he said, 'and we're all familiar with Lisa's work here.'

Lilya eyed Guggenheim more closely.

The young woman, Lisa Strassburger, had put down her notepad, wrapped the blanket around her legs and crossed her arms across her chest as if to warm her body. She seemed to be following Guggenheim's talk calmly and intently.

'Without education and training, these people won't have a chance in Palestine, or wherever it is they want to settle down,' said Guggenheim. 'No one's waiting for them to arrive. They have to be able to offer something. Our schools and evening classes are just as important as food, clothing and' — he paused for a moment — 'weapons.'

'Thank you,' said Harold, casting his gaze across the crowd again, about to end the meeting.

'But books aren't weapons.'

Silence.

She had said something after all without meaning to.

Guggenheim looked over at her. 'What are you suggesting?'

'Blankets, medication, camp beds and books alleviate suffering, no doubt. But they're not enough,' she said. 'Without a political approach, you won't find a long-term solution.'

There was murmuring in the room and Lilya felt uneasy.

Harold asked for quiet. 'Let the comrade finish what she's saying,' he said.

But Guggenheim ignored him and his voice had a hard edge to it. 'I'm quite prepared to discuss your theories and listen to your political suggestions,' he said, turning to face Lilya. 'Come to my office. You know the way. My door is always open for a good argument — a qualified one, mind you.'

Guggenheim didn't wait for her to answer and jumped down off the stage. Lilya wanted to react to his rebuke but Harold beat her to it by saying, 'Thank you, the session is now over.'

They went back out, squinting in the bright sunlight, Harold walking alongside her. He laid a hand on her arm. 'You may be right,' he said, 'but in some situations what seems appropriate is precisely the wrong thing. We wouldn't be where we are today if it wasn't for David. He's sometimes difficult or hard, and maybe not always fair. But we can only fix the essential things with the means we have, and he uses all the influence he has.'

'Well, Harold, what's the score?' Guggenheim was suddenly standing next to them. He didn't seem to take any notice of her.

'A draw, or at least it was before the meeting.'

'Perhaps we can make it back before the game's over and catch a goal or two,' he said. He turned to her. 'Commissioner Wasserfall, would you accompany us? It could be something for your report: sweating, fighting Jews, all happy together.'

She was taken by surprise for a moment. 'Just like back home,' she said.

Guggenheim laughed and, for a moment, the tension in him seemed to relax.

# CHAPTER TEN

'What is it, Lev?'

'A message,' he said.

He'd knocked on her door, come in and automatically sat down on the edge of her bed. He was holding a piece of folded paper. Although she'd only been in Föhrenwald for a few days, she already felt as if she knew him well. She liked and trusted him.

On the day after their tour, she had explored the camp on her own. She'd been to the infirmary and school, crossed the market square between the camp entrance and the railway tracks, and had met Lev there, who was delivering clothes from the tailor shop to one of the stalls in his car. His face had lit up when he saw her — she'd seen him smile for the first time — and she'd helped him out, taking a pile of blouses out of his car, folding them neatly and diligently as she had been trained to, then lining them up on a plank resting on wooden trestles. Lev thanked her, letting the trader know with a certain pride that he and the young lady were acquainted.

Now Lev stared at the floor, the piece of paper in his hand.

Quite abruptly, he handed it over to her. It was a telegram. She sat down opposite him on a chair.

'Ezer gave it to me,' he said. 'You've only been here a few days, and you're already one of us. He's visited you too now.'

She opened the telegram: it was from Shimon Ben Gedi. His message was as short as it was puzzling.

*REQUEST IMMEDIATE REPORT AND CONTACT+STOP+*

The last time they'd met, a good three weeks ago, he had commanded her to weave any usable information about the Lind affair into her camp report. If it fell into the hands of the decryption experts in Baker Street, their eyes should pass over it without noticing a thing.

Albert Green, *Nature,* Whitehall, Terry, Sir Lucius Honeywell — Ben Gedi would be astonished and go looking for Elias Lind. But what was the rush? Something must have happened.

Lev was still sitting on her bed, sunk in thought, as if a telegram had reached him

161

too, but one he could barely understand. Lev had led her through the camp twice, with an upright, decisive bearing; but both times she had sensed his agitation and the edginess that showed in the way his hands constantly moved. Lev still said nothing.

'It's nothing to worry about, just a wire from a friend,' she said and folded the telegram again.

Lev did not react. He made no sign of getting up. She came over and sat down next to him.

'A wire,' he said, and at that, without waiting to be asked, he started to recount his story, first quietly and falteringly, then more and more fluently. He told her about his life in a village near Cernowitz, under Imperial Austrian and, later, Romanian rule, his wife Rivka and his daughters Ruth and Hannah. There were always new rulers arriving, the Russians, Romania again; over the years they had taken on many different nationalities, but they had remained *Jews* throughout. There had been good times and bad — until the Germans had arrived, that is, and then it all ended. His family had fled and after a few days, separated: he went to find out whether they could all go into hiding with distant relatives in Russia. And so he left them behind.

When he returned with good news a few weeks later, the houses in the village where he had left them were all abandoned, with truck tracks leading away.

He'd fled again, always heading east and mostly at night, and every step had torn his heart to shreds. He'd hidden and walked until he found work and lodgings with a woodcutter. He tried many times to get information about his girls. People told him not to ask too loudly if he wanted to keep his job.

When the war had ended, he'd made his way back west. En route, he was attacked in a forest and his assailant, whoever he was, tried to kill him. But he survived and dragged himself on.

He lifted his cap and leaned forward so that she could see the scar. In Poland, sapped of strength, he'd eventually come across people from an aid organisation who gave him essential supplies and told him about Föhrenwald and Bavaria. They also searched for information about his family. One day a message had arrived: there was no hope. They had pushed a piece of paper into his hand on which the name Ancel was written three times: Hannah, Rivka, Ruth.

He fell silent.

'It's better to be certain,' he said into the

silence. 'Then you can slowly start to bear things. Uncertainty, on the other hand, grows and if you're not careful, it can bury you alive.'

Abruptly, he sat up straight. He wanted to know what she was going to do now she'd read the telegram. His hands began working and moving again; he smoothed out the bed cover. Then his fingers found the wooden frame of the bed and started to feel its underside.

She would wire Ben Gedi to say that her report would be ready in the next few days. He would know what to do with it. But the only way to send a cable quickly and safely was from the UNRRA office in Munich. She'd have to contact David Guggenheim and ask for his help; there was no alternative. Could Lev drive her there tomorrow?

'It's practice,' he answered, his face lighting up.

David Guggenheim was not around when she arrived in Munich the following lunchtime. She asked a woman in uniform when he'd be back. 'Some time in the evening,' she replied.

Lilya was undecided whether or not she should wait for him.

Lev explained that he had to return the

car; he was needed in Föhrenwald. But she could go back on the Isar Valley train — the Jerusalem Express. That was what everyone in the camp called it.

She decided to stay and look around the city, and call in at the UNRRA office again late that afternoon. Lev drove away and she set off in the direction of the English Garden, where she came across people with carts, rucksacks and prams, gathering wood for winter. A school class sat on one of the large greens, being instructed by a nun.

Crates were being carried out of the Haus der Kunst gallery, supervised by a delegation surrounding a young female soldier. Around her stood other soldiers, passers-by and people who could be art experts. A man hung about in the background, and she wondered for a moment if he belonged to the group or if he'd stopped out of curiosity. She slowed down.

His gaze rested on her for longer than decency or tact allowed, then he turned back to the group. He was wearing a brown, worn-out suit and a dark, wide-brimmed hat that partially covered his face. He was sturdy, small and had a full beard. When she drew level with the group, he looked at her, then back at the young soldier.

She crossed the road behind one of the

few cars parked by the kerb. It was an old pre-war model with a tarpaulin roof. She carried on walking without turning around until she reached Theatine Church: bombs had blasted a hole in its roof. It was covered with scaffolding, and a group of teenagers, women and elderly men were putting bricks into piles. A crane spewing black soot was lifting coarse blocks of stone and putting them down elsewhere. The odour of mortar and dust lay in the air.

Before she continued towards Marien-platz, she looked around again. In the distance, four lions pulling a chariot stretched their paws up into the air; the Siegestor was buried by their fall. The entrance to the Hofgarten was hidden under heaps of debris and rubble. A man was standing there, his back to her. Had she been followed from the art gallery? She decided to err on the side of caution.

In her training, she had learned that in situations like these she had two options: the first was to take the most circuitous route possible: not to go straight to Marien-platz, but to zigzag into side streets and back on herself to check whether she was being followed. The second was to approach her suspected stalker and see whether he tried to avoid her.

It was also possible to use both methods, one after the other. This was time-consuming but gave a more reliable result.

She walked the few yards towards the entrance of the Hofgarten through clearings in the piles of debris, as if she wanted to look at the field marshal's hall from another angle. On the same spot where the stranger had been standing, there was now a black market trader wearing a baggy coat. He addressed her, holding out a fan of postcards depicting a line of uniformed men marching in high leather boots.

The man in the brown suit had vanished.

Good, she said to herself. Now for the cross-check.

Later she didn't know how many twists and turns she'd taken, how many streets and alleys she'd turned into, how many ledges, scaffolding sites and shopfronts she'd used to measure the distance she'd covered with her trained eye. But there was one thing she was certain of: the man stayed on her heels for a while with a skill and routine learned through years of practice. Then he disappeared. Who was he? One of Whitehall's snoops? She hadn't forgotten Major Terry's words: *I had to follow you for an awfully long time . . . A car will pick you up in Clapham.* Since then, they might have found out that she was searching for Raphael Lind and perhaps were now in pursuit of her.

Or was it a completely different person?

She would be better off among crowds. In front of the barely damaged town hall, tables and chairs had been set out and shaded by threadbare parasols. Guests held their pale faces up to the sunlight; nearly all the tables were taken. She went down the steps of the Ratstrinksstube Inn whose windows were bricked up and into a dank cellar chamber. Two men were sitting at the far back of the bunker-like room; one of them, who was dressed like a priest, was wearing a black cloak. Spread out in front of them were papers, and what looked like photographs. The younger of the two seemed to glance in her direction. She was almost certain it was David Guggenheim and felt a pounding in her throat. She headed back out with a glass of lemonade and sat down at a table that people had just vacated. Should she talk to him if he came out? Perhaps it was better to let him attend to his business and try to visit him later in his office as planned. In her bag was Elias Lind's text. She looked around once more, but there was nothing strange to be seen. The place was crowded, she felt safe. Then she opened up the dossier.

## Chapter 2

Perhaps it's all rather simple (although no less terrible) and Raphael has met his death, like so many of our people. I should start getting used to this thought — to everything we don't want to know or hear about in this turbulent country. People here are supposed to be strong: the motto is 'reconstruction, battle and youth', and the humiliation of torture and annihilation are things we don't want to see. We don't want to look into the lifeless eyes of ashen-faced people who tell us stories about a distant country that is not ours. Or so we think.

I was also young once and strong, just like Dahlia, whom I have dreamed of every night since our meeting in Ascher Levandovsky's haven; and every morning, my hope that she's still alive is quashed again. When I arrived in this country only a few years after the Great War, I wanted to leave the past behind and only look forward to a new tomorrow.

In May 1923 I announced to Father that I was leaving for Palestine. It was a proper speech. I'd prepared it for weeks. We were sitting in armchairs in the living room. Father was leaning back and I was sitting on the edge of my seat. In the background, I could hear the large grandfather clock ticking: I could barely take in anything else.

He listened to me in silence, not asking me a single question or interrupting once. When I'd finished, his head sagged to his chest. Then he stood up, walked over to the high windows that were bright with sunlight and looked out at the street without saying a word. The long curtains hung almost symmetrically to the left and right; he looked like an actor waiting for the curtain to fall. I could only make out his backlit silhouette, his large stature, his angular shoulders and his hands; he was wringing them behind his back, and they seemed to have taken the place of talking.

'Eli, I'm appalled,' he said eventually.

He turned around and looked at me. I tried to hold his gaze.

'I can't approve of your plans,' he began, 'because you are destroying everything. Everything we have ever built.'

He had fought for years for recognition and equality, he said, in a trembling voice. He'd gone through years of suffering because they were not wanted. They had been driven away because they didn't belong to anyone or anything.

'But now, Eli, we've finally reached our goal,' he said and pointed to the window. 'Look at our city. Look at Raphael and his achievements. Now we're seen for who we really are: Germans of Jewish faith. Patriots. Schiller and Goethe's heirs. Scientists, lawyers, doctors and bankers. The desert lies behind us, Eli.'

I'd often heard these arguments before. Father's words had a weight, and he spoke as if his life depended on it, as if all our lives did. I should have interrupted him because I knew he was wrong. The desert didn't lie behind us: it lay in front of us. But I didn't dare.

I had no inkling of the events that lay in store for us. And if anyone had predicted them back then, I wouldn't have believed them. I just felt the venom of all the small humiliations I had suffered. I began to tell Father about them. Just as I told him about all the things that had happened to me in the army, at university and every day — things that he turned a blind eye to. And the constant fear that everything might be taken away again: the looks, the whispering behind my back, the unmistakable feeling of being tolerated, but never gladly.

'Good morning, Dr Lind, congratulations on your PhD. Wonderful,' the professors would say to me in passing. But they were barely out of range before I heard them whispering, 'Such a nice, clever fellow, so cultivated. If only they were all like him, then we'd be able to get on. But when it comes down to it, that's not what they want; they just pretend they do to gain the benefits. It's actually quite a shame. He's an extraordinary young man and his father is most agreeable. Not to mention his brother, Raphael Lind, an expert! The Kaiser Wilhelm Institute! And what strapping young men! Who would have thought that Jews could grow so tall . . .'

Father listened to me and I was sure he understood. But I wasn't allowed to be right, because everything I was saying put his life into question: our life. Everything he stood for. I had placed myself outside the family.

Father looked at me and said he would think over what was to be done. He insisted that I speak to Raphael. At the end of our conversation he said, 'Take a leaf out of your brother's book. He knows where he belongs, and that Jews don't run away any more . . .'

I'll never forget that sentence, and it chokes me still to think of it.

Lilya peered over the papers towards the entrance. There was no one to be seen. She continued reading.

Afterwards Father must have talked to Raphael. He asked me to meet him in the Romanisches Café. I'd never much liked it, but it was a second home to Raphael.

We pushed our way through the small room

to his regular spot by the window. Whereas Raphael greeted people left, right and centre, shaking hands with people at every other table, slapping shoulders or bending to kiss the hands of ladies in pearl necklaces, a charming smile on his lips, I was eyed warily.

As soon as I sat down, I had the feeling that Raphael was more relaxed than he had been in the past few weeks. The day before, there had been a great commotion at home. Father had arrived back early from the office, embraced Raphael and then disappeared into his study. 'Raphael is happy today,' Mother said. 'He's been given permission to work again.'

Raphael waved the waiter over and ordered drinks for us both. Then he drew a cigarette out of his case, lit it and gave me a challenging look.

I didn't want to have an argument with him. All I wanted was to confirm my decision, speaking to him in my own words: I knew that if I started to discuss it with him, we'd end up getting nowhere.

'Palestine?' cried Raphael, who burst out laughing after I'd laid out my plan. 'What nonsense! What colossal nonsense!' Then he leaned over the table, his eyes piercing me. 'Father will throw you out. On your ear,' he said, more calmly. 'Think it over, Eli.'

When coffee and cognac were served, he came back to my plans and I made it unmistakably clear that I was going to stick to my decision, whatever the consequences.

Raphael made a few more attempts to convince me of the opposite: he used the same arguments as Father. But I remained firm. I said I knew what I was doing. Gradually, he lost his composure. He seemed totally unprepared for my decisiveness; it was completely unfamiliar to him. I'd never seen my brother so rattled.

'Then go, for all I care! Go, in God's name, Eli,' he finally concluded as he threw back his cognac. 'But it's the wrong decision, you'll see.' Then he turned to the window and I thought I heard him say in a strangled voice, 'It's all wrong . . .'

Lilya noticed that the man she took to be a priest had stepped out, and was squinting into the sunlight, shortly followed by David Guggenheim. He fished for his sunglasses in the pocket of his uniform and put them on. The men shook hands and the priest left.

She was still unsure whether she should approach him or wait until later in his office. But Guggenheim was already coming over to her.

'May I take a seat?' It didn't sound like a question.

'Be my guest,' she said, and tidied her papers.

'Sorry, have I interrupted your reading? The report?'

He laid his hat, sunglasses and a pack of cigarettes on the table.

'No, it's more like a letter in a bottle,' she said. 'It's private. In a reckless moment, I promised to help a friend as I'm in Germany anyway. He can't travel any more.'

'Out of generosity,' said Guggenheim, and smiled at her, 'or true love?'

'Neither nor. Let's call it necessity. It's a long story.'

'And you're not prepared to tell me?'

'To be honest, no, otherwise we'd still be here tomorrow.'

'Perhaps it'd be worthwhile,' he said and leaned back, interlacing his fingers behind his head. Lilya didn't respond.

A waitress came up and asked if they wanted another drink. She indicated her half-full glass and Guggenheim politely declined.

He leaned forward again. 'What's your impression of this city and this country? Will we ever be able to forgive them?'

She was puzzled by this abrupt change in

topic. 'I think there are much more pressing questions right now.'

He looked at her expectantly.

'I'm less interested in what happens to this country. In any case, I haven't been here long enough. What's important is the country that needs to be created, after all that's happened.'

'And its new citizens who are stuck behind my fences, waiting for the day they can emigrate at last?'

'No one has to go to Palestine, but there are many who want to and Britain is not letting them in — with armed force. And America is just sitting back and watching, without lifting a finger.'

'Is that an accusation?'

'It's nothing against you personally. Your duty is to the camp, and that's a big enough task. And it'll get even bigger in the weeks to come. I'll cover it all in my report: the suffering of so many, the shortage of everything, the failure of politics and politicians.' She noticed that Guggenheim was growing restless.

'Global politics are for people who have enough to eat,' he said. She was tempted to interrupt him: this was a discussion she wanted to avoid. 'My politics are rather smaller in scale, but you can see and feel their results. That's why I talk to Germans and the priest, who I was with just now. He passes on requests to trace missing persons, putting on necessary pressure and keeping his faith in the ways of the Lord. Even though he spent the last months before the end of the war in a concentration camp unsure what would happen to him.'

'He helps you and the camp occupants?'

'Yes,' said Guggenheim and looked at her. 'On an individual basis.'

After the scene at the camp cinema, Lilya had resolved not to broach this subject any more. But she wasn't finding it easy. She sipped her lemonade.

Guggenheim seemed to be deliberating whether he should continue the conversation; he suddenly looked tired, even though his blue eyes had a steely shimmer.

'I have a great deal of respect for everything I've seen here,' she said, and lowered her voice, 'especially what you and your people are doing. I've noted many things and I'm grateful to you all for the candour and hospitality I've been shown. But there's one thing: soap washes but doesn't erase dirt. You are not going deep enough. That's why I'm here.'

'You'd like to break up the camp tomorrow if you could?'

'I'm highly appreciative of what you and the UNRRA are doing. But you are managing misery without any kind of political perspective.'

'We're not a government. We're an aid organisation.'

'You're an American. You have all the influence you need, right at your fingertips.'

'Oh, if only it were that easy. You think Uncle Sam just has to click his fingers and all the misery in the world is eliminated? And if he doesn't, then he's not doing his duty? Don't you think your expectations are a little high? The war ended only a year ago.'

She sensed that he was agitated and tried to fight her rising anger. She had nearly managed to make him lose his composure again. Even if this discussion would be just as pointless as their first one at the villa. Some vague impulse drove her on against her better judgement. 'I'm only trying to put what I see here into a larger context,' she said. 'I'm not taking inventories of camp beds.'

Her ploy seemed to work. 'Of course you're not!' cried Guggenheim, raising his voice. A few people at the neighbouring tables turned around.

He leaned in close. She could see the veins in his neck and feel the warmth of his body.

'Instead you're stuck up in your ivory tower of paper forms, reflecting on greater contexts in the hope of changing the world with a choicely worded report. Start at the bottom! Where people need to get their hands dirty!'

Had she gone too far? David Guggenheim hadn't done anything to her. He'd given her a free rein to carry out her work, and write whatever she liked and felt was important. He hadn't once asked to see her report before she handed it in. In the end, she didn't want to convince him of anything; she wanted something completely different. She tried to start again, making her voice more appeasing. 'Perhaps all we're talking about here is an effective division of labour.'

He looked at her in surprise.

'I mean, each of us has to make his or her own contribution so that the situation improves. Perhaps we can reach an agreement — camp beds *and* politics.'

'The pipes of peace?' he said and reached for his cigarettes.

'For the time being. But without any smoke signals in my case.'

'And without fire?'

'It depends where you're looking from,' she said.

Both of them laughed. 'Okay. Offer

accepted,' he said and offered her a cigarette again. With feigned disapproval, she declined.

'Have you seen everything you wanted to see? Before your journey continues or you head home?'

'Enough to write my report.'

'I mean here in the city. Munich must once have been very beautiful.'

'Using a great deal of imagination, I've mentally rebuilt the odd church here and there,' she said.

'I hope they don't fall down again as soon as you leave.'

'Well, then the Americans will turn up with shovels and diggers.'

'And it'll be your job to hold the construction plans.'

They laughed again.

'Division of labour: I could warm to that idea,' he said and took a deep breath.

Neither of them said anything for a while. Perhaps only to break the silence, she said, 'I went to visit you in your office. But you weren't there. And to kill time, I took a look around the city. I was going to try later.'

'Try what later?'

'To ask for your help. I have to send a cable. And it has to reach Palestine as quickly as possible. It's quite urgent.'

A jeep drove up. At the wheel sat Harold, the young officer from the camp meeting; he turned off the engine and waved to them. She felt both relief and disappointment that their talk was over. Guggenheim offered her a lift to Siebertstrasse where she could take care of her cable. They walked over to the vehicle and, with blatant curiosity, the young officer asked her to climb in.

# CHAPTER ELEVEN

Lilya was sitting at her small attic desk by the open window. Pencil in hand, she looked at the report in front of her. Work done. *Test? Not failed. Trust me.*

She had decribed the situation in Föhrenwald: detailed, clear and without any compromise. Jews still being held behind barbed-wire fences; children who had never experienced anything like freedom in their lives. Thousands and thousands of Jews arriving from Eastern countries, desperately seeking shelter in Germany. She had talked to people, and visited the infirmary, constantly surrounded by children tugging at her trouser leg. She had been allowed to inspect lists and pore over statistics; she'd asked how the German population near the camp was managing and what people expected to happen in the coming weeks. Time and time again, she'd been told: *nothing good.*

These Jews were stuck in Germany but Britain was still placing an iron hand across the gates to Palestine, the only safe haven for them. A haven that could become Israel, if they succeeded: she, Ben Gedi and the others.

Would her boss be satisfied with her? If he was, he would know what to do with her sharp-edged report, her conclusions: funnel it into the broader political discussion, leaking it to newspapers and members of parliament in Britain and influencial congressmen in the US. Putting more and more pressure on the British government in London.

After just over a week, it was time to move on. She hadn't seen David Guggenheim for a few days since their impromptu meeting at the Ratstrinkstube. In any case, he didn't figure in her report. But the thought of him had stayed in her mind. She had caught herself hoping to bump into him while she was asking questions and conducting investigations on her camp rounds — a look, perhaps a quick exchange of words. But it hadn't happened.

Cordelia had already registered Lilya's planned visit to the Offenbach Archival Depot, although Lilya hadn't told her why she wanted to go there. The US Army had set up the OAD in a factory warehouse on the banks of the Main to store recovered looted Jewish property, including millions of books. Lilya wanted to see if she could pick up Lind's trail there using the leather-bound catalogue, *Alexandria*. She would pack in the morning. And if the trail went cold in Offenbach, she would travel on to Berlin to look for Desirée von Wallsdorff.

Her report on the Displaced Persons Camp should generate pressure from the outside in a more general way. However, the Lind affair, as Ben Gedi put it, should hurt the British from the inside. That is, if there was something to reveal. It was time to find out.

She knew that Raphael Lind had worked for the British during the war, passing on his research to them with Albert Green's help. Had Raphael Lind known what he was doing back then? He was a traitor, even if it was for the right cause. Had the Germans found out and come to fetch him? Perhaps under torture and interrogation, they'd squeezed him for every last drop of information before putting him up against the wall. That might explain his disappearance from the German bureaucratic system without a trace. *Deleted from record.* She imagined him in some cellar captured by the Gestapo, his black suit and torn white shirt unfastened at the cuffs, a splintered pocket watch lying on the floor, a pool of blood and excrement, snatches of words in Hebrew, a prayer. An order, then a shot.

She lifted her head and looked out of the window. She remembered the photo of the house in the woods. Before she left, perhaps she would find someone in the camp who could decrypt the smudged writing on the back.

Putting her pencil between her teeth, she leaned back. Through the attic window, she saw a bird of prey the size of an eagle. It was coasting on the wind, circling to lose height before rising again, its wings opened wide. There wasn't a cloud in the sky, just this solitary bird continuing its course until it vanished from sight.

She heard someone on the stairs. The door was flung open.

'Pfaff sewing machines!' cried Lev, and entered the room. 'An entire truckload! From Kaiserslautern, straight from the factory.'

She looked at him, puzzled.

'They just found them in a warehouse and David Guggenheim brought them here. Just like that, without asking anyone. We can start a company with the sewing machines and sell whatever we don't use in the camp to the whole country! And I'll have a suit at last, like a proper chauffeur.'

'I'm happy for you, Lev, and I'll use your services whenever we meet.'

His face fell and he turned serious. Had she said something wrong?

'You're really going to —' He broke off and seemed to be thinking something over. 'You're really going to leave. Is that what you're saying?'

'It's high time. I've done what I came to do. There's just one more thing on my mind.'

'I'll drive you anywhere you want.'

She laughed. 'It's something different this time. I have a photograph with a puzzle on the back. It belongs to a friend and he asked me to decipher it for him. But I don't understand what it means, and perhaps you can help, Lev.'

She went over to her rucksack and pulled out the *Book of Books,* inside which the photo was wedged. But Lev appeared to be more interested in the leather-bound book with its gilt bookplate: he came closer and looked over her shoulder.

Lilya explained that it was the catalogue of a library whose books were missing; that she was going to use the rest of her time in

Germany to find out what had happened to it.

She handed him the book, and he ran his fingers over its surface, touching the gilt inscription. Then he opened it and leafed through its pages. He was about to shut it again when he paused for a moment. He had spotted something and seemed to be trying to remember something.

'That inscription — I've seen it before.'

He pointed to the ERR stamp: he'd seen it somewhere here in the camp; he didn't know what it meant but he recognised it. He racked his brain and then he remembered: in the room next to the camp library. He could take her there. But first, he wanted to see the photograph.

'I'm looking for someone who can first make the text visible and then decrypt it,' she said and held out the photo.

'Those are two different things,' he said, smiling. But there were all kinds of experts in Föhrenwald, even those who could make the text invisible again after reading it. Lev took the photo and stuck it into his jacket pocket.

'I'll see what I can do,' he said. 'I'll get back to you by tomorrow.'

It was only a short journey to the camp by

car. Lev drove her straight to the Tarbut Szul, the Main Camp School, hoping they would find Lisa Strassburger there. She wasn't only in charge of the school and library, Lev said, but was a leading member of the camp board of directors too.

Lisa Strassburger was poring over some lists at a library desk and looked up when they entered the room after knocking gently. Her hair was red and she had a reserved but charming smile. Despite the heat and quite out of keeping with the season, she was wearing woollen stockings and a cardigan. Lilya had heard it said that some kind of trauma made her constantly feel cold. The slightest draught was like a steel blade slicing through her. The warmth of her voice when she greeted them belied this. She knew Lev and remembered Lilya from the meeting.

'Welcome to my arsenal,' she said with a wry smile, alluding to the silly row over Lilya's comment.

Lev explained their purpose and told Lisa about the black book and its stamp.

Lisa sighed and asked them to follow her.

In an adjacent room — a warehouse for paper, writing equipment and unusable books — there were two crates standing in a corner. On one of them, Lilya spotted the letters *ERR.*

Lev began to fiddle with the seam of his trousers again.

'May I look inside?' Lilya asked.

'Be my guest,' said Lisa.

Inside the crate were bookends made of metal, beech, ebony, oak and teak, some very simple, others richly adorned or inlaid; some even resembled sculptures. They nestled in crumpled paper, as though they had been carefully and lovingly packed, then forgotten.

Lilya turned around. 'Where are they from?'

'I expect they're from Offenbach. But I don't know exactly. When I started here a few months ago, the crates were already here.' Lisa Strassburger hugged herself, shivering. 'But what am I supposed to do with bookends when we don't have any books?'

She had asked the Americans at the book depot in Offenbach for support with the camp library many times, but in vain.

She sighed again. 'We've asked the UNRRA for help — after all, we're their responsibility. David Guggenheim's done his best. But whenever he asks for the books we need so urgently for our school and library, they turn a deaf ear or bring up legal reasons why it's not possible. We fill in application after application, but there's no sign of any progress. At some point, I'll just send the bookends back with an angry note.'

Lev was becoming agitated. Lilya could sense that he wanted to get involved. 'Perhaps you can help?'

Lisa Strassburger looked at her, wide-eyed. 'Are you planning on going to the depot?'

Lilya sketched out her plans, saying that Offenbach was indeed her next stop, even if just for a flying visit.

Lisa turned up her collar. 'Perhaps *you* can try?'

'Why would they listen to me?'

Lisa smiled. 'Because you could make them believe that the last thing Palestine needs are dumb Jews.'

Together, they went out into the sunshine. Lisa turned to Lev, who had escorted them out.

'It was a nice evening last night, Lev,' she said, 'and the occupants learned a great deal from Harold. Some of them have changed plans: they aren't interested in Palestine any more. They want to go .to Pennsylvania instead.'

'Perhaps Miss Wasserfall can put them

right?' said Lev and gave Lilya an impish grin.

'That would be wonderful,' said Lisa. 'Once a week,' she explained, 'the people from UNRRA and the Joint get together and tell the other aid organisations and army staff about their home countries. Crowds of people turn up to listen. Lev persuaded a young American officer, Harold, to come last night. It was terrific. There's another meeting tomorrow.'

'And what should I do?' asked Lilya.

'Talk about your home. Your family, the way of life, what people do. Do you have siblings? Perhaps a brother you admire? They'll hang on to your every word. But they all have an infallible instinct for spotting the truth. They'll know if you're glossing things over. It would be marvellous if you came.'

Lilya reached for Lev's arm and looked up at the sky. The bird was back.

'Don't think for too long. Just say yes,' said Lisa. 'Tomorrow at six o'clock in the cinema. And then you can leave this place, knowing you've done a good deed.'

Lev gave her a hopeful sidelong look: she wanted to say no, but instead she found herself saying, 'Sure. I'll be there.'

■ ■ ■ ■

In Wisconsin Street, some boys were playing football. They were wearing short trousers, and running barefoot and bare-chested
through the dust with red, dirt-smeared
faces. Their stripped-off shirts served as
makeshift goalposts. A woman shouted
something to them in Polish, brandishing a
broom. When she saw Lev, she waved to
him.

They made their way to Yehuda, to whom
Lev wanted to show the photo. If anyone
could make the writing on the back visible,
Lev said, he could. The ball flew over their
heads and landed in the scrub brush.

'This is a little town like any other,' Lev
explained. 'People argue, work, hope, cheat,
have children, make plans and die. And
they're also worried about balls smashing
through a window and landing in their
soup.'

He fished the ball out of the scrub, put it
in front of him and tried to kick it back to
the boys. But instead, it flew steeply up into
the air, lingered there for a moment and
plummeted almost vertically back down
towards Lev: he had to jump aside to avoid
it. The boys roared with laughter and Lev

joined in. He had a high-pitched laugh, almost a whinny: an onlooker might have thought he was crying.

They carried on to Independence Square. Yehuda was sitting on a bench in front of a building, a young man with wire-framed spectacles and tousled, brown hair. Lev asked Lilya to wait where she was for a moment. She saw the young man take off his glasses, stick the arm in his mouth and hold the photo close to his eyes. Then he held it up against the sunlight as if trying to see through it, before putting it into his jacket pocket. Lilya couldn't hear what they were saying. Lev came back over.

'He thinks the Joint is doing a good job in Föhrenwald and wants to help us.'

She didn't feel comfortable about letting a stranger pocket the photo. But did she have a choice?

'He thinks you're nice,' said Lev.

'He doesn't even know me.'

Lev smiled. 'Everyone knows you here,' he said.

'What makes you say that?'

'Everyone's curious. You can't do anything here without people noticing. Like I said, it's a small town.'

'And what do people think of me?'

Lev hesitated.

'Come out with it, Lev.'

'Oh, this and that.'

'I see,' she said, and poked Lev gently in the side.

'They think you're pretty.'

'Is that all?'

'And that your report might help. And . . . that you're sad.'

'Sad? What makes them think that?'

Lev hesitated again. 'It's hard to say,' he began, 'perhaps because of a man . . .'

'What man?' She realised that Lev was finding it difficult to carry on. But he was the one who'd started the conversation.

'Some people have heard about your loud discussion with Mr Guggenheim,' he said, 'and now they think you and Mr Guggenheim — that you didn't really . . . well, that he was very unfriendly towards you and perhaps that's the reason why. They feel sorry for you.'

'Nonsense. What do you think, Lev?'

'Nothing.'

She poked him again.

'I think you're looking for something. You're strong, but fragile at the same time — you don't want to be here, but you don't know where your place is yet. In Palestine, of course, like all of us, but that's not what I mean. You can even be unhappy in Palestine. Or sad. When you have no goal.'

'Carry on, Lev. What else do you see?'

'Men, many men.'

'What do you mean?'

'I'm not sure. But they all want something from you.'

'Lisa is a woman. And she wants me to talk about Palestine.'

'And you agreed.'

'Yes, I did. But I'm only going there if a man accompanies me,' she said, and gave Lev a sly look. He sprang to attention and smiled.

'I won't let you down,' he said.

Lev offered to take her for a walk after the meeting the following evening — her last one in Föhrenwald. He showered her with compliments and congratulated her on the talk. But he was in a serious mood. They left the camp and found a path through the woods; the evening sun was filtering through the treetops like glass splinters. Past the edge of the woods, they saw a farmer ploughing a field; the plough was being pulled by a gaunt brown horse.

The evening at the cinema had been a success. She had talked about Jerusalem, her home, the city of hope and hatred, a real place but at the same time otherworldly, a windy village in the mountains off the beaten track, a provincial setting and a global stage. She talked about the hope of creating a country for everyone, about plans, discussions, gatherings and the need for fighting and politics. She had painted a loving portrait of her parents Deborah and Ehud, and had taken the audience on a trip down the streets of Rehavia. She'd left out any mention of Yoram.

All this had sapped her energy. But the enthralled, open expressions of the people in the audience swept her along. Lev had stood next to her and translated into Polish and Russian. She'd listened to her own words coming from Lev's mouth, foreign in a comforting way. When Lilya finished her talk, Lisa asked the audience if there were any questions. Although the hall had been quiet, people now flung up their hands: How did she see the future? What did she think about British politics in the Mandate? Could you swim in the Sea of Galilee, and was it true what they said about the healing powers of the Dead Sea? Was the fruit from the trees as large and juicy as people said?

Lev pointed to a glade in the woods. 'The drill square. Not for me, but for the boys who can still run, jump and hop.'

She saw traces in the sand, broken branches, rough markings hewn into tree trunks, a hollowed-out pit.

She stopped. 'Lev, there's something you want to say, but instead you speak to me about young soldiers and praise my talk to the heavens. It's putting me on edge.'

In his hands Lev had the photo. The young man with the wire-framed spectacles had managed to decrypt the inscrutable letters on the back in a single day. Now they were legible to anyone. He'd carefully retraced them in pencil. She could read the text now, but didn't understand it. No figures or formulas, just a sentence.

*Det bugter sig I bakke, dal.*

What language was it? What did Raphael Lind's note mean?

She looked up and searched the sky above the trees. Where was the bird?

Lev continued walking for a few paces in silence.

Lilya turned to face him. 'I'll miss you, Lev.'

He embraced her, quite unexpectedly, held her for a moment, then pushed her away again. 'Talk to Mr Guggenheim,' said Lev. 'He should know that you're going to Offenbach.'

'Why, Lev? I have the impression that I

only aggravate him. It doesn't take long for him to get annoyed with me. I don't want to bother him any more. Really, I don't want to . . . I . . .'

'That's not it,' said Lev. He looked at her. 'I think it'd be far worse for him if he knew you were a long way away,' he said with a smile.

With that, they started off back to the camp in the dwindling light.

■ ■ ■ ■

# OFFENBACH

THE HOUSE OF BOOKS

■ ■ ■ ■

# CHAPTER TWELVE

Lilya wound her way around bomb craters overgrown with weeds. Alongside the old streets, a net of paths had cast itself across the city. Dirt tracks and channels that cut a swathe through gardens and backyards led past hollow façades, heaps of debris, twisted steel girders and windows streaked with dirt. Women in aprons and headscarves were knocking the mortar off bricks and piling them into small heaps. An ageing couple in field-grey overcoats were pulling a handcart on which they'd piled wooden crates, an old mirror and a wicker laundry basket. In it a small girl was lying on a pile of clothes, asleep. Greenery was growing out of the tumbled-down stumps of walls: grass, fern, moss and clover.

Lev had driven her to the station in Wolfrathausen. The UNRRA office had called the camp administration in Föhrenwald and asked him to be a replacement driver for the director. This was good news. As they said goodbye on the platform, Lev had taken off his cap and waved it above his head. He became smaller and smaller as the train set off, and Lilya felt a lump rise in her throat.

Near Offenbach in Frankfurt, 250 miles north of Munich, she had been assigned lodgings with US Sergeant Harvey Ladenbruck. She still felt Cordelia's hand over her, invisible yet effective, helping her out when she needed it. Since his war injury, Ladenbruck had been working as a warehouse clerk. His world consisted of ladders and lists, corned beef, sweetcorn, peas, French's mustard, beer, dried eggs, coffee and powdered milk.

He was climbing down a ladder in the warehouse when she came looking for him, wiped his hands on his uniform trousers and looked her up and down. He stood lopsidedly as if he could only put weight on one leg.

'Lilya,' she said, reaching out a hand to him.

He smiled. 'Harvey,' he said.

'Okay, no point hanging around here then. Let's go.' His eyes were dark and he spoke rapidly. 'Come along then, miss.'

A woman was just leaving the building when they reached Harvey's quarters. She must have been in her late twenties, wearing a little too much make-up and a tight-fitting dress that looked like she had sewn it herself, and light-coloured stockings with a hole in the knee that she'd darned with different coloured thread. After they went in, Harvey told Lilya that when he arrived in the evenings she was nearly always on her way out. Her name was Anita Renneberg and her husband was missing — either fallen in the war or in captivity somewhere. The house belonged to her mother, who still lived in a garret upstairs but could no longer leave her home. Harvey lived on the first floor, through which they had to go to reach the second floor, where Lilya would stay.

They climbed up the narrow staircase to the first floor; to the left and right, plaster was falling off the walls.

Two guitars were propped on wooden stands and cables were lying next to them; on one of the chairs was a black Bakelite radio with its back removed. Mouth organs of different sizes and pitches lay strewn over the floor as well as electricians' manuals and all kinds of tools — screwdrivers, pincers and metal saws — were scattered across Harvey's quarters, as well as nails and spools of thread on the bedspread. The yarn was the same blue as Anita Renneberg's darned stockings. Harvey picked up the things and threw them into a box.

'Les Paul,' he said, pointing to the guitar. 'He's opened up a completely new world of music. Heard of him?'

Lilya said she hadn't.

'Hitler's dead, long live hillbilly, that's my motto. Music makes people good. Except for the really bad guys. But let's go upstairs so I can show you your room.'

He reached for a key that was lying on his chest of drawers where handwritten sheet music was spread, opened the door and, with a gallant gesture, indicated that she should go first.

Lilya's room was on the second floor with a view on to the backyard. There was a bed, a chair, and on the floor in the corner lay two dismounted chandeliers. The room was spacious and empty. She could hear a ball being kicked against the wall down below and boys shouting. Next door, a saw whined.

'That dreadful thing,' said Harvey, and left. If she needed anything, she knew where to find him.

The next morning, she set off for the Offenbach Archival Depot. She reached the River Main, which divides the city, by crossing the Römerberg, Frankfurt's historic main square, where only three single façades were left standing, their stepped gables looking like a pair of ribs. The broken steel arm of the Eiserner Steg footbridge rose up through the water; on the far bank of the river, Lilya saw workers with shovels approaching a wheezing digger.

After securing a place on a ferry barely bigger than a dinghy, she felt a growing unease. Would she be able to trace Lind in the OAD with the *Alexandria* catalogue?

The depot was situated on a bend in the river. After she'd passed Offenbach's bombed-out port, she saw two trucks on the river quay in the distance. Soldiers were carrying crates to a ship.

'Please be careful!' she heard a man shout, who had a clipboard of lists in his hand.

'Books from the Alliance Israélite Universelle in Paris — think of them as precious china, gentlemen.'

The man was wearing a white coat, like a doctor or chemist, talking to the men who were panting with the effort of carrying the crates. He encouraged each one of them: thank you, that's the way, just be careful, yes, carry on.

An officer joined him and looked at Lilya. 'Could you possibly give them a hand?'

Lilya arched an eyebrow. The man with the clipboard looked at Lilya and waved her over. She wanted to point out the mistake but the man looked so determined that she simply went over to the open truck bed, took a crate and carried it to the ship; a bare-chested docker took it from her and disappeared into the ship's hull. She helped until the second truck was also emptied. By then, Lilya was thoroughly drenched in sweat. The late afternoon July sun was high in the sky. She wiped her forehead with her upper arm.

The officer who had asked her to help stood in front of the group.

'This is a moving moment for all of us. A homecoming, a partial reconciliation. The books will be sent back to Paris.' He laid a hand on the shoulder of the man in the white coat. 'And we also need space. We're bursting at the seams.' Then he said to Lilya, 'Now you can return to your desk,' and left.

Lilya watched him, dumbfounded, until the man in the white coat eventually reached out his hand.

'Welcome to Noah's Ark,' he said. 'A rather unconventional greeting, admittedly. My name is Nathan Westmann and I'm in charge of identifying books. You have already been announced. And I have read your brief letter.'

Cordelia, Lilya thought.

'Can I freshen up somewhere?' she asked.

'Come with me, I'll show you where everything is,' he said. 'Captain Bernstein will never learn to decipher military badges and stripes. He can decrypt any bookplate in the world, almost better than I can. But as far as military rank is concerned he's a dead loss. That's academics for you! You could have refused to help: you're a member of the Joint if I've interpreted the badge on your uniform correctly.'

Lilya accompanied Westmann through the gate where two GIs were standing guard. The OAD building was several storeys high and its windows were metal-framed. It was solidly built, and the main entrance consisted of a heavy, steel door.

'This used to be a chemical plant,' said Westmann. 'IG Farben. I don't know what they produced but it's now home to our books.'

Lilya stopped behind the entrance in front

of a pile of crates made of coarse wood; on the side stood NIRO in large lettering.

'We're dependent on abbreviations here, and sometimes even I lose track of what's what. NI stands for the Netherlands, and RO is the Bibliotheca Rosenthaliana. They're on their way back to Amsterdam. We found these extraordinarily precious books stashed away in Hungen, very near here. A rich citizen of Amsterdam called Leeser Rosenthal once donated them to his home city.' He laid a hand on one of the crates as if he wanted to give it strength for its long journey ahead. 'Come with me, let's go up to Director Bernstein's office. I'll introduce you properly.'

The Offenbach Archival Depot was one of the American force's central collection points, Westmann explained. The IG Farben factory premises were perfect: they had a quay equipped with loading facilities, a crane, a ramp and railway tracks running from the depot to the river.

They crossed a room on the fourth floor: the sunlight strained through the windows. Thousands of books were lying around, loosely piled in crates. The room was quiet: no one was working here.

'These are our biggest headache,' Westmann said. 'We haven't given up. Our bookplate investigators have looked through them all, over and over again — but no luck.'

Lilya picked up a book and weighed it in her hand as though she were determining its origin and former life by its weight. She imagined it sitting in a large, venerable library — in *Alexandria* — where there was a smell of paste, leather, paper and dust, and where the clacking of hooves and the shouts of newspaper hawkers could be heard from the street. Where the floorboards creaked and Chaim Friedrich Lind came in through the door, solemnly fixing his spectacles on his nose with a measured, almost ceremonial gesture, then reaching for a book from the shelf.

'Hold it for a moment. The warmth of your hand will do it good,' said Westmann. 'Mozart's complete works, Ludwig von Köchel, Breitkopf & Härtle, Leipzig, 1862. First edition. Take a look, KV. 525.'

Lilya thumbed through the pages.

'*Eine kleine Nachtmusik,*' explained Westmann. 'No bookplate, no personal notes, no trace of the owner, nothing. Like all the books in here.'

Captain Isaac Bernstein was sitting in his office at a large, dark wood desk at right angles to his secretary, who was dwarfed by a huge Underwood typewriter. 'I owe you an apology,' said Bernstein, rising.

He had a pleasant, sonorous voice. He'd taken off his tie, which was lying on the desk.

'One of my subordinates has pointed out my mistake. But you carried those crates like you were one of us!'

'I've done my share of carrying,' she said.

'Where, if I may ask?'

'In a kibbutz in Palestine. If you live there, you can't avoid learning how to carry.'

'We won't be able to give you much time. You can see how busy we are. More and more books keep arriving here, need sorting and sending back to their owners: and now even the Displaced Persons camps are demanding books. They want to set up libraries! Dr Westmann will assist you with your enquiry. If he can't help you, no one can.'

He escorted her to the door where Westmann was waiting for her.

'Come with me,' he said. 'You haven't seen the half of it yet.' There was pride in his voice.

On the third floor, long tables filled the room, criss-crossed by washing lines. A young soldier with rolled-up sleeves was stirring paste in a bucket.

'This is where we treat damaged books. We try to restore everything we can within our means.'

Nathan Westmann went over to the soldier and cuffed his arm in comradely fashion. 'This is the director of our "medical unit". He brings these dead cases back to life by cleaning, drying, gluing, patching and binding. That's what the washing lines are for — to hang up the pages to dry.'

She began to wonder how long Westmann's tour would last. It wasn't that she found it boring: on the contrary, she was following everything intently, with curiosity and compassion. It all interested her. But she also wanted to know whether she was in the right place. 'Dr Westmann,' she said, 'when can we talk about my search?'

'Tomorrow. Bring everything you have with you. And some patience. I'll be up here on the second floor with the bookstamp investigators. Or come to our morning conference at nine o'clock. I'll tell Mr Bernstein you'll be there.'

The following morning, Lilya joined the people standing at the open door of the OAD's conference room on the first floor. Employees were sitting on chairs, stepladders or on the edge of tables; many more were standing. One of the corps officers was taking minutes in a notebook.

When Westmann saw her standing in front of the door, and realised that she was reluctant to enter, he waved her in. Next to him was Captain Bernstein; Westmann pointed to a free space by the window. 'Good morning, ladies and gentlemen — officers,' intoned Bernstein. 'At ease, make yourselves comfortable.'

A tall, strapping GI who was standing next to her whispered, 'That's his standard opening.'

Bernstein asked for quiet. Another soldier next to her got up and stepped forward. He produced a note.

'The heating has been repaired again,' he said. 'Three windows on the upper floor have been replaced and the pile of rubble next to the building will be removed today. The security staff will be increased again by two MPs and we have 149 employees, volunteers and armed force members, eight liaison officers and, as usual, guests.'

At this, he looked over and winked at her.

'Thank you, Sergeant. More on that later. Dr Westmann, over to you.'

Nathan Westmann stood up, a sheet of paper in his hand that Bernstein's secretary had given him. 'Receipt of 830 crates, wooden, standard format, approximately 200 tons,' he said without consulting the paper. 'Transport from Hirzenhain. Origin: various European countries, especially Belgium and Holland, Jewish texts as well as Freemason books. The material is in a deplorable state.'

He paused and looked around to see if people were following him. 'All the books in interim storage in Frankfurt City Library have arrived here to be inspected: twenty trucks, approximately two and a half tons each. Torah scrolls and other religious books are on their way here from Wiesbaden. Inspection is scheduled. Output: sixty wooden crates from the Biblioteca Rosenthaliana. Destination: Amsterdam, loaded and shipped. No confirmation of receipt as yet. Alliance Israélite Universelle, Paris. Shipping completed.'

'Thank you, Dr Westmann. Especially for the careful loading operation. And also to those who helped. And now for the general situation: as you all know, the General Clay Office report has arrived, and from now on Offenbach will be the central, unique collection point for looted books.'

He paused for a moment. 'Any questions? None, I see. The number of visitors announced for arrival or already here is once again very high. The list will be handed out to you in a moment. I would ask you to stand by for upcoming talks in my office.'

The sergeant read out the list: Lilya heard Russian, French, Dutch and English names. A jolt went through her.

'Guggenheim, David. UNRRA, Munich.' For a moment, she was anxious that she'd misheard. 'Library for the Displaced Persons Camp Föhrenwald.'

After Bernstein had ended the session, he asked Lilya to come into his office. He handed her a letter from Cordelia.

'We aren't a post office,' he said, 'but we help where we can.' He sat down behind his desk. 'Even though it's difficult for us and we aren't supposed to do this in the first place, the DP camps are crying out for books as much as soap and milk powder. You've just come from one of these camps, and that's why I'm interested in your opinion. If we send some of the books we've rescued to one of these places, we enter a legal grey zone. Because then we lose control over what's been entrusted to us for survivors, dependants and legal owners. But as time drags on, we're hard-pressed, even forced, to find a way to deal with this.'

She pictured the empty bookshelves in the school building, Lisa Strassburger's helpless smile and the box of bookends from the ERR's inventory. And Lev, pointing to a crate and looking at her expectantly.

'I think that whoever you send bookends to should also receive books,' she said.

Bernstein looked up. 'I'm afraid I don't quite follow you.'

Lilya told him about her visit to Föhrenwald library and the crate with the ERR stamp.

'People from Bavaria are arriving today. So you don't think I should send them away empty-handed?'

'If you're really interested in my opinion — no, you shouldn't.'

Bernstein looked at her challengingly. 'And why not?'

Lilya told him about the poverty in the camp, people's hunger for life; education was imperative for them to be able to start over again. It was also a weapon in the struggle for freedom. Increasing numbers of children would grow up in camps who would have to be educated for life through books. It was everyone's duty to help, she said. Without education, there could be no hope.

She paused, surprised at how committed she was to this cause. Bernstein had taken off his glasses, as if by not seeing her he could understand her better.

'I like your expertise. For all its lack of scholarliness, it's very convincing. It would barely stand up to legal scrutiny. But still.' He looked at her with paternal mirth, even though he couldn't have been more than a few years older than her.

'It's not about scholarliness,' she said. 'You don't have to test my hypothesis in front of a dissertation panel.'

'True,' said Bernstein. 'In any case, this evening, an UNRRA employee is arriving from Munich. We're on good terms with him, but he's a stubborn guy. I'll see how he reacts to your opinion. Because he's searching for any way he can to make his camp's claims legitimate.'

She had to go; Westmann was waiting for her. But she would have liked to hear more about this 'stubborn guy'. Was he coming alone, for how long and where was he staying? Did he know that she was in Offenbach? *Just forget it,* she told herself.

Before she went to find Westmann, she opened the letter.

My dear friend,
   If we can raise Jesus from the dead, we must be capable of greater things too. Like flying without fear? Sleeping with-

out nightmares? Loving without suffering? Well, at least a reunion in Berlin? If duty brings you here, you are more than welcome to stay with me during your visit. I'm looking forward to seeing you again.

C

P.S. Did you arrive safely in Offenbach? I hope they are treating you well there.

Underneath was Cordelia's address: Berlin, Winterfeldtplatz, and the number of her apartment. Lilya was glad to have a place to stay in Berlin, and was looking forward to seeing her again. She wanted to find Desirée von Wallsdorff and talk to her. She must know much more than she had written in her letter to Elias. She put Cordelia's letter away and set off to find Westmann.

The bookstamp investigators were sitting at long tables, bent over books with magnifying glasses and lights. They carried out their work diligently and in silence. Nathan Westmann's workspace was set up in a niche consisting of just a desk, on which was set out a large magnifying glass, a pair of tweezers, scissors, an eraser and an open book. Various bookplates were glued inside the book. He took a form out of a drawer. He seemed happy to see her. 'I'd like to offer you a seat,' he said, 'but you can see the state of things around here. Pull up a crate. I'm going to make a note of everything, and you can leave what you have here for inspection.'

Lilya placed the book that Elias Lind had given her on the table.

Westmann picked it up, placed a magnifying glass over the gilt inscription on the cover and opened the book. He browsed the pages in it for a while, read an entry here and there, then closed it again. He reached for the catalogue with the bookplate, then his gaze travelled back to Lind's book.

'A catalogue, meticulously produced,' he said, placing a hand on it. 'From Berlin you say?'

'The library was called *Alexandria.*'

'If I understood your letter correctly, it's not so much the books that you're in search of but a trail they might have left behind? You're looking for a lost person — the person this book belongs to and everything that is so carefully and thoughtfully catalogued here.'

'Yes,' she said, 'that's right.'

He leaned back as if he were about to tell a long story.

'Sometimes, cases are simple: books turn up, we know who they belong to and that the owners are still alive. We return them via the quickest route possible.' He paused briefly. 'But in most cases, the owners aren't alive, and that's where things start getting tricky. At least then, we can save the items and find heirs or institutions willing to accept them. But if we don't even have the books, it's a hopeless case.' He gave her a searching but friendly look. 'I have the feeling that this is the kind of case you want to present me with, am I right?'

'We do have this book, a name and . . .'

He took a pen and bent over the form. 'Okay, who are we looking for?'

'Lind, Raphael, Berlin Dahlem,' she said. 'Professor, Kaiser Wilhelm Institute of Physical Chemistry, probably murdered in 1941 or '42.'

She suddenly stopped talking. Westmann had laid down his pen and all the colour had drained from his face.

'Lind?' he said and stared at the book.

'Yes.'

'The Vilna Ghetto,' said Westmann quietly, as though talking to himself.

He looked up at her. 'Does that mean

anything to you?'

'A place of Jewish culture and terror . . .'

'Terror, yes.' Westmann got up. 'Lind arrived in the city with German troops. When everything was over at last, the SS troops followed them in.'

Lilya looked at him incredulously, keen to find out how he knew this. But Westmann, still pale-faced, held out his hand to her.

'Pick me up tomorrow morning at ten o'clock at the gate downstairs,' he said. 'Then I'll try to help you. But don't be too hopeful. Many things have happened — and many things haven't.'

# CHAPTER THIRTEEN

NEW SESSION, NEW MUSIC!
The magnificent Allies
Come and be ELECTRIFIED at the
legendary Senkenburg

The *Stars and Stripes* had advertised the concert. On the street in front of the bar a queue had formed of US soldiers, army personnel, civil clerks and German women who might have been lonely and in search of a new life. They were waiting for the doors to open; a military police jeep was parked at a distance to keep an eye on the goings-on.

Harvey had invited her: it was going to be a very special concert, as he put it. When she came back from the OAD, he was pulling a wheeled handcart loaded with his two guitars and all kinds of technical gear and left the house soon after.

Lilya had grown up with music. Her father

had a gramophone, and Schubert, Brahms and Bach were his idols. When he listened to music, he seemed to submerge himself in a different world. In the youth group and kibbutz, she'd danced around a flickering campfire to the guitar, even though she'd never really been a fan of Jewish folk music. Nevertheless, she had only a vague idea what she was letting herself in for that night: she had but sketchy notions of Harvey's modern music.

She could hardly wait for the next day and her meeting with Westmann. In fact it seemed inappropriate to be going to a concert after whatever she had triggered in Westmann. But something made her want to go: Harvey's inviting expression, perhaps, or the desire to do something out of the blue. Or maybe just the lure of hearing music again, and letting herself fall into a cosmos of noise, rhythm and glamour in the company of others. It was a million miles from the Vilna Ghetto.

Nearly all the tables were already taken when Lilya finally managed to squeeze through the crowd at the door and into the hall. Smoke hung in the air like fog over water, and waitresses were ferrying glasses of beer to the tables. It was noisy inside. She glimpsed red lipstick, the peroxide blonde of pinned-up hair and uniforms that ranged from the highest to the lowest echelons of the US Army. Over the stage hung a mirrorball. She thought she spotted Harvey's neighbour Anita Renneberg in the corner of the hall. A soldier had placed his arm around her shoulders and was kissing her ear. She threw her head back and laughed, but then slid away from him and pointed to the stage.

The Allies, with Harvey at their head, jumped up to perform. Applause broke out; one of the musicians sat down behind the drum kit and began a solo. Everyone wanted to hear Harvey play guitar; there were boos and whistles, and beer coasters flew on to the stage. Finally the others joined in and Lilya had the feeling of being aboard a ship as the hall began to sway to and fro.

Eager and agitated, she listened to the first set, which consisted of three songs. A GI sitting with a group of army people offered her a beer. It tasted bitter, like half-baked bread, but she felt lighter after a mouthful, as if she could gently give in to the pulsating room. She took another sip.

During the break, some of the tables were abandoned while others were taken. 'The changing of the guard,' said the GI in front of her and raised his glass again.

At that moment, David Guggenheim entered the hall. She saw him heading towards a table behind the pillars in the middle of the room, accompanied by a tall, dark-haired captain. They sat down and took out their cigarettes. Evidently they didn't have a light because Guggenheim turned around to the table behind him to ask for matches.

Guggenheim's companion was Captain Bernstein, the director of the US book depot: she hadn't recognised him at first without his glasses.

Had they not seen her? Or maybe they didn't feel it was necessary to say hello or invite her over to their table?

A soldier who was smaller than she was appeared next to her and offered her a cigarette, which she politely declined.

The Allies tuned their instruments, and Harvey put a new string on his guitar. There was a short lull. She scoured the crowd and noticed that Guggenheim's seat was empty.

'Your little discussion with Bernstein worked a small miracle. I'd like to thank you.' Lilya started and turned. Guggenheim was standing next to her, smiling, then indicated the table where Captain Bernstein was waving to her and pulling up an extra chair.

She followed Guggenheim through the room, feeling the effect of the beer. It wasn't the floor that was swaying: she was. He explained that Captain Bernstein was an old friend — but despite this, or perhaps for this very reason, he was a difficult partner to negotiate with. Bernstein shook her hand and winked at her.

Two other GIs sauntered over to their table, but their greeting was drowned out by the opening bars of 'Tiger Rag'.

The atmosphere intensified, the music grew louder and more compelling, the beer flowed and the first couples began to dance on the small floor in front of the stage. They whirled, grasped each other tight then let go again.

In the break between two numbers, Bernstein turned to her. 'Nice to see you again,' he said. 'David is immensely grateful to you. He was concerned.'

'Concerned?'

'That you might leave without him being able to thank you. David hadn't expected anyone or anything to change my mind: our friendship was put to a tough test. Now we're simply going to give it a go — the crates will be packed tomorrow.'

Guggenheim reached to take three beers from a waitress's tray as she squeezed past their table; he put a dollar bill in their place.

The Allies began to play a slow number in three-four time, and Lilya noticed that Bernstein threw David a look. Then he leaned over to her again. 'He's a good dancer, but he never shows it,' he said. 'His only partner these days is the serious side of life.'

'Meaning? No girl?' The question just slipped out and now she bit her tongue.

Bernstein looked at her with playful solemnity, and gave her the thumbs down. *'Nada,'* he said.

Guggenheim leaned forward towards them. 'I'm afraid I'll have to interrupt your little debate on life,' he said, standing up and pulling Lilya on to the dance floor without so much as asking. She had no choice but to follow him.

He put one hand on her waist, the other on her shoulder. Gently, his energy focused on her, he began to spin her around, leading her across the dance floor, then letting her go again. She moved through a jungle of arms, legs, bodies and glistening eyes. Harvey's guitar seemed to be singing. 'How did you manage that?' he asked. She could feel his breath on her ear. 'It's like Bernstein's a convert. If your report on Föhrenwald has the same effect, the camp occupants will all get a visa tomorrow. We can just close up and I'll have to set off on my pilgrimage to Jerusalem.'

She laughed. *Not failed.* 'I'd prefer you to send my greetings to Lisa Strassburger: I did it for her, more than anyone, because of all the work she does. And in any case, it was all your friend's decision. Bernstein has always wanted to help you and Föhrenwald — that's always been the case. I could tell right away. I just provided him with an excuse. It wasn't a miracle, just tactics, and a bit of luck.'

'Luck?'

'Call it what you will.'

'I'll stick with luck. I like luck,' he said and pulled her closer to him.

Harvey continued singing. He had a beautiful voice.

Guggenheim spun her around. They passed the table where Bernstein was sitting and he waved at them as if they were travellers setting off on a journey. She felt the warmth of Guggenheim's hand on her hip.

He'd only just found out the real reason for her trip from Bernstein, he said: so it wasn't Föhrenwald, his work and the UNRRA. And, if he was honest, he was relieved to hear that she had other, clearly much more important things to do in Germany.

She felt an urge to tell him about her plans in the same way that she'd felt in Cordelia's company a few weeks ago. But she held back. One dance didn't make a friendship and she'd already told Cordelia way too much.

The song came to an end, but Guggenheim still held her in his arms.

'Short break!' shouted Harvey.

'I think I'll just go and say hello to my friend,' she said. 'Come with me, I'll introduce you to Harvey.'

Guggenheim followed Lilya up to the stage and after she'd waved Captain Bernstein over, he got up and joined them too. The men greeted each another: Harvey leaned down and shook hands with the two officers. He called the other band members over; hands were grasped in criss-cross fashion. Lilya lost track of who was introducing who to whom, only noticing that she and Guggenheim stayed close together.

'The guys have to get ready for their last set,' Harvey said in apology and reached for the glass of beer on the floor. He put two fingers to his temples in salute and turned back to his band.

Lilya, Guggenheim and Bernstein went

back over to their table and sat down. She noticed an almost imperceptible shift in Guggenheim's mood. Had she come on too strong? Or was he annoyed because she wouldn't tell him anything? He grabbed his cap, saying that he needed some fresh air. She wanted to say something, but Bernstein laid a hand on her shoulder. 'Let him go,' he said. 'It's better not to place any obstacles in his path. And anyway, he'll be back in a few minutes.'

'He's changed so much since he came to Germany,' Bernstein continued. 'You should have seen him in college: easy-going, charming, ambitious as hell — but he wasn't bitter. He won everyone's heart. This country has set him on edge.'

'This country?'

'Didn't he tell you why he came to Germany?'

'To help? He's a big fish in the UNRRA.'

Bernstein's face turned serious. 'Sometimes I think that the things he does for others are the things he needs most himself.'

'What do you mean?'

Bernstein took a sip of beer and put the glass down carefully, as if he were considering something. 'He's in search of answers and reassurance here. He's restless, very earnest and, sometimes, like a stranger to me.'

'He didn't make it very easy for me in Munich. I waited for him in his office after I arrived and went looking for him in the garden in the end. I know I hadn't announced my arrival, and that was something he didn't take kindly to.'

'Did you see the photograph on his desk?'

'I couldn't miss it. Such a pretty, unusual woman.'

'His mother,' explained Bernstein. 'He never knew her. The photo is the only thing he has left of her. She put it in his cradle after he was born, or, more accurately, she gave it to the people who took him in. Right after his adoption, they left Germany and took him to America where he grew up. When he joined the army to fight against Germany, they gave him the photo — he'd never seen it before. Since then, he's kept it with him, day and night. When the war was over, he wanted to stay in Germany any way he could, in the hope that he might find her, and so he volunteered to join UNRRA. They snapped him up immediately, of course, a man like him.'

The concert was over and the hall was emptying. Backstage, Lilya went looking for

Harvey and offered to wait for him. But when he said she should go on ahead, she was almost relieved. She'd have time to herself and that suited her. She'd lost Bernstein, Guggenheim and the other soldiers in the throng after a brief goodbye and hadn't seen them after that.

Outside, it was pitch black; none of the streets were lit. The stump of a streetlight kept vigil. Small groups of soldiers, civil clerks and German women were still standing around in front of the bar, laughing and smoking in groups. Across the street, the MPs were leaning against their jeep.

'Next time it's our turn, and you can wait outside,' shouted an MP to a sergeant, who immediately crossed the street and offered him a cigarette. She heard the pair of them laughing behind her.

The voices died down. She shuddered. From the distance, she heard a bottle smash, high-spirited squeals, then the MPs' voices. She carried on walking. Silence.

Until tonight, she'd managed to stop herself thinking about David Guggenheim too much, or letting him get to her. Perhaps she should have refused to dance with him. Now thoughts of him crowded her mind and heart, sudden and unbidden. She felt his hand, his breath. But she didn't want to and couldn't let that happen. He wasn't part of her life and she didn't belong here.

She stopped at a crossroads next to heaps of rubble and tramlines piled on top of each other that gleamed in the moonlight. She'd lost her sense of direction. Should she go back towards Harvey after all? She decided to try the left-hand street. It was narrow and the façades of the buildings were grey and mute. She slowly made her way forward in the dark.

A stone must have dislodged from the heap of rubble behind her because she heard it hit the ground. She held her breath. Were those footsteps?

Lilya continued walking as if into a dark tunnel, or so it seemed. She could sense that someone was following her. *Just keep going.* This street would lead to a bigger one soon, a crossroads where perhaps there would be people.

Until the last minute she blocked out the thought that someone was closing in behind her. But suddenly she was certain of it. She stopped, turned around and saw the silhouette of a man in front of her. He was so close that she could smell his hair cream and feel his breath. Then a grip, as tight as a wire-cutter. He twisted her right arm behind her back. She tried to break loose but it was hopeless. Her face contorted in pain, she was forced to kneel down in front of the stranger.

With her free left hand, without moving her upper body, she cautiously felt around on the ground. Her fingers touched sand, dirt, a stick, then something hard and jagged. A piece of brick? Heavy enough in any case. She managed to pick it up.

She only had one shot.

Lilya leapt up, trying to make out the stranger's face in the dark, and struck with every ounce of her strength.

She must have hit him somewhere around the neck, not on the head: he staggered slightly but managed to keep hold of her. His breathing was coming hard now and he released his grip for a moment. She tore herself away, pushing him hard: he staggered and let out a grunted curse. She dropped the stone and shoved past him, running back into the darkness.

She ran without knowing where she was going, just on and on. After a while she was sure that he hadn't followed her, and stopped. When she finally arrived at a street that she recognised, she doubled over, put her hands on her knees and gasped for breath: Glauburgstrasse. The lights in the hall were almost all out but two officers were still standing and smoking on the steps of the Senkenburg. The MPs were about to drive off in their jeep.

Lilya recognised David Guggenheim's silhouette, and he must have seen her too. Had she forgotten something? The other officer briefly raised his hand and left. 'No,' she said, still panting. It must have come out as a shout.

One of the MPs climbed out of the jeep, a torch in his hand. Guggenheim came down the steps and came over to her. He seemed to study her from top to bottom in the torchlight, then he threw away his cigarette and pulled a handkerchief from his jacket pocket.

'Your face,' he said, 'may I?' Gently, he rubbed the dirt off her forehead.

'Tell me what happened. What are you still doing here anyway?'

'One still has to be careful these days. It's still Germany,' commented the MP, who shone the torch down the street and turned it off. If she wanted, and this officer didn't insist on taking her for a walk on this summer night, he could give her a lift and drop her off somewhere safe.

'Take us both,' said Guggenheim. And no sooner had she sat down in the back than she felt his uniform jacket across her legs.

Only then did she realise that her entire body was shaking.

'And now tell me what you're really doing here. And this time, I want all the details I might need. I won't take no for an answer.'

# CHAPTER FOURTEEN

She sat bolt upright and opened her eyes. It was already light outside. She pushed up the sleeve of her nightshirt and inspected her lower arm: it was black and blue with bruises. Last night's events seemed unreal. First the unexpected dance with David Guggenheim, which had ended much too soon; then the attack, which she'd only just been able to escape. And finally, the ride home together in the jeep while she told Guggenheim, his warm jacket lying over her lap, about what had happened to her on her way home and about her mission to find Lind. Had she said too much?

She could still recall the terror she'd felt in the dark. She got dressed, and after hastily drinking a coffee, she set off.

Nathan Westmann was waiting outside the gate when she arrived at the OAD. Despite the warm day, he'd slung a light-coloured coat over his shoulders.

'We're going to take a little walk, not far,' he said after he'd greeted her.

They walked past the loading ramp down to the Main, taking the path between the river and the railway tracks. A tugboat was towing barges with steel ropes; a floating crane was making its way towards Frankfurt, black smoke belching from its funnel. They walked downriver side by side in silence.

Westmann stopped in front of an imposing, shell-sandstone building. It had a large dome and was still intact.

'The Nazis turned it into a cinema. Propaganda films to boost flagging spirits, Nazi Party events. Now it's been handed over to the Jewish community to use as a synagogue, but there aren't any Jews left.'

Westmann's tone changed; he seemed to lack strength, almost as if someone else was speaking. Little was left of the engaging, approachable person she'd met the day before.

They turned off at Goethestrasse. After a few yards, Westmann knocked at a door. They listened. There was the sound of steps approaching and a man in his thirties opened up, wearing US Army uniform trousers, the braces hanging down, and a vest. Lilya spotted ink or paint on his hands. He seemed both surprised and happy to see Westmann, and ushered them in.

The man led them through to some kind of workshop. On a trestle table lay scattered drawings and pens, on the shelf was a pile of *Stars and Stripes* journals and on the floor by the wall there were paint pots with rusty lids and flaking labels. Next to them was a ladder and a shop sign saying: *Fehlberger adds colour.* Over the table hung three light bulbs, shining brightly.

'You wanna see the pictures?' he asked, first looking at Lilya, then Westmann.

'Yes please, Jeff . . .'

The man climbed up the ladder, pulled a box down from the top shelf and took out a large black portfolio.

Jeff Tulitz was an illustrator for the army press corps, Westmann explained, and quite a celebrity at home. He gave war stories a face for the folks back there. Westmann invited Lilya to take a look at one of the pictures. Jeff lit a cigarette and wisps of smoke curled around the sheets of paper.

The drawings had been done in black pen: a village street, a moon, a dog and soldiers in German uniforms. Books, a den, a hiding place behind a cupboard, handcarts, fire and distorted faces with wide-open eyes. Then alleys, wooden houses, a grave full of piled-up bodies. Standing there was a man in a white coat next to an officer in German uniform with a gun in his holster. She carried on thumbing through the pictures, and when she'd finished, she started over again.

'Rosenberg's people, the Führer's ruthless and official thieves, were based in Sigmuntstrasse,' said Westmann. 'The Kulturhaus was in Straschunstrasse; it housed the museum, the library with reading room, the archive and the Statistics Office. And the collection point.'

Westmann paused before continuing with his story: 'They sent 47 crates to Germany, 20,000 books in all. The rest was pulped. A leather tradesman was also involved — 500 Torah scrolls were sent to a shoe factory to line boots. The Germans came with an entire unit: they had people with them who spoke Hebrew and Yiddish. And scientists.'

'Why scientists?' she asked. 'What did they have in mind? Besides, Lind was a biochemist, not an expert on the Torah, language, book trade or ancient literature.'

'They brought him selected books and he had to look for something. No one knew what. I once heard Lind saying, "Knowledge is being fed to the wrong people." '

Lilya picked up a sheet on which the man with the white coat was drawn. He was tall, and to his left and right Wehrmacht soldiers were guarding him with carbines. They were standing in front of an open trailer. She couldn't make out the cargo.

'Is that Lind?'

'Well, it's not a photo,' said Jeff, lighting another cigarette. 'I drew what Nathan described to me . . .'

She looked at Westmann.

'Like, he was imposing, tall,' Jeff continued, 'and at the same time bitter and driven as though he belonged there with the Germans.'

She saw that Westmann was following the conversation intently. 'They were in awe of him,' said Jeff, 'even though he was their prisoner.'

Now Westmann chipped in. 'Afterwards, outside the city,' he said, 'they shot all the Jews and all the witnesses. They ferreted them out of their hiding places. One house after another. The whole city was assassinated. Only a handful were able to flee . . . only . . .' He faltered and looked around for a chair to sit down on.

'I think that's enough for today, Nathan,' Jeff said. He closed the portfolio and put it back in the box.

Westmann apologised, said he was going out for some air, and she heard the door close behind him.

Jeff Tulitz turned to Lilya. 'He's never

240

brought anyone here to my studio. I always thought that he could only get closer to the things he saw in Vilna by looking at the pictures I drew for him. They're too huge, too painful. It's a miracle he survived. Not many did.'

Lilya wanted to know more about the pictures. Jeff lit another cigarette. He didn't know that much because Westmann had mostly described individual scenes to him, and hadn't told him a whole story.

Westmann was from Berlin, that much Tulitz knew, like his colleague Raphael Lind. They'd had to work for the Germans in absolute secrecy in a house in the city centre. They were supposed to collate highly specialised knowledge from the looted books, each in his own field. Nathan managed to flee east before the shootings began. He almost made it to the Ural Mountains. In a small village, a family found him and took him in.

'He's convinced he's the only survivor,' said Tulitz, 'and he can hardly bear it. By telling me about the things he saw, and me drawing them, he can start letting them go. He and Lind were part of some kind of group — I've forgotten what they were called, he only mentioned it once. But the name Rosenberg cropped up, and the word

*Einsatzstab*: it means "mobile unit". But it makes it sound like they were a part of a machine! Only the Germans could come up with a name like that!' Jeff laughed. 'Like, hard and metallic. Pass me the *Einsatzstab*. So, everything screwed on nice and tight? German workmanship.'

He turned serious again. 'Be careful with Nathan. He's strong, and everyone appreciates him here in the OAD, but there's this whole other side to his story.'

Once they reached the Main again, Westmann's steps grew assured once more. He seemed almost buoyant. 'I expect Jeff told you about our work together,' he said. 'It helps me enormously. Jeff paints the pictures and, by doing so, they disappear from my memory. Now they're lying in a black box in his studio, and we look at them now and again, just the two of us.'

He paused.

'And now there are three of us,' he finished off. 'If you hadn't brought up Raphael Lind's name, it would never have happened. But it's better this way — much better.'

Lilya wasn't sure what to say in reply.

'I'll visit Berlin again when all this is over. I'll take a look around the city and then leave the country. But first, you have to go there, as soon as possible.' He stopped. 'I don't think I can really help you here in Offenbach. We haven't come across any of Lind's books in our archive, not yet. I know the lists. I looked through them again even though I knew what the outcome would be. If anything changes on that score, you and Elias Lind will be the first people to know.'

He set off again. 'Go to Berlin, and I'll tell you who to look up there. I'm sure Dr Durlacher can help you. Let's go into my office and I'll tell you what you need to know.'

# CHAPTER FIFTEEN

The car turned and came to a halt not far from the depot gates. The engine spluttered, then died. Through the windscreen, she thought she could make out the driver, talking to the car.

The driver's door opened and out climbed Lev, who slowly donned his cap. It was different from the one he normally wore. He adjusted it to the right position and looked over at her. She walked towards him and stretched out her hand. Lev shook it with solemn formality. His uniform was finished off with meticulously polished black boots that gleamed like new. He was freshly shaven and gave off an overpowering scent of eau de cologne. On the passenger seat, she glimpsed a pair of leather gloves.

'I'm under orders to pick you up, ma'am,' he said, imitating an official tone. But the 'ma'am' came out like a goat bleating.

'Who gave you those orders, sir?' she said.

'Furthermore, unless something rather important has escaped my notice, I am still "miss", and quite happy that way.'

Both of them laughed, happy to see each other again on this unexpected occasion. She should have realised that David Guggenheim hadn't come alone. Why have a new driver, after all?

'Föhrenwald, then Offenbach, then back again, all in two days,' said Lev. 'He obviously wants to see how good I am, our boss.'

'Practice,' she said. 'You can never have enough.'

Lev suddenly seemed awkward. 'He told me what you've done for him, for all of us. Don't you want to stay with us? There's so much left to do.'

'My journey's taking me in the opposite direction: to Berlin,' she said.

'So you're not going home yet?' asked Lev. There was curiosity in his voice.

'No.'

Lev shuffled from one foot to the other. Suddenly his face lit up. 'I have an idea. I'll join you,' said Lev. 'What do you think of that?'

She laughed. 'That would be wonderful, Lev, but our boss won't agree to it.'

'If you ask him, he'll think it over.'

David Guggenheim came through the gate

with a suitcase in hand, along with Captain Bernstein. They were engaged in a lively discussion. Guggenheim glanced over at Lilya, but continued talking to the captain while looking at her. He shook Bernstein's hand and walked over to the car. She liked the way he walked: it was only when he pushed his hair back that she thought he looked like a college kid. He should just cut it. But that wasn't any business of hers.

'Did Lev suggest that we drop you off in Berlin on our way to Föhrenwald?' Guggenheim asked with a smirk when he reached the car. 'Those few hundred miles are no big deal. At least that was his plan when we were driving over here.'

Lev took his case and shook his head.

'Lev would get so much practice that he'd be qualified to chauffeur the President of Palestine in a year,' he said. 'We should think it over.'

'Israel,' she corrected him.

'Whatever you say. The most important thing is that it turns out to be a really nice country. Founded on the Wasserfall constitution.'

' "All men shall be brothers" is my slogan. But not many people share my view. I'd be happy if you came over and provided me with some company. In any case, the invita-

246

tion stands. We don't have to talk politics.'

Guggenheim laughed.

Lev sat down behind the wheel, carefully pulled on his gloves and started the engine. Guggenheim opened the door and invited her to sit with him on the back seat. The evening before, when he'd dropped her off in Liebigstrasse after the incident, he'd said that he wanted to make sure that she at least caught her train on time: it was important that she arrived safe and sound in Berlin. Through army channels, he'd reserved a seat for her on a military train.

At a wooden shack on the forecourt of the station, Guggenheim bought her a coffee. Lev had already said goodbye and was waiting back in the car. But the scent of his aftershave still lingered on her cheek, which she tried to rub off with a handkerchief. Trams crawled haltingly around the square, as if they had to learn how to drive again; she heard the scraping of their wheels. The coffee was bitter and weak, and tasted of chicory. Pigeons hung around her feet. A few yards away from her, a man opened his coat and showed passers-by cigarettes that were hidden in the lining.

Guggenheim was clearly in a good mood and she didn't want to rule out that he was happy because they had a little time alone together.

'Yesterday . . .' he said. He hesitated. 'I've not danced for a long time.'

His tone took her by surprise. 'It's something you never forget, isn't it?'

'But you can lose interest.'

'I didn't notice last night,' she said.

He looked down at the ground. Then up again. 'Yesterday . . . was different.'

The ghost of a smile crossed his face again. 'And I like Harvey,' he said, as though trying to gloss over the situation. 'The way he plays. So wild. I've never heard an electric guitar before. But I'm not so sure it'll catch on — it's so loud.'

'It forces us to be quiet. Perhaps that's the deeper meaning.'

He laughed.

She looked at his hands, which he'd laid on the table next to his cup, just as she had. With one finger, he touched the tip of her index finger. A wave of warmth went through her body, all the way to her toes.

'The deeper meaning,' he said. 'Perhaps that's it. A question that drives us on without us ever finding the answer. But perhaps it's the wrong question.'

'Or perhaps expecting there to be only one answer is wrong.'

'It would only take one to change the

world, I think.'

He glanced at his watch again. Should she mention what Bernstein had told her about his search for his mother? But before she could start, he was getting ready to leave.

'It's time to go. Your train to the Reich's capital won't wait for you,' he said. He reached for her rucksack and hoisted it on to his shoulder. As they walked through the station hall, he touched her hand for a second time. Then he took both her hands and squeezed them, but immediately let go again.

'It's better like this,' he said.

'Yes,' she said, knowing it wasn't true.

On reaching the carriage — having pushed their way through the milling passengers, making her worry she'd miss her train — he put her rucksack down on the platform. She climbed up the metal steps and turned around to face him.

'Safe journey,' he said, raising his hand, 'and be in touch. Let me know what's going on in the Big Smoke.'

He turned and walked away. For the first time, he seemed almost embarrassed.

She had a window seat. Two American officers sharing the carriage gave her a friendly look, and one of them heaved her bag into the overhead net. She pushed down the window and looked out again. Not far away, she spotted David Guggenheim in the crowd. From up here, he seemed smaller, somehow more approachable, as if she could touch him. Not long afterwards, a double whistle sounded and the train set off. Without turning around again, David Guggenheim disappeared in the hordes of people.

■ ■ ■ ■

# BERLIN

## WINTERFELDTPLATZ

■ ■ ■ ■

# CHAPTER SIXTEEN

People jostled across the square pushing her aside, pointing to an egg or plucked chicken, then pulling something out of their pockets to use in barter: a silver spoon, a fountain pen, an ivory comb. From afar, the market had looked like a scene from a silent movie dipped in matte colours.

Farmers had sparse clusters of eggs, leeks, potatoes and turnips spread out in front of them. A book dealer was sitting behind his table reading; despite the heat, he was wearing a woollen scarf around his neck. A man was hanging up pre-war dresses and suits on a cord between two trees, and a few uniforms dangled there too, their rank badges missing or ripped off. Military police walked back and forth, smoking. In front of a partly bombed-out church, people stood patiently waiting for the free food being handed out. Searching for Cordelia's house, Lilya looked up.

Her journey to Berlin had seemed never-ending; Lilya had spent almost twenty-four hours getting there. The train had constantly come to a halt, sometimes not moving on for a long time. She had stared out at the landscape: endless yellowing fields that looked like the dying embers of a sunset. She'd had to change trains twice, and both times there was a mute, dogged fight for seats. But Guggenheim had even made provisions here too: she always found a seat reserved for her. The faces of the people in the carriage were serious, as if they had turned their gazes inward to search for the people they had once been. She felt their stolen, listless glances, as if they were looking at her but not seeing her.

She took advantage of the hours on the trains to carry on reading. Raphael and Elias, Elias and Raphael. When the morning broke, she'd made some notes and developed something of a strategy: a plan for Berlin. And the closer she got, the more keenly she felt Cordelia's inquisitive look.

She was going to try to find Desirée von Wallsdorff and talk to her. And she also intended to look up Dr Erich Durlacher, who Raphael Lind had known and who might be able to help her. Westmann had given her Durlacher's address. After that, she'd get in touch with Elias Lind. It was time to give him an initial report.

She found Cordelia's house: Lilya knew her apartment was on the second floor. There was a sign hanging on the door: *Ring Gertig, the janitor. C.*

A man who was missing three fingers on one hand opened the door, gave her a wary look and handed her the key.

Cordelia had given Lilya one of her two rooms. There was a cupboard and a bed, which was made up with a starched sheet and covered with a bulky white blanket. Cordelia had placed a lavender-scented towel on her pillow. The morning sun shone through the window overlooking Winterfeldtplatz.

On the small night table next to her bed there was a well-thumbed city map and a note: *See you tonight! C.*

In the kitchen she found some bread, margarine and milk. She wanted to take a walk to explore the city and then go looking for Durlacher in the afternoon.

A black market was set up in front of the Reichstag. The cupola was gutted by fire, and its steel construction sat on top of the ruin like a skewed hat. The buildings still standing nearby were pockmarked; only the golden Victory Column in the distance remained upright, the angel on top looking down on the destroyed city.

Westmann had given her a carbon copy of a densely typed page. Some of the words had been marked with a pencil. There were places, names and locations of looted goods: *Hungen, Schloss Schlesiersee, Berlin, Pleikershof, Niemes, Altausee, Neu Pürstein, Böhmisch Leipa, Hauska, Schloss Banz . . .*

Westmann had marked two entries: Eisenacher Strasse 11 and Emser Strasse 12/13; *BERLIN!* and *Durlacher* were written next to them. Erich Durlacher had lived in Schlüterstrasse before the war, Westmann had said.

After she'd passed Savignyplatz, she kept a lookout for Schlüterstrasse. Durlacher had lived in the rear building of one of the houses.

She found the building. The side facing the street was undamaged: angels, stucco and caryatids adorned the front and the flush-mounted balconies. She went through the gateway to the courtyard, which was flanked by roughly plastered grey walls.

Dustbins stood in front of the door. In the small rectangle between the front and rear building, she recognised potato plants.

She looked around, searching for a doorbell with a nameplate. Faded pieces of cardboard were stuck next to the door, and only a few of the notes scribbled on them were still legible. *INGE, please get in touch, we're alive! Your parents,* was written on the wall in chalk. Underneath was an address in Berlin Friedenau. She read the names again but didn't find Durlacher among them.

A woman in a tatty apron came out with an axe in her hand and walked over to the potato plants. Perhaps she would be able to help.

'I'm looking for someone who used to live here . . .'

'You can't be Inge . . .'

Lilya mentioned the name Durlacher.

The woman's expression hardened. 'We have enough troubles of our own.'

Lilya tried a new tack. She only wanted to know if he'd lived here, before the war.

The woman put her axe down, leaned against the wall and crossed her arms over her chest.

'What do you want? Did he send you or was it his lawyer? It was all above board, the apartment sale, you can go to the land registry and see. It's all documented, just talk to my husband . . .'

'I'm not interested in the apartment. I'm looking for Dr Durlacher — I have a message for him.'

'Then you've come to the wrong place. And if you do find him, you can tell him that he and his whole *mishpocha* should leave us alone. You're the second person today who's asked for him.'

Lilya was just about to give up. But the last sentence made her snap to attention.

'I'm sorry for the inconvenience,' she said, trying to inject warmth into her voice. 'Especially if someone else has already been here today.'

'Oh, I didn't tell him anything. He didn't say he was looking for Durlacher anyway. He just wanted to know if anyone else had asked for him today.'

'Do you happen to remember what he looked like?'

'Ask me something easy! I don't know. Sturdy. Not that it's any of your business.'

Lilya thanked her and left. She took a good look around once she was back on the main street: there was no one to be seen. On the opposite side of the road, she saw a hairdresser's. The shop was empty, and the owner was sitting on one of the chairs with a newspaper open on his lap, asleep. A bell rang when Lilya pushed open the heavy door. The man looked up, folded his newspaper and stood up.

'Can I help you?'

She was looking for some information, she explained, and said the name Durlacher.

He thought it over.

'The professor?' he said. 'A nasty business. The things those people had to go through.'

He gave her the number of a house on Leibnizstrasse, but he wasn't entirely sure. She thanked him and left.

Who had been here before her that morning? Perhaps it was just a coincidence? After all, Durlacher was a scientist and she might not be the only one trying to contact him to ask for his advice. But still, she felt uneasy. She'd been sure that the stranger from the Haus der Kunst had followed her in Munich, and a man had come out of the dark and attacked her in Offenbach. Was she on the point of unearthing something buried deep in the past? Whatever was behind it all, she was here now and she wouldn't want it any other way.

She arrived at the house in Leibnizstrasse: E.D. was written on a ground-floor nameplate.

There was no bell. She paused for a moment, looked around and knocked. Someone fumbled at the spyhole and pushed the cover to one side.

'He's not seeing any more students today,' said a woman's voice from behind the door, then Lilya heard footsteps walking away and the clattering of a typewriter.

She tried again, this time by squeezing her Joint ID through the letterbox. A key rattled and the door opened.

A middle-aged woman in a beige woollen dress took stock of her. Around her neck hung a pair of spectacles on a rough piece of string.

Lilya explained that she was here on official business and explained her report, the OAD and Dr Westmann.

The doctor was expected at around three o'clock, said the woman flatly.

Lilya looked at her watch, thanked the woman and went back out on to the street where she would wait somewhere nearby.

At ten to three she spotted a man in the distance making a beeline for the house, and she knew immediately that it must be Dr Erich Durlacher. A few minutes after he'd disappeared through the gate, she made her way back to the building again. The woman who had opened the door earlier came down the steps outside towards her, obviously on her way out.

'He's expecting you,' she said.

When she arrived at the front door, Erich

Durlacher was already standing in the hallway and welcomed her politely, almost effusively. 'So, you must be the report-writer. It's a dangerous life if you root around too deeply. Please come in. You can have tea, or tea. It all tastes the same.'

They walked down the dark passage to his living room whose walls were lined with overspilling bookcases. As she passed a mir-ror, she glanced briefly at her reflection. A door led from the living room to the kitchen.

Durlacher must have been about sixty. He took short, energetic steps, slightly unevenly, as if one of his legs were longer than the other or had been injured. He offered her a seat.

'Thank you for taking the time to see me,' said Lilya, and sat down.

'Your German is excellent. The Joint clearly picks only the best,' said Durlacher and disappeared into the kitchen.

Through the open door, she saw him add-ing a briquette to the stove; the kettle was already giving off steam.

'Extraordinary for someone who has grown up in Palestine. Was it your parents?' she heard him saying from the kitchen.

'Yes. And literature.'

'You like reading? That's wonderful. Who still dares these days?'

Durlacher poured the tea and came back into the living room. 'Nathan said that you were coming.'

'Dr Westmann?'

'He wasn't sure whether you'd definitely make it in these uninviting times for public transport. His telegram was sent to my former address in Schlüterstrasse, but the postman knows what's what.'

'So you know why I'm here?'

'It has to do with Raphael Lind, who I met in rather exceptional circumstances. It's a long story — or a short one, depending on how much you want to know. You don't want to write his biography, I take it. I saw Lind for the last time in early summer 1942.'

She told him about her meeting with Elias Lind: that he assumed his brother Raphael had been alive until at least 1944. Durlacher gave her a probing look but she couldn't make out what he was thinking.

'Well,' he said, 'how much time do you have?'

'As long as you need.'

He leaned back, blew into his teacup, took a sip and put it down again. 'You have to know who we were if you want to understand how we became what we are today. All of us, including Lind, were born in the heyday of the nineteenth century, which seems so far off these days. We had faith in that era — its future, its progress. And in the emancipation of Jews. The institute in Dahlem enshrined this progress. The Kaiser Wilhelm Institute for Biochemistry. With the Kaiser himself as its patron! It was where world knowledge was acquired. Then came the Weimar Republic in 1918, our first democracy and again a time of even more progress in the world of sciences in Berlin. Our knowledge was spread across the world.'

He swallowed another sip of tea, pausing as he did so to look abruptly out of the window. A shadow slid past. Durlacher seemed to consider for a moment whether he should investigate who was skulking behind the house.

'Odd,' he said. 'It must be the janitor.'

But he couldn't ignore it. He looked up at the window again, but continued. By now, Lilya was also distracted. She kept glancing outside but there was no one to be seen. By the mid-1930s, they'd all been laid off, Durlacher continued. A handful of those who stayed in Germany continued their research for a few years at private institutes. They somehow carried on with their lives, but were cut off from social and cultural events:

all the more reason to devote themselves to their work. They were waiting until something happened that would make things better for them. A flicker of hope kept them alive.

Once a week, the Rositzkys had invited them to free meals near the new synagogue. Ladislaus Rositzsky and his wife Marja, who had already lived in Germany for a long time and came from an old Polish noble family, always invited them. Katzleson, Liliencron, Lewy, Reichenow, Esslinger, Lind and a few others met up there. Not long before, this group had been the leading representatives of the German scientific world: enzymologists, lawyers, biochemists, scientists, researchers, physicists and fuel experts. Now they were dependent on charity from friends so that they didn't starve. Some of them had entered the once grand apartment as though it were their surgery, university or institute. Lind always wore a three-piece suit with a silver pocket watch and matching cigarette case — things that most others had long since misplaced.

Lilya listened raptly. She imagined the Raphael Lind she saw in the photograph with Elias from 1932, only a few years before he was banned from his profession and became dependent on the Rositzkys.

'What kind of impression did you have of Lind during that period?'

'He became more and more reticent as time went on. Sometimes he'd disappear for several days and we always thought he'd been taken away. But then he'd turn up again, pale, stiff and with a very determined look. Rumours circulated. He had contacts abroad, said some; others said he had a rendezvous with a woman and a handful claimed he'd offered his services to *them*. The last rumour was the worst and I never believed it.'

In the early summer of 1941 they eventually took away the Rositzkys and some of their guests.

'They took me away too,' he said, and looked at the floor. He seemed to have difficulty continuing. 'I thought it was all over,' said Durlacher. 'I thought I was going to be deported. But they took me to Kurfürstenstrasse. They told me I was going to stay in Berlin and gave me a labour card at the SS Headquarters. I was put to what they called voluntary service within the Reich Association of Jews. This organisation was forced to work for the Nazis and as a Jew you could either cooperate or be killed outright.'

'Durlacher and other scientists, lawyers, librarians, art historians, teachers and musicians had to evaluate cultural artefacts that the Gestapo had confiscated from Jewish houses, libraries, parish halls and laboratories, especially texts in Hebrew. They were to look for anything among the looted books that was particularly valuable or contained information. Anything of use: Jewish knowledge. Secret knowledge. They wanted to find out by examining our books why and how the Jews were able to secretly rule the world. The worlds of finance, industry, the sciences. An absurd concept!'

'Wow, a lot of people must have been working with you.'

'There were ten of us, and then, one day, very early in the morning, Lind appeared, guarded by a tall SS officer.'

'Can you recall when that was?'

'Oh yes — it was November 1941. "And so we meet again," he said in greeting. He'd grown very thin in the few months since our meetings at the Rositzkys and his hair seemed whiter. He looked dishevelled. But then, we'd all undergone some kind of transformation.'

Lilya cupped her tea with both hands. She felt a shiver. Durlacher's living room was gloomy and the only window looked out on to the wall of the building next door. How had he lived before? she wondered. She took a sip of tea.

'It was my job to train him up — introduce our rules, or, rather, the rules of survival,' Durlacher continued. 'They were really quite simple: in the mornings, you had to be prepared for a visit from the SS, and again in the evening. The grounds were surrounded by a high fence. We weren't allowed to talk to anyone outside our group, let alone make contact with one of the guards. We were even given our own toilet and when an air-raid siren went off, we had either to carry on working, or we were bundled into a cellar with weapons and munitions.'

Durlacher paused briefly, and with a jittery hand he fished out a handkerchief from his jacket pocket to wipe his forehead. Unlike Lilya, he seemed to be feeling hot. He stood up, walked a few paces back and forth in the narrow living room, breathing faster now. He wiped his forehead with his handkerchief once more and fetched a glass of water from the kitchen. When he sat down again, he seemed calmer. From the very beginning, he told her, Lind had been exclusively assigned the task of evaluating scientific books and libraries. His reports were filed separately and collected in the evening by a messenger, who must have taken them to someone high up in the SS.

'And how long did Lind stay in your group?'

'Until early summer 1942. Then the ERR came for him. People from the SS were always coming and going, but *these* people hadn't turned up until then. Does that mean anything to you?'

'I heard their abbreviation many times last week: Einsatzstab Reichsleiter Rosenberg. The head of the occupied territories in the eastern zones and the Führer's chief thief.'

Durlacher nodded. 'In any case, that was the last time I saw Lind.'

'They probably brought Lind to Vilna. At least that's where Dr Westmann met him in 1942.'

'Yes, he told me about that. But at the time he had no idea, of course, what would happen to Lind. We both had our assumptions but they were different.'

Lilya sat up. 'How were they different?'

Durlacher sighed. 'I don't know for sure. There were rumours, nothing more. It was said that there was a project, and that Rosenberg or some people from the very top were responsible.'

'Did it have a name? Do you know anything about it that could help me?'

He hesitated. 'Operation Fire Storm.'

'That sounds unusual.'

'Nazi speak. It was all about research: facts, knowledge, progress and power. Destruction. In Frankfurt Rosenberg and his people had set up an Institute for the Study of the Jewish Question. This institute was meant to investigate how Jews had become so successful all over the world. How they thought, what they thought and what they knew. We supposed that they'd taken him there to support Operation Fire Storm. But it was never more than a supposition.' His tone was sour.

'Do you know any other details about Operation Fire Storm?'

'No. Raphael had a special task to do, that's all we could be sure of.'

'Do you have any idea what it could have been?'

'Lind was a biochemist. He'd worked in the First World War on research into poisonous gases. I take it that you've read his texts.'

Of course she had. And she knew that Raphael had paid a high price for his research: the gas he'd developed led to his professional ban for a few years after the war. Had the Nazis wanted to use Raphael's knowledge — Jewish knowledge — to secure victory?

Durlacher got up, went over to a cupboard

and came back with a dossier.

'This is being sent to Nuremberg, along with the report. I am writing almost day and night. The true and little-known story of our slavehood under thousands of books,' he said. 'Our conversation might very well find its way into the document, if you agree to it. Or even your search results, which are beginning to interest me very much too. I want to help find these people and bring them to court. Even if justice can never be done — it's as ephemeral as the truth. Read this: an internal memo from the Reich Main Security Office, the SS's headquarters. Someone passed it on to me. It must be the third carbon copy, but it's still very legible. And valuable, even for you.'

He handed it to Lilya and sat down again.

To IV B 4
Attn. of SS Sturmbannführer Eichmann
    internal
Subject: Jewish librarians

Procedure: verbal consultation on 14.01.41 between SS Stubaf. Eichmann, H.stuf. Steindorf and Dr Wartenberg
    As a result of the examination carried out by SS Hauptsturmführer Wartenberg on the Jews supplied to the IV B 4, it

has been established that the following Jews are viable for local work:

Dr Julius Israel Lewkowitz, 65 years old, resident of Berlin, NW87, Jagowstrasse 23

Dr Erich Israel Schlesinger, 57 years old, resident of Berlin Charlottenburg, Schlüterstrasse 52

Dr Ernst Israel Friedmann, 40 years old, resident of Berlin Charlottenburg, Gustloffstrasse 11

Dr Nathan Israel Braunstein, 55 years old, resident of Berlin Schöneberg, Bahnstrasse 2

Dr Raphael Israel Lind, 51 years old, resident of Berlin Dahlem, Königin Luise Strasse 123

Dr Berthold Israel Landauer, 59 years old, resident of Berlin Charlottenburg, Elizabethstrasse 22

Jakob Israel September, 51 years old . . .

The above-mentioned Jews are to be used initially for half a year at the VII A I and should start work on Monday, 3 November 1941. The Jews shall be engaged every day from 8.00 until 4.30 in functional tasks concerning Jewish-Hebrew literature, for which no other labour can be supplied. The Jews listed under 1,2,3,4 and 7 will continue to receive their salaries from the Reich Association of Jews.

The Jew listed under point 6 will receive a state pension as a retired civil servant.

The Jew listed under 5 will live off his own means, according to his own statement. If necessary, this Jew could receive remuneration from the Reich Association of Jews if required.

Before starting work, the Jews will be made aware of their duty of confidentiality and will work in a room that provides no insight into the matters they are working on. They will be assigned their own WC and will be under the constant surveillance of Hauptscharführer Fechter. The direct superior for their work will be Dr Kummler. After finishing work each day, they will be inspected by an SS guard.

VII A I
StSS Standartenführer
Signed Steindorf

After Lilya had read the document, she gave it back to Durlacher. This was proof that Lind was indeed forced to work for the SS and the ERR, Rosenberg's people. She felt relieved and yet also a deep rage. Or was it sorrow?

'You said something about rumours. Lind disappeared for days during the time of your meetings at the Rositzkys. Did you think that Lind might have left the country at some point? Would that have been possible?'

'Of course. In England, his standing as a scientist was high and he would have been welcomed there for certain.'

'I found out that after he was laid off by the Kaiser Wilhelm Institute, he carried on working in close cooperation with London. Up until 1941, perhaps longer.'

'That's impossible!'

She told him about Albert Green and *Nature;* about the secret publications after Lind was banned from working for *Die Naturwissenschaften.*

'An important journal, I know,' said Durlacher. 'I can imagine that Raphael, despite being such an unerring, strait-laced fellow in every respect, would have got involved in this kind of thing — just to pass his knowledge on to the British. You can't imagine how often I regretted staying behind and being forced to work for these people. What must have gone through Lind's mind when they finally arrived to take him away?

Unimaginable fear.'

'There were also rumours that Lind stayed behind for a woman,' said Lilya and waited for Durlacher's reaction.

He got up and seemed exhausted all of a sudden, as well as keen to end their conversation. 'I have no knowledge of that. People do the most irrational things for all kinds of reasons.' He sighed.

# CHAPTER SEVENTEEN

**Chapter 3**

How I hope that Desirée von Wallsdorff is safe and in good health. You know what she meant to me. The longer I sit here and mull things over, the closer even the distant past feels.

What I'm about to tell you happened in our childhood. It happened a long time ago and yet it runs through my life like a leitmotif.

Summer 1906. We were in the Harz: Father, Mother, Raphael and me. The von Wallsdorffs were staying at a hotel very near ours. The daughters were beautiful, and Desirée was like a flower. Theodora, the younger girl, was still a child.

Although I was only twelve, I loved Desirée. I couldn't stop gazing at her. She was a few years older than me and, of course, only had eyes for my brother. I must have seemed very young to her.

All day long I wandered with Raphael and Desirée through the forest. The paths were steep and we could hear the rustling of wild boars. Raphael had a compass and went in front. He made markings on the trees with a knife. He rubbed leaves between his fingers, held them to his nose and said 'Smell'. He knew the formulas of scent off by heart.

We arrived at a glade. A troop of soldiers was squatting in the grass, their carbines stacked together like a hay sheaf.

A young officer came over to us. He was chewing on a blade of grass. Raphael went towards him. They talked, and my brother nodded. Raphael then suggested that we play hide and seek on the way back down to the town.

Everyone would take turns, he said. 'You first, Eli, no cheating!' I had to close my eyes and count to ten. Then I called out and my voice echoed through the woods. A bird answered back. I set off, looking and listening, cutting down through a small path, but then climbed up the hill again. I walked in a circle around the spot where Raphael and Desirée were supposed to run when I found them. I kept stopping and listening. It went on for a long time: nothing.

Then I heard branches cracking and a soft rustling sound up on the slope. I sat down in a hollow and waited. Were they going to get bored soon and take their turns?

The rustling got nearer and, from further up on the left, I heard something else. Then it was on the right. I didn't even dare call out. Something was crawling towards me. Soon I could hear it below me too on the path that led down to the valley. I was trapped.

I became frightened.

I ducked down in the hollow; the entrance to a fox's den formed a nest beneath me. I heard whispering. A shadow loomed over me. Then a hand grabbed me and pulled me up.

'Raphael!' I screamed. It was the officer, staring at me with a grim expression. 'What are you doing here?' he barked. 'It's dangerous. I already warned your brother.' He took out a whistle and blew twice sharply. Heads appeared everywhere and the officer continued to hold me up by my collar.

'A spy!' he shouted and the woods echoed with laughter. I was trembling.

The officer indicated the path back down. 'Safe passage for the young man! Run, Moses,' he said. 'Before your God has second thoughts.'

Mother was outraged when I got back to the hotel: wet, covered in dirt and pale. Father was sitting by the stove with Raphael.

Where had I been? she asked. Raphael looked over at me. I suddenly understood what was going on. 'Behind the house,' I said, 'on the slope. I was trying to climb trees.'

Desirée had asked after me, Mother told me. She'd been quite upset and had had an argument with Raphael. Mother wanted to know if anything had happened between us.

'Nothing,' I said. 'I just wanted to do a bit of climbing.'

After supper, a note arrived for me. Raphael glared across the table.

'Postal secrecy,' my father said over the rim of his glasses, when he saw Raphael's expression. 'One of our country's great achievements.'

I started reading.

It was my fault. I should have stopped him.
I was so worried about you. I won't sleep
tonight. But I deserve worse.
We'll see each other tomorrow, Eli.
Please forgive me.

Yours, D

The house was by the Kleiner Wannsee. Lilya opened the gate and walked down the garden path. There was no bell, just a heavy metal doorknocker. She looked up at the house, protected by tall trees to the left and right; moss and pine needles covered the shingles on the roof.

A woman opened the door to her, around

thirty years old and slim, her blonde, mid-length hair pulled back carelessly.

'How nice of you to come,' she said and shook Lilya's hand, smiling. 'My aunt's friend Elias already announced you by letter, and she hoped you would visit. I'm Janne.'

Lilya followed her into the large hallway and into a spacious drawing room that housed a grand piano. Books covered the high walls and the window looked out on to a large garden. Beyond it she could see the sheen of a lake. Somewhere in the house, a bird screeched.

'I'll go and check on my aunt,' Janne said.

Lilya heard the muffled steps of the young woman: she must be walking over a thick carpet on her way upstairs.

'Hugo,' screeched the bird, then chattered away to itself.

She tried to make out where the bird's cries were coming from. During training she had learned that the higher the frequency of sounds, the easier they were to localise; low sounds were a problem.

'My father's name was Hugo,' said Janne when she came back into the drawing room. 'We tried to teach our cockatoo other things — my mother even tried Mozart and Proust but Father drummed "Hugo" into him without asking us, until the bird surrendered. Father died two years ago. Mother and I wanted to give the bird away because we couldn't stand listening to him saying Father's name all the time. Aunt Desirée took him in, like she has so many other things in her life. She's waiting for you in the retreat.'

Janne led Lilya into a room that adjoined the drawing room and faced the garden. There was a smell of cigarette smoke and fresh coffee. One of the windows was open and an elderly, crooked man in green overalls was busy with a large watering can at the end of the garden.

In the retreat, two sofas stood at right angles to one another and the walls were lined with shelves. Next to the sofas there were two coffee tables and a large wing-backed chair with a footstool, half turned towards the window and garden. Smoke curled from behind the chair. Somewhere in the distance, she heard the cry 'Hugo!'

Janne led Lilya to the chair, bent over, kissed her aunt and left the room.

Desirée von Wallsdorff was slim, and her hair, fixed on one side with a golden hair-clip, was dyed blonde. She was wearing a red dressing gown with a velvet collar and flat slippers that tapered at the toes. Her perfume was heavy and she was holding a meerschaum cigarette holder with an amber-coloured mouthpiece. When Lilya stood in front of her, she got up slowly, supporting herself on the arm of the chair, swayed a little and smiled. Her lipstick was slightly smudged in the left corner of her mouth. She had a mature, austere beauty. Although her eyes seemed a little tired, they shone a startling blue colour as if reflecting the sky.

'Let me look at you, child,' she said, placing a hand on Lilya's upper arm; she proceeded to study Lilya from top to bottom. She swayed again a little and Lilya wished that she would sit down. Instead, she opened her arms.

'I am truly happy that you've come: Elias announced you. You should have read what he said, the words he used.'

She offered Lilya a seat opposite her and gracefully sank back into the armchair.

'I hope you have some time. Tell me, how is Elias? He told me a bit in his letter, but men tend to give their feelings and experiences short shrift. Well, do put me out of my misery.'

Lilya talked about her meetings with Elias, their conversations about his work in the

Jewish Agency, his love for Dahlia and her death a few years ago. Finally, she talked about her assignment to look for his brother and his guilt at not having done enough for Raphael.

Desirée listened attentively; but at the world 'guilt', she narrowed her eyes as if to say, *What nonsense.*

'Once he'd made up his mind to leave, he paid a high price. His father disinherited him and his only brother declared to the whole world that he didn't understand what Eli was doing. It was hurtful, humiliating even. Nonetheless, Elias was full of hope. He believed in a new country, and in its founding as a new state for Jews. And he was right, wasn't he? But his hopes weren't realised as quickly as he thought. Perhaps your generation will be more fortunate.'

She offered Lilya coffee, which was keeping warm under an embroidered cosy. She took a sheet of paper from the table beside her. Written down were various dates, names and facts. She pushed it towards Lilya, reached for her cigarette again, which had been smouldering in the ashtray, and said in a firm voice, 'I would very much like to help you, and, at the same time, I have some misgivings. Perhaps it is a breach of trust, even a betrayal, if I tell you everything

I know about Raphael. But all the same, I feel indebted to Elias out of love and respect. It's always the same with the Lind brothers — ever since my childhood, they've caused these conflicts of loyalty in me.'

She sighed to emphasise the last point and glanced at Lilya as if checking how much she knew about Elias's unreciprocated love, or what he might have told her about their early years, and how in the end she chose Raphael.

'I can't describe how close I was to Raphael. But there were times when I also doubted him. And sometimes we didn't make it easy for Elias.'

She sighed. 'I knew that Raphael and I would never be a couple. And yet I got involved with him. It only lasted a year, and we parted on good terms with a kiss. War was imminent — it was spring 1914. It came to an end so easily that I was convinced Raphael had never loved me; I thought he might have been incapable of love. You're a woman — perhaps you understand. Men are always so wrapped up in themselves. They only let a woman into their hearts who won't intrude on their love of themselves.'

She reached for her cigarette holder, pulled out the extinguished butt and probed for a new cigarette in a wooden case. Rather laboriously, her hands quivering, she inserted a new cigarette. Lilya passed her a silver, slightly worn lighter from the table. Desirée inhaled deeply and looked up at the ceiling. Then she turned back to Lilya. 'And then it happened after all! My God, she was beautiful.'

Lilya looked at her, mesmerised.

'Raphael met Vivien Olsen in 1921. He was in a terrible state at the time, waiting to see if he would be allowed to work and get back to his research. I tried to distract him — we remained friends after we split up. We often went to bars and cabaret shows. I had a large automobile and money. My God, those were sad, wild times for us.'

She took another deep drag on her cigarette. 'Vivien had come to Berlin with her fiancé. She was ten years younger than Raphael and had a laugh that could shake trees.'

Desirée lowered her voice as though about to impart some bad news. 'She was engaged to Bert von der Lohe, a tall, charming man of nationalist persuasion. They were a striking couple; wherever they turned up, people stopped and stared. And Bert was the envy of every man.'

She looked at Lilya to see if she was following. 'Raphael completely fell for Vivien — it must have happened as soon as he laid eyes on her. Not typical of him at all! I barely recognised him. Or should I say, it was love at first sight? I don't say this lightly and I know that most people who knew him well found this implausible — because Raphael was often dismissive and withdrawn, unapproachable even. He devoted his entire life to his research.'

Desirée looked out at the garden, but her eyes seemed to be focused inward on the distant, unforgotten past.

'You know, Raphael also had a gift for music. Life had lavished an indecent number of talents on him. He was a gifted violinist, spent countless evenings at the opera and the Philharmonie, and even composed his own pieces. They were not nearly as abstract as the new sounds coming from our generation. All those scores and signatures and figures! So mechanical! No, his pieces were lyrical.'

She looked through the open door into the drawing room at the grand piano as if she imagined Raphael sitting there. 'He used to host salons, sometimes here in my house. They'd rehearse at the institute amid the vitrines and phials. Vivien must have heard him on one of those occasions. After that, she always came to the recitals. Bert was unmoved by the arts, but for her a new world opened up. Raphael had placed a spell on her. I was happy for him about their affair, but despite this I didn't know it was much more than that. *Much* more.'

Desirée pointed with the tip of her cigarette to Lilya's empty cup, but she politely declined.

'Then Vivien became pregnant. She began to wonder whether she could pass the baby off as Bert's. He was away on business for several months and Vivien decided to take the pregnancy to term.'

Desirée paused and pulled her dressing gown more tightly around her, as if she felt cold.

'Raphael urged her to give up the baby for adoption. He didn't see himself in a position to marry her and raise the child because of his professional situation but he couldn't have endured it either if Bert had assumed he was the father, and brought up the child as his own.'

She stubbed out her cigarette, fished the next one out, stuck it into the holder and lit it.

'It was a terrible period, and I tried to persuade Raphael to face up to his responsibility. It's your child, I said to him again and again. But in vain. Just after the birth when she was still in hospital — it must have been May 1922 — Vivien gave up her baby for adoption. The family had money and opportunities and would be good parents. I don't know anything else about them. They would never see each other again.'

Lilya saw that Desirée's eyes were shining with tears. She pulled out a handkerchief from her dressing-gown pocket and dabbed them away. 'Vivien parted from Bert when he came back without telling him the real reason,' she carried on in a choked voice. 'And with Raphael . . . they tried being together but Vivien had lost her spark, and from that day on there was something between them that they couldn't overcome.'

All at once, Desirée seemed exhausted. She sank back in her chair, looking quite suddenly small and fragile. 'Raphael seemed to work more then ever. He seemed like a changed person.'

She paused again, the handkerchief crumpled into a formless ball in her hand.

Lilya gently took the handkerchief from her hand and wiped away the tears.

'Thank you,' she said, barely audible.

Her skin was as pale as chalk and her strength seemed to have been sapped.

She thanked Desirée for her candour, took the photograph of the house out of her bag and laid it on the table in front of her. She explained that Elias had found it in the catalogue and had discovered the reference to his fiftieth birthday on the back, written in code in Raphael's handwriting. Lilya turned over the photograph and showed her the puzzle. Desirée took the photograph and looked at it closely. She said she'd never seen it before. Lilya read the sentence on the back aloud: *Det bugter sig i bakke, dal.*

Desirée sighed; no, it meant nothing to her. It was a beautiful house, she added, but for certain, it wasn't near here.

Lilya sensed that it was time for her to go. As she left, Desirée stayed sitting but pressed the paper with her notes into Lilya's hand. Lilya imagined that she was adrift in her memories, brighter since their talk, and that no one would be able to rouse her from them.

# CHAPTER EIGHTEEN

The car, which was driving from the direction of Friedrichstrasse, was going fast. Lilya was on her way to the black market at the Reichstag building on Unter den Linden, the prestigious boulevard that had seen the last act of the Battle of Berlin. At the market she wanted to watch the traders, scan through books and talk to the vendors, in the hope of finding some new trace of Raphael Lind's books, or just to have time to think. She didn't turn and look when she crossed the boulevard. She should have. By the time she saw the car, it was too late. It hit her hard. All around her, the houses seemed to tumble; she only saw sky, an endless dark blue. Her body felt deadened, as though preparing for the onset of pain. Something warm and comforting ran down her forehead and she could feel the heat from the asphalt, warmed by the sun. Absurd that it should have happened here, in Berlin. A hand touched her throat. Something was pushed underneath her head. She could hear voices asking questions. 'Yoram,' she said. Then darkness enveloped her.

Where was she? Snatches of conversations, hands gliding over her body, a stabbing pain in her arm, her head throbbing.

'It'll stop soon,' someone said, and then it was night-time again.

Cordelia's red lips were moving. 'Dr Valentin . . . it could have been worse . . . serious concussion and a cut, major bruising. Nothing broken. Valentin . . . a friend of the family . . . to look after you . . . and move wards . . . you were lucky.'

She could smell Cordelia's perfume. She tried to concentrate on what she was hearing but she couldn't make sense of it. Then her eyelids drooped.

When she woke up again, Cordelia was still there. But she had a different dress on: brighter, more friendly. Lilya looked at her.

When Cordelia saw that she was awake, she gave a relieved smile. 'Welcome back,' she said, and took Lilya's hand.

'What day is it?' Lilya wanted to know.

'Wednesday.'

She thought for a moment. 'I was in town

on Sunday.'

'Dr Valentin let you sleep. With a helping hand — the best kind of medicine.'

Cordelia stepped back and a man in a white coat bent over her. One arm of his glasses was broken and taped together. He only had one hand, or was it just that she couldn't see the other? Her head ached, and every movement caused pain to sear through her body. His name was Hellmuth Valentin, her doctor.

'Just a few more days and then you'll be out of here. You were very lucky,' he said.

The cut on her temple pounded. She lifted her hand, counted her fingers, put her index fingers together and was relieved that she could make them meet.

The doctor was having a quiet word with Cordelia. They'd both turned away from Lilya and she couldn't make out what he was saying. Cordelia kept looking over at her with a worried expression.

'He's an old friend of the family,' said Cordelia and sat down again beside Lilya's bed. 'I marshalled him over here as soon as I heard. You didn't turn up at home on Sunday evening, and so I started calling all the hospitals. Luckily there aren't that many. I was really worried about you, Lilya.'

■ ■ ■ ■

She hadn't been able to glean much from the police, said Cordelia the next day. The car had been driving very fast and didn't stop. They assumed it was an accident. She didn't want to be a pessimist, Cordelia continued, but it was equally possible to assume that it had been intentional.

On Friday the nurse came and sat Lilya up for the first time. She clenched her teeth in pain.

'You've been sleeping a lot,' said the nurse, 'and you speak in your sleep — so many names! There's a visitor here for you.'

The nurse groomed her hair with a coarse hairbrush and braided it into a loose plait. 'You look nice,' she said. 'Where are you from?'

'Palestine.'

'Never heard of it. Do they speak German there?'

'Some of us do. Most of them speak Hebrew. And English. The British . . .'

'Then that's where your visitor is from.'

A small man who must have been in his forties stood next to her bed. The nurse pulled up a chair for him and left.

'May I sit down?'

She lifted her hand in assent.

He spoke a refined English with a lilting tone, and seemed to weigh up each word carefully before he said it. He'd taken off his hat and was holding it in his hands.

She recognised his voice.

'I've come to check on you and wish you a speedy recovery.' He looked intently at her.

She noticed how handsome his face was. Where had she seen him before?

'And to offer you my services,' he said, leaning forward in his chair. He raised his hand as if he were about to rest it on her shoulder, but paused. He leaned back again and looked at her thoughtfully.

'But you should regain your strength first,' he said, and got up. 'As soon as you're back home, we'll see each other again.'

Back home? What did he mean? Palestine? A wave of pain shook her body, expelling any thought. When the stranger was almost out of her sight, she suddenly remembered who he was: Major Terry. It had been weeks since she'd seen him at the meeting with Honeywell in London. But what was he doing in Berlin?

A few days later, after Dr Valentin had arranged for her to be transported home and prescribed bed rest, Major Terry turned up at Cordelia's apartment. Lilya was alone. She had just finished reading a note from Desirée, which she found on her bedside table when she arrived back at Cordelia's flat. Her hands still trembled.

Dear Lilya,

I am very sorry for having you leave my house without a word or a goodbye: please pardon an old lady who has seen more than she ever wanted to see.

There is one thing I hesitated to tell you. And I still don't feel right in revealing it to you. Yet I am convinced that you must know the full story.

I told you about Raphael and Vivien. Their love, Vivien's broken marriage, the pregnancy, the adoption. What I didn't dare say at the time is that a few days after the SS came for Raphael in Dahlem in October 1941, a terrible story made the rounds: a woman had been found drowned in Wannsee. It wasn't reported in any of the newspapers. They suspected it was suicide. I was the only one who knew it was Vivien. So I lost both of my dearest friends within days, Raphael first and then her. God must know why them!

Desirée v. W

When she opened the door, still shivering and feeling pain again all through her body, Major Terry suggested that they go outside and have a chat together, if she was able and agreed. She didn't have the strength to say no.

He linked arms with Lilya and helped her down the stairs. They found a bench on Winterfeldtplatz with trees offering shade and sat down. Major Terry looked up into the canopy of the trees above them, where birds were singing. A horse and three-wheeled carriage clattered across the square, while boys were playing marbles against a wall, squabbling loudly as they did so.

'You already look much better, and Miss Vinyard seems to be an excellent friend to you,' Terry began. He lit a cigarette. 'We have a penchant for benches, don't we?' he said, exhaling smoke. 'First Hyde Park and now here, in this Faustian city.'

'Major,' she said, 'I am deeply honoured that you've lured me out into the sun. But I'd prefer it if you came to the point and told me what it is you want. I'm in pain and I would rather be in bed.'

For a moment, Terry seemed taken aback by her resolute tone, then drew in very close to her. He obviously didn't want anyone to overhear them.

'We know that you're looking for Raphael Lind,' he said. 'We suspected it when you turned up at Ben Gedi's office in Tel Aviv, just a few days after we gave Elias Lind notice of his brother's death. But when you looked up Albert Green in London, we knew for certain.'

So Whitehall was interested in Raphael Lind.

'Sir Lucius asked me to keep an eye on you,' Terry continued, 'after you left London without contacting us.'

Lilya suddenly felt uneasy, even afraid. Terry hadn't seemed to want to harm her up until now. She didn't even feel threatened by him. But how could she be sure? She looked across the square. There were enough witnesses to feel safe. She pushed her fear aside and sat up.

'So it was you? Ever since I've been in Europe, I've felt that someone was tailing me. But are you on my side, Major? Is it one of your men? If so, please tell him to be a little more discreet.'

'You're being tailed, beyond a doubt. But I see it slightly differently. We are probably tailing the one who's tailing you.'

Lilya threw him a puzzled look.

'We have to assume that someone was trying to kill you, or at least deliver a clear

296

warning. There's hardly any other explanation.'

'Even if that were true, why should it be of interest to you and Sir Lucius?'

Major Terry sighed. 'Well . . .' He paused again. 'Because we should cooperate in this matter from now on, not confront each other. You are on to something that is also important for us and for whoever is out to do you harm. I am here to warn you. You're in danger and we can help you.'

He scanned Winterfeldtplatz and then fixed his gaze on her again. Lilya sensed that something else was coming now. 'But you can also help us,' he said.

So that was it. 'Why should I trust you? You're British, and you've admitted that you're tailing me.'

Terry seemed to be having difficulty maintaining his studied politeness. 'We were in contact with Lind. Rosbaud set it up, the editor of *Die Naturwissenschaften*. Lind's knowledge was highly relevant to us. I myself was posted to the British Embassy in Berlin during the thirties,' Terry continued. 'It was my duty to build secretly, under the cover of a third-grade diplomat, a network of scientists and experts who were working against the Nazis. Until Lind was banned from his profession, he was a specialist in

what the Germans call "resistance re‐
search". In the First World War they used
poisonous gases: a dangerous, unpredict‐
able weapon. Not only did they injure the
enemy but also their own people. Lind was
working on an antidote, improved chemical‐
based gas masks and treatments so that such
a thing could never happen again. We were
highly interested in what the Germans were
planning and researching. And when war
broke out in 1939, even more so. Would
they use poisonous gases again? We had to
be prepared for that eventuality. We hoped
that Lind, since he didn't, to our surprise,
leave the country when he had the chance,
would cooperate. And he did.'

Terry took out another cigarette and lit it.
Lilya was finding it increasingly difficult to
sit. Her hip was starting to hurt even more,
and a large graze on her elbow had started
burning beneath the bandages.

'Were you personally in contact with Ra‐
phael Lind?'

'Only very briefly,' said Terry, and took a
deep drag on his cigarette. 'I had to leave
the embassy in Berlin at the end of 1939.
Things got too risky after the war started.
One of our agents was supposed to stay in
touch with Lind and pass his articles on to
Green. But he vanished without a trace. We

presumed that the Germans had caught him.'

'Why didn't you simply offer Lind a chair at Cambridge and invite him to England?'

'We did. In vain. He refused to emigrate when it was possible. But because we were worried he'd be deported, we even forged a plan to abduct him. To save him.'

Terry gave a caustic laugh, threw his cigarette on the ground and crushed it with his heel.

'The enterprise failed,' he continued. 'Someone must have tipped off the Germans. A disaster for us, and a personal setback for me. Lind was our man, after all. And the Gestapo got to him before we could. Then came the period in Eisenacher Strasse — we know you've been to see Durlacher. He will have told you about that. We don't know what happened to Lind after that. No sign of life from him. Not a thing.'

So that's why they'd tracked down Elias Lind in Jerusalem. Now it made sense to Lilya. They'd wanted to remove all trace of Raphael Lind and their failed rescue attempt from their files. It would prevent someone from looking into the details and uncovering their fiasco; this embarrassing mishap on the part of the British, with all its strategic consequences.

Lilya wondered if she should mention this to Terry. But then again, no. She'd save it for Ben Gedi. He could decide whether it represented a suitable weapon. Something else was on her mind right now.

'Your plans were leaked, you say? So you suspect a hole in the spy network?' Lilya said. 'And you assume that the person who tipped off the Germans behind your back and double-crossed you and Whitehall is not happy about my search for Lind?'

'That's one way of putting it.'

'And who is it, Major? This man. The one tailing me?'

Terry hesitated before he continued. 'First we checked everyone who returned from Germany to Britain either before the war or shortly after it broke out. Many of them still work for us. They're all clean. Then the ones who have come back since: all clean too. What's left is the list of "Lost in Action" — and it's very long. We've been through it over and over again, but we haven't come to any concrete conclusion so far. There's no one left we can still check or ask.'

The matter was complex and now it was vital that she kept a level head. 'Even if everything you say is true, and one of your people foiled Lind's abduction, why would he have me in his sights? And how does he even know that I'm looking for Lind?'

Terry looked across the square as if the trees or walls might provide the answer. 'In Whitehall, only Honeywell and I know about your search mission. Perhaps you should think hard about whether you remember talking to anyone on your trip? Did anyone overhear you? Did you notice anything?'

There was a hard edge to his voice all of a sudden. She wanted to retort but Terry put a placatory hand on her shoulder.

'Whatever the case,' said Terry in a gentler tone of voice, 'the man who is after you seems to want to prevent you finding the professor somewhere among the rubble.'

'I thought that your entire concept was based on the fact that Lind is no longer alive?'

'Ours, yes. But not the man who's tailing you.'

'So you have doubts yourself?'

'Just suppose Lind is still alive and you find him, he might be able to tell you who his contact was on the British side. Name, address, appearance, everything. The one he passed his knowledge and articles to. And with this information, you could denounce this man as a traitor and notify us about him. High treason still carries the death penalty in Great Britain. So you are a great danger to this man and it seems he does not like you getting so close to the truth.'

The three-wheeled carriage clattered by again, this time loaded with coal. Boys in short trousers ran after it in the hope of catching falling pieces.

'Your stalker is just as interesting for us as for you,' continued Terry, his voice infused with friendliness again. 'Whether you like it or not, there is an overlap of interests between us.'

She didn't fully understand what he was trying to say. 'So you want me to lead you to your traitor? I'm supposed to be your bait?'

Terry inhaled deeply and leaned back, crossing his arms across his chest. 'That's not how I'd put it. Let's say: we're inviting you to work with us.'

She let all this sink in, not wanting to react too quickly. Keep him in suspense, she thought, and she closed her eyes to consider. She opened her eyes again. 'What if I say no?'

Terry fidgeted on the bench. She saw his features tensing. He appeared to be losing patience: after all, he had obviously intended to return with a result. And not with a bunch of unresolved issues and lessons in tactical manoeuvres from a young, politically unpredictable woman.

'Then you're on your own. And we'll see what happens.'

She breathed heavily. Was it her condition? No, her body was calm; nothing was going on. Just the pain becoming worse. She knew she hardly had a choice. Terry would stick to her heels as best he could, and her stalker would too. She could make it harder for them, but whether she'd actually succeed in shaking them off seemed doubtful after everything that had happened. And perhaps she might benefit from Terry and his contacts?

'Think it over,' Terry tried, his voice friendly again. 'If you cooperate with us, we can also protect you.'

Lilya looked at Terry closely. 'There's one small but important detail missing from your story.'

She waited a beat. 'There was a woman in Raphael Lind's life named Vivien Olsen and they had a child together. She killed herself after Raphael was taken away. I think you know about it.'

Terry looked at her, waiting for her to go on.

'Find Vivien's family for me,' Lilya added. 'I'm sure that you have the contacts. Find out what I can't find out myself and I'll lead you to your man.'

Terry seemed to consider how he should respond to this for a moment. 'The child was illegitimate — it's possible that the family knew nothing about it,' he said. She didn't hear much opposition in his voice.

'Nevertheless I want to try. I'd just like to know if any of the Olsens are still alive,' she said. 'Perhaps the family can help me. Well, what have you got to lose, Major? Your country will give you a knighthood if you find your traitor with my help. Cooperation not confrontation, isn't that what you said? Shall we make a start — or does the deal only apply to me?'

Lilya gave Terry a challenging smile; he looked annoyed. He scanned the square again. The boys with the marbles had disappeared. Music from a radio drifted from a window. A woman called out that lunch was ready.

The major sighed and reached out a hand. Then he smiled. 'All right then. I consider this our arrangement from now on.'

He helped her to her feet, linked his arm in hers and they walked carefully, one slow step at a time, back to the apartment.

'I have to admit I'm impressed,' said Terry after a while, and she felt him pull her closer. 'Where did you learn to be so stubborn?'

# CHAPTER NINETEEN

Cordelia had covered the beds with blankets and Gertig the janitor had fetched chairs up from the cellar. Glasses of all different sizes were standing on the kitchen table and empty jam jars served as ashtrays. The party was Cordelia's idea. She had invited friends and colleagues to help ease Lilya back into the outside world.

Lilya tried to stop her; she said she still didn't feel completely well and wasn't in the mood for conversation, laughing and drinking.

But there was no dissuading Cordelia. In a light-coloured, tight-fitting dress, with a white band in her hair, she stood at the open window, smoking and looking across Winterfeldtplatz, keeping an eye out for the first guests. The scent of her perfume filled the room.

Joint employees, army and military administration, as well as men and women from the broadcasting station were all invited; in next to no time the apartment was teeming with people laughing, talking and smoking. Everyone had brought something along: food, whisky, beer or cigarettes. A corps lieutenant had brought a smoked fish. She knew the man who arrived last and did the rounds with a shy smile. He had angular yet refined features, and a pair of horned-rimmed glasses stuck together on one side. It was Valentin, the doctor.

After everyone was settled and their glasses had been filled, Cordelia tapped her ring on her glass and asked for silence.

'Has everyone got a drink for a toast? I'd like to present to you my friend and colleague Lilya . . .'

Everyone turned to look at her.

'And to celebrate that we have her back. She must have a terrible impression of Berlin and I think we should change that. We are both indebted to Dr Valentin' — she pointed to the doctor who shrank away rather than taking a step forward — 'who performed a small medical feat.'

Applause; some shouted, 'Hear, hear!' Lilya blushed. Someone standing next to her pressed a glass wordlessly into her hand. It was half filled with a shimmering amber liquid that looked very tempting. Everyone raised their glass to Lilya and drank to her health.

She swallowed deeply and felt a powerful burning sensation shortly followed by a soothing warmth that spread throughout her body.

Lilya shook many hands and was asked to drink a toast here and there. She admired the ease with which Cordelia got people talking. Lilya watched her as she joined one group, then left again with self-confident, fluid movements, weaving her way in and out of the throng of guests. She allowed people to embrace her, holding out her cheek to be kissed in her unaffected way.

Lilya wanted to thank Dr Valentin who was lost in a reverie by the window. The last rays of sun glanced off the rooftops. The left sleeve of his suit was tucked and sewn under the shoulder; his eyes were alert, but very sad.

'Naturally,' he said in response to her thanks, 'that's my job.'

Then he drew in closer as if wanting to avoid being overheard. His demeanour was serious. 'I'm very relieved that you've recovered. To be honest, your condition was critical. You slept for three days and I was worried that you wouldn't wake up again; it wasn't a minor crash.'

'You don't think it was an accident, do you?'

He sighed. 'Cordelia has already asked me that, and the little Englishman in the grey suit. He doesn't think it was an accident. And neither do I, quite frankly. Given your injuries, the car must have headed straight for you.'

He sighed again, his gaze focused out of the window. 'This has to end some time. Enough is enough. Too much has been destroyed and we need a fresh start.' He paused for a moment. 'But try not to think about the incident too much,' he said. 'Just be glad that you're feeling better. The world still needs you, especially in these times.'

Cordelia joined them. She had taken off her white hairband and seemed relaxed and blissfully happy. She stopped in front of Lilya and refilled her glass with whisky before advising her to eat something from the kitchen. She shouldn't underestimate the whisky.

A brief while later, in which Lilya emptied her glass for a second time, she heard music in the next-door room. Someone must have brought along a gramophone, but after a few spins on the dance floor she had to sit down and hold on to a chair. Lilya wondered if she'd ever be able to stand up again. But why should she anyway? Sitting down was so nice, the music was so nice — everything was so nice. If only the walls would stop tilting to the side. Fresh air would do her good.

The balcony that looked out on to the garden was deserted; a lone, glowing cigarette stub smouldered in a glass. She leaned against the balustrade. The music seemed very distant now. She spread her arms akimbo to grip the railing and closed her eyes. Just for a few seconds, then she'd be all right. She felt the cool evening breeze on her back, the light wind, but it made her even dizzier. She breathed in deeply, wanting to gulp down the evening air. She was grateful for . . . the music, where had the music gone? Happiness, where was it? Harvey's guitar had gone silent, just one more spin, his hand, the warmth of his body, yes, that's better, yes, don't stand in the way . . . David, what are you doing?

She stayed out on the balcony lost in thought until Cordelia came out to find her.

'Lilya, you should go to bed. You can't sleep standing up!'

Where had everyone gone? Had they all left? The world wouldn't stop spinning.

When she woke up in her bed, everything

was quiet. Cordelia had already left the house. Someone was knocking on a door in the courtyard, dull thuds that she felt reverberate through her body. She rolled out of bed, crawled across the hallway to the bathroom, held her head over the toilet bowl and vomited. Panting for breath and crouched on the floor, she leaned against the wall. Images rose in her mind without meaning or logic. A sour, furry coating covered her tongue. Propped against the edge of the sink, she cleaned her teeth for several minutes until a red trail mixed with the white foam. She decided to take a bath.

After the bath she got dressed and went into the kitchen. Glasses and plates were piled high in the sink and the bitter smell of cold ash wafted up from the bin. Every glass was a mammoth task. She had trouble standing up, but she wanted to make herself useful and have everything in order by the time Cordelia came home.

The bell rang. She put down the tea towel and walked down the hallway to the front door. Through the spyhole she saw a grey suit. She took off the chain and opened the door: it was Major Terry again. She stepped aside, and asked him in.

He strode purposefully into the living

room, and waited until Lilya had sat down before he took a seat too. He looked around the room. 'I hope you enjoyed your party last night,' he said with a strained smile, fingering the rim of his hat, which he'd taken off when he'd come in.

He looked at her, as if compelled by a question, then abruptly stood up and disappeared into the kitchen. She heard him turning the tap on and off. He came back and sat down again, his face taut.

'Running water. How lucky you are. You look a little pale. Was it a late night last night? Have a good time?'

Lilya suppressed a yawn. Terry took out his silver cigarette case and looked around for an ashtray. He found one on the windowsill, fetched it and sat down again. Lilya's patience was starting to wear thin.

'Well, Major . . . ?'

After the first drag on his cigarette, he seemed to relax. He cleared his throat. 'We've found her father.'

Involuntarily, she leaned forward. Had she heard right? It wasn't even a week since she'd spoken to Terry. She had to admit that the British were quick.

'It wasn't easy but we eventually found him via his daughter's name. He's from Denmark.'

'And?' Lilya burst out. 'Did he know that his daughter had a child, did he say anything on that subject? Does he know Raphael Lind?'

Terry placed the cigarette in the ashtray and took off his jacket. Beads of sweat were running down his temples.

'Yes and no.' He took a handkerchief out of his pocket and wiped his forehead.

'Can you be a little more specific?'

'He knows. But he's put it all behind him. He tried to understand his daughter for too long — why she got involved with Lind in the first place and stayed in Germany with him, why he wouldn't marry her, what happened to the child. But he's old now and it's all in the past.'

Terry shrugged and looked out of the window. 'Resignation is sometimes the only way to survive when there's no hope. You can reconcile yourself to it.'

They sat in silence.

'But I haven't given up hope,' Lilya began. 'Perhaps Vivien had contact with him until the end, and left behind some clue as to Lind's whereabouts.'

'Forget it.'

'Could you give me Olsen's address?'

'What for? You're not thinking of visiting him, are you?'

That was precisely what she'd been considering. But she thought it made more sense to contact him first by letter.

'No, but I want to write to him. Perhaps I'll find out something that could be important to him too.'

'Believe me, it's a dead-end street.' Terry stood up. He hesitated for a moment and then placed a card on the table.

'You didn't get it from me, understand?' He looked her in the eye.

She thanked him and saw him to the door. He turned to face her one last time.

'And any news for me?'

Lilya pretended not to know what he was angling for.

'You still haven't thought of anyone you might have confided in too much?'

Since their last meeting, she'd thought a great deal about this question, retracing her journey every step of the way from the first meeting in Ben Gedi's secret office in Tel Aviv, the bus journey, London, Föhrenwald, Offenbach, to the present — but to no avail. She'd told her story to David Guggenheim in Offenbach, and to Cordelia. It was absurd to imagine that either one of them had anything to do with the matter.

'I see,' said Terry and reached for the doorknob.

Out of the blue, a name flitted across her memory. 'Have you ever heard the name O'Madden? Colm O'Madden?' she asked.

The major stopped and looked at her in surprise. 'No,' he said.

'It's just an idea. We talked a couple of times after leaving Cyprus on the ship to Southampton. He tried to embroil me in conversation and it was difficult to shake him off.'

Terry raised his eyebrows. 'Colm O'Madden, you say? And he travelled with you from Palestine?'

She nodded.

'Thank you,' said Terry and walked out into the stairwell. He turned around one last time. 'We'll look into it.'

# CHAPTER TWENTY

'There are some rumours going around the camp. I thought you should know . . .'

David Guggenheim's tone was serious. She asked him to repeat what he was saying.

'Just a story, but . . .'

Rumours? What about? The connection was bad, but at least she had one.

Cordelia let her know the evening beforehand that she'd arranged a phone call with UNRRA in Munich. During the telephone call that afternoon, Lilya finally got to see Cordelia's workplace — her small, thirty-square-foot but very practical Joint office in Dahlem. The call from Munich came in at three o'clock.

'People say the man worked for Rosenberg but I can't guarantee that . . . no idea . . . trial . . . well, it was important to tell you anyway . . .'

'Do you know where he lives?'

'North of . . . -unich . . . check.'

The line was crackling and Lilya reluctantly held the receiver away from her ear. There was a sound of static and then Guggenheim's voice again — this time loud and clear.

'Hello?' he said.

'Yes, I'm still here. Do you know any more about this man?'

'The military police haven't found him yet apparently. But they think he might be hiding in Bavaria.'

'Is there a name or another indication?'

The line went dead for a couple of seconds but it was still connected: then she heard a rustling noise.

'Are you still there?'

'Just a minute, I've found a note . . .'

'And?'

'War —'

Silence.

Lilya held the receiver closer to her ear. Cordelia made a pacifying gesture. *Be patient.*

'Wartenberg . . . does that ring any bells?'

'Wartenberg . . . not straight away, no, I'll have to think . . .'

'I thought it'd be good if you knew the name.'

'No doubt about it. Thanks for the

information.'

. Silence again. She didn't want to put the phone down just yet, but she didn't know what to say either. Images surfaced from their time dancing together. She felt the blood rising in her head. Perhaps it would be better to end the conversation now. She was about to say goodbye when Guggenheim cleared his throat and said, 'I was told you had an accident?'

'Yes, I didn't see the car until it was too late.'

'Do you feel better now? Do you need anything?'

There was a warmth in his voice that did her good. Like on the back seat of the jeep in Offenbach. 'No, I was lucky — I'm in the best hands and almost completely recovered.'

She sensed that Guggenheim wasn't going to leave it at that.

'Really? I don't like the sound of it at all.'

Lilya wanted to calm him down, but the line was interrupted again.

'Let me . . . know, what I can . . . and what your plans are . . . Please.'

That was the last thing she heard, then the receiver went dead. She looked at the telephone for a while.

Wartenberg. Now she was sure she'd

heard that name recently. But in what context? It must have been here in Berlin. She would go and see Erich Durlacher again the next day.

Leibnizstrasse was still scattered with puddles, and it smelled of fresh mortar and damp cardboard. A few clouds, stragglers from the night before, scudded across the sky between the rows of houses.

Lilya had heard the rain coming and felt the wind long before it whipped up. She'd lain awake, listening into the darkness until the first thunderclap came, announcing a major storm. It had rained on until the morning hours. Since the accident, her body had become more sensitive, as if the car collision had awakened new senses.

Elias Lind had told her that his bones were a barometer, hydrometer and seismograph, as if his advancing blindness gave him ways of seeing in these other, useless ways. The *khamsin* caused a tugging feeling in his left leg. Approaching frost was signified in his wrists. 'My skeleton is just one big weather station,' he'd said and laughed.

Erich Durlacher wasn't at home this time either. The woman who worked for him opened the door and immediately recognised Lilya. The doctor had left the house the previous day, and had not said when he'd be back. Her tone was coloured with impatience, perhaps anxiety. She looked back at her typewriter.

Lilya couldn't work out whether the woman was really on her own. She thought she could hear a creaking sound in the apartment like someone walking across floorboards.

The woman looked up at the ceiling. 'It's hell,' she said. 'The Spielhagens above us, three children, and then the soldiers in billets on top. How is anyone supposed to work?'

'Are you typing his report, the one that is supposed to go to the Nuremberg Trial?'

'No, he took it with him. I'm typing letters, entries and my never-ending correspondence with the land registry. For the apartment in Schlüterstrasse. I've told him over and over again that he should get himself a lawyer.'

'So Dr Durlacher has finished his report?'

'More or less. A man recently called in and said he'd check it and have it translated, so that Dr Durlacher can send it to the authorities in Nuremberg.'

Lilya stopped short when she heard this. 'What man?'

'My God, there have been so many here

recently. I think he said he was from the British military police but he spoke very good German.'

Lilya asked if she could come in for a moment.

'Please do,' said the woman, and led her along the passage to the living room. She didn't have anything to offer her, she said, and, besides, she had to get on with her work.

Lilya followed her into the small study and asked if she could describe the man in more detail.

'I only let him in, then I went back to work,' she said curtly. She took a stack of papers from her desk and put them on the shelf. Then she made a visible effort to remember. 'Well, let me think. He was small, stocky, smartly dressed and had a pleasant voice. Almost like a famous actor.'

'Did Dr Durlacher know him from the past?'

'I don't think so. The man showed him an ID card. They left in his car, which the man had parked in the courtyard. I saw it through the window.'

'What kind of car was it?'

'Wheels, a black roof — a soft top, I think. One of the headlights was damaged — I noticed that because they were so big.'

Lilya looked out of the window into the courtyard. She felt a little dizzy and asked if she might sit down for a moment.

The woman indicated an armchair — Dr Durlacher's reading spot, as she called it. Lilya was welcome to wait here, but it might take a while before the doctor came back. The woman put on her glasses and began typing.

Lilya looked at the clock. She'd wait for an hour. In her mind's eye, she saw the car coming towards her, felt the dull pain of the collision again and blood trickling down her temple. The sound of a car engine interrupted her thoughts, shortly followed by keys jangling in the door. She pushed herself up and out of the armchair, and leapt over to the window — but the car had already vanished. Durlacher's secretary had taken her hands off the typewriter and was peering intently over her glasses at Lilya.

Durlacher seemed to be in a good mood; he was whistling as he shut the front door behind him. He was about to say something when he glimpsed Lilya. A broad smile spread across his face; he seemed happy to see her.

'Still in town?' he asked. 'Things are moving along here. I was just able to see for myself, during a car ride. But my English! A catastrophe. All the better that the good man spoke such excellent German. Almost accent-free too, just imagine. Otherwise it would have been a fine excursion.'

He asked Lilya to follow him into the living room. There he plopped down into the armchair. He'd laid his briefcase on the table.

'Frau Marbach?' he called into the study. 'Have you anything to offer us except paper?'

Mrs Marbach came in and threw up her hands. 'The water's been turned off, and there's no milk until tomorrow.'

'Then we'll drink champagne,' said Durlacher.

Frau Marbach sighed and went to the coat rack to fetch her jacket.

After she'd gone, Durlacher wanted to know what had brought Lilya here and if she was making any progress in her search for Lind.

'Yes,' she said, 'that's why I'm here. It's just a small matter, but I keep coming back to it. I don't even know if you can help. The last few weeks have been very turbulent and perhaps I'm getting a few things mixed up —'

'Enough of the preamble,' he said, interrupting her.

'It's a name. A name I think you mentioned: Wartenberg.'

'I mentioned? I'm not sure I did. But you might have read it on a document that I showed you. Just a moment . . . I asked Frau Marbach to make copies . . .'

He got up and went over to his briefcase, paused, turned around and appeared to be thinking. Then he disappeared into the room next door and came back with a document in his hand. Lilya took it, immediately recognising it. He was right: it said *Wartenberg* at the top.

'There are apparently some rumours in the camps in Bavaria that Wartenberg is still alive, hiding somewhere in Bavaria, I was told,' she explained.

Durlacher listened attentively as he held up the document. The value of this file would increase enormously if this were true, he said.

Lilya asked him whether he knew anything about this Wartenberg character, and what connection he'd had to Raphael Lind. After all, according to the document, he'd been the one to choose Lind for the work in the loot depot.

'I only saw him once,' said Durlacher. 'He was clever, tall, well-mannered . . . I'd have classed him as a Wehrmacht man, an aristocratic officer, rather than one of the Party mob. I never spoke to him. He was in the SS and there were rumours about him.'

'What kind of rumours?'

'That he was in charge of Operation Fire Storm. He might have asked for Lind and had him transferred from Eisenacher Strasse. But that's just speculation. He only came to the depot once. And when the top men turned up, it was better not to look at them, but simply carry on working and keep your eyes on the ground.'

Durlacher paused and looked at her almost mischievously. It was rather odd, he said, that so many people were suddenly interested in him; there was so much coming and going in his normally quiet apartment. Seeing Lilya's face, his expression sobered again.

'Dr Durlacher, as you know, you're not accountable to me in any way. But would you mind telling me the name of the Englishman you're working with? I've also met a few Englishmen over the past few weeks and perhaps there are overlaps,' she said.

Durlacher looked surprised. 'Really? How strange. He introduced himself as Major Burnside — or was it Turntide? Or perhaps something else altogether.'

He lifted his head and looked in the direction of the kitchen.

'Frau Marbach, perhaps you can remember the name of that polite Englishman . . . ?'

He started when he saw Lilya's face. Frau Marbach had left a few minutes earlier.

'What did he offer you?'

'Legal support. A translation of my report and a talk with a military prosecutor. I gave him a copy of my report today to translate and assess.'

Lilya tensed. 'How did Major Turntide, or whatever his name is, come across you?'

Durlacher looked as if he'd been caught out. 'Oh. That's a good question. To be honest, I hadn't thought to ask him that.' He paused for a moment. 'And you'd be right to say that it was an oversight.'

'Well, to say the least, you have given him highly valuable information, which took a lot of effort to put together — information not to everyone's liking.'

Durlacher seemed embarrassed. 'So many people turned up this week wanting to talk to me: Englishmen, Americans, Russians and French, former colleagues, people writing reports.' At this, Durlacher smiled pleadingly, as if hoping that she would still hold him in high esteem and that their unspoken alliance wouldn't be affected.

'You could say that at an advanced age I've become a little hub where people exchange knowledge. But it's made me lose sight of things.'

He looked down at the floor, thinking. Then, looking up, he said, 'Perhaps his name was Burnside after all.'

# CHAPTER TWENTY-ONE

The woman on the other end of the line was polite yet firm: Major Terry was not available.

Lilya felt her temper rising. How was she supposed to reach Terry? By phoning Whitehall and asking to be put through to Berlin?

It had taken her a while to fit together the pieces of the puzzle after her visit to Durlacher. Something in her had wanted to deny the way things seemed, even after her talks with Major Terry. But she had to admit that everyone had been right: David, Lev, Cordelia and even Terry. She was on to something serious. Everything Durlacher had told her about his new English friend pointed to the fact that he was the one following her. He had approached Durlacher because he was tailing her again. She remembered the car crash — the collision and the dull pain — and shuddered. Terry had offered her protection, but now he wasn't available.

Lilya looked over at Cordelia who had put her feet up on the desk in her office and was smoking. She could see the camp through the window: a place of refuge for European Jews who had found their way to Berlin. The window was open and inhabitants walked past and said hello. Cordelia stood up to give a cigarette to a one-legged man on crutches.

She'd try one last time. Cordelia beat her to it and laid her hand on Lilya's before she could pick up the receiver.

'Let me do that,' she said. 'What's a well-connected father for?'

She dialled a number and spoke to a man — Lilya could hear a croaky *Yes* on the other end. After a few minutes, she hung up and smiled at Lilya.

'Give Derek a few minutes and then you can phone His Majesty's Government again.'

When Lilya called the second time, she'd barely finished saying her name when the receptionist, who only minutes earlier had insisted that Major Terry wasn't there, asked her to hold the line. Shortly afterwards, she heard his voice.

'Please excuse me,' he said. 'My mistake. I should have left your name with her. That would have saved you setting the entire American General Governor's apparatus in motion. You might as well have shouted out my name from the top of the Brandenburg Gate — now the whole world knows about us.'

Lilya ignored Terry's reproach. There was no time for an exchange of blows. 'I have some news,' she said, 'and I dare say it'll interest you.'

She briefly described what had happened at Durlacher's: the Englishman's visit, his offer to take the report and a rough description of the car he was driving.

Terry was silent.

'You're not saying anything.'

'I'm thinking.'

'Do you have a hunch who this Englishman could be?'

'Not on the telephone.'

They met at six o'clock on Winterfeldtplatz.

Terry looked around and they sat down on their bench. Again, he seemed on edge and moved in close to her.

'About this Colm O'Madden chap. We don't have a Colm O'Madden on our list in Whitehall. But he'd have been very sloppy to call himself by his real name. What we do know based on our intelligence is that the chap who took over from me in the Lind affair when I left Berlin at the beginning of the war — the one who disappeared into thin air shortly afterwards — could be a suspect. He was down on our books as Everett Harp. We should entertain the possibility that he and O'Madden are the same person.'

'Entertain the possibility?' she said, outraged.

'We're only at the beginning. It's like this.' Terry started to recount the longer version of Harp's story.

Harp had been born Ernst Hartmann in Hanover in 1899 to an English mother and a German father, which is why he spoke both languages without accent — a highly favourable qualification for a career as a spy. As a boy, he and his mother had been involved in a tram accident: she had died. It left him with the tips of two fingers missing on his left hand — or perhaps it was his right one, the documents were not clear on this. His father was violent, so Harp went to live with an uncle in Chester soon after his mother's death. Due to his German background, however, he was constantly taunted. As a young man, he returned to Germany and worked as a chauffeur, messenger and film extra, and was regarded as reliable, discreet, patient and clever. After the Nazis rose to power, Whitehall took an interest in him.

'What you should know,' said Terry, 'is that Harp is not stupid to a high degree — like many of our recruits — but intelligent to a small degree. That's what made him so unpredictable.'

Lilya compared Terry's image of Harp with her picture of O'Madden and her unknown stalker. The glove on O'Madden's hand was etched on her memory.

'In September 1941,' continued Terry, 'Harp suddenly vanished into thin air. As I've already mentioned, we presumed that the Germans had caught up with him. In any case, shortly after we lost him, Lind vanished too and our carefully planned rescue mission fell through.'

'Did Harp know Lind personally?' Lilya asked.

'We have to assume so. Even if the chain of transfer for German documents was often long, for security reasons. In Nazi Germany we had to exercise extreme caution. We sometimes worked with the German resistance. Very few people knew the name of the person on the receiving end: an envelope would be hidden, a code word cited, then the envelope received and passed on. Harp also worked under a code name. But it's highly likely that he was the last link in the chain to Lind.'

'His code name didn't happen to be Turntide or Burnside, did it?' said Lilya.

Terry looked at her, dumbfounded. 'Turntide actually, yes . . . how do you know that?'

Lilya blanched. 'I told you about my last meeting with Durlacher. The British military employee who offered to translate Durlacher's report? He thinks his name was Turntide.'

Terry whistled softly. 'I'm impressed, Miss Wasserfall. It seems as if you're about to solve one of the British secret service's cold cases.'

'I only hope I'll be able to celebrate it with you — if Turntide, Harp, my stalker and Colm O'Madden turn out to be the same person.'

There were a dozen ways she could go underground. Whichever one she chose, she had to slip away noiselessly. Should she let Cordelia in on it? When would be the right time? She wanted to find this mysterious Wartenberg — and to do it alone. Without being followed.

There was one last thing to finish. She was waiting for an answer from Hans Olsen in

Copenhagen. She had written to him in English. His reply came in German. His handwriting was straightforward and clear, and matched his message: he had nothing else to add and after years of self-reproach and grief for his daughter, he had made peace with both her and his own fate. Between the lines, she could tell how much strength he'd needed to put the pain behind him, stop asking himself questions, continue living and put aside all the anger and despair that Raphael Lind had caused him — this distant man whom he had never met.

I would like to thank you for taking up the search again, which I failed to do, and which nearly destroyed me. I am sorry that I can't help you. I wish you the best of luck and hope that you find the answers you are looking for.

That's how the letter ended. And with that, Lilya's path was decided: she would head south and find Wartenberg.

She told everyone that she would go and visit Erich Durlacher again in three days' time — and that she had 'new, important information'. That gave her a head start. Enough time to get back to Bavaria and the American zone.

■ ■ ■ ■

# Bavaria

## KIBBUTZ NILI

■ ■ ■ ■

# CHAPTER TWENTY-TWO

Lilya's head kept falling forward on to her chest but sleep remained elusive. She had found a place in the third-class compartment and was wedged in between suitcases and bags by the window. The sun was beating down on her and the carriage was stuffy and hot. An aching fatigue washed over her, thoughts came and went; scenes, images and snatches of conversation from the past three weeks in Berlin. Since her accident, her conversations with Terry and everything that she'd found out and experienced, a change had come over her. She was glad to leave the city behind — it had nearly cost her her life. Was her agitation simply fear? She would soon see David Guggenheim again. And after the attack in Offenbach she hadn't forgotten how happy she was to have him by her side; his voice, his company, a male presence protecting her. She imagined his hand on her and felt her body tense.

She looked out of the window. In the distance she noticed a castle. They were pulling into a devastated town lying at the foot of a fortress. Then the whistle sounded, there was a jolt and the train set off again. She closed her eyes.

At Munich main station, she struggled through the crowds towards the exit. The splintered steel girders of the roof were still stacked by the railway tracks, which had only been cleared and straightened a few months ago; the entrance hall was still an expanse of rubble. On the station forecourt she spotted a US Army jeep. Two soldiers were leaning against the vehicle and smoking. She straightened her uniform jacket, tidied her hair and walked over to them.

She was entitled to military transport, Guggenheim had told her. The soldiers, clearly happy to have a change in their routine, agreed on the spot to drive her to the UNRRA office. They flicked away their cigarettes, and one of them held the door open to let her climb into the back.

The soldier in the passenger seat, a black GI from Louisiana, turned around a couple of times and tried to engage her in conversation. But she only managed to catch snippets of what he said. He soon gave up, laughing.

She was relieved when the jeep turned into the familiar street and pulled up under the shady trees; it felt like a homecoming. She felt a pounding in her throat — anticipation, impatience, but also uncertainty. What would it be like to see David Guggenheim again? How would he greet her?

She went through the house to the garden; the swing had been unhooked and the frame stood there, abandoned. But David Guggenheim was sitting on the veranda, lighting a cigarette as he leaned back in his wicker chair. Next to him on a round table, papers were spread out, weighted down with stones, and a ballpoint pen. He didn't seem to notice as she approached him.

'Oh,' is all he managed to say when he looked up to see her standing in front of him.

His expression was a mix of astonishment, joy and perhaps a hint of embarrassment that she had never seen before.

'Made it,' she said.

He stood up, neither of them really knowing how to greet the other, and after a moment they shook hands.

'Escaped from the big, scary city?'

He looked at Lilya. She couldn't make out what he was thinking.

'You're leaning a little to one side. The

accident?'

'Yes. But I've stopped believing it was an accident.'

He shuffled the papers into a pile and pointed to a chair.

'We'll get round to that. But please sit down first. I'll get you a coffee. A proper one.'

She set down her rucksack and took a seat at the table. A glass of water would be fine, she said, and reached for the carafe on the table. In the beech tree overhead two birds were bickering noisily. They now shot out from the branches.

Guggenheim looked up. 'They've been at it the whole time,' he said, 'while I've been trying to work.'

She had the feeling that she had to talk to avoid an awkward silence. She pointed to his papers. 'Looks like you've got your work cut out. More reports about the camp?'

She needn't have worried. Guggenheim was clearly in a good mood.

'The file on reports and miracles is closed. That's your department anyhow. These here are invoices, petitions and all kinds of applications and missing persons' reports. The more people arrive in Föhrenwald, the more staff we have to deploy.'

'Any information from the priest?'

340

'Nothing tangible. He's been able to help in many cases, bringing families together, raising the dead, and producing missing people from some corner of the world. But in this case . . .' He rested his hand on the top page.

'Is it a particularly complicated case?'

He hesitated for a moment. 'I'd say averagely awful and fashionably hopeless.'

He laughed but she sensed a strain behind his laughter. He pulled his hand back as if wanting to change the subject. She hesitated, wondering whether she should continue to press him, and then decided to risk it. 'It's your case, isn't it?' she asked in a low voice.

Guggenheim's expression turned to stone. Had she gone too far? Would he stand up in a moment and ask her to leave? Or use some pretext to disappear? As quick as a flash he could erect a wall around himself — she'd already experienced this on several occasions. But this time, she didn't want to give up.

'It's your mother, isn't it? And the priest is helping you?'

He looked at her, slack-jawed. 'Did Bernstein tell you that?'

She nodded. Suddenly his face brightened. 'I love my adoptive parents: I have them to thank for everything. They gave me the best childhood you can have. I grew up in New Jersey and often went to New York with my dad. He's from there. Every morning, he went by train to his law firm near Times Square — it was on the twenty-third floor and the elevator was quick as a bolt. When I got older, he often took me with him in the school vacations, and I'd spend the day in the city while he worked. In the evening, my mother came too. She'd devote all her time to setting up a county museum for local art. But those evenings we all went to eat at Tishman & Fry's. They served steak and French fries, thick like your thumb. The waiters wore white uniforms like navy captains, with gold stars on the lapels. Each star stood for five years' service. One of the waiters had five stars. It was a real shame when I found out that Tishman and Fry had never even existed. The owner was an old guy called Ginzburg who picked out a couple of names from his circle of friends.'

He smiled and seemed to be lost in his thoughts of New York.

'But your birth mother gave you a photo of herself, didn't she?'

'Yeah. A kind of delivery slip, you could say. A clear breach of German regulations.' He laughed, rather awkwardly, like someone who wasn't used to talking about himself and his feelings.

'And now the picture has travelled back here with me. Mom and I have come a long way together. I sometimes talk to her. But she never answers. Then I tell her that maybe she's not my mother after all, and she gives me this scolding look, then starts to laugh. I don't think she could ever be mad at me.'

'Could you be at her?'

He hesitated for a moment. 'No. She must have had her reasons back then.'

She let a few moments pass. 'May I see the photo?'

'Just a moment.'

He disappeared through the veranda door and came back out not long later holding the photograph.

The woman was more beautiful than Lilya remembered. She was standing in front of a bookshelf, which filled almost the entire frame. Her head was tilted to one side, and her eyes had an air of gentle melancholy.

Guggenheim slid the picture back into the envelope before straightening up in his chair. It was obvious that he wanted to bring this part of their conversation to an end. It was time to talk about the really important things, he said. About work and their progress in the camp: Föhrenwald had survived the first great influx of refugees. Lisa Strassburger had been appointed site director so that he could concentrate on politics, administration and contacting army and civil authorities. Lev was now chauffeuring him around confidently and had started talking to the car. He was a great help to him, on a personal level too. He thought Lev's job was helping him find a way to return to life.

Guggenheim's tension seemed to have completely evaporated, and Lilya wondered how she could drag out this chatty mood, which was also doing her good. His voice was warm in a way that she'd rarely heard in their talks so far.

He smiled at her and leaned towards her, touching her shoulder with his hand. 'But look at me yakking away here. There are much more important things to talk about, like how you are. I can't get your accident out of my mind. So it wasn't one after all, huh?'

'Perhaps someone was trying to kill me.'

How easy it was to say. But she still wasn't sure.

'The way you say it, you sound pretty convinced.' Guggenheim leaned towards her. 'Is there any other explanation,' he said, faltering, 'other than . . . murder?'

She was worried he would lapse back into his more official tone: the conscientious, matter-of-fact, strategic-minded officer, who didn't want to make mistakes or miss anything. But he stayed silent and continued to fix his gaze on her.

'If we rule it out as an accident — and we should,' she said, 'then we have to assume it was deliberate. Maybe to stop me doing anything else here in Germany. A warning shot, if you like.'

He looked at her and asked for details.

She told him about her meeting with Terry, the hole in the British spy network, and her deal with the major; about her talks with Durlacher and his mysterious English friend who was likely to be the British link to Lind. And the man who seemed bent on killing her.

Guggenheim leaned back, his eyebrows knitted. 'But you won't break off your journey? It sounds like you're taking a huge risk.'

He stood up and fished a pack of cigarettes out of his trouser pocket. 'I wonder if it's worth it, Lilya. You seem to be stirring up something that is too big for you. And I'll be frank: I don't like your deal with the British major. Have you ever thought about just dropping the case?'

Of course she had. Several times over the past few days, in fact. But the result was always the same.

*A Test. Won't fail. Trust.*

'I've already come this far and there's no way back. It's too late.'

Guggenheim lit another cigarette with studied insouciance. Then he looked at her again.

'I've made up my mind. I'm staying here to look for Raphael Lind. I made Elias Lind a promise. If I give up now, it will all have been for nothing.'

'And what about the stalker who's still at your heels? He might find you again. Wherever you happen to be. I don't like that idea at all.'

'I don't think he suspects where I am. I spread a rumour in Berlin that I was going to visit Durlacher in the next few days to give myself a head start.' She paused briefly and grinned. 'Unless there's something you want to tell me, Lieutenant Guggenheim . . .'

Guggenheim smiled. 'Aha, caught red-handed,' he said. 'I just didn't want to let you out of my sights. And so I sent someone after you. But the whole thing has got out of hand.'

He sat down again, suddenly more serious. 'But this isn't a game, Lilya. And because I know what you're doing, *and* I am a soldier, I will have to act too at some point.'

Lilya suggested they talk again before doing anything. She hadn't yet followed up all her leads. Durlacher had confirmed that a man called Wartenberg had business with Raphael Lind. And it was very likely that he was the one who had apprehended Lind in Eisenacher Strasse: Durlacher had shown her a document with Wartenberg's name on it.

'Camp rumours have it that he was a big fish in Rosenberg's task force — SS Headquarters or the Weapons Agency — I couldn't work it out exactly,' said Guggenheim.

'Do these camp rumours also say where this big fish can be caught? If he is still alive?'

'Rumour says that he is.' Guggenheim leaned back and looked closely at her. 'I was afraid you might ask that. You want to visit him and ask him how things were in the Third Reich, just like that? Oh, and by the way, Wartenberg, while you're at it, where did all the Jews get to? One dear to my heart in particular?'

'Something like that,' she said. 'But I'll put it slightly differently.'

'Have you ever heard of Pleikershof? It's a kibbutz nowadays, Kibbutz Nili. It was a farm in Franken. A survivor who works on the kibbutz mentioned Wartenberg in connection with the ERR.'

'And now comes the catch . . .'

'The survivor refuses to talk to us and made it clear that he'd like to get out of Germany as soon as he can.'

'I see. So, if we offer him the opportunity to get into Palestine, he'd talk?'

'We can't do that. Even if we could, we wouldn't know how reliable his statement was. Perhaps he'd tell us anything just to get a passport out of here.'

'He can't have made up the name Wartenberg. Durlacher's document proves that. There could be something to it.'

The man who'd tipped off Guggenheim was called Jossi Schierlinger — he was the one she should visit. Perhaps he'd tell her who his source was. Perhaps not.

Guggenheim seemed to be having an internal debate. 'I'll give you two days,' he said.

She looked at him in surprise.

'Two days with Lev and the car, that's all I can spare. I'd feel happier if you weren't

travelling alone,' he said and looked her in
the eye. 'Think about it.'

# CHAPTER TWENTY-THREE

Lev clung to the steering wheel, his arms outstretched. They had parked in the courtyard and the engine was already switched off. On the final stretch, they'd driven down a long, never-ending country road. At the end of a column of birch trees that stood to attention in straight rows, they'd discovered the hidden farm. They turned off into Pleikershof. It was an enormous estate of farm buildings grouped around a courtyard, consisting of one house and three barns. The barns and stable roofs were caved in, but the half-timber walls had survived. Lilya was in awe: no kibbutz in Palestine was comparable to the size and layout of Kibbutz Nili. But those kibbutzes had been built on freedom whereas this was a product of vileness and misery. None of the kibbutz inhabitants could be seen but two large, shaggy dogs had noticed their arrival and were running around the car, barking loudly.

Lilya saw that Lev was watching them out of the corner of his eye. She went to open the door.

'Please don't!' His voice had a note of panic. He continued to cling to the steering wheel.

She and Lev had set off from Munich at midday. After they'd left the city, the route took them through the countryside. Lilya's nerves were jangling and she'd even snapped at Lev for not noticing a tractor in the right-hand lane until it was nearly too late.

She wanted to find out where Wartenberg lived — and then? What was her plan? Guggenheim had warned her not to do anything from now on without first consulting him.

The sun was beating down on the roof of the car and sweat was running down their necks. Suddenly she heard a whistle. One of the dogs trotted off. The other sniffed around at Lev's door.

'Rasso, down!'

The voice came from the house, followed by another whistle.

Lev had told her that he'd often been chased by dogs while he was fleeing from the East. They had trailed him through the woods, and he'd only be able to shake them off when he reached a river.

'I'll get out and make sure the dogs back off,' she said.

A boy came out of the long main building and walked towards them. He was holding a stick and whistled again. Just before he reached the car, he flung the stick through the air; the dogs chased after it.

Lev didn't move. Lilya got out.

The boy, who must have been about sixteen, raised a hand when the dogs returned. They sat down in front of him. '*Beseder*. These German dogs speak Hebrew,' he said. 'I'm Giora.'

He reached out his hand and blinked, his eyes watchful. Then he shooed the dogs into the house in front of him.

The car door opened and Lev climbed out.

'How can I help you?' Giora asked, returning.

'We'd like to speak to Jossi Schierlinger,' replied Lilya. 'We hope we've come to the right place.'

The boy smiled.

Giora walked a few paces over to the barn and called out in a surprisingly loud voice, 'Jossi! Visitors for you!'

The dogs barked from behind the closed front door and Lev tensed. A man came out

352

of the barn, walked over to them, wiping his hands on his trousers, and shook hands with them.

'You're from the Joint, I see. I hope you haven't come to write one of those useless reports — no offence but if they weren't, we'd have been irrigating the Negev Desert instead of German land long ago.'

He turned around and looked out across the fields. Then he invited them into the garden behind the house: there, a large herb and vegetable patch flaunted the fertility of Franken's soil. For Lilya, it brought to mind how difficult the first few years had been back home: they'd only just managed to scrape a harvest from the dusty earth, while the kibbutz was constantly in danger of being attacked or ambushed by Arab groups. But in the long term, the harvest had been a resounding success. A feeling of homesickness hit her for her tough but orderly life during those months on the kibbutz near the Lebanese border. Lev was standing next to her, his fingers fumbling with the seams of his trousers again. Lilya saw that his eyes were fixed on Jossi, only looking away once he'd locked the gate behind them.

'I hope Giora gave you a proper welcome. He does the cooking. In a few months, the crowds will be queuing up outside his restaurant in Dizengoff Street, Tel Aviv.'

He offered them a seat at the heavy garden table, which was shaded by an old linden tree. A carafe of water and five glasses were already set out. They sat down.

'If you like, you can have fresh milk instead — the best north of Haifa,' said Jossi.

Lilya and Lev politely refused: the sun was already setting but the heat was still oppressive. The pungent smell of straw and fresh soil hung in the air, and the crickets had begun to chirp. A wasp circled above their heads.

Jossi leaned back in his chair, felt around in the breast pocket of his shirt, and asked Lilya what had brought them to this wilderness. As he listened, he pulled out a pack of tobacco and a pipe with a chewed tip and began to stuff it. 'You've made a wasted journey, I'm afraid. Mr Guggenheim has already squeezed me for all I know. Wartenberg isn't the only one in hiding. If you want to go rounding up underground Nazis in Bavaria, your little car won't be big enough for them all. There are plenty to fill a whole bus — one-way to Nuremberg.'

'The man I'm looking for isn't just any old Nazi,' she said.

'None of them were just any old Nazis.'

Jossi told them that some of the members of the kibbutz had made it their mission to hunt down Nazis after the liberation: to drown, strangle, poison or shoot them.

He hesitated and looked at his pipe, which he'd stuffed but hadn't yet lit.

Although they were bent on revenge after everything they'd been through, hardly a soul among them actually managed to do violence to Nazis when they found them: they either didn't have the strength or couldn't bring themselves to do it. He held a burning match to the pipe bowl and inhaled.

'Schlomo, a comrade here on the farm, discovered Wartenberg by accident at the market in Erding. He'd driven over there for a big delivery of seeds. Wartenberg was standing in front of the post office together with a blonde woman. When they left, Schlomo managed to follow them to a large farm on the edge of town without being noticed. He lives in the servant's house with the woman.'

Jossi sucked deeply on his pipe. 'Schlomo stalked him for a while, nothing more. He could have killed him, or at least reported him, but instead he returned to Pleikershof after twenty-four hours, his head hanging in shame. He felt like a coward.'

Jossi shrugged and squinted into the setting sun. Then he turned to Lilya. 'And what do you want from him?'

'He has some information I'm interested in,' replied Lilya.

'So you don't want to have him arrested?'

'I want to ask him some questions.'

'And you think he'll just confess to his evil deeds when you ask?'

'Just *one* would do.'

'I'm all ears.'

'I'm looking for a missing Jewish scientist who was very likely to have been in contact with Wartenberg. That's what I want to talk to him about.'

'I admire your resoluteness. I hope you've brought something that will make him talk.'

Jossi eyed her closely before getting up and calling Giora. They exchanged words and then Giora disappeared again. They would have to be patient, said Jossi and also left.

A short while later, the men and women returned from the fields. The sun was sinking behind the house and the smell of burning wood drifted across the courtyard. Lilya and Lev sat for a good hour under the linden tree and watched the farm's goings-on. Finally, Jossi came back over. Behind him trotted a young man, his hands in his trouser pockets and his bowed head covered in a mass of curls.

Lev and Lilya stood up to shake hands with the young man, who introduced himself as Schlomo. He didn't even dare raise his head.

'Thank you for helping us,' said Lilya. 'Do you really think you can tell us where to find Wartenberg?'

He wordlessly handed them a note, pulled from his trouser pocket like a crumpled handkerchief. Then he looked up at Lev as though he were searching for help. Lev was shifting his weight from one leg to the other. 'Death, that's what he deserves. Without a trial. Without . . .'

He looked down at the ground again and thrust his hands back in his pockets. 'Hand him over to the Americans. Tell them who helped you. And the British. When the next group of refugees is let into Palestine, think of me.'

'I promise I'll do everything I can,' she said.

'That's not the same as goodwill and hope,' added Jossi and laid a hand on Schlomo's shoulders. 'We've heard about you from David Guggenheim. You can work miracles. When you want to.'

'He's mixing up miracles and political will.'

Lilya unfolded the note and held it up to the light. On it was written *Hermannshof* and an address in the American zone, not far from Erding.

'Thanks,' she said and smiled at Schlomo, who looked like a weight had been lifted from his shoulders.

'Think over carefully how you're going to handle this,' said Jossi. 'When you corner the fox in its den, you have to be well prepared.'

Especially when you already have the wolf at your heels, she thought later, as she was walking back to the car with Lev.

# CHAPTER TWENTY-FOUR

She held the letter against the light and ran her finger over the back. It appeared not to have been tampered with. The sender was *Elias Lind, Jaffa Road, Jerusalem.* It was lying on her table when she returned from Pleikershof. For the short time she'd been in Munich, she had been staying in a small guest room in the attic of a villa on Sieberstrasse, which David Guggenheim had arranged.

She swallowed hard when she read the name of her home town, held the envelope to her nose and inhaled deeply. In Föhrenwald, she had been able to talk about Jerusalem without shedding a tear. But now something came over her, and her spirits went into a tailspin.

She sat on the bed feeling utterly powerless. She listened to her body: exhaustion was the road to hell. She'd come so far and still had to hold out for a little while longer.

She couldn't afford to be weak. And yet, with the memories of Jerusalem, thoughts of Yoram returned.

Grief, she'd once heard, was like a cat: it came and went when it felt like it. In her mind's eye, she saw Ofer Kis again, in a room not much bigger than this one. He'd come to give her Yoram's bloodstained cap.

She tried to swallow back her tears — she had to be strong and carry on — but it was too hard. The sobs rent her almost in two; she placed the letter on her bedside table and curled up on the bed.

Did he, wherever he was now, want her to forget him? Was that what her tears meant?

At some point she fell into a deep and dreamless sleep. When she woke up she heard birds singing through the open window and cars trundling over the cobblestones. The morning sun streamed in and Lilya sat up, smoothed the pillow flat and stretched. Elias Lind's letter was still lying on the bedside table.

As arranged, he'd addressed it to the UNRRA in Munich. It was written in block capitals; the sentences looked like rows of crooked houses. He'd pressed so hard with his fountain pen that the letters had left dark blue stains on the back. She imagined him bent over the paper, his magnifying glass in one hand and his pen in the other.

Dear Lilya

Please don't put it down to impatience, let alone ingratitude, if I write before I have received news from you. Shimon Bed Gedi came to visit me after your report arrived and told me what you'd gone through in London and Föhrenwald. What you have written in your report for him is such a strong plea, and yet a powerful political statement underlined by hard facts and wisdom. Ben Gedi has told me that he will use it to stir international public opinion for our cause.

Yesterday I received a letter from Berlin from Desirée Wallsdorff. You can imagine how much it moved me. It was like a sign of life from my brother — an unexpected one, as if he were talking to me. I felt deeply ashamed. How foolish I was! Had I known about Raphael's hopeless personal situation, on top of all the difficulties caused by the times, would I have been able to do anything? I've never heard the name Vivien Olsen before. So Raphael's reluctance to leave Germany was for love. And he mustered the courage to work against that abhorrent regime.

A few days ago, I saw the silhouette of a man standing in front of a shop window on the other side of the street, his back turned to me. He had Raphael's build, his upright posture, his stiff neck and the same hair — I thought it was him. I felt the urge to cross the street to look at the man's face. But you'll be surprised at what I did. I took my stick, put it to the ground and carried on. I walked away without looking round, and then turned into the next street.

It brought home something painful. But it was also an endless relief: I know enough about my brother now to let go.

Perhaps you should not have been drawn into the affairs of an old man in the first place. I can now live with what I know: and I would never be able to forgive myself if you got deeper into danger, or if something happened to you.

She placed the letter on the bedside table again, stood up and went over to the window.

Perhaps he was right? She imagined the streets of Rehavia, felt the wind as light as a feather brushing her skin, pictured the tree-lined boulevards, a roof over her head shad-

362

ing her from the sun, protecting her from the world. She saw the view from Mount Olive over the city in the evening light, on stones and walls as brown as baked bread; on the other side, the desert, rugged and craggy, crowned by the shimmering sun. In the distance was the Dead Sea basin, deep and mysterious.

But would it be wrong to break off her mission now? She knew that she was closer to Raphael Lind than ever before. And her search had set things in motion that she had never anticipated. She had met people she had become close to and fond of and had traced countless destinies that were all linked to Raphael Lind in some way: people looking for answers, just as she was. Now she would do everything she could to find and help him — if he was still alive.

*Won't fail.*

And then there was David Guggenheim's expression when she had turned up in his garden: the way he'd said, 'Oh!' He'd looked at her as if he never wanted to take his eyes off her again. If she left now, she'd never see him again.

She folded up the letter and put it carefully back in the envelope. Then she sat down at the table to write an answer.

I've come this far and, as so often, I'm now at a crossroads. But I know which path I have to take from here. And when it runs out, I'll come home.

You would never forgive yourself if anything happened to me, you wrote. And I could never forgive myself if I gave up now. You know enough about Raphael, you say. I want to know everything. Do you understand?

That's how her letter ended.

# CHAPTER TWENTY-FIVE

They passed through a village where farmers were squatting with baskets full of vegetables and potatoes for sale at the side of the road. A convoy of US Army trucks was parked in a side street. At the edge of the field, there were tank tracks and a gutted jeep. Beyond the village the landscape opened up again. Lilya felt as if they were plummeting through a huge void.

Lev steered the car to the side of the street, got out and disappeared behind a bush. On the way back, he fished a pack of cigarettes from his trouser pocket.

'It can't be much further,' she said.

She leaned on the door until he'd finished smoking. The sun was getting stronger.

David Guggenheim had lent her Lev and his car again. But this time, he wanted to know in more detail where she was going, what time she intended to arrive and how long she would stay. And what on earth she was planning on doing there.

'We should arrest and question him. No big deal, just following our orders,' Guggenheim had said. His tone was admonishing, like a superior, trying to prevent a young recruit from doing something rash. 'The man is a criminal and dangerous.'

'Either Wartenberg will talk or he won't let me enter in the first place,' she said. 'He won't be waiting for me at the window with a loaded shotgun.'

'He's part of a system. Since the Germans were defeated, it's one of silence, denial and relativisation. Anyone who dares to break down this wall is in for . . .'

'What?'

Guggenheim raised his hands as if in surrender.

'Don't you find you're exaggerating a little?' said Lilya.

'Okay then, you win. But from now on, I'm going to call you Lilith.'

'I prefer Lilya.'

'But Lilith suits you better.'

'Why?'

Guggenheim folded his hands behind his head.

' *"And wild cats shall meet jackals, and a goat-haired demon shall call out to his partner,*

*and this is where the Lilith shall settle . . ."*
Isaiah, it's in there. The man was a prophet.
That's why.'

Lilya laughed. 'Let me try at least. Lev
will be with me. And I will jump into the
bushes at the first hint of danger. Then you
can move in with the military police and
take him away for interrogation. I just think
I'll get more out of him without handcuffs
and weapons. He'll either speak, or he
won't.'

Quite unexpectedly, Guggenheim took her
hand. It was clear from his look that he
wasn't sure what he was doing either. She
felt his warmth and her heart thudding.

'We had an agreement,' she said and tried
to extract her hand. But he held on tight.

'Perhaps we can extend our agreement a
little,' he said.

'What do you have in mind?'

He drew her towards him, put his arms
around her body and his lips to her mouth.
It was like falling; Lilya's body relaxed, and
the contours of the world around her
blurred. He let her go, stroked her cheek
and looked at her: the expression in his eyes
took on a different solemnity.

'I know I shouldn't. You're caught up in
everything. I can feel it. And we can't stay
in this place where our paths have crossed.

We have to move on and rescue our worlds — you yours and me mine. But I sometimes wonder what would have happened if we'd met in a different time and place. Say, across the tables in Tishman & Fry. If you'd smiled and raised your glass at me, I'd have helped you into your coat and we would have left together.'

'But I'm through with drinking,' she said.

Guggenheim laughed.

Before he could continue, she ventured: 'But when I listen to your daydreams, you don't sound like you're averse to the idea, Lieutenant Guggenheim.'

He only took a second to answer. 'No, Lilya,' he said. 'And you?'

'I have a long car journey ahead of me to think it over.'

'And will you let me know the result?'

'I'll tell you everything I discover.'

She picked up her bag, pressed her cheek to his, and left.

Lev saw the sign too late. He braked sharply and reversed. Along the country road to Markt Schwaben, a sloping entrance on the right led up to the farm building marked Hermannshof. The wooden sign was weathered, barely legible, and hung crookedly on an old linden tree. They took the turning and some buildings grouped around a courtyard came into view. The yellow paint of their façades was peeling off, shingles were missing from the roof and the tail of the weather vane was broken.

Lilya left Lev in the car, asking him to keep his eyes peeled, and went the last few yards on foot. Hens ran across her path and a peacock called from a wall leading to the stables. She was in plain clothes, wearing a high-necked, simple dress: she'd left her Joint uniform back in Munich.

According to Schlomo, Wartenberg was living outside the courtyard, in one of the outbuildings.

She found the right place, smoothed her dress and held the black notebook, which she'd borrowed from the UNRRA accounts department, pressed to her chest. Her hands were shaking. She took a deep breath and rang the bell.

Steps approached on the other side of the door. A woman opened; she had blue eyes and light blonde hair tied at the neck. Lilya guessed she must be in her early forties.

In the hallway behind her, a man appeared. He must have been about twenty years older than the woman, tall and slim, with a neat parting and alert eyes. He was wearing a white shirt over his carefully pressed suit trousers and a grey tank top; his shirtsleeves were pushed up to his elbows.

'I'm here on behalf of the American military administration,' Lilya said. 'I'm writing a report about the supply situation among the people in south Bavaria, and I'd like to ask you a few questions if I may. On my list, this house is in the name of Wartenberg.'

The man pushed past the woman, looked left and right across the courtyard and towards the road, then ushered her in.

'You're Jewish, from Palestine judging by your accent,' he said. 'I hope you've come alone.'

This took Lilya by surprise.

'I have the greatest respect for your race,' he added, and closed the door behind her. 'It has always interested me. Come, follow me.'

Wartenberg led the way. The ceiling in the hallway was low, and from the kitchen wafted a smell of chicory coffee. A crucifix had once hung on a wall next to the entrance. All that was left now was an outline etched by sunlight. In the living room, which also served as a dining room and study, he cleared a chair for her to sit on.

'The things we have to discuss can also be

done standing up,' said Lilya.

Wartenberg looked at her, his eyes narrowed. 'Tell me what you want. You haven't come to count the potatoes in my pantry, have you?' he said.

'Karl, don't,' said the woman, who had followed them into the living room and laid a hand on his upper arm.

'I'm looking for any signs of Professor Raphael Lind,' said Lilya.

On the way there, she'd thought long and hard which tack to follow in order to get the man to talk. And in the end, she'd decided to get straight to the point if Wartenberg let her in. It was a tried and tested method.

Wartenberg let out a low whistle. 'I like it when people don't beat around the bush.'

'Me too,' said Lilya, and opened her notebook. Then she looked back up at him.

Wartenberg stood motionless, but his mind was clearly in a whirl. 'Why do you think I can help you?'

Lilya consulted her notebook as if checking something. 'I expect you remember Dr Durlacher?' she said. 'He showed me a document from the Reich Main Security Office which had your name on it and also Lind's. Raphael Lind.'

Wartenberg shoved his hands into his

pockets and turned to the window. 'Good work, young lady,' he said, before turning back to her. 'All right then, let's see if I can actually help you. But let's save our chat for a short walk together. The air is fresh at this time of day. My morning walk in the woods is a ritual I've come to love. So much so that I find it hard to miss out on. Things seem clearer afterwards.'

He looked down at Lilya, who hesitated.

'Have you got the right shoes on? We have some from Wehrmacht stocks,' said Wartenberg and turned to the blonde woman. 'The highest quality.'

Just behind the house, they took a footpath that ran along the edge of the wood. She should have told Lev: he ought to know where she was and what she was doing. But Lev would be sitting in his car with the window wound down, unsuspecting, dozing and smoking a cigarette between naps.

Wartenberg led the way and pointed to a hide. 'The landscape to the north of Munich isn't comparable to the south,' he explained. 'But if you want to take a look at the view, climb up. You should be able to see all the way to Thalkirchen, which is famous for its painted ceiling. It served us well for a long time.'

'As a depot for loot?'

'No,' said Wartenberg, 'as a place to conserve assets! Out of duty to our German national treasures. We had to hide them away from the Allied terror.'

She was annoyed with herself for trying to provoke him. She still couldn't work out who Wartenberg thought she was and whether he was really prepared to talk to her. In fact she was amazed she'd made it this far. Wartenberg was up to something: he obviously had some plan in mind. Otherwise he could easily have turned her away. In any case, he had imperceptibly taken the lead and she had to be on her guard.

The path they were taking led into the woods. Lilya saw dog tracks that disappeared into the leaves. It was cooler here; the dampness of the morning was still in the air. Dew glistened on the ferns. Lilya shivered.

Wartenberg must have noticed it. 'Just a little further,' he said, 'then we'll reach the glade. It'll be sunny there — not your desert sun, that's for sure, but even the German sun can be quite something.'

The glade was circular, as if drawn by human hand. There was a dip in the centre with a fire pit. Charred wood and what she thought were animal bones were lying there. A light wind rustled the tips of the trees;

the sky was now completely blue.

Wartenberg sat down on a fallen tree trunk and motioned her to sit next to him. He looked around into the woods and indicated that she should be quiet. He lifted his head and scanned the edge of the glade.

'I assume I can be sure that no one followed you?' he said.

'No one,' she answered.

He placed a finger to his lips. 'Did you hear that? The cracking? Perhaps an animal.'

Lilya straightened up. It was highly unlikely that anyone had followed her. Yet something nagged at her. Perhaps it was just experience that taught her that the unlikeliest event could become the most likely in the blink of an eye.

Wartenberg listened carefully again. The wind was the only sound to be heard besides the twittering of birds and leaves rustling up above their heads. He turned back to Lilya.

'I'm not naïve. It's just a question of time before your friends come and pick me up. Most of my comrades are dead or waiting to go on trial in Nuremberg. As you can imagine, I'm not keen on joining them.'

Lilya didn't know where this was leading.

'Now that you're here, it's in my interest for you to find Raphael Lind,' he continued.

'I protected him, and if he's still alive, it's thanks to me. I saved him. That would shed a completely different light on my case in front of a tribunal.'

Lilya raised her eyebrows. So that was it: yet another individual out to use her for his own ends. But she had no choice: Wartenberg offered her a unique set of clues. And he would talk. Secretly, she hoped it wouldn't save him.

'You're truly heaven-sent, young lady, if there is such a thing,' said Wartenberg.

They had needed Lind and his research into chemical resistance, Wartenberg explained: with no research, there would be no victory.

Lilya thought about one of her conversations with Terry. The deployment of chemical weapons in the First World War had taught the Germans that they were not just a danger to the enemy, but also to the home troops: because the response to gas was gas. You needed an antidote, or protective measure — and that was where Lind entered the picture.

In this phase, they had received an unusual tip-off, said Wartenberg. A man had contacted them who claimed he could help them. He had a slight accent, mentioned Lind and had said he'd reveal his whereabouts in exchange for a large sum of money.

'I had no idea that Lind was even still in the country. A scientist of his standing! Or that he was even —'

'Still alive,' finished Lilya. 'Which must have seemed unlikely to you, considering the way you and your people behaved.'

Lilya bit her tongue, but Wartenberg ignored her remark.

'Do you know who wanted to hand over the professor? Did you pay for the information?'

Wartenberg guffawed. 'Come on! Lind was our man. Why should we pay for him? It was child's play for our people to find him. We compared a few notes, made a few phone calls and asked a couple of questions. We had him in next to no time. He was still living in his house in Dahlem. He was rounded up and his entire research material was confiscated.'

'So the informer went away empty-handed?'

'Of course. He had contacted us by phone. We made it perfectly clear to him that he shouldn't do so again,' said Wartenberg. 'But then, the following happened: to step up the pressure, and to lay his hands on the money, he tried a different tack. The man said he knew from a reliable source that British agents were planning on abducting Lind and bringing him to England. But by then, we'd already brought Lind in.'

Lilya's ears pricked up.

When Lind returned from Vilna, where he'd been sent by Rosenberg, he was hollow-eyed, gaunt and unsettled. There wasn't much left of the stiff, self-assured, often dismissive scientist Wartenberg had known.

'I went to see him in Eisenacher Strasse,' explained Wartenberg, 'and told him what we expected: research to seal our victory.'

What a pair of brothers they were, Lilya reflected. While Elias was writing a novel in Palestine, half-blind from mustard gas injuries and spurned by his family, his older brother let himself be roped in by the Nazi war effort. At the same time he was a spy and informer for the British, undetected, unhappily in love and forsaken, no matter what he did. Lilya was curious to know how the rest of the story went.

'When the attacks on Berlin became more intense, I had to remove Lind and his equipment to safety. That was in summer 1943,' said Wartenberg.

In Lobenberg am See, not far from Berlin, Wartenberg found an old manor house, situated in woods and barely visible from the outside. He had the boathouse converted into a laboratory, and even managed to get hold of a transformer. He also gave Lind a car. They tried to furnish his hideout as comfortably as possible, fetched his desk, even mended his violin and had it tuned. The only condition was that he was not allowed to leave the estate grounds past the woods and fields.

Wartenberg looked at her with a cryptic smile and paused for a moment. With unmistakable pride, he said that Lind soon became a kind of secret personal doctor to the Führer. And why? Because Wartenberg had spread the rumour all the way to the upper echelons of the Nazi Party that Lind was on the brink of discovering a cure for cancer. Not any old kind of cancer, but cancer of the larynx. All he had to do was wait until this information reached the ears of the Führer. Because since Hitler had contracted a laryngeal infection, he had lived in fear. Kaiser Friedrich III's death from cancer of the larynx in 1888 haunted him and this played into Wartenberg's hands. Ultimately, Lind was allowed to continue his research on the Führer's secret orders — although the Germans were already being driven back on the Eastern

Front and a firestorm attack on England was no longer a top priority. But gas was still a weapon and an option.

One day, the SS turned up at Lobenberg am See to take Lind away. When Wartenberg finally found Lind in the SS headquarters on Prinz Albrecht Strasse, they were in the middle of their interrogations. They wanted to find out about his foreign contacts and who he'd passed on information to — but there was not enough solid evidence. And so Wartenberg managed to take Lind back to Lobenberg with a referral from the Führer. After that, the SS kept an eye on Lind around the clock.

'At the end of 1944 research into poisonous gas was stopped,' said Wartenberg, rounding off his story, 'but I didn't want to give up and said nothing to Lind. The SS still thought he was doing research into a cure for cancer. In April 1945 the Führer died. Then I knew the time had come when I had to look after myself.'

'Do you know the theory that the German secret services had been working on when they came for Lind?' Lilya asked.

'*Nature,*' said Wartenberg. 'You know the journal? There were indications that Lind had been working together with these people in the thirties even after he was banned from working in Germany. But nothing could be proven. I looked into it, remembering the telephone informer: suddenly, I was convinced that he had something to do with the matter, in one way or another. Otherwise, how did this stranger know what Lind knew, or that his knowledge was so valuable to us?'

'And you left it at that?' said Lilya.

'Yes. Lind and I had struck up a kind of friendship,' replied Wartenberg.

'How touching,' said Lilya. 'But I think it's much more likely that you were bent on changing the course of history with Lind's help. After all, you'd set up his laboratory by the lake at great personal risk and effort. Didn't it ever occur to you that Lind had leaked your secrets? The results of your research into poisonous gases?'

He smiled thinly. 'Following the interrogation in Prinz Albrecht Strasse, Lind no longer had any contact with anyone abroad. He was watched day and night. And before that? I don't know. But it was too late to do anything in any case.'

'Any ideas who the informer was?' said Lilya. Up until now, everything that Wartenberg had said corresponded to what Green and Terry had told her. Perhaps she wouldn't just find Lind through Wartenberg, but identify her stalker as well.

'No,' said Wartenberg, 'but I suspect that it might have been a defector from White-hall. In any case, there's much that points to this: the slight accent, the *Nature* theory, the planned abduction. There was an agent with an English mother and German father, who'd even been hired by the Russians at some point — they paid better than the British, promised a great future in Stalin's empire. It all fitted into place.'

Everett Harp. Colm O'Madden. Major Turntide. Terry would be amazed.

'Do you think that Lind knew he'd passed on information to the wrong people at any stage? Traitors, backstabbers, profiteers?'

'He gave it to the British — he can't have known any more than that,' said Warten-berg.

While they'd been talking, it had turned warmer: the sun was now high above the treetops. Lilya had no idea how long they'd been sitting there. And she still hadn't got to the most important part: when had War-tenberg last seen Lind?

She was about to begin along these lines when Wartenberg pre-empted her. 'And you said that you found me via Dr Durlacher? May I ask how you know him?'

'I have a long journey behind me. But

381

what brought me here in the end was a book,' said Lilya.

'Lind's *Book of Books*? I know it. He was very attached to it. It contained a list of thousands of volumes, all of which we confiscated. The fact that I left him the book with the gilt bookplate might have got me into bother had Rosenberg got wind of it. But there were times when I needed to cheer up my professor.'

'What do you mean?'

'He suffered a great loss,' said Wartenberg and paused for a moment.

'Vivien Olsen? Lind found out about her death after all? How did he react?' asked Lilya.

'I only told him much later — in 1943, I think — and it jeopardised our project. But he kept asking about her, wanting to see her and know how she was. He must have loved her a great deal. After I told him the truth about what had happened, I was afraid he'd do something to himself. There was a photograph in the book of a house in the woods: nothing special but he looked at it constantly.'

'And what happened to Lind after you decided to save your own skin?' Lilya asked.

Wartenberg stood up and buried his hands in his pockets again. His gaze scanned the edge of the glade once more. 'Orders were to shoot him. Wipe him out, and all his knowledge besides. I was in charge of carrying out the order.'

Lilya got up too and looked him in the eye. 'But you didn't carry it out.'

'No! I saved him. Several times over. He was becoming more and more despondent — perhaps he was convinced I would shoot him in the end. In any case, he tried to poison himself. I didn't know what to do — the Red Army was closing in on Berlin, the Führer was dead, and I had to make sure I found a hideout. But Lind and I were close. I dragged him to the station and put him on a train going west. It was one of the evacuation transportations, which was heading for Belsen, I think.'

Lilya exhaled. 'That's it? You never heard from him after that?'

'No. So it would make me all the happier if you found him.'

They left the glade in silence and walked back through the wood, the light now brighter. At the hide, when the house was already in view, they heard the sound of engines. Cars approached the estate.

On reaching the house, two US Army jeeps pulled into the courtyard and braked sharply. Military police jumped out. In the front vehicle sat an officer. He got out and walked towards the house, flanked by two soldiers. The other jeep drove around to the back of the house and stopped there, its engine still running.

The officer and his two men came up to Lilya and Wartenberg.

'Mr Wartenberg,' said the officer, 'my name is Jonathan Lustig, a captain of the US Army. I must ask you to come with us.' His German had almost no trace of an accent.

Wartenberg stood to attention and threw Lilya a pointed look. She knew what he was thinking. *You said no one had followed you.* The blonde woman appeared at the front entrance, fear written all over her face.

'You'll surely allow Miss Stock and myself to pack a few things? I don't expect we'll be returning tonight,' said Wartenberg.

The officer nodded, and one of the armed soldiers accompanied them into the house. Wartenberg looked back at Lilya; this time his expression seemed to say: *Find Lind!*

# CHAPTER TWENTY-SIX

'Can we speak or should I expect a summary execution?'

'First one, then the other,' she said, taking a sip from the glass of water in her hand.

David Guggenheim was standing near her. She was sitting on a bench at the rear of the villa garden. She could still feel the tension of her morning with Wartenberg — the creeping sensation of unease during their long conversation. Right up to the end, she'd grappled with the feeling that Wartenberg was simply setting a trap for her. She had a headache and she still felt nauseous from the long journey. Now Guggenheim was standing in front of her: but something had also come between them. He hadn't kept to their agreement. Instead, he'd sent the MPs before she'd returned to Munich. Perhaps she would have got more information out of Wartenberg, but Guggenheim's premature rescue mission had foiled her plan.

'I had no alternative,' he said. 'It might not have been the ideal moment. But when you were gone long enough to put all your questions to him, I had to act. Besides, I violated my duties with our operation: I should have arrested Wartenberg on the spot as soon as I found out where he was hiding. Instead I gave you a head start.'

'You're not a soldier. You're an UNRRA employee. It's an aid organisation.'

'We report to the army. And I'm an American.'

She sighed. Even if the whole thing stank, she knew Guggenheim was right. If the situation with Wartenberg had got out of control, she would have been glad of Guggenheim's sense of duty.

He stood in front of her, his hands in his trouser pockets, his head inclined towards her, and smiled.

'Okay then,' she admitted, 'mitigating circumstances. But I know how to look after myself.'

'You're a seasoned fighter, I know. But it didn't really help you in Berlin.'

Before Lilya could reply, he sat down next to her on the bench and put his arm around her.

'I know what you have accomplished, Lilith, and I hardly know another soul who has come as far as you. But sometimes you still seem unaware of what you've got yourself into. The British secret services, a Nazi with a certificate of good conduct, all blood and lies, an unknown stalker — none of these people will be easily scared off.'

She couldn't brush off Guggenheim's arguments. But they didn't help. It was her mission and she knew what she was doing. 'That's nothing I don't know. Since I set off on my assignment, I've had to live with this knowledge. And I'm still alive.'

Guggenheim stood up and began pacing to and fro. Then he abruptly stopped and turned to her. 'Then at least stop playing the lonesome heroine! I just want to help you, that's all!' He looked her up and down. 'How did you get to be so stubborn?' he said, shaking his head.

Lilya couldn't help laughing. Major Terry had accused her of the same. She stood up and reached for his hand. 'Okay, David, but you have to promise that you won't make any more deals, knowing full well you can't keep them. Out of concern, your sense of duty, or whatever.'

'Deal.' He drew her hand to his lips and tenderly kissed her fingertips. Then they both sat back down on the bench. 'Then I'll tell you what I've found out about Wartenberg.'

Lilya looked at him, open-mouthed.

'I couldn't stop thinking about it, and so I checked up on him in a few files. I wanted to know exactly who this guy is you're dealing with. Wartenberg was in Vilna, supervising shooting squads after the ghetto was cleared. Perhaps he even joined in. We're still tracing evidence, witness statements, documents, that kind of thing. And he employed forced labourers. Detainees in concentration camps were forced to fill his bombs with tabun gas. He knew about the human experiments carried out by Karl Brandt, Hitler's doctor, and chose people to be human guinea pigs in poison gas tests. He must know that we know all this.'

'He put much more of a spin on his version. It was the tale of the good soldier. But he was very keen for me to find Lind.'

Guggenheim looked at her in surprise.

'He claims he saved him by using Lind as a researcher into gas resistance. He said he protected him from the SS and I think he expects Lind would back up his statement if he were found.'

'Ludicrous!'

'Absolutely. But Wartenberg sees it as his

only chance if he's put on trial in Nuremberg. That's what he's banking on. Which is why he was extremely happy to give me information, and told me things that coincided with Terry's and Green's theories. And then he went on to say where he'd seen Lind for the last time.'

'Now I'm all ears.'

Lilya leaned back and stretched her legs. 'When the Red Army was close to Berlin, Lind tried to poison himself because he was sure he would be executed. And with Wartenberg's help, it seems that he survived. Wartenberg claims that he put Lind on one of the last evacuation trains heading west.'

'Did he say where it was going?'

'Bergen-Belsen.'

Guggenheim reached for the cigarette pack and she saw that his hands were shaking. 'Well, another trail,' he said. He lit a cigarette and blew out the smoke slowly. 'Give me a few days and then we'll know whether it leads to the end of the story.'

She hadn't bargained on seeing Wartenberg's captor in Guggenheim's office. Captain Lustig was sitting next to David with a map covered in handwritten markings spread out between them. Through the open door to the garden, there was the sound of birdsong; the frame of the swing was visible above the hedge. A large silver coffee pot was standing on the table, next to which there were two half-empty cups. Sugar was sprayed carelessly across the tabletop and the ashtray was brimming over.

Guggenheim looked up from the map and smiled. He came over and led her to the table.

Captain Lustig stood up too and greeted Lilya with a handshake. He was about to say something but Guggenheim beat him to it. 'Jonathan and I have known each other for many years. He's a good friend and a brilliant soldier.'

'David, I don't think Miss Wasserfall wants to hear compliments but facts instead. Especially if all that I assume is true, then we should make haste.'

Guggenheim pushed a cup towards her, but she didn't want any coffee.

'Captain Lustig has a plan,' Guggenheim said and looked at Lilya with the trace of a smile. 'And I think it's quite a good one. Jonathan?'

'A vast number of trains travelled inland towards the end of the war, first from the concentration camps near the front, then from the east and south of the country. The Nazis called them "evacuation transportions".'

'When in fact they were death marches or death trains,' added Guggenheim.

'That's right,' confirmed Lustig. 'Bergen-Belsen was one of the destinations. Wartenberg knew this when he decided not to kill the professor, or arrange for him to be killed.'

Lilya became restless. 'How likely is it that a man who had tried to poison himself like Lind would have survived the journey?'

'Hard to say,' said Lustig, 'but I'm afraid it's low. Even if he did survive the journey, Bergen in 1945 was like a scene from the Apocalypse: around 60,000 prisoners, and nearly 10,000 corpses when the British arrived. The camp was only built for a couple of thousand occupants.'

'Let's assume that Lind managed to make it there. Is there any prospect that we're going to find anything that leads us to him?'

Lustig looked at her. 'Put it this way: looking for a needle in a haystack would be easier. Without a torch, at night.'

She realised he was trying to make a point.

Lustig lit a cigarette and leaned back.

'However . . .' He paused. 'I've made a few local enquiries.'

The door opened. One of Guggenheim's employees came in and handed him a telegram. He thanked him, glanced at it and gave it to Jonathan Lustig. His features lit up.

'Dr Alfred Caposi, our man.'

Lilya gave him a puzzled look.

'He was one of the first to arrive at the site in 1945 and helped with the medical organisation. The doctors there did what they had to do in different ways. Everyone had to process the experience in their own way. Like all the others, Caposi functioned well for about a year. He put all his strength into helping the survivors back to life. Until a fuse blew . . .'

'Can you be more precise?'

'He started acting strangely, wasn't able to take any pressure. He could have gone back to England. Should have. He was highly respected among the troops and the camp occupants. But he refused.'

'And now?'

'Caposi is tolerated. He lives in a big house there. He now has time on his hands and knows his way around the place.'

Guggenheim looked at Lilya.

Lustig seemed to feel a little awkward when he noticed. 'I know it's a rather unusual suggestion. But right after the liberation, Caposi helped the survivors write lists of the camp occupants after the German records had all been destroyed by the guards before they fled; each name was individually noted. If anyone knows about Raphael Lind, then he does.'

'The likelihood that Lind's name will be found on one of these lists is small. And even if it is, we can't assume that he's still alive,' said Lilya.

Guggenheim looked at her in astonishment. 'You're not going to give up now, surely?'

Lustig looked at them both. 'Think it over, the offer stands.' He glanced at his watch. 'I'm two hours overdue. Please excuse me — duty calls.' Lustig took his pack of cigarettes from the table, tipped his forehead briefly with his index and middle finger and left.

Guggenheim took Lilya's hand.

'What's the matter?' he asked.

'I'm just trying to stay realistic. I have the feeling that Lind didn't survive the evacuation transport. And I'm starting to get tired. You have to know when enough's enough.'

Guggenheim came closer to her.

'If I looked soberly at the chances of finding my mother, I'd have given up long ago.'

'What do you mean?'

'Hope is a tenacious thing.'

'That's kitsch for cowboys,' she said,

almost laughing.

'No, Lilith, it's just Guggenheim idealism. Or roaming realism. You might like it and it might give you strength.'

■ ■ ■ ■

# BERGEN-BELSEN

## GLYN HUGHES HOSPITAL

■ ■ ■ ■

# CHAPTER TWENTY-SEVEN

The jeep pulled up on the market square in Lüneburg. Red- and brown-brick merchants' houses lined the square; a row of intact stepped gables rose against a backdrop of blue sky. A large church, its front entrance hidden behind huge trees, lent the entire ensemble a century-old serenity and naturalness that Lilya immediately took to. The local famers selling potatoes and other vegetables on the market square moved more slowly and in a more measured fashion than their Berlin counterparts, or so she thought.

It must be close by, said the driver, leaning over a city map that he'd spread out over the steering wheel. On David Guggenheim's orders, two Canadian sergeants had picked her up to the north of Kassel. Once again, he'd secured a military escort for her. They'd driven through the night, taking just a quick break to sleep in the jeep after eat-ing dinner at a guesthouse.

The soldiers had chattered almost non-stop but she barely understood a word. It was all about women, Nazis and war experiences. Rogues were still hiding in woods and villages, they said, motioning across the fields. This is where Himmler had been caught and brought to Lüneburg. Somewhere not far from the city, they'd started singing national anthems that they'd probably learned back home on some clean-swept drill square — and never needed. Lilya clambered out of the jeep. Its engine roared as it drove away. Her hip was hurting. She could still feel the after-effects of the accident in Berlin, now nearly four weeks ago. Her stay in Munich had passed without further incident; her plan of leading her stalker astray had evidently worked. Would he catch up with her here? she wondered. She stretched. A trader showed her the way, looking at her with curiosity, almost pity. She couldn't miss it — the house belonging to the English doctor and the German woman on Uelzener Strasse.

It was a red clinker-brick building, its roof patched up with black tar paper. On the left, a path led through an entrance into the garden. In front of the house, sitting on a bench, was a woman dressed in a blue-grey striped housecoat; her bare feet were stuck inside men's brown shoes. She had a bowl in her lap and was peeling potatoes.

Lilya opened the gate.

The woman looked up. 'Alfred!' she cried into the hallway of the house. Then she paused and listened. She stood up, walked towards Lilya and shook her hand.

'Probably sitting up in the trees again,' she said, shrugging, with a fleeting smile.

Lilya introduced herself but she had the impression that the woman had been expecting her.

'Mama, who is it?' A small, barefoot girl in a short, grimy dress appeared in the hallway.

'Uncle Alfred has a visitor. Hella, say hello to the lady. She's come a long way.'

'From the camp?'

'No, darling. Not everyone comes from the camp.'

Hella raced out of the dark hallway and into the garden. Her blonde hair blazed brightly in the sunlight.

'Follow her,' said the woman, 'it seems Alfred isn't coming down.'

She went into the garden, which was full of fruit trees. A wooden ladder was leaning against one of them. The girl shook it.

'Hey, be careful!' shouted a voice from above.

'Dr Caposi?' Lilya called up into the treetops. She spotted a face among the branches.

'Step up so I can take a better look at you.'

She climbed on to the first rungs of the ladder.

The doctor was sitting astride the branch like a rider on a much-too-thin horse, holding a small pair of pruning shears in his hand. His hair was reddish-blond and beads of sweat stood out on his forehead. Besides a pair of faded uniform trousers, he was wearing a vest, criss-crossed by a pair of red braces.

'Snip: scissors, forceps, swab — nearly done,' he said.

'Dr Caposi . . .'

'You can stay with us. Please, drop the doctor. I'm not one any more. Fallen off Mount Olympus now. The birds up here are going quite crazy.'

Lilya climbed down. Caposi grabbed a large branch and swung down, jumping from a great height. He rolled over and shook her hand.

'Give me an earthquake rather than the so-called rock-hard truth any day. Ruptured times we're living in, don't you think?'

He walked with her over to the house.

The woman who had been sitting in front of the house was called Alma, and she showed Lilya to the room at the back. She heard birdsong through the open window.

'As long as it doesn't rain, it's fine,' said Alma, tapping the long, streaky water stains on the wall.

The doctor stuck his head around the door; wood shavings covered his bare under-arms, which were damp with sweat. 'Tomorrow at eight,' he said. 'I'll take you to the camp. We can talk during the journey.'

After a brief, meagre meal with the family, which consisted of a thin soup and some bread, she went up to her room. She sat at the window until late into the night, staring out at the garden. Now and again, her chin nodded on to her chest.

For a brief moment, she'd hoped that David Guggenheim would come here with her, as ridiculous as that was. She'd hoped but hadn't dared say it. He must have felt it. Unfortunately, he was indispensable, he'd said, but there was a hint of hesitancy in his voice. Every day, more survivors were arriving from the East. But if he was required, he'd be on the quickest route via military transport to see her. He'd suddenly lapsed into his matter-of-fact officer's tone, and she was sure he was protecting himself. The time they'd spent together in Munich had been so wonderful, so unexpectedly light-hearted that she'd almost forgotten he could suddenly turn away without warning.

Hella muttered in her sleep. Church bells sounded on the hour and Lilya still flinched at the noise of trucks and jeeps. She caught Alfred Caposi's voice in the room next door, groaning as if trying to shoo someone away or defend himself. Then she heard Alma's soothing whispering.

In the morning, the doctor was like a different person: he stood in front of the house, freshly shaven with a neat side parting in his hair. Alma straightened his tie once more and stroked her hand across his uniform jacket, which he probably wouldn't have to wear much longer.

Caposi went into the garden and over to a garage then disappeared inside. An engine started and exhaust fumes billowed out of the door.

'He hardly ever uses it,' said Alma. 'They were going to scrap it but he managed to wangle it out of the district office.'

Caposi reversed. It was an ancient, open-top jeep: a crack ran through the front windscreen and the exhaust pipe was dangling dangerously low.

'In you get,' said Caposi.

Outside the city, the view through the window changed to woods and meadows: Lilya saw heather, pine trees and juniper bushes. After a few miles, Caposi pulled up at the edge of the road. They sat on a tree trunk and surveyed the hilly landscape. The doctor took out a pack of Old Holborn.

He lit a cigarette, took a deep drag and stared at the sand by his feet. Then he bent down, took a branch and began to draw lines: oblong shapes, a street, a gate. When he'd finished, he rubbed it all out again.

'I'll bring you to the camp. I haven't been there for a long time. Let's see.'

'Thanks for helping and coming with me.'

'Well . . .'

'I've thought hard about how we should proceed,' she said.

'We'll start by looking,' he said.

'Of course, but . . .'

'We'll look through lists, ask questions and more questions. It's a bit like sowing seeds,' he said. He made a sweeping gesture with his arms. 'Patience is a virtue, miss.'

He stubbed out his cigarette with the toe of his shoe.

'Jonathan Lustig,' he continued, 'is a hard man to refuse. He put me in the picture. If the man you're looking for has made it this far, then it wasn't the end of his journey but just the beginning . . .'

He lit another cigarette.

'The stench. Very few people will ever understand that. I'm always afraid it'll come back. Especially at night. I arrived here in April '45 with the Royal Army Medical Corps. They were lying inside the camp gates. Tens of thousands of them. Just corpses, as far as the eye could see. Even the living looked dead. If they were lucky, they had crosses marked on their foreheads for the carriers. I hope your man was given a cross; what's his name again?'

'Raphael Lind.'

'They took their clothes off and burned them, that's how it was done. Wrapped in blankets, like newborns, they were carried into Camp 2 where we'd set up a military hospital. Into the horse stables to be washed. Washing humans. Did your man make it that far? Who knows. Next their hair was shaved off, they were scrubbed all over, some of them screamed as we did it. Then we sprayed them with DDT. Only then did we look for a bed. The rooms were too full. We kept putting up more beds in the court-yard, on the street. The buildings were full. There was an officer responsible for each block, and then there were aid workers from

Britain, Switzerland or other nations. And nurses. So many people.'

He took a deep breath and scraped the ground with his foot.

'The barracks were in Camp 1. Once everyone was out, we set light to them with flamethrowers. Many of the inmates were frightened and panic almost broke out. Perhaps your professor was there. The flames soared and a black cloud rose up.'

He cleared his throat.

'We fed those starving people with the wrong food. Many of them died at our hands because we didn't know any better. Hungry people need to eat, we thought. Then we called in specialists. Some of those we'd liberated also helped and gave us advice. We had to change methods.'

'How do you mean?'

'There were scientists and doctors among the inmates, and they helped us find the right mixture. We called it the Bengali mix: milk powder, flour, sugar and treacle. That was the solution.'

Caposi stood up very abruptly, trod on his cigarette and went over to the jeep. Lilya followed him. They drove on in silence.

At the end of a long section of forest, they saw a large sign mounted on a wooden frame. Caposi braked.

THIS IS THE SITE OF **THE INFAMOUS BELSEN CONCENTRATION CAMP**
Liberated by the British on 15 April 1945

10,000 UNBURIED DEAD WERE FOUND HERE, ANOTHER 13,000 HAVE SINCE DIED

ALL OF THEM VICTIMS OF THE GERMAN NEW ORDER IN EUROPE, AND AN EXAMPLE OF NAZI KULTUR.

He parked the jeep under the shade of a tree. Caposi was pale with beads of sweat on his forehead.

As in Föhrenwald, the buildings were made of stone, but they were bigger, and the paths were surfaced and clean. They would go directly to the American zone, said Caposi.

'Camp jargon,' he explained. 'There are Russian, British and American zones here. We just gave them those names. The people who were still alive when we arrived are now the old guard. First class. American zone. The other zones accommodate those who came at the end from the East. When did your man supposedly arrive?'

'At the beginning of April 1945, I suspect.'

'American zone, if he was still alive when

he got here,' said Caposi.

He went over to one of the long buildings. 'When you arrive as a stranger in the camp, you should know in advance who you want to talk to: UNRRA, the Joint, the Jewish Relief Union, the Jewish Agency, the Central Committee of Liberated Jews. Everyone's here and everyone talks at the same time. You can't hear yourself speak.'

'What do you suggest?'

'The registrar's office. It's being managed now by the Jewish Relief Unit.'

The registrar's office was on the first floor and the door was ajar. A man in a doctor's coat was perched on the edge of the desk and sitting on a chair behind it was a woman in uniform. Lilya heard her laugh.

Caposi knocked on the open door. The woman looked up and the doctor turned around.

'Alfred!' the woman called out, getting up.

She had red hair, tamed by a large, horn hairgrip and her uniform bore the JRU's insignia. Lilya guessed her to be in her mid-thirties.

'So you're back again? How nice. Welcome,' she said to Caposi, shook his hand and beamed at him.

The man in the doctor's coat looked at him with a friendly expression.

'We were worried about you,' said the woman. 'I was told you had left for England long ago.'

'No, I'm still here. Well, we'll see.' He took out a handkerchief and wiped his forehead.

It was only then that the woman took any notice of Lilya. Caposi explained that Lilya was looking for someone who was believed missing and would like to take a look at the register. He wasn't there in his capacity as a doctor, but as Lilya's escort.

Caposi went to a cupboard as though he had done so many times before. The drawers were divided into alphabetical sections. He opened the *L-N* drawer, fished out a thick file and placed it carefully, almost like a holy script, on the desk. He rummaged around in his jacket pocket for a pair of glasses, put them on and asked Lilya to take a seat too. Shortly before the liberation, the SS had destroyed the entire camp register, he said, opening the file. And so in spring 1945 they'd started again from scratch.

He began to thumb through the pages, paused, flicked some more and then back again. It went on like this for quite some time. Then he shut the file, looked up at the ceiling and opened it again. 'L,' he said, and placed a finger back on the top of the page, running it downwards lightly as if touching a scar.

Lilya could barely stand the suspense. Before she could say anything, the doctor leaned back with a sigh.

'Well . . .' he said.

She tried to interpret his expression, in vain.

'He's not in here. Other routes . . . we have to try other routes,' said Caposi.

Lilya had tried to prepare herself for this. But without succeeding. Now she felt her strength ebbing away. Durlacher, Westmann, Wartenberg, Guggenheim, Lustig, the journey to Pleikershof. All for nothing? She had let herself get carried away. And here was Caposi, as stubborn as he was eccentric. 'Are you completely sure, Dr Caposi?' she asked.

Caposi wriggled back and forth in his chair.

'As things stand, we have to assume that the man we're looking for never arrived here. This is a list — of the living.'

Lilya sensed that Caposi had something else to say but was holding back. She pushed on. 'If we rule out his death for a moment,' she said, 'is there any reason why a survivor wouldn't be listed?'

'There's no reason to believe that,' said

Caposi, 'although I'd never claim that these lists are infallible.'

Lilya waited for a moment to see if he'd carry on.

'Well,' said Caposi eventually, 'now and again, survivors weren't listed.' He paused for a moment. 'A few refused — I witnessed it myself. They were frightened. Death lists, lists of deportations, abduction and destruction. Never again, they said.'

Lind had tried to poison himself, Wartenberg had said. Perhaps he'd refused help? Lilya wasn't going to let it go, just like that. 'Any other possibility?'

Caposi looked at her. 'There might have been cases where the survivors no longer knew who they were themselves,' admitted Caposi. 'They didn't know their own names, where they came from, or what had brought them here. Their past had been destroyed.'

'Even after you'd nursed them back to health? With medicine and your Bengali mix? Didn't they recover their identities after that?'

'I don't know of any such case, but it would be plausible, I think. The liberation of the camp took place less than a year and a half ago. Traumas of this kind often take years to resolve, if they resolve themselves at all.'

Now she didn't want to loosen her grip. 'How can we look for cases like this here? Is there a way?'

'Not in the register. Only —' Caposi broke off, as if he felt that the thought he'd just had was unfeasible. 'I can ask around,' he said eventually. 'But it might take a while. And I don't know if you have the time . . .'

'Would you try to do that for me?'

Caposi sighed. 'Okay then. Let's see; but don't get your hopes up. Your man is probably dead. That's harsh, but harshness is the mother of truth.'

# CHAPTER TWENTY-EIGHT

She squatted by the open window of her room overlooking the garden and held the photo that Elias Lind had given her to the light. The day before, Caposi had asked her to be patient after their visit to the camp registrar. Now she wanted to use the time she had to wait to approach her mission from a new angle.

How often had she looked at the photo: the house at the edge of the woods with its brightly lit window? On the reverse side, the note, retraced in pencil by Yehuda in Föhrenwald: *Det bugter sig i bakke, dal.*

No matter how often she looked at the photograph, she couldn't find any signs or clues. It was just a mute, lifeless picture. But an unusual kind of memento.

Suddenly she froze. It was an impulse, not even an intuition or anything she could put into words. She held the photo close to her eyes. If she were lucky, there would be a magnifying glass somewhere in the house.

Lilya found Alma in the garden, working barefoot in the vegetable patch, her shoes lying on the lawn. She had not seen Caposi all morning. He'd left early for the camp again, Alma had told her.

Alma sent her to look in the kitchen: there she'd find a magnifying glass. Lilya found one in a drawer filled with odds and ends. She sat down on the garden bench under one of Caposi's pruned trees, laid the photograph on her lap and pored over it.

She knew what she had to do. Rather than look at the photo again she had to enter the house through the open window into the brightly lit room, make out what was on the shelves and go through them, title by title.

She held the magnifying glass over the open window on the photo. Yes, she'd been here once before, seen these books, these shelves, but she hadn't paid them attention before. She bit her lip. Why couldn't she put her finger on this elusive memory that was so hard to shake off?

She screwed up her eyes and stared through the magnifying glass. The books weren't in German. It wasn't *Alexandria.* The titles on the spines were written in a foreign language. She read the message on the reverse again.

*Det bugter sig i bakke, dal.*

She turned the photo back over and looked once again at the books on the shelf. If she wasn't mistaken, they were in the same language.

She looked up. Caposi was coming down the garden at a flying pace. His hair was windswept and he was holding the jeep keys in his hand. He seemed worked up. He waved over to her, calling across the lawn, 'I've found someone that might fit the description!' She should get her things and come with him, quickly. She stuck the photo in her pocket, along with the photo of Elias and Raphael Lind, thanked Alma for the magnifying glass and went to the jeep with Caposi who was already waiting in the driver's seat in front of the house.

He drove fast and Caposi told her in leaps and bounds, muddling things up, how he'd found the man they were about to visit. Was this the day she'd waited so long for? Would she send a telegram to Elias Lind this very evening? *I've found him — your brother is alive!*

It wasn't far to Camp 4.

'The man works in the printing press,' said Caposi. 'The newspaper *Unzer Sztyme* has been going for almost a year now. They're just preparing the anniversary edition.'

The printing press was set up in a shed; the door stood wide open. Even from afar, they could hear the rattling of the machinery.

'Wait here,' said Caposi and went in.

Not much later, the rattling stopped. Caposi appeared at the door and waved her over. A younger man in work overalls with oil-stained hands was standing next to the machine. It smelled of paint. Rolls of paper were stacked on a shelf. An older man was sitting at a table in front of the machine, chewing on a piece of bread. He paid no attention to the visitors. He'd gathered the crumbs up into a pile and wouldn't take his eyes off them.

'That's Menachem,' explained the man in the work overalls. 'We gave him that name at some point. He has no papers, no memories, no real name.'

Lilya went over to the table but the man didn't look up. 'Good morning, my name is Lilya Wasserfall. I'm from Palestine,' she said to Menachem. There was no reaction. 'I am a friend of Elias Lind,' she ventured. Nothing. Menachem seemed to be ignoring her.

Lilya turned back to the young man in the overalls. 'What job does Menachem do?' she asked.

'This and that. He sorts the printing paper, cleans the machine. He even repaired it once. He might not know who he is but his hands are skilled. I guess he was a mechanic or something like that.'

'How long has he been here?'

'He saw the British arrive. We don't know anything else.'

She looked around for a chair, found a stool and pulled it up to the table.

Menachem must have been around sixty; he was tall and his eyes were alert. She'd rarely seen men in the camp as old as he was. She had Raphael Lind's photo in her pocket but first she wanted to rely on her observation.

Menachem licked his finger and dabbed it on the remaining crumbs. He searched the entire table until he was sure he hadn't missed one. Then he looked up and seemed uneasy all of a sudden.

'Menachem leads a very ordered life,' said the printer. 'You can't fool his body clock. Half an hour, not a minute longer, then his break is over. He'll want to go back to the machine to check the paper feed.'

'I just want to ask him a question.'

Menachem seemed nervous and was squinting. He clearly felt Lilya's presence to be a threat to his time schedule.

'The Kaiser Wilhelm Institute in Berlin.' She spoke as if she were spelling the name out loud. 'Have you ever worked there?'

The man glanced towards the printing press. Any moment he'd stand up and leave.

There was perhaps one last chance, one more question that might act like an electrical impulse. 'Karl Wilhelm Wartenberg. Does that name mean anything to you?'

He looked at her with a blank expression.

She tried to read something from his face. Was there any indication of this man's identity? Please. Anything.

Then she saw it. Yes, there was something and it was unequivocal. Why hadn't she noticed it in the first place? Without going to the trouble of looking at the photo. She felt a physical change take place in her; as if a fluid level inside had suddenly dropped. As if her body were leaking.

She stood up, steadied herself on the table and went to the door. The light outside glittered brightly, hurting her eyes. Caposi followed her and looked at her quizzically.

'There's no doubt about it — it's not him,' said Lilya, her arms hanging limply by her sides.

'Give me the photo. You didn't even take it out.' His voice was unusually forceful.

Lilya gave him the photo of the brothers.

He glanced at it for a second and then disappeared back in to the printing room.

She heard voices. Then the machine in the shed started up again. Caposi came back, his head stooped. 'The scar,' he said.

'Yes, you can't miss it. The man in there doesn't have one,' said Lilya.

They went back to the gate. Lilya's gaze turned upwards. A never-ending canopy of treetops and leaves filled the sky above them. Beams of light fell through the gaps but she couldn't feel the warmth of the sun. She thought of Elias Lind. It was all over now: she'd have to write to him — and didn't know how she would break the news.

Caposi chatted away on the journey home, evidently trying to distract her. She was only half listening. She sat slumped in the passenger seat, feeling shattered, but this time for a different reason. It was definitely all over.

Her thoughts went around in circles, again and again. And there was nothing but a void.
*Failed.*

She'd failed: this is exactly what she'd have to write to Elias Lind before she met him in person. He himself — if she'd understood his letter correctly — would be able to live with the result. But would she?

As they drove into Lüneburg, she sat up

again and turned to Caposi. 'I'm sorry, Alfred, I'm not a good listener right now, as you'll understand. But thank you for all you've done for me.'

'Thank me when it's over,' he said, and turned sharply into Uelzener Strasse.

In front of the house there was a parked jeep bearing a red cross. They got out and went into the garden.

The doctor from the JRU office was there. He seemed relieved to see Lilya and Caposi. Alma was sitting stiffly on a garden chair. The two of them seemed to have been struggling to make conversation. After a brief greeting, Dr Persson got straight to the point. He'd clearly been waiting for them for a long time.

'Alfred said you were looking for someone. He told me your story. It kept going round in my head. The lists . . . I came across something in them that might interest you.'

Lilya felt like interrupting him: she couldn't bear to hear any more about nameless people, lukewarm leads or dubious signs that would lead nowhere.

Her expression must have showed this. 'If you prefer, I can come back another time,' he said.

'No, please, carry on,' she said feebly.

'There's a rumour,' began Persson, 'a

419

nurse . . . I don't know her but it's said that she . . .'

'Come out with it, fellow, what have you found?' said Caposi. He was more resolute than ever and drew himself up in front of Persson. 'What about the nurse?'

'She's taken a patient home to look after. Against all the rules, but no one wants to intervene. It's a man, in his mid-fifties.' He turned to Lilya. 'Alfred told me this morning that Professor Lind must be about that age now.'

Lilya was finding it hard to take in what he was saying. Stories, stories, stories. How many stories had she heard by now? And here was yet another with many loose ends.

'I thought you might want to look into it. The woman works at the Glyn Hughes Hospital.'

'Thank you very much, Dr Persson,' said Caposi. 'I haven't been there for a long time, even though I helped build that hospital. I should stop by. What do you think, Lilya?'

Lilya took a deep breath and looked at Caposi with a serious expression. Where had his sudden decisiveness come from?

'All right,' she said.

Dr Persson looked at his watch and made a move to leave. Lilya remembered the photograph of the house at the edge of the woods, the books and the titles in a foreign language and the sentence on the back.

*Det bugter sig i bakke, dal.*

'Dr Persson,' she said, and looked up at him. 'You're Swedish, if I remember rightly. I have a photo I'd like to show you. Perhaps you can help me to understand it.'

Persson looked at her, a tentative expression on his face. 'I can try,' he said, 'but I'm already rather late.'

'It'll only take a few minutes,' she said. She fished the other photo out of her pocket.

'My goodness, how beautiful,' he said, holding the photo in his hands. 'I shouldn't look at these things nowadays. Too painful — reminds me of my home, Scandinavia.'

'Please read what's written on the back.'

He turned over the photo. 'Hard to decipher . . .'

'Do you need a . . . ?'

'No, it's okay.'

He slowly began to read aloud.

*'Det bugter sig i bakke, dal.'* He smiled. 'Do you want to hear it? I can't sing it though.' Persson stood up, cleared his throat and began to recite.

There is a lovely country

In the shade of the broad beech
On the salty Baltic beach . . .

'And then comes: *Det bugter sig i bakke, dal*, which means: *It winds itself in hill and valley.* It's the Danish national anthem.'

'Could this photograph have been taken in Denmark? I mean the books on the shelf, could you look at them for a moment?'

He held the photo close to his eyes. 'Danish books, as far as I can tell.'

Now she was sure.

*Stop.* She had to be careful not to get carried away again. Before she did anything else, she had to be absolutely sure. Perhaps Cordelia would be able to help her. She would try to call her. Ask her if she was crazy. Her friend would be frank and honest.

'Thank you, Dr Persson, you've been a great help to me. More than you'll ever know. I'll come to the hospital. I can hardly wait.'

# CHAPTER TWENTY-NINE

Not far from the camp, in a large clearing in the woods, lay the hospital. It was a long, red clinker-brick building. Above the entrance, like the spire of an invisible church, rose a small tower. An odd silence engulfed the place.

They walked towards the entrance. Most of the windows were tilted or opened a slit. In the distance she could see figures moving slowly. Some of them were propped on crutches or sitting in old-fashioned wheelchairs. One patient was being pushed in a lying position. In between, the white caps of nurses bobbed about as if in a ghostly pantomime.

When they entered the building, it was clear that Alfred Caposi knew the way. He guided Lilya along the corridors. Doctors and nurses walked past them, some greeting Caposi effusively or in surprise. He had to tell them over and again how he was and when he was coming back.

'She's waiting here in the meeting room,' said Caposi. 'Karen Dove is one of the best — I made enquiries. Tell her that you want to help her.' He opened the door to a small, sparsely furnished room.

The woman was sitting at the table. She had a pale complexion and large, green-blue eyes. Her blonde hair was cut short, evidently with a coarse pair of scissors. She looked almost boyish despite her clean, freshly starched nurse's uniform. Lilya guessed that she was no more than a few years older than herself.

Lilya greeted her, sat down at the table and introduced herself. 'Thank you for coming.'

'I'll clutch at any straw. I'm always wondering who he is, if he is missed by anyone, whether he still has family. I'm putting as much faith in you as you are in me.' The nurse had a young, slightly grating voice. 'You're bound to want to know first how I found Dr Chaim?' she continued.

'Dr Chaim?' Lilya looked at her quizzically.

A smile crossed Karen Dove's lips. 'I called him that at some point. In the first weeks, he often said the name Chaim to himself. I never managed to understand why but it seemed to mean a lot to him. He helped out in the camp, never flagging, working alongside the doctors — which is why I called him "Doctor".'

Chaim — a reference to Raphael and Elias's father?

'I noticed him in spring 1945 when we walked in through the gates to hell. He was weak but I saw straight away that he wasn't suffering from dropsy. In fact he seemed unusually strong. I arranged to have him brought to Camp 2. The whole procedure. You'll have heard about it.'

Caposi's account ran through Lilya's mind.

'He quickly got his strength back, which seemed to suggest that he hadn't been in the camp for long, or on one of the death marches. Only he didn't know who he was or where he came from. No name, no address, no story. But he soon helped look after the ill and starving.'

'Dr Caposi told me about the Bengali mix.'

'It took a while for them to hit on it. They had to go through a lot of experiments first. I often had the feeling he must be a doctor. He was someone who knew about the human body.'

She paused and looked briefly out of the

425

window, as if a far-off thought had occurred to her. 'In February this year, his strength failed. He became weak, as if there were something inside him still making him ill. He came here to the Glyn Hughes Hospital. But we couldn't find anything, not with our limited means. After a few weeks, we realised that his condition wasn't getting any worse, but no better either. Lots of people looked after him in the beginning but then fewer people came as time went on. In the end, no one at all.'

'So you decided to take him in?'

She looked back out through the window.

'Everyone here advised me not to, said I was overstretching myself. "You'll make yourself unhappy, you'll never be able to keep it up," they said. But I'd made up my mind. Sometimes the strangest methods are the right ones, aren't they?'

Karen Dove had tears in her eyes. Lilya placed a hand on her arm.

'It must have taken a great deal of strength and I'm sure you did a good job.'

'That's not the point,' said Karen, and pulled a handkerchief from her sleeve to blow her nose. 'He's not well.'

She stopped again. 'I don't know what's what any more: whether he's running out of life or life's running out on him.'

She dabbed her tears away with the handkerchief. 'Sometimes I'm afraid of the time when he passes away — but at other times, I wish for it more than anything. So that he finds peace — a peace that he wasn't granted here on earth. Is that allowed?'

Lilya squeezed her arm again gently and then pulled her hand away. She took out the photo of the two brothers. 'It's an old print,' she said, 'but I'd be grateful if you would look at it. The man on the left is Professor Raphael Lind. That's who I'm looking for. Does he have any similarity to Dr Chaim?'

Karen Dove took the photo and looked at it almost fearfully. Lilya watched her closely. Someone was pulling a squeaky cart outside the window. In the distance, an engine roared.

The nurse's face remained impassive. She laid the photo on the table, still looking at it. 'If you want to see him, then come soon,' she said.

# CHAPTER THIRTY

The orderly didn't want to leave until Lilya had opened the invitation. The soldier stood there motionlessly at the gate facing the street. Hella had pulled herself up in front of him as though she were guarding the house. Alma peered through the kitchen window. Dr Caposi was tending the garden.

In Palestine, the British would have liked nothing more than to lock her up; here, the same people were delivering her a personal, sealed invitation. She had long since understood that as far as the British Empire was concerned, there was a fine line between an invitation and a summons. This was certainly the latter. It was about time she let the young soldier go. She scanned the lines.

'I accept the invitation,' she said.

The soldier saluted, and left.

It wasn't far to the British officers' mess hall. She was wearing a fresh uniform shirt, ironed by Alma, and she'd prepared herself for the conversation. The previous evening, before going to sleep, she'd made notes so that she could deliver all the news she had to her host, sorted and weighed. She'd realised the major would turn up here sooner or later: she was in the British zone and he had his sources.

An orderly escorted her into the officers' mess hall, not far from the market square. Major Terry had chosen a table set apart from the others. When he spotted Lilya, he got up and smiled at her from a distance. She saw him in uniform for the first time, which made him appear taller.

'I hope you've got a proper appetite. Our canteens might not be on a par with the French zone. But we do more than just try our best. The only thing we don't have are kosher dishes.'

Terry pulled one of the chairs from the table and indicated to Lilya to sit down. She did.

'I doubt you'll be offering me pork.'

'Lamb. From Lüneburg Heath.'

Terry sat opposite her, leaned back in his chair, folded his arms across his chest and beamed at her as if she were a prize.

'We found you,' he said.

'I wasn't hiding. But I felt it was in the

interests of my own safety to disappear from Berlin without letting you know. You yourself said when I called the embassy that everyone knew about us.'

Terry laughed softly, shook his head and looked her in the eye.

'Always a step ahead. I've never come across anyone quite like you. In any case, it's an honour to receive you in our zone — quite officially. I hope you feel comfortable.'

A uniformed waiter put water on the table.

'Your zone — and you want to hand it over to the Germans now, all neat and tidy, no stains, no mess?' asked Lilya.

Terry wordlessly poured her some water, his beam giving way to a strained smile. He changed the subject. 'I heard you're staying with an Englishman here. I'm glad. Even if Caposi gives us cause for concern. He should leave the country before he goes completely bonkers. And a German wife to boot. Not a blessed match, I imagine.'

'You didn't invite me so that we could chat about my host, surely? Caposi has been a great help to me. More than any other Englishman.'

Terry leaned back again and eyed her. 'I heard you've come considerably close to solving your case?' he said after a short pause. 'There are indications that Lind is really alive?'

'There is a sign, yes.'

'In the camp?'

'No, outside,' she said.

Terry looked at her in surprise.

An officer and his adjutant walked past the table. Terry greeted them curtly, almost without looking up. He made it clear that he didn't want to be disturbed.

'And has our stalker showed up again?'

'No, not yet. I know that must be disappointing but that's the way things stand at the moment. And I suppose that if I'm only being stalked by your people when I find Lind, you've got less of a chance of receiving that medal.'

Lilya was suddenly so tickled by this idea that she nearly giggled. Why hadn't she thought of this before? The British might go home empty-handed because she'd been so good at shaking off the man they were looking for.

The major had slumped down in his chair and was looking at her with quiet contempt in his eyes. The officers at the neighbouring table glanced over furtively. Terry's discomfort was visible.

'I'm sure he'll turn up sooner or later,' he said, straightening up again. 'You may find it amusing to think that things will turn out differently. But this little escapade will end in a showdown on the street.'

'Perhaps you're right. After all, you managed to find me. And my stalker — even you have to admit this, Major — was always a tick faster than you.'

Terry leaned forward and grasped her hand. 'Lilya, please,' he said, and then lowered his voice. 'If you have a hot lead to Lind, it's only a question of time before whoever's hard on your heels shows his face here. And then it's not only you who'll be in danger, but Lind too — if he's still alive — and Caposi. That's why I asked you to come here. You might be our bait, as you put it, but that also involves responsibility — our responsibility. It is my wish and my duty to prevent you from coming to any harm. And even if you don't like it — you need us. You need our protection. And together, we need to come up with a plan.'

Lilya turned serious again. Up until now she had always thought that there was a solution — a political solution, a greater solution, an ultimate goal, which she had to serve. She'd always agreed with Yoram on that point, even if they had completely different ideas on how to go about it. Perhaps Yoram would laugh at her now if he were still alive: she'd let herself be exploited by the British. She'd struck a deal with them. Perhaps he'd say: *You've lost, Lilya. They've got you!*

And so what if he did? Let him. Let him laugh at her. The thought was as clear as it was liberating. Let all of them — the theorisers, ideologists, debaters, tribunes and fighters — let them all laugh at her! The pig-headed and the ignorant. She'd finish off her job here, even if it involved collaborating with the British.

Terry had taken a cigarette out of his case and was sitting back in his chair, watching her and the effects of her thought processes.

'I found a man living near Erding by the name of Karl Wilhelm Wartenberg,' said Lilya. 'He ordered Lind's arrest in 1941 from his home in Dahlem. And he'd received a telephone call prior to this.'

Terry sat up and took notice. 'How do you mean?'

'The caller had a slight, almost imperceptible British accent. It was autumn 1941 and it was very obvious that he wanted to sell information. He knew that Wartenberg worked for the Weapons Agency and might be interested in Lind's research.'

'In autumn 1941, you say? Shortly after Harp disappeared off our radar?'

'Exactly. And everything that Wartenberg

was able to find out about this anonymous informer corresponds almost exactly to what you told me about Harp.'

Terry leaned over the table. 'Did he also tell Wartenberg about the planned abduction?'

'Yes. But at the time, Wartenberg's people had already arrested Lind. Wartenberg didn't consent to blackmail, or receive information: he said that he didn't need the man's information.'

'That means that Harp wanted to trade in Lind and his information to the Nazis for payment?'

'Yes, and Wartenberg also claimed that he tried it later with the Russians too, and they took the bait.'

Terry let out a whistle. 'I'm impressed, Miss Wasserfall.'

He reflected on this for a moment. Then he calmly laid out his plan: she would receive round-the-clock surveillance. Discreet and effective.

'From now on, we're not going to leave your side,' said Terry. The smile had returned to his face and he waved over the waiter. 'And now, you should fortify yourself, young lady.'

The lamb *was* rather good. Terry hadn't made an empty promise. After coffee, it was high time for her to leave. She stood up, thanked him and turned to go. After a few steps, she turned back again. 'Send my greetings to Mr Honeywell in Whitehall,' she said. 'He should think over what kind of offer he'd like to make. I have a few ideas — I can send him a list when I get to Jerusalem. I hope he still remembers who I am.' She smiled, nodded to Terry and left the room.

That night she listened at the window from time to time, tossing and turning in her bed. All was quiet in the house. She could only hear Caposi snoring or speaking in his sleep now and again, and soon after, Alma's soothing voice that sounded almost like a song.

First thing next morning, she would drive over to see Karen Dove. Caposi was unaware of her agreement with the British major; unaware of the danger she might be putting him in; unaware of the man whose hand was like a wire-cutter; of her 'accident' and of the traitor whom Terry called Everett Harp; unaware of her agreement with Whitehall. If she acted as bait, she would make Caposi her stalker's target — and the stalker would try his best to prevent them both from finding Lind.

A car drew up in the still of night. The engine was cut immediately and a door clicked quietly. Not right in front of the house but somewhere further down the street, she picked up the sound of muffled voices, almost whispering. She tried to ignore it. But she'd learned from Ben Gedi to trust her instincts. After pushing back the covers and carefully putting her feet on the floor, she grabbed her trousers, put them on and slipped on a shirt. With her shoes in her hands, she crept down the stairs. Slowly, on tiptoes, she put one foot in front of the other. Effortlessly, she found the front door in the dark. The key was in the lock. She gripped it and turned it around slowly. She heard the mechanism of the lock being released, making a quiet *click*.

It was foolhardy to go out on her own, without waking Caposi. Nonetheless, she opened the door a crack and peered out. The moon had gone behind the clouds but it was a balmy night. She put on her shoes and went down the steps. Her eyes swiftly got used to the dark. She could now make out the outline of the garden and spied a folding spade that Caposi had stuck into the soil near the entrance. She grasped the handle, pulled it out without a sound, cleaned off the dirt and opened the gate to the street.

Now she could see the car parked no more than a hundred yards from her. The street-lamps were off and there was no one to be seen. The voices had also gone quiet.

She looked around again and then ran, ducking behind the hedge, towards the car. A cat scurried across the path and she jumped. But she wanted to be certain by looking at the headlamps of the car. She wanted to know whether it was the same car . . .

Again, she heard voices. But she couldn't work out how many people there were. The men spoke with an English accent. She paused at the end of the hedge and raised the spade over her head. If they were about to move towards the house, she'd know how to protect herself.

She heard footsteps on the other side of the hedge then one of the men seemed to stop. Lilya's heart thudded. The sound of unzipping, then splashing. Lilya didn't move a muscle.

'Okay, Bill. Best we go home.'

'Just a minute.'

She heard the man fastening his trousers, walking away and returning to the street. Lilya lowered the spade. Now she could see the men's uniforms in the moonlight. So these were supposed to be her protectors! She peeled herself away from the hedge and stood next to the car on the street. 'Good evening, gentlemen,' she said in a firm voice.

One of them spun around, his shirt still hanging out of his trousers, as he fumbled with his gun holster. The other turned on a torch and the beam of light searched frantically all around.

'Here,' she said, holding up her spade so they could find her.

The men stared over at her.

Once more, the beam of light swept the ground and then climbed her body. She had to close her eyes.

'That could've backfired, miss,' said the one called Bill.

'It was my understanding that you were supposed to be guarding me, not the other way round. If someone had wanted to pay a call on me at home, you'd have shown him the way.'

'That's not quite true, miss. But please excuse us. I hope you won't feel the need to tell Major Terry about our little meeting here —'

Bill interrupted and pointed to the spade that she was still holding. 'You didn't really think that trowel would protect you, did you?'

'More effectively than the British Army,' she said, and turned to go.

The two soldiers escorted her to the front door and waited until she had gone in.

'Good night, miss. You'd better get a few hours' sleep. And we'd be ever so grateful if you kept this to yourself.'

Back in her attic room, she flopped down on the bed and curled up under the covers. Her heart was still hammering. She longed for sleep yet knew that it wouldn't come to her that night. Her thoughts spun in circles, and her fear had returned. What if they hadn't been her protectors? And her stalker had been lying in wait around the corner, first grabbing her from behind then pulling the wire noose so tight that she dropped the spade? She pulled the cover over her head and listened to the silence of the night without stirring a limb.

The images of the night before came flooding back to her when she was woken by footsteps. They approached her across the landing to her apartment. She sat up and measured the distance to the rear area of the building. She could jump through the kitchen window into the inner courtyard — with a bit of skill, it might work. Avoid the street, through the garden and backyards, doubling back on herself. She knew Jerusalem like the back of her hand. Quietly, she pulled on her shoes and grabbed her rucksack that always stood packed next to her bed.

She listened again. It seemed to be a man. Perhaps there was another waiting down on the street? Or behind the building. It must be the British.

She hesitated. Someone knocked on her door. Three times. Pause. Twice. It was their sign.

Yoram always came unannounced. Even though they had a rule that meetings had to be announced. He'd made it himself.

She opened the door very slowly. It was Ofer Kis. He came in without saying hello, looked around and gently pushed the door to behind him.

'Are you alone?' he asked. She nodded and he went past her to the room that faced the street.

He was holding a cap in his hand. It needed washing, she thought, and mending. It had a large rip in the side, and was covered in black stains. Perhaps it was even past being saved.

She followed Ofer into the room, was overcome with dizziness and had to grip the table.

They could try soaking the cap; they really should try everything they could. She looked over at the sink.

Ofer went to the window and looked out. 'I know it wasn't me you were expecting,' he said, so softly that she could barely catch his words. He turned to her. The muscles in his face were rigid.

She wondered whether he still played the violin, the way people think absurd things in these kinds of situations.

They had to make a plan now. 'A tentative one,' he said and looked out of the window once more.

A plan. Why?

The cap. Why was he carrying it? His always had salt-edged stains.

She heard snatches of what he was saying: *North . . . hiding place . . . better this way.*

'No!' she said, interrupting him mid-sentence.

He was lying. It wasn't true. It was all a trick — a bitter, nasty one that they were playing on her. If Yoram knew what they were doing in his name, behind his back — and his friend Ofer, of all people!

'A bomb,' said Ofer and glanced at her, 'killed him and two others in the cellar. A mistake, some kind of carelessness, a technical problem, we don't know.' His voice cracked, he shook his head and looked down at the floor.

She wouldn't play this game, ever. Suddenly, she was holding the cap — he must have given it to her. It was hard and cracked. She could have broken off a piece. She held it to her belly.

'Why are you telling me these things, Ofer?' she heard herself say.

He didn't answer. He laid a hand on her shoulder.

'Come, Lilya,' he said, 'the car's waiting downstairs.' He hoisted her rucksack on to his shoulder and led her to the door.

The north.

The cap.

Yoram's cap.

Down below on the street, her legs buckled. Two men grabbed her, one left, one right, pulled her upright and pushed her through the open door of the car.

'You're lying!' she screamed. 'I want to see him!'

The car moved off. Ofer was sitting next to her. He turned his face to the window and stared out.

The buildings disappeared slowly and were replaced by barren hills, brushwood and desolate landscape. The roads led downhill and when a British outpost suddenly appeared, Ofer placed a revolver on her lap. But they were waved through.

'It's better this way,' Ofer repeated, and turned back to the window. 'When all this is over, you can come back again.'

'But Ben Gedi, I have to . . .' Her voice sounded like a stranger's.

'He'll find out,' said Ofer, 'and wait for you.'

She turned on to her side. Outside everything was quiet. When the dawn chorus began, she sank into a brief, dreamless sleep.

# CHAPTER THIRTY-ONE

The house was at the end of a dirt track. Immediately beyond, large trees made it only visible from the front. The garden around the house had gone wild but signs of order could still be seen here and there. The flowerbeds were bordered by stones and a broad path led to the door; a few smaller ones trailed off into the garden. An orphaned greenhouse stood between the flowerbeds, a few of its panes broken. Inside there were some cracked flowerpots containing dried-up plants. A house martin came flying out.

Lilya could feel the stillness all around. Caposi wanted to wait by the car, but she asked him to escort her into the house. He shrugged and followed her up the path.

She looked around. There was no one to be seen. He might be somewhere out there. And somewhere out there were Terry and his men too.

Karen Dove looked pale and overtired. She wiped her hands on her apron. 'He's very weak today. I already thought about postponing the meeting.'

She asked them to come in. 'His room faces the garden. That way he's woken by the morning sun,' she said as they entered the hallway. 'He's bedridden now.'

Karen Dove asked Lilya and Caposi to wait in the living room.

It contained two armchairs, a bed, a washbowl and a cupboard; she could make out packets of medication behind its milk-glass doors. A book was lying open on the table: *Stamboul Train*. It looked as though Karen Dove lived in this one room. Lilya took a brief peek out of the window.

After a few minutes, the nurse returned, and she looked as if she were trying to make up her mind. 'If we keep it brief, he should be okay,' she said.

Lilya was distracted for a second; she'd heard a noise outside — branches cracking.

'I'll take you to him now,' said Karen.

'Is the front door locked?'

Karen Dove looked at Lilya in surprise. 'Of course, why?'

'I'd like to make sure that we're not disturbed.'

Karen Dove led them down the hallway

and opened a door quietly. The room was bright and through a half-opened window Lilya could hear birdsong. Somewhere further away a woodpecker was at work. The bed stood with its foot to the window. She breathed in and out deeply. Then she went in.

Dr Chaim was sitting upright in bed, propped up by two large cushions and looking out of the window. He had a white, carefully trimmed beard. There was only one place where his skin shimmered through: a thin line on his left cheek. He still had a full head of hair but it was almost as white as paper; his torso was sturdy. His eyes had a sheen like dying embers, as if he wasn't taking anything in, or what he saw was consumed by their afterglow.

He sat there, stock-still except for his hands, which were slowly fiddling with the cover.

Lilya stepped closer to the bed. His similarity to the man whose photograph she had been carrying for weeks was overwhelming. As well as to Elias Lind.

'Talk to him,' said Karen. She pulled a chair up to the bed for Lilya.

His breathing was shallow and came fitfully.

'Professor Lind,' she said.

He looked at her listlessly.

She tried again. 'I'm looking for Raphael Lind. From Berlin.'

He raised his eyebrows. His hands stopped moving.

She could sense that something had struck a chord. 'Elias, your brother, sent me to you. Elias Lind, he lives in Jerusalem.'

His hands began kneading the cover again, but more intensely this time.

'What you're saying seems to be having a strong effect on him. I've never seen him this way,' said Karen. She moved closer to the bed and looked at him. He didn't seem to want to let Lilya out of his sight.

'Tell him something about yourself.'

Where should she start? Her mind went blank. How long had she worked towards this day? And now she couldn't find the words. 'I have been looking for you . . . for weeks. I'd almost given up hope . . .'

'Tell him about his brother,' said Karen.

'I met Elias several times in Jerusalem; he'd like to see you again. He's well . . .'

Out of the corner of her eye, Lilya saw a movement through the window. Perhaps Caposi had gone out? She would have to warn him. But what was he doing behind the house?

But no, Caposi came into the room with a

camera. And now she saw them clearly: ducked British soldiers were slinking through the garden, weapons at the ready. 'It would be good if we could take a photo of Dr Chaim,' she said, rather too loudly and emphatically, turning briefly to Karen as she tried to distract her from what was going on outside the window.

While Caposi pointed the camera at Dr Chaim, her words tumbled out, jumbled up: how she'd found him, her weeks of searching. She blurted out names: Durlacher, Wartenberg, Terry and Green, Desirée von Wallsdorff, Ben Gedi, Guggenheim. Whenever she mentioned the name Lind, the doctor, otherwise apathetic, showed emotion.

Suddenly she noticed that he'd fallen asleep. His features seemed to have relaxed. The nurse's hand rested on her shoulder.

'Come, it's enough for today,' said Karen.

At that very moment, a shout rang out in the garden, cutting through the air like a barked order. Then a shot was fired. And another. Caposi threw her to one side and away from the window. She heard footsteps behind the house, a man yelling. More shots were fired. Next door in the living room, a windowpane shattered and there was a thudding sound as if someone were hammering nails into the wall.

Caposi pulled her to the floor. Karen Dove was cowering in a corner at the foot of the bed, her arms wrapped tightly around her body.

'We have to get him away from the window,' Lilya said to Caposi, who was lying on the floor next to her. Glass shattered again. Shards lay scattered on the floor in front of Lind's bed.

Thud, thud, thud, the shots went. She saw Karen Dove duck her head even lower; then she sat without moving a muscle. Lilya slithered across the floor on her stomach, gripped the bedstead that was on wheels and pulled. Caposi came from the other side and grabbed hold of it too. Together they tried to move it but it was heavy.

She called over to Karen Dove, who was still not moving, then crawled over to her. She was now leaning up against the wall with her eyes wide open. Her face was as pale as snow, veins stood out on her temples and her breathing was coming hard and fast. Lilya touched her leg and Karen Dove looked at her in astonishment: she didn't appear to be injured.

Suddenly, all went quiet. Lilya lifted her head and listened. Someone called from the garden, 'It's all clear, you can come out now. It's over.'

The nurse stood up shakily, smoothed down her dress, went over to the bed and placed a hand on Lind's forehead. He didn't seem to be injured either.

Lilya sat up and leaned against the wall. She saw Alfred Caposi going over to the window, glass splinters crunching underfoot. She tried to get up but her body was leaden. Caposi came over to her, reached out his hand and pulled her up. Her legs quivered slightly as she held on to his shoulder.

'Everything okay?' he asked.

She breathed in and out deeply, nodding. 'Yes, thank you.'

Caposi linked arms with her and led her out of the house. Jeeps were parked on the driveway. British soldiers were leaning against the bonnet, their weapons lodged between their legs, lighting each other's cigarettes. In one of the jeeps, Lilya saw a man bent forward in the passenger seat, nursing a bloody arm. It was Major Terry. A medic was standing next to him, unravelling bandages.

'It's just a scratch really,' said Terry between clenched teeth, sitting up as Lilya went over to him. 'We've got him, that's the main thing. It was Everett Harp all right. He was on his own.'

Then he yelped in pain. 'Not so tight!' he yelled at the medic.

Once his arm was bandaged, he clambered down off the seat and pointed in the direction of the greenhouse. 'Back there,' he said. 'Come and take a look at him.'

Feet protruded from the greenhouse, and broken glass was lying everywhere. A sergeant was standing with a carbine under his arm next to the dead man.

The man was lying on his side, one arm outstretched, the other hidden by his body. Next to him, Lilya saw an army revolver. Terry touched the dead man with his boot, causing him to roll on to his back. Lilya now saw his face and his left arm that had been concealed by his body. He was wearing a thin brown leather glove and underneath his brown suit jacket, a sheath containing a sharp, jagged knife poked out.

'Well? Do you recognise him?' asked Terry.

'I'm afraid so,' she said. 'He was with me on the ship.'

'The man who called himself O'Madden?'

'The very one.'

Terry shook his head. Ernst Hartmann, Everett Harp, Colm O'Madden, Major Turntide. The truth was a slippery business.

'I'd like to show you something else,' said Terry, and took her by the elbow. 'A little further into the woods, there's a parked car. A Wanderer — smart car, a coupé, built in 1932 in top condition. Just the headlamps are a little too big, ruining its proportions. I'd be interested in knowing whether you've seen it before.'

They walked around the house towards the edge of the woods. Two soldiers were standing on a narrow path that opened up between the pine trees and led along a gravel path to a small clearing. The car stood there. One of the headlamps was dented and the glass was shattered.

'He obviously parked the car here and then lay in wait for you in the woods.'

Yes, it was the same car. She went closer and touched the damaged headlamp.

'We'll check the number plates and take the car to Berlin. Perhaps Dr Durlacher will recognise it. Major Turntide indeed! I'm curious about its previous owner. Didn't I mention that Lind had to sell his car before he was abducted?'

When they arrived back at the house, Caposi was already waiting in his jeep. She got in and saw that the speedometer had been destroyed. A bullet hole the size of a finger made the five-mile mark unreadable.

Caposi went to start the jeep but Terry sprang to attention in front of him. 'Thank you, Dr Caposi. We are greatly indebted to you. Without your participation, we would be . . . well. I'll be communicating this to the higher ranks.'

Caposi lifted his arm. 'Very well. Ruptured times, eh? That's what they are . . .'

'Certainly,' said Terry, turning to Lilya. 'And yourself? I expect you've come to the end of your journey now?'

'Not quite,' she said, 'but I've never been as close as I am now.'

# CHAPTER THIRTY-TWO

Terry had immediately sent the roll of film with the photos that Caposi had taken of Raphael Lind on an RAF aeroplane via Hanover to London. From there, it would be sent to Palestine. As soon as the pictures had been developed, Elias Lind was to send a telegraph. Terry had assured her of transport, this time with the Royal Air Force.

Now she was alone in his office and the telephone seemed to be looking at her. 'Please forgive me if I'm wrong,' she said faintly to herself. It had to be the Olsens' house in the photograph: Vivien's parents' house. That's why the picture was so important to Lind. It was his last remaining memento of Vivien after he was taken away and she killed herself.

But there was something else: the house, the brightly lit room, the shelf with the books. The thought had come back to her many times and her heart had always beaten faster. It was the Olsens' house. But could it also be . . . It was such a far-fetched thought, barely more than an intuition, taking shape in all its baffling beauty and audacity.

She picked up the receiver and hesitated. Then she dialled the number in Munich that she already knew off by heart. There was only one question he had to answer.

'David, can you hear me?'

'Yes, clearly. How are you, Lilya?' It was obvious that he was happy she'd called.

'I found him, he's alive,' she said and wanted to scream for joy. All the tension and fear of the past weeks and months finally fell away.

'Are you sure?'

'Almost positive. And the others say there's barely a doubt.'

'That's wonderful! Congratulations, Lilya! What a success!'

'Thank you. But I'm actually calling for a different reason . . .' — Lilya hoped that the line wouldn't fail her, that the connection would hold — 'it's about the photograph of your mother.'

'I'm just trying to get used to the idea that —'

'Please fetch the photo.'

'Right now?'

'Yes.'

He seemed to hesitate, then asked her to wait a moment.

'Okay, I've got it in front of me.'

'Then listen to me please, and look carefully at the photograph. You don't have to answer straight away.'

It started raining in the morning and a pungent odour of soil, grass, blossoms, leaves and bark came in through the window. The entire world seemed fragrant. At around midday, the clouds drifted away. The air was velvety and pure, and the lawn in front of the house gleamed. She kept her ears open for the sound of an engine.

Eventually, a car pulled up in front of the house. She peered through the kitchen window and saw David Guggenheim climbing out of the car. He was wearing a pilot's cap and a parachute silk scarf. She could see that he was tired by the way he walked. Lev, sitting behind the steering wheel, got out of the car after him, picked up an army rucksack from the back seat, slung it over his shoulder and followed Guggenheim through the garden gate.

'So that's the man,' said Caposi, who had taken up position behind Lilya at the window. 'Well, let's see.'

They went outside to greet the pair. Alfred saluted and took the rucksack from Lev. 'Welcome, gentlemen,' he said.

Guggenheim beamed when he saw Lilya. He looked at her for a second, then hugged her.

Lev stood next to him, shifting from one foot to the other. 'I've been her friend for much longer, you know,' he said, once David had let her go, and pulled her clumsily towards him.

Coffee was already prepared and waiting for them in the kitchen. Alma had even managed to rustle up some cake. Caposi asked them to sit down. 'Please help yourselves,' he said, 'we don't have much time. We should set off in half an hour.'

Lev sat down at the table, let Alma pour him a coffee and immediately struck up a conversation with little Hella, who had settled in beside him. Guggenheim threw her a pleading look, as if to say, *please don't keep me on tenterhooks any longer.*

She took him into the living room and closed the door behind them. 'The photograph, do you have it with you?' she asked.

He took off his cap and produced an envelope from his pocket. 'I would like you to look at the photo of your mother very carefully.'

She placed the photograph of the house in the woods next to it, the one that meant so much to Raphael Lind and which she'd taken with her everywhere on her journey. 'I'd like you to tell me whether you see what I see.'

He gave her a searching look, bent over the photographs, touched them, shuffled them around on the table, placed them next to one another again, and laid one half on top of the other.

Neither of them said anything; just his breathing could be heard. In the kitchen, Alma was clearing the plates and cups away, and she could hear voices at the front door. Lev and Caposi must have gone outside to smoke a cigarette before they set off. She stole a look at Guggenheim. He was leaning forward with his hands propped on the small table, still staring at the pictures. His upper lip was thrust slightly forward and a small furrow had appeared between his eyebrows. She looked at his profile: his ears, his shoulders, his dark-blond crop of hair that wasn't tamed with brilliantine today. It was wavy. Was there a similarity or was she just imagining it?

'Is there a magnifying glass in the house?' he asked, without looking up.

She passed it to him. Bending over the

magnifier, Guggenheim stared again at the pictures. Then he picked up the photos one by one from the table and held them at arm's length, moving the glass over them with the other hand. Finally, he put everything back on the table.

'I have no idea what it means — what the photo of this house is all about. But it is astonishing. The books.'

'They're Danish books,' she said.

'And the house? What kind of house is it? Who does it belong to?'

'What do you see exactly?' she asked.

He seemed to hesitate for a moment, as if he didn't understand the question or as if the answer was so obvious that there was no need to explain. 'The books on the shelf are the same,' he said slowly, looking to her for help. 'In both pictures.'

'They're the same,' she said and laid a hand on his arm. 'The photo of the house belongs to Raphael Lind. He took it with him everywhere for many years and it meant a great deal to him. In all probability, it's Vivien Olsen's parents' house. In Denmark, where she grew up.'

'Who is Vivien Olsen?' he asked, almost abruptly.

'Raphael and Vivien met in 1921. She moved to Berlin from Denmark to be engaged to a young man called Bert von der Lohe, but then fell helplessly in love with Lind. They couldn't leave each other alone — that's what an old friend of Lind's in Berlin told me — but Raphael couldn't or didn't want to commit to her. Not even when Vivien became pregnant with his child. When the child was born, she called him Hans, after her father — and —'

'Lilith,' he interrupted her. 'I can't follow you any more. What kind of story is this? What does all this have to do with me?'

'And gave him up for adoption,' finished Lilya with a steady voice. 'The child ended up with a couple who emigrated to America.'

Guggenheim snapped to attention and looked at Lilya. He appeared to want to say something but couldn't manage to get a word out.

'David, if all that I've found out is true . . . There seems to be a lot of evidence that the woman in the photograph is Vivien Olsen. The photo is of her parents' house in Denmark, the same books, the same room. This is your mother in the photograph.'

He halted, as if the sentence he was trying to say was too big, too unwieldy — absurd.

'And Raphael Lind might be your father,' she said gently. 'Go on, say it.'

460

David Guggenheim didn't move. Perhaps she had said it all too quickly.

She took his hand. 'We want to try to find out.'

David followed her to the car without saying anything. Caposi was already waiting.

'Where are we going?'

Lilya smiled. 'To visit Hans Olsen junior's father.'

# CHAPTER THIRTY-THREE

David Guggenheim seemed to be struggling to find his place in this version of events. Instead of inundating Lilya with questions, he sat silently, his eyes focused straight ahead, as though he were concentrating on a fixed point in the distance. He had sat down in the passenger seat next to Caposi. Lilya placed a hand on his shoulder. He gripped it with his right hand and held on tight: his fingers were cold.

'I've been looking for my mother since I set foot on this continent,' he said.

'And your father?'

'It's like he doesn't exist. There isn't a single clue. Perhaps I'm just the result of some forgotten one-night stand. And the people who have forgotten have died.'

'What about your parents in America? Couldn't they tell you anything?'

'No. It was an anonymous adoption. These things were done properly in Germany.

They never saw my birth parents, not even my mother. So they know nothing about who they were, where they lived or the events around my birth.'

'That must make you feel bitter.'

'Not any more.'

After the turbulent events of the day before, Karen Dove had brought Raphael Lind to the Glyn Hughes Hospital for a check-up. Two military policemen were assigned to keep an eye on him around the clock. Everyone assumed that Harp had acted alone but no one wanted to take any risks.

Karen Dove was waiting for them at the entrance. There wasn't a trace of acrimony in her voice about the events that Lilya had drawn her into — only relief. Dr Chaim was completely unhurt; Karen wasn't sure if he had even noticed the ruckus.

The hospital ward' where Lind was being looked after was on the second floor; it wasn't possible to see in from the outside. One of the soldiers on guard was sitting on a chair, and the other was walking up and down the corridor, a gun slung over his shoulder.

Raphael Lind was lying in a bright white bed, bolstered by two large pillows. Someone had placed a large bouquet of flowers next to him. The window was open a crack and the fragrance of freshly cut grass wafted in.

David Guggenheim had the photograph of his mother with him, the woman who might have been Vivien Olsen. He stood in front of Lind's bed: what was going through his mind? Lilya had never seen this normally resolute man so guarded and wary. His expression pleaded with her to start the conversation. And in truth, when she leaned over Raphael Lind in greeting, she had the impression that he recognised her. His features seemed relaxed and his eyes twinkled with friendly curiosity. His fingers gripped the bed cover like the last time, but they were calm.

'Professor Lind,' she said, 'this is Lieutenant David Guggenheim, a good friend of mine.'

*What was he supposed to make of this information?* shot through her head but she couldn't think of anything better. Lind seemed to be listening to her attentively and mildly, detached from his surroundings. She explained in a few brief sentences, emphasising in a few words why they had come: *a question, please, look, search, photo, name, woman, mother, hope.*

Guggenheim stepped forward and handed

her the photograph. 'This is the woman we are looking for,' she said, and held it in front of him. She would mention her name later.

Lind glanced briefly at the photo and then turned his face to the window. Patience, she thought, don't give up just yet.

Lilya looked at Guggenheim and gripped his hand. A light breeze came in through the window, billowing the curtain. She heard Karen Dove's voice in the corridor and those of the two guards.

Then Lind's gaze fixed on the photograph of the young woman and seemed to linger there. He suddenly opened his mouth as if to speak but no sound came out. He moved his lips and formed silent words. Lilya tried at least to lip-read how many syllables he spoke. Later both she and David agreed that there were three: *Vi-vi-en.* But equally, didn't *Sum-mer-time* have three syllables? As did, *Don't know her, What was that?, I don't know* or simply *Please go now.*

But his hands had started kneading the cover again.

Lilya fetched Karen Dove; perhaps she would understand what Lind was trying to say. The nurse stood next to Lind's bed and placed her hand on his shoulder. Then Lilya said the name Vivien Olsen: but Lind just continued staring blankly at the photo. Not even Karen Dove could interpret what he felt.

They left the hospital and walked back to the car. Karen stayed behind to keep Lind company: she would send news if her patient said anything.

Suddenly, David stopped. 'She's dead, isn't she?' he said. 'Vivien Olsen. Otherwise you would have found her too.'

He was looking at her in a way that she couldn't make out.

'Perhaps I should have told you as soon as you arrived. But I thought it better not to tell you everything at once. And we weren't even sure before we came here . . . we're still not sure —' She broke off. David was standing there motionless. Gently, she touched his upper arm and carried on with her explanation. 'She took her own life when she heard that the Gestapo had taken him away. She couldn't know that they weren't going to murder him, and use him for their purposes instead. She had to face the fact that she might never see him again.'

She held back for a moment. 'Or her son.'

David thrust his hands into his trouser pockets and gazed off into the distance.

'David, I'm sorry.'

He turned back to her and took a deep breath. 'I can't be angry with you. Why should I be? You've helped me so much. Now I know who the woman in the photograph was, what her name was, who she loved, and what happened to her. That's more that I ever dared to hope for.'

Lilya looked at him and narrowed her eyes. 'I met someone in Berlin — an admirable, unusual woman. I'm sure that she will want to tell you about Vivien Olsen. Take the photograph with you. She'll be able to say whether our theory is right.'

She linked arms with David and on the way back to the car she told him about Desirée von Wallsdorff and her friendship with Lind and Vivien. If she were able to identify the woman in the photograph as Vivien Olsen, then Lilya's hunch would be confirmed.

'What's more, I've been in touch with Vivien's father in Denmark,' continued Lilya. 'Hans Olsen is old and ill, but perhaps you'll find a way to go and visit him. So, there's still a great deal ahead of us,' she said.

David Guggenheim stopped again, grasped Lilya by the shoulders and kissed her on the cheek. 'Then let's see what we can get straight among all these possibilities,' he said, linking arms with her, and pulling her along.

# CHAPTER THIRTY-FOUR

She put all the papers together: the little batch of rather unsorted sketches Elias had given her before the journey, her own notes, Hans Olsen's letter and, finally, a note with Desirée von Wallsdorff's address in Berlin. On top, she laid the letter she had written to David as a covering note, a summary, a farewell: she wasn't sure herself what it was meant to be.

Dear David,
The whole story is so long, and perhaps it's not over yet. I wanted to tell you everything in detail, but then I'd have to write a novel.

Still, you should know everything I know. That's why I'm leaving you all the papers that I have collected on my trip, as well as the address of Desirée von Wallsdorff in Berlin, which will give you final certainty, I'm sure.

The story of Raphael and Elias Lind, and of Vivien Olsen and her son, has also become my story over the past few months. At first I tried to fight it. I cursed my mission and wanted to stay where I was among the hills in my hide-out near the border with Lebanon. To fight, not look for people who are strangers to me, wasting my time on the stories of individuals. But now I've understood that the overall picture is only made up of whatever small things we do. Life is a series of individual stories, and an entire cosmos at the same time.

You once said that it's not the right time and place for us both: each of us belongs in a different world. But still, I hope that we who search find ourselves and each other again. I've learned and understood, also through you, that there might be a new beginning for me too. This has been painful and liberating at the same time. That's the way it's meant to be.

Thank you,
With love, your Lilith

P.S. I've added my address in Palestine. And Elias Lind's, who I'm sure cannot wait to see me again.

Alma had given David the attic room: Lilya laid the bundle of papers in front of his door, knocked softly, and went quietly back downstairs before he had the chance to open it.

On the day before her departure — Terry had booked her a seat on a military flight — Alma had laid a table in the garden under a tree with all manner of food, cakes and drinks from the British officers' mess, delivered by Major Terry.

The major himself was still at headquarters with David Guggenheim to arrange for Raphael Lind to be transported to a hospital in England. From there, as soon as his condition allowed, he would be brought to Palestine, to his brother. That was the plan.

Terry had reached an agreement with Honeywell in London, who, after some hesitation, had given clearance for 'entry beyond the normal immigrant quota for Jews into Palestine' — not without first emphasising how generous Whitehall was.

Nevertheless they had to delay the transfer until they had received confirmation from Elias Lind: Caposi's photographs hadn't arrived yet. Only Elias could identify his brother beyond all doubt.

The car that Everett Harp had parked at

the edge of the woods, however, was swiftly inspected. The British Embassy in Berlin reported that the car was registered in 1932 in Lind's name in Berlin. Evidently, Harp had not only stolen Lind's knowledge.

From the garden, voices reached Lilya's ears in her room. Alma was giving Caposi instructions and was running back and forth between the kitchen and the garden. In the room next door, Hella was scolding her doll, then laughing. Warm air breezed in through the window.

Lilya had set out her belongings on the bed. Before she packed everything in her rucksack, she reached inside. She had kept the cap in a cloth bag. Now she took it out, raised it to her lips and kissed it. Then she put it back in the bag and stuffed it into the rucksack.

She heard someone calling her from outside. She went to the window and waved. She turned back to the bed, fastened the buckles on her rucksack and wiped the tears from her cheeks. She stopped for a moment in front of the mirror and breathed in and out deeply. 'Another rule, Lieutenant Guggenheim,' she said. 'Crying doesn't count.'

Everyone was already waiting when she arrived in the garden. For the umpteenth time, Caposi was recounting the story of their eventful visit to Karen Dove: the shoot-out, and his surprise at what he'd walked into.

As they ate and drank, telling each other all kinds of anecdotes and laughing, the light changed in the garden. The sun broke through again as if saying its goodbyes, then it disappeared behind the house. They fetched lanterns.

Alfred Caposi tapped on his glass and made a toast to Lilya. He thanked her for showing him that there was still hope in these 'ruptured times'. They all stood up and raised their glasses.

All eyes were on her. She looked into their faces, lit by the shining lanterns.

David Guggenheim did not take his eyes off her. He gazed at her and raised his glass. She saw his lips moving and he smiled. The following day, he'd be setting off back to Föhrenwald with Lev. He'd sort out a few things there, and then drive to Berlin to meet Desirée. Had he already discovered what she'd left outside his door?

The table had to be laid again for dessert. She took advantage of the break to have a few moments to herself; she stood up and strolled to the end of the garden, where a meadow began. Behind her she could hear the clattering of crockery; the tang of cigarette smoke hung in the soft night air. Caposi must have set up a gramophone in the garden: strains of a waltz reached her ears. The first stars had come out.

'It'd be nice if we could . . .'

She turned. She could see his outline against the lights hanging in the trees.

'. . . dance again.'

He reached for her hand, pulled her to his lips and kissed her. 'Lilith,' he said. His voice was tinged with warmth and impatience. 'I've read your letter. Not just once. And I think I even understood most of it . . .'

She stayed near him and didn't move. He pulled her closer.

'Lilith, I wish you could come with me on my trip to see Desirée, and perhaps further on to Denmark.' He looked at her with a smile. 'It's almost a tradition now.'

She looked at him with mock reproach. 'Traditions make you lazy and complacent,' she said. 'And I have to return to Palestine.'

'Lilith Tova Wasserfall, Ben Gedi's fiercest weapon, and facing a new mission, no doubt?'

Lilya laughed and shook her head. 'No, I just want to tell Elias everything at last. He was the one who wanted me to go to Germany. He has a right to hear my report.

Besides, I miss my parents. And I have to report to my boss, Shimon Ben Gedi. Mission completed? He will let me know.'

'When are you leaving?'

'Tomorrow,' she said. 'Alfred is taking me to Hanover airport. A military plane. I've never seen our country from the air . . .'

'It's breathtaking, I bet,' he said.

'I'll let you know,' she promised.

'You have to report back, even on the nice things. We should add that to the rule book,' he said.

'Consider it added,' she said.

He embraced her tightly as if he never wanted to let her go again and she pressed her face into his chest. She heard his heartbeat. His lips touched her hair and he breathed in deeply.

Lev came running through the almost pitch-black garden. 'Cake!' he shouted. 'Everything's ready. Where are you?'

'Where are we, Lilith?' David asked. She felt his breath in her ear.

'I don't know,' she said.

'Perhaps we'll find out.'

'Most likely. We're already on our way.'

She drew away from him and reached for his hand. 'Let's go then, Lieutenant Guggenheim, before Lev eats all the cake.'

# EPILOGUE

After the midday heat receded, life returned to Jaffa Road. Shutters flew up, and stools were placed in front of shops. The shadows began to stretch. Traders who had been dozing behind their tables or in the shade of a wall rearranged their wares. Boys carried silver trays with coffee down the street. Others offered bread, skewered on sticks for carrying. British soldiers were on guard up on the roofs. Buses and overladen trucks inched their way through the throngs of people with handcarts, camels and heavily packed mules.

Elias Lind had invited her to his home. He had something up his sleeve — but what?

Since her return, Lilya had spent many evenings with him, and turned up to see him without appointment or invitation. She had decided never to return to the north, and was living in her parents' *caidal*. She wanted to be on her own, and to focus on how her future might look. Twice she'd met Ben Gedi in Tel Aviv. He hadn't revealed what he was up to, but had simply said she should be on standby. She would be hearing from him. But she could tell from his voice that he was proud of her.

During their evenings together, Elias Lind wanted to hear stories about Germany. Every time, he asked for more details and she had to describe sights, smells, bombed places, colours of wood, stone and walls, how cars looked and street signs, shoes and clothes. He wanted to know what she'd eaten and drunk, the sound of voices, the idiosyncrasies of all the people she'd met on her trip. Gestures, hair colours, the way they talked, mannerisms. As if the writer wanted to keep it all in his head, and write it down after she'd left.

At some point, she'd asked, 'Has our book already got a title?'

He seemed embarrassed and even blushed. 'It's just an attempt — I'm feeling my way towards it. You said yourself. I should feel the strength in me again — and the necessary recklessness.'

His brother had been there with them at all those meetings. At least he was watching them from the desk. Caposi's photo of Raphael stood there, in a simple wooden frame.

But even before preparations for his transportation had been finalised, Raphael Lind had died. He'd left the world peacefully, Elias was told. When Lilya learned of his death, she thought of Wartenberg: so his plan had not worked out. A few days later, she read a notice in the newspaper about the Nuremberg trials: his name was among those sentenced to death.

He would learn to live with the fact that he'd never see his brother again, said Elias Lind. Perhaps it was meant to be that way.

Once, he picked up the photograph. 'Did you notice what extraordinary pyjamas he was wearing? Very elegant. That's how he was. Only the watch chain is missing. Where did he manage to find clothes like that in these times?'

He put the photo back down. 'But confining him to his bed for posterity wouldn't have been to his liking. What kind of impression does that make? He'd have preferred a lectern or a laboratory at the very least.'

David Guggenheim had taken care of everything back in Germany. And thanks to Major Terry, a burial in Berlin was arranged for Lind — in Weissensee next to his parents. Desirée von Wallsdorff had confirmed that the woman in the photograph really was Vivien Olsen. But the letter that Guggenheim had sent to his grandfather in Copenhagen announcing his arrival didn't reach old Olsen: he had died a few days before it came.

Desirée had told Elias all this in a letter and had enclosed a photo of Raphael's grave. It was an especially beautiful cemetery, Desirée wrote, almost unscathed by the destruction found elsewhere in the city. Since then, Elias and Desirée had resumed their correspondence and she had already announced her intention to visit him in his 'Promised Land' as soon as she'd gathered all the necessary papers.

'Past love never dies,' said Elias Lind, and smirked, 'and who knows — perhaps she'll like it here.'

Elias Lind's house was halfway between Jaffa Tor and Mahane Yehuda market. It was cool in the stairwell as Lilya climbed up the steps and knocked. Elias opened the door, and a certain festivity lay in the sweep of his movement. He smiled at her and led her through the hallway into the living room.

'You already know the way.'

The half-drawn curtains fluttered in the breeze. There were two plates on the table in the room and two cups. There was a smell of fresh coffee.

He asked her to sit down. Then he gave her a look that she couldn't make out behind his thick spectacles.

'And now, to our matters. I know I should have said something long ago. But I wasn't allowed to. Not before I knew for sure.'

Lilya straightened up.

'Today's the day. I wanted you to be there. Just you. Just the two of us.'

He looked at the clock on the wall, almost as big as a railway clock. There was a truck parked outside the house. The engine died with a sigh. Doors banged.

Lilya walked over to the window and pushed the curtains to one side.

'British troops,' she said.

Elias Lind pretended not to be interested.

She wasn't sure what was going on. 'I'll go and take a look.'

'Please do, and then let me know.'

The truck was parked right outside the front door and the driver's cab was empty. Someone was up on the truck bed. The tarp was rolled back and she heard voices.

As she was walking around the side of the truck a soldier jumped out, almost knocking her over.

He held her arm. 'I'm sorry,' he said, then

let her go again. 'I should've been looking where I was going.'

A second soldier jumped down from the truck bed. Five wooden crates were piled inside the truck with the markings OAD/LIND/PALESTINE/JAFFA ROAD in chalk on the side.

'We were told that someone would be expecting us in front of the house.'

The soldiers pulled the crates to the edge of the truck bed. 'Perhaps someone should tell the owner that we're going to fill his house to the rafters.'

Lilya went up ahead to notify Elias and heard the soldiers panting behind her. Slowly, they piled up the crates one by one in the hallway. Lind had to sign for the delivery from the American zone.

'Captain Bernstein okayed the cargo,' announced the soldier. 'Hope there's no weapons in there or Zionist propaganda.' He winked at Lilya.

The men saluted and turned to go. The sergeant lingered for a moment and said, 'Are you Lilith Wasserfall?'

She nodded. Elias looked at her, flummoxed.

'Then this letter here is for you.' He pulled out an envelope from the folds of his uniform, gave it to her and left. In his heavy boots, he stomped his way back down the stairs, as she turned the letter back and forth in her hands indecisively.

Elias Lind laid a hand on the crates. 'Dr Westmann put in a word for our cause. They found the books in a barn in Lobenberg am See. *Alexandria*. Offenbach accepted it and Westmann wanted to deliver it as quickly as possible to Palestine . . .' He stopped and looked at her. 'You're not even listening!'

'Yes, I am.' She felt the letter in her hand. He had written after all. Hardly a day had gone by since her return when she hadn't longed for a sign of life from him. She stared at the letter and felt her heart hammering.

'Will you help me sort them? You read out the titles and I'll put them on the shelves? We should celebrate!'

Lilya started. 'Of course, yes, I will.'

He shook his head. 'Come on, open it. So we can talk again normally.'

She ripped open the envelope.

Elias looked at her in expectation and grinned. 'Is he coming?'

'Yes,' she said, without looking up from the letter.

'Is that good or bad?'

'He wants to meet you . . .'

'When should we expect him?'

'Soon. Lev will be accompanying him.

With permission from the British. He's managed it!'

'The man who is always saying . . .'

'No, that was Alfred Caposi.'

'So many men,' he said, shaking his head, and then he began gingerly to open the upper crate.

He looked up again.

'Is he coming for your sake or mine?'

'We'll see,' she said.

# AFTERWORD

Germany, summer 1946 was a 'time between times'. Everything was displaced; nothing was where it used to be. The injuries caused by the war and the dictatorship went deep and could be seen and felt everywhere. And it is through this shadowy world, marked by stray hopes, fears, traumas, guilt and wounds, that we accompany a young woman from Palestine on her journey to Germany.

As an author who lives in Germany and who was born not much more than ten years after the events described here — and who is aware of his Jewish roots — I wanted to describe this country in the shadow of catastrophe, this 'time between times', as it were, from an external perspective. I wanted to approach it from a different, tentative angle with the foreign and clever point of view of a young woman, who is inextricably linked and affected by everything that she learns — and is yet unaffected.

Lilya, born to German-Jewish parents in 1924 in Palestine, is completely committed to a project: the founding of a Jewish state. She is aware of the ambivalence of this undertaking, as even her own family has been torn apart by it. But she is given quite a different mission, which displaces her — she, of all people, who is in search of a homeland.

Similar to many of the other characters in this book, this makes her a child of her time. Like, for example, the other central characters of the book, the brothers Raphael and Elias Lind. Outcasts ever since the collapse of the German Empire and the brief but formative heyday of Berlin in the 1920s, they have been in search ever since of a viable way of life, a place to settle, a future, salvation and — a homeland. Both of them do this in very different ways, and it exacts a high price from both.

But not only the characters in this book — and here, explicitly, the survivors of the Holocaust — are displaced. This term also applies to objects, feelings, hopes and old securities. Hardly anything is in the place where it belongs. Not even love, in Lilya's painful personal experience.

*Displaced* is a book about loss, placeless-ness, the search for a homeland and something like deliverance. It is set many years ago in the past yet it reaches, I hope, far into our present times. Because the search for roots is becoming increasingly important in these times of crisis, violence and radical change; of disintegration and collapse of communities and states. This is something we witness every day in a world of asymmetrical wars, ideologies veiled in religion and states that are paralysed, unable to take action. People take huge risks to find new places to live because they have been displaced from their homelands. This is also a theme in *Displaced*, as well as hope, stubbornness and courage.

# HISTORICAL BACKGROUND

## Jerusalem

At the point of the story's beginning, the Second World War has been over for a good year; while the future of Palestine continues to be uncertain. While Holocaust survivors await emigration visas in devastated Europe, the British Mandate government, a recipient of a League of Nations authorisation for Palestine after the First World War, rigidly adheres to its strict immigration restrictions. In this country torn between the Orient and the Occident, violence is rising at a rapid rate. Both Jewish and Arab resistance groups fight for Palestine's independence.

In 1946 underground activities directed against the British Mandate powers reach a new peak. At the end of July, Jewish underground activists set off a bomb, destroying a side wing of the King David Hotel in Jerusalem. Ninety people are killed.

## London

Britain has won the war but its resources are drained. The war prime minister Winston Churchill has been thrown over by Clement Attlee. The British Empire seems to be on the point of collapse: India, like many other countries, is struggling for independence, and the Palestine issue is still unresolved. Manoeuvring precariously between Arab and Jewish interests, and increasingly more subject to public pressure, the British government seeks a route through the problems. In 1947 the newly formed UN decides to divide Palestine. In 1948 the State of Israel is proclaimed and the British pull out of the country.

## The Displaced Persons (DP) Camp Föhrenwald in Bavaria

The situation in the DP camps, many of which were set up by the US Army in southern Germany under the administration of UNRRA, is worsening every day one year on from the end of the war. Increasing numbers of Jewish survivors are migrating in waves from Eastern countries towards Germany, looking for protection in the US zone.

One of the biggest camps is Föhrenwald near Wolfratshausen, which up until 1945 was a settlement for forced labourers at a secret German munitions factory. For many Jews, Föhrenwald is a port of safety as well as a transit camp — and, eventually, an overcrowded waiting room. The camp existed until 1957. Here, as in other places in the middle of southern Bavaria, a Jewish *shtetl* was formed, complete with shops, a cinema, synagogues, schools, cafés, a camp library and a market. And a football team, a section of the Jewish DP league.

But the situation is explosive: the camps are overcrowded and everyone is determined to emigrate. Obtaining a visa for Palestine or the USA is a very difficult procedure.

### Offenbach and the Offenbach Archival Depot (OAD) of the US Army

In the premises of IG Farben on the River Main in Offenbach, the US Army set up the biggest depot for books looted by the Nazis and rescued after the war in 1945 — complete with loading bay, rails and a jetty.

The depot was a central collection point where millions of books awaited their rightful owners, most of whom were no longer alive. What should be done with these cultural artefacts, which were looted from all over Europe on Hitler's orders by the

Einsatzstab Reichsleiter Rosenberg? Or did the OAD find the people who owned the looted goods?

## Berlin

Berlin is in ruins, divided into sectors and already a pawn in the imminent Cold War. The city faces an uncertain future. The black market is thriving and in Tiergarten, the city's largest park, Berliners grow their own vegetables. For everyone, whether victims, perpetrators, collaborators, innocent or guilty, the main thing is survival. But Berlin is also a dangerous city, because here where the powers have clashed, secret services are present and everyone is out to further their own interests.

## Pleikershof near Nuremberg/Fürth, Kibbutz Nili (formerly Streicher-Hof)

Pleikershof near Nuremberg was the former farm of the agitator and Gauleiter of Nuremberg, Julius Streicher, the editor-in-chief of *Stürmer*. After his arrest in 1945, this was turned by the US Army into a kibbutz for survivors. It was called Nili by its inhabitants, who tried to prepare themselves there for Palestine.

## Bergen-Belsen

The Apocalypse: this is how it must have seemed to the British liberators who opened the gates to the camp in April 1945. A so-called *Austauschlager* or exchange camp up until 1944, Bergen-Belsen was also a concentration camp and entry point for 'evacuation transports' from the Reich, which in fact were death marches and death trains. Typhus, starvation, cramped conditions and tens of thousands of dead were waiting behind its gates. Even after the arrival of the British and their medical units, including that of Glyn Hughes, the dying did not stop. Hospital beds were set up on paths, SS barracks and hospitals were requisitioned and the infested camp huts were incinerated with flamethrowers. But the tall, black columns of smoke fanned more fear than hope. In 1946 Bergen-Belsen was a camp for survivors, organised by UNRRA, numerous aid organisations and the Central Committee of the Liberated Jews.

# ACKNOWLEDGEMENTS

No writer is an island. I am deeply thankful to a number of marvellous people who travelled with me along a long road.

My wife and always my first reader, Bettina Abarbanell. My children and partners in everything, Sophie, Julius and Sebastian. My friends and collegues Jan Philipp Sendker and Alexander Fest. The fantastic team at Random House Germany: Ulrich Genzler, Holger Kuntze and my editor Katrin Sorko.

Mark Richards at John Murray in London, who believed in the book from the start. Claire Wachtel in New York and Hannah Wood at HarperCollins US, who are opening the book to a new world.

Lucy Renner Jones, my translator, who gave me and my book a new and uncomparable voice. And my editor Becky Walsh at John Murray; I am thankful for her guidance, insights and never-failing advice.

# FURTHER READING

Numerous books have guided my writing and have offered me invaluable insights. Here is a selection:

**On the History of Israel and Palestine**

Nusseibeh, Sari (with Anthony David), *Once Upon a Country: A Palestinian Life,* London, 2007

Rosenberg, Göran, *The Lost Land: A Personal History of Zionism and Messianism and the State of Israel,* Stockholm, 1998

Segev, Tom, *The Seventh Million: The Israelis and the Holocaust,* New York, 1995

——, *One Palestine, Complete: Jews and Arabs Under the British Mandate,* London, 2005

Shavit, Ari, *My Promised Land: The Triumph and Tragedy of Israel,* London, 2014

## (Auto-)biographies, Letters and Diaries

Andreas-Friedrich, Ruth, *Schauplatz Berlin: Ein Deutsches Tagesbuch* (Scenes from Berlin: A German Diary), Munich, 1962

Arendt, Hannah, *The Aftermath of Nazi Rule. Report from Germany,* Berlin, 1950

Arendt, Hannah, and Gerschom Scholem, *The Correspondence: Hannah Arendt and Gerschom Scholem,* Berlin, 2010

Ben-Natan, Asher, and Susanne Urban, *Die Bricha: Aus dem Terror nach Eretz Israel — Ein Fluchthelfer erinnert sich* (The Bricha: From Terror to the Land of Israel — A Memoir of an Escape Helper), Düsseldorf, 2005

Blumenthal, W. Michael, *The Invisible Wall,* Berkeley, 1998

Frisch, Max, *Tagebuch 1946:1949* (Diary 1946–1949), Berlin, 2011

Oz, Amos, *A Tale of Love and Darkness,* New York, 2004

Sahl, Hans, *Memoiren eines Moralisten* (Memoirs of a Moralist), Munich, 2009

Scholem, Betty, and Gerschom Scholem, *A Life in Letters, 1914–1982,* ed. and tr. Anthony David Skinner, Cambridge, Mass., 2002

Scholem, Gerschom, *From Berlin to Jerusalem,* tr. Harry Zohn, Schocken, New York,

1980, *Briefe,* Bd. I, 1914–1947 (Letters, Vol. I, 1914–1947), Munich, 1994

Stern, Fritz, *Five Germanys I Have Known,* New York, 2006

Sutzkever, Abraham, *Vilna Ghetto 1941–1944,* Zurich, 2009

Willstätter, Richard, *From My Life,* New York, 1965

## On Looted Books and Art

Bertz, Inka, and Michael Dorrmann (eds.), *Raub und Restitution: Kulturgut aus jüdischem Besitz von 1933 bis heute* (Loot and Restitution: Jewish Cultural Artefacts from 1933 to Today), Göttingen, 2008

Dehnel, Regine (ed.), *Jüdischer Buchbesitz als Raubgut* (Property of Jewish Books as Loot), Zweites Hannoversches Symposium, Frankfurt am Main, 2006

Kurtz, Michael J., *America and the Return of Nazi Contraband,* Cambridge, 2006

Nicholas, Lynn H., *The Rape of Europa,* New York, 1995

## Scientists in the Third Reich

Deichmann, Ute, *Flüchten, Mitmachen, Vergessen: Chemiker und Biochemiker in der NS Zeit* (Escape, Collaboration, Forgetting: Chemists and Biochemists in the Nazi Era), Weinheim, 2001

Schmaltz, Florian, *Kampfstoff-Forschung im Nationalsozialismus: Zur Kooperation von Kaiser-Wilhelm-Instituten, Militär und Industrie* (Biological Weapons during National Socialism: On the Cooperation of the Kaiser Wilhelm Institutes, Military and Industry), Göttingen, 2005

## On the Situation of Jewish Survivors

Königseder, Angelika, and Juliane Wetzel, *Lebensmut im Wartesaal: Die jüdischen Displaced Persons im Nachkriegsdeutschand* (Optimism in the Waitings Room: Jewish Displaced Persons in Postwar Germany), Frankfurt am Main, 2005

## And

Noam Zadoff helped the beginning of my journey with his enlightening essay, *'Reise in die Vergangenheit, Entwurf einer neuen Zukunft: Gerschom Scholems Reise nach Deutschland im Jahre 1946'* ('Journey into the Past, Plan for a New Future: Gerschom Scholem's Journey through Germany in the Year 1946'), *Münchener Beiträge zur Jüdischen Geschichte und Kultur,*

Heft 2, 2007.

When this manuscript was finished, Mirjam Zadoff's remarkable book, *Der rote Hiob — Das Leben des Werner Scholem* (The Red Job — The Life of Werner Scholem), Munich, 2014, was published, an effectively narrated biography of two brothers and of life as a Jew under National Socialism and in the twentieth century.

# ABOUT THE AUTHOR

**Stephan Abarbanell** was born in 1957 and grew up in Hamburg. He studied protestant theology and general rhetoric in Hamburg, Tübingen, and at the University of California, Berkeley, and worked as a chaplain at the University Hospital San Francisco. He served as chief of programming at rbb Broadcasting for many years, and is now in charge of cultural affairs with the public rbb Television and Radio in Berlin. He lives with his wife in Potsdam, Germany. *Displaced* is his first novel.

The employees of Thorndike Press hope you have enjoyed this Large Print book. All our Thorndike, Wheeler, and Kennebec Large Print titles are designed for easy reading, and all our books are made to last. Other Thorndike Press Large Print books are available at your library, through selected bookstores, or directly from us.

For information about titles, please call:
  (800) 223-1244

or visit our website at:
  gale.com/thorndike

To share your comments, please write:
  Publisher
  Thorndike Press
  10 Water St., Suite 310
  Waterville, ME 04901